Great Stories Remembered

FOCUS ON THE FAMILY

presents

Great Stories Remembered

compiled and edited by Joe Wheeler

PUBLISHING

Colorado Springs, Colorado

GREAT STORIES REMEMBERED

Library of Congress Cataloging-in-Publication Data
Great stories remembered / compiled and edited by Joe Wheeler.
    p. cm.
    ISBN 1-56179-459-7
    1. Family—United States—Fiction. 2. Domestic fiction, American. I. Wheeler, Joe, 1936– .
    PS648.F27F63   1996
    813'.0108355—dc20   96-7879
                                      CIP

Published by Focus on the Family Publishing, Colorado Springs, CO 80995.

Distributed in the U.S.A. and Canada by Word Books, Dallas, Texas.

The author is represented by the literary agency of Alive Communications, 1465 Kelly Johnson Blvd., Suite 320, Colorado Springs, CO 80920.

Focus on the Family books are available at special quantity discounts when purchased in bulk by corporations, organizations, churches, or groups. Special imprints, messages, and excerpts can be produced to meet your needs. For more information, contact: Sales Dept., Focus on the Family Publishing, 8605 Explorer Dr., Colorado Springs, CO 80920; or phone (719) 531-3400.

Editor: Michele A. Kendall
Cover Design: Bradley L. Lind
Cover Illustration: Christi Baughman

Printed in the United States of America

96 97 98 99 00 01 02 03/10 9 8 7 6 5 4 3 2 1

Table of Contents

Introduction

"A Certain Man Had Two Sons . . ."
Joseph Leininger Wheeler

. . . And so begins one of the oldest and most famous short stories we know: Christ's parable of the prodigal son in Luke 15. It is a masterpiece of story construction, even by today's critical standards.

For reasons known only to Him, our Lord rarely spoke in abstractions or in generalities—the Sermon on the Mount is a rare exception. Rather, He told stories . . . lots and lots of stories.

Obviously, His apostle Matthew felt called to explain; in the thirteenth chapter of his book, he makes one of the most incredible statements in Holy Writ:

> All this Jesus said to the crowds in parables; indeed he said nothing to them without a parable. This was to fulfill what was spoken by the prophet:
> "I will open my mouth in parables, I will utter what has been hidden since the foundation of the world."
>
> Matthew 13:34 (RSV)

X

Earlier in the same chapter (verses 10–15), the question "Why?" is posed to our Lord by His own disciples—and for this, I prefer J. B. Phillips's translation:

> At this the disciples approached him and asked, "Why do you talk to them in parables?"
>
> "Because you have been given the chance to understand the secrets of the kingdom of Heaven," replied Jesus, "but they have not. For when a man has something, more is given to him till he has plenty. But if he has nothing, even his nothing will be taken away from him. This is why I speak to them in these parables; because they go through life with their eyes open, but see nothing, and with their ears open, but understand nothing of what they hear."

Stories . . . they are as old as time itself. Genesis begins with narration, with stories. Our modern conversation fairly swims with them as well:

> "What did I do this weekend? . . . Oh, wait till you hear what happened to me! You see, I'd just locked the house when suddenly . . ."
>
> "How did my interview go? . . . Well, sir . . . uh . . . I'm afraid it didn't go too well. You see, as soon as his secretary came for me . . ."
>
> "How was my day? . . . Oh Mom! You'll never believe it—that dreadful new boy at school . . . oh, I hate him! I hate him! . . . He . . ."
>
> "What happened on *Days* today? Wait till you hear this. . . ."

Stories. We speak in stories to each other.

Let's change the setting. You are sitting with your family in church. The minister gets up, puts on his spectacles, opens his Bible, and says, "Turn with me in your Bible to Deuteronomy 4, verse 1, where it reads . . ."

You look around you. What do you see? People are getting glassy-eyed, beginning to sink back into their seats. Heads start nodding.

But what if, at any time along the way, the minister should take off his glasses and say, "Now this reminds me of a story. . . ."

What will happen? A veritable resurrection of the entire slumbering congregation, that's what!

What happens if it's a children's story? "The story I'm going to share now is just for kids . . . so you older folks may take a nap until I'm done."

To nobody's surprise, the adults listen, if anything, even more intently than the children. *Trying to leave me out, huh? Not on your life!*

Why Use Stories?

Why indeed! Perhaps because they alone remain in conscious, easy-to-access memory. My mother, Barbara Leininger Wheeler, was and still is an elocutionist of the old school. Since she knew so many stories, poems, and readings by heart, her "reading" was in reality a performance, for the story came *alive* through drama. Her stories were vivid, and every syllable was enunciated correctly. Whether it was Longfellow's "Courtship of Miles Standish," *Evangeline*, or *Hiawatha*—the latter being two full-length books—"Lasca," "Kentucky Bell," or her wonderfully wacky "Sewin' on her weddin' clothes" reading, she knew every word, every inflection, every laugh spot, and every tear spot. I have long since forgotten most of what I have been exposed to in life, but Mother's stories are a part of my psyche, who I am, and hence key factors in how I live, how I treat people, how I perceive God.

I have become convinced, beyond a shadow of a doubt, that few things have a greater potential for good, for enrichment, for developing values, for creating empathy, for instilling kindness into the hearts, souls, and minds of children than does reading out loud to them.

And few more enduring bonds can exist on this planet than those created by reading to a child nestled on your lap or one encircled by your arm.

That is why I urge parents to turn off the television for the first 10 to 12 years of their children's lives in order to create in them a love of the printed word, develop their imagination, make it possible for them to write well, instill the right sort of values—and so much more!

The Golden Age of Story Writing

So where does one go to find worthwhile stories? Well, they are still being written . . . but far fewer than was true during the period I call the Golden Age of Christian Stories (1880–1950). Today, the best writers are writing for television, the movies, or advertising; not so during the Golden Age, especially before 1930, when the best talent pool wrote for print publications.

Furthermore, the values portrayed then were the Judeo-Christian values our nation was founded upon. Up until the twentieth century, if you wanted your audiences to understand your allusions, you would refer to incidents in the Bible, *Pilgrim's Progress,* and the McGuffey Readers.

There existed then an implicit understanding between parents, schools, churches, and publishing houses: that children were to be protected from harsh adult realities until they were old enough to face them without being destroyed in the process. Children were free to be children. Books such as Alcott's *Little Women,* Twain's *Tom Sawyer,* Tarkington's *Penrod,* Wilder's *Little House on the Prairie* series, and Moody's *Little Britches* series reveal a world where freedom and responsibility went hand in hand, and one learned to live by the principles found in Scripture.

Certain writers, like cream, floated to the top: Margaret E. Sangster (both of them, grandmother and granddaughter), Grace Richmond, Annie Hamilton Donnell, Grace Livingston Hill, Temple Bailey, Christine

Whiting Parmenter, Elizabeth Goudge, Pearl Buck, Zane Grey, Gene Stratton Porter, Harold Bell Wright, Lloyd C. Douglas, James Oliver Curwood, Zona Gale, Edison Marshall, Agnes Sligh Turnbull, and so many more. They carried the Golden Age on their capable shoulders.

Today, that wonderful adult partnership has ceased to exist: Parents let the media run amok in their own homes; the schools are either as permissive or as selective as their leaders permit; the church wrings its hands, ostensibly powerless to act without parental consent—and the poor child is let loose among the wolves.

It is long past time to rebuild that collaboration, starting with the home and the church. But in reality—since half of what we learn in a lifetime we assimilate by the age of six—the court of last resort must be the home. Parents must moat their bastion against the forces of evil and ever so gradually prepare the child to face adult realities, but from the ethical and spiritual perspective of the Christian home.

If the mind, heart, and soul are not filled with media amorality, they can be filled with something positive instead. For this to happen, we need stories. Deeply moving stories. Stories that have the built-in power to induce both joy and wrenching tears. Stories that add up to a Judeo-Christian philosophy of life.

This First Collection

You will note that the stories are arranged according to seasonal appropriateness. This way, you are likely to find stories to mesh with the time of year indicated. As was true with the McGuffey Readers, the stories represent pieces of life itself, stories that deliberately challenge the amoral media on a wide number of fronts.

Tennyson declared in his great poem "Ulysses" that each of us, like Ulysses, can say, "I am a part of all that I have met": the sum total of what we have been exposed to, what we have seen, what we have heard, what we

 XIV

have read. If we would like our children to grow up to be loving, caring, and kind Christians, then we have to start doing something about the influences that mold their characters while there is still time.

Coda

We appreciate hearing from our readers. If you have any comments, positive or negative, about this collection, or have any stories you would like us to include in future collections, please send them to

Joe L. Wheeler, Ph.D.
c/o Focus on the Family
Colorado Springs, CO 80920

Winter to Spring

His "Innymunt"

Author Unknown

"When anybody does naughty things and bweaks your playthings, he's an innymunt."

Mr. Rogers was thinking. His thoughts went back 20 years, and he saw himself a young man doing a prosperous business, and although not in partnership, still intimately associated with one who had been his playmate, neighbor, and close friend for years. And then Mr. Rogers saw the financial trouble that had come upon him, and he thought bitterly that if the friend had played the part of a friend, it might have been averted.

He saw the 20 years of estrangement and felt again the bitterness of that hour.

Mr. Rogers rose from his chair, and going to his safe, drew from it three notes for $5,000 each, due on the following Monday.

3

"Twenty years is a long time to wait for justice," said he to himself, "but now, and without my lifting a finger, these notes have come into my possession, and I know, Robert Harris, that it will be hard work for you to pay them. I knew justice would be done at last."

And Mr. Rogers replaced the notes in his safe, and closing his office, went home to tea.

Many a man will cry out for justice when it is revenge he desires.

On Monday morning, Mr. Rogers went to the station to take the 8:00 train for Boston. He had just taken his seat when he heard his name spoken and saw Mr. Palmer, his neighbor, standing by his side.

"Are you going to town?" asked Mr. Palmer.

"Yes," was the reply. "Anything I can do for you?"

"I wish you would take charge of my little girl as far as the next station. Her grandmother will meet her there. I have promised her this visit for a week and had intended to take her down myself, but just at the last minute I received a dispatch that I must be here to meet some men who are coming out on the next train."

"Why, of course I will," said Mr. Rogers heartily. "Where is she?"

At these words, a tiny figure clambered onto the seat, and a cheerful voice answered, "Here I am!"

"Thank you," said Mr. Palmer. "Good-bye, Betty; be a good girl, and Papa will come for you tomorrow."

"Good-bye, Papa; give my love to the baa-lammie and all the west of the fam'ly," replied Betty.

People looked around and laughed at Betty's putting the lamb at the head of the family. They saw a very little girl under an immense hat, with a pair of big blue eyes and rosy cheeks.

Mr. Rogers put her next to the window and began to talk with her.

"How old are you, Betty?" he asked.

"I'm half past four; how old are you?" promptly returned Betty.

"Not quite a hundred," laughed Mr. Rogers, "but pretty old for all that."

"Is that what made the fur all come off the top of your head?" she asked, looking thoughtfully at his baldness, for the heat had caused him to take off his hat.

Mr. Rogers said he guessed so.

Betty pointed out various objects of interest and made original comments upon them, not at all abashed by her companion's age and gravity.

Suddenly, she looked up and said, "I go to Sunday school."

"Do you? And what do you do there?"

"Well, I sing and learn a verse. My teacher gave me a new one 'bout bears, but I don't know it yet, but I know the first one I had. Want me to tell it to you?" The big blue eyes looked confidingly up at Mr. Rogers.

"Why, of course I do, Betty," he replied.

Betty folded her hands, and with her eyes fixed on her listener's face, said, "Love your innymunts."

Mr. Rogers flushed, and involuntarily put his hand on his pocketbook; but Betty, all unconscious of his thought, said, "Do you want me to 'splain it?"

The listener nodded, and the child went on: "Do you know what an innymunt is?" Receiving no answer, she said: "When anybody does naughty things and bweaks your playthings, he's an innymunt. . . . Wobbie Fwench was my innymunt; he bweaked my dolly's nose and he sticked burrs in my baa-lammie's fur, and he said it wasn't baa-lammie, noffin' but just a lammie." The big eyes grew bigger as she recalled this last indignity.

Mr. Rogers looked deeply interested—and who could have helped it, looking at the earnest little face? Betty continued to "'splain."

"It doesn't mean," she said, "that you must let him bweak all your dolls' noses nor call your baa-lammie names, 'cause that's wicked; but last week Wobbie bweaked his bicycle, and next day all the boys were going to wace, and when I said my pwayers, I told the Lord I was glad Wobbie bwoke his bicycle. I was.

"But when I wanted to go to sleep, I feel bad here," and Betty placed a tiny hand on her chest and drew a long breath. "But by and by, after much as a hour I guess, I thought how naughty that was, and then I telled the Lord I was sorwy Wobbie had bweaked his bicycle and I would lend him mine part of the time, and then I felt good and was asleep in a minute."

"And what about Robbie?" asked Mr. Rogers.

"Well," replied the child, "I guess if I keep on loving him, he won't be a 'innymunt' much longer."

"I guess not either," said Mr. Rogers, giving his hand to help her down from the seat as the cars slacked speed and stopped at the station. He led Betty from the car and gave her into her grandmother's care.

"I hope she has not troubled you," said the lady, looking fondly at the child.

"On the contrary, madam, she has done me a world of good," said he sincerely as he raised his hat, and bidding Betty good-bye, he stepped back into the car.

Mr. Rogers resumed his seat and looked out of the window, but he did not see the trees, nor the green fields, nor even the peaceful river with its thousands of water lilies, like stars in the midnight sky.

Had he told the Lord that he was glad his "innymunt" had broken his bicycle and could not join in the race for wealth and position? When he came to put the question straight to his own soul, it certainly did look like it.

It was no use for him to say the notes were honestly due. He knew that he could afford to wait for the money and that if Robert Harris was forced to pay them at once, he would probably be ruined. He heard the sweet voice of the child saying, "Love your innymunt," and he said in his heart, using the old familiar name of his boyhood days: "Lord, I am sorry Rob has broken his bicycle. I'll lend him mine until he gets his mended."

Had the sun come out suddenly from behind a dark cloud? Mr. Rogers thought so, but it had really been shining its brightest all that morning.

A boy came through the train with a great bunch of water lilies, calling, "Lilies, cent apiece, six for five."

"Here, boy!" called Mr. Rogers. "Where did those come from?"

"White Pond, Lily Cove," said the boy, eyeing Mr. Rogers with some perplexity. He had been a train boy for five years and had never known Mr. Rogers to buy anything but the *Journal*.

"What'll you take for the bunch?"

"Fifty cents," replied the boy promptly.

Mr. Rogers handed him the half-dollar and took the fragrant lilies. "How do you get into the cove now?" he asked as the boy pocketed the money and was moving on.

"Get out 'n' shove her over the bar," replied the boy as he went on.

Mr. Rogers looked at the flowers with the streaks of pink on the outer petals, at the smooth pinkish-brown stems, and thought of the time 40 years before when he and Rob, two barefooted urchins, had rowed across White Pond in a leaky boat, and by great exertion dragged and pushed it over the bar, and been back home at 7:00 in the morning, with such a load of lilies as had never been seen in the village before. Yes, he remembered it, and Rob's mother was frying doughnuts when they got back, and she gave them six apiece. Oh, she knew what boys' appetites were! She had been dead for 30 years now.

Just then the cars glided into the station, and everybody rushed out of the train. Mr. Rogers followed in a kind of dream. He walked along until he came to Sudbury Street and stopped at a place where he read, "Robert Harris, Manufacturer of Steam and Gas Fittings."

He entered the building and, going up one flight of stairs, opened the door and entered a room fitted up as an office. A man sat at a desk, anxiously examining a pile of papers. He looked up as Mr. Rogers entered, stared at him as if he could not believe his eyes, and, without speaking, rose from his chair and offered a seat to his visitor.

Mr. Rogers broke the silence. "Rob," he said, holding out his hand, "these came from the cove where we used to go, and—and—I've come around to say that if you want to renew those notes that are due today, I am ready to do so, and—and—"

But Mr. Harris had sunk into a chair and, with his head in his hands, was sobbing as if his heart would break.

Mr. Rogers awkwardly laid the lilies on the desk and sat down. "Don't, Rob," he said at length.

"You wouldn't wonder at it, Tom," was the reply, "if you knew what I have endured for the past 48 hours. I can pay every penny if I have time, but to pay them today means absolute ruin."

"Well, I guess we can fix all that," said Mr. Rogers, looking intently into the crown of his hat. "Have you any more paper out?"

"Less than 200 dollars," was the reply.

The 20 years of estrangement were forgotten like a troubled dream, and when they finally separated, with a clasp of the hand, each felt a dozen years younger.

"Ah!" said Mr. Rogers as he walked away with a light step. "Betty was right. If you love your 'innymunt,' he won't be an 'innymunt' any longer."

A Sandpiper to Bring You Joy

Mary Sherman Hilbert

A lonely child, a wounded mother, and a pain-racked daughter dealing with the suffering of her aged mother. The setting: the sea.

She was six years old when I first met her on the beach near where I live. I drive to this beach, a distance of three or four miles, whenever the world begins to close in on me.

She was building a sand castle or something and looked up, her eyes as blue as the sea.

"Hello," she said.

I answered with a nod, not really in the mood to bother with a small child.

"I'm building," she said.

"I see that. What is it?" I asked, not caring.

"Oh, I don't know. I just like the feel of the sand."

That sounds good, I thought and slipped off my shoes. A sandpiper glided by.

"That's a joy," the child said.

"It's what?"

"It's a joy. My mama says sandpipers come to bring us joy."

The bird went glissading down the beach.

"Good-bye, joy," I muttered to myself, "hello, pain," and turned to walk on. I was depressed; my life seemed completely out of balance.

"What's your name?" She wouldn't give up.

"Ruth," I answered. "I'm Ruth Peterson."

"Mine's Windy." At least it sounded like Windy. "And I'm six."

"Hi, Windy."

She giggled. "You're funny," she said.

In spite of my gloom, I laughed too and walked on.

Her musical giggle followed me. "Come again, Mrs. P.," she called. "We'll have another happy day."

The days and weeks that followed belonged to someone else: a group of unruly Boy Scouts, PTA meetings, an ailing mother.

The sun was shining one morning as I took my hands out of the dishwater. "I need a sandpiper," I said to myself, gathering up my coat.

The never-changing balm of the seashore awaited me. The breeze was chilly, but I strode along, trying to recapture the serenity I needed. I had forgotten the child and was startled when she appeared.

"Hello, Mrs. P.," she said. "Do you want to play?"

"What did you have in mind?" I asked with a twinge of annoyance.

"I don't know. *You* say."

"How about charades?" I asked sarcastically.

The tinkling laughter burst forth again. "I don't know what that is."

"Then let's just walk." Looking at her, I noticed the delicate fairness of her face.

"Where do you live?" I asked.

"Over there." She pointed toward a row of summer cottages. *Strange,* I thought, *in winter.*

"Where do you go to school?"

"I don't go to school. Mommy says we're on vacation."

She chattered little-girl talk as we strolled up the beach, but my mind was on other things. When I left for home, Windy said it had been a happy day. Feeling surprisingly better, I smiled at her and agreed.

Three weeks later, I rushed to my beach in a state of near panic. I was in no mood even to greet Windy. I thought I saw her mother on the porch and felt like demanding she keep her child at home.

"Look, if you don't mind," I said crossly when Windy caught up with me, "I'd rather be alone today."

She seemed unusually pale and out of breath.

"Why?" she asked.

I turned on her and shouted, "Because my mother died!"

"Oh," she said quietly, "then this is a bad day."

"Yes, and yesterday and the day before that and—oh, go away!"

"Did it hurt?"

"Did *what* hurt?" I was exasperated with her, with myself.

"When she died?"

"*Of course* it hurt!" I snapped, misunderstanding, wrapped up in myself. I strode off.

A month or so after that, when I next went to the beach, she wasn't there. Feeling guilty, ashamed, and admitting to myself I missed her, I went up to the cottage after my walk and knocked at the door. A drawn-looking young woman with honey-colored hair opened the door.

"Hello," I said. "I'm Ruth Peterson. I missed your little girl today and wondered where she was."

"Oh, yes, Mrs. Peterson, please come in. Wendy talked of you so much.

I'm afraid I allowed her to bother you. If she was a nuisance, please accept my apologies."

"Not at all—she's a delightful child," I said, suddenly realizing that I meant it. "Where is she?"

"Wendy died last week, Mrs. Peterson. She had leukemia. Maybe she didn't tell you."

Struck dumb, I groped for a chair. My breath caught.

"She loved this beach, so when she asked to come, we couldn't say no. She seemed so much better here and had a lot of what she called happy days. But the last few weeks, she declined rapidly. . . ." Her voice faltered. "She left something for you . . . if only I can find it. Could you wait a moment while I look?"

I nodded stupidly, my mind racing for something, anything, to say to this lovely young woman.

She handed me a smeared envelope, with MRS. P printed in bold, childish letters.

Inside was a drawing in bright crayon hues—a yellow beach, a blue sea, a brown bird. Underneath was carefully printed:

A SANDPIPER

TO BRING YOU JOY

Tears welled up in my eyes, and a heart that had almost forgotten how to love opened wide. I took Wendy's mother in my arms. "I'm sorry, I'm sorry, I'm so sorry," I muttered over and over, and we wept together.

That precious little picture is framed now and hangs in my study. Six words—one for each year of her life—speak to me of inner harmony, courage, undemanding love. A gift from a child with sea-blue eyes and hair the color of sand—who taught me the gift of love.

Their Word of Honor

Grace Richmond

The two boys had never known their father to give such absurd directions. Should they follow through or not?

The president of the Great B. railway system laid down the letter he had just reread three times and turned about in his chair with an expression of extreme annoyance.

"I wish it were possible," he said slowly, "to find one boy or man in a thousand who would receive instructions and carry them out to the letter without a single variation from the course.

"Cornelius," he continued, looking sharply at his son, who sat at a desk close by, "I hope you are carrying out my ideas with regard to your sons. I have not seen much of them lately. The lad Cyrus seems to me a promising fellow, but I am not so sure of Cornelius. He appears to be acquiring a sense of his own importance as Cornelius

Woodbridge III, which is not desirable, sir—not desirable. By the way, Cornelius, have you yet applied the Hezekiah Woodbridge test to your boys?"

Cornelius Woodbridge, Jr., looked up from his work with a smile. "No, I have not, Father," he said.

"It's a family tradition; and if the proper care has been taken that the boys should not be told about it, it will be as much a test for them as it was for you and for me and for my father. You have not forgotten the day I gave it to you, Cornelius?"

"That would be impossible," said his son, still smiling.

The elder man's somewhat stern features relaxed, and he sat back in his chair with a chuckle. "Do it at once," he requested, "and make it a stiff one. You know their characteristics; give it to them hard. I feel pretty sure of Cyrus, but Cornelius—" He shook his head doubtfully and returned to his letter. Suddenly, he wheeled about again.

"Do it Thursday, Cornelius," he said in his peremptory way, "and whichever one of them stands it shall go with us on the tour of inspection. That would be reward enough for anyone, I fancy."

"Very well, sir," replied his son, and the two men went on with their work without further words. They were in the habit of dispatching important business with the smallest possible waste of breath.

On Thursday morning, immediately after breakfast, Cyrus Woodbridge found himself summoned to his father's library. He presented himself at once, a round-cheeked, bright-eyed lad of 15, with an air of alertness in every line of him.

"Cyrus," said his father, "I have a commission for you to undertake, of a character I cannot now explain to you. I want you to take this envelope"—he held out a large and bulky packet—"and, without saying anything to anyone, follow its instructions to the letter. I ask your word of honor that you will do so."

The two pairs of eyes looked into each other for a moment, singularly alike in a certain intent expression, developed into great keenness in the man, but showing as yet only an extreme wide-awakeness in the boy.

Cyrus Woodbridge had an engagement with a young friend in half an hour, but he responded instantly and firmly: "I will, sir."

"On your honor?"

"Yes, sir."

"That is all I want. Go to your room and read your instructions. Then start at once."

Mr. Woodbridge turned back to his desk with the nod and smile of dismissal to which Cyrus was accustomed. The boy went to his room, opening the envelope as soon as he had closed the door. It was filled with smaller envelopes, numbered in regular order. Enfolding these was a typewritten page, which read as follows:

Go to the reading room of the Westchester Library. There open envelope No. 1. Remember to hold all instructions secret.

Cyrus whistled. "That's funny! It means my time with Harold is off. Well, here goes!"

He stopped on his way out to telephone his friend of his detention, took a Westchester Avenue car at the nearest point, and in 20 minutes was at the library. He found an obscure corner and opened envelope No. 1.

Go to the office of W. K. Newton, Room 703, tenth floor, Norfolk Building, X Street, reaching there by 9:30 A.M. Ask for letter addressed to Cornelius Woodbridge, Jr. On way down in elevator, open envelope No. 2.

Cyrus began to laugh. At the same time, he felt a trifle irritated. *What's Father up to?* he questioned in perplexity. *Here I am way uptown, and he orders me back to the Norfolk Building. I passed it on my way up. He must have made a mistake. Told me to obey instructions, though. He usually knows why he does things.*

Meanwhile, Mr. Woodbridge had sent for his elder son, Cornelius. A tall youth of 17, with the strong family features, varied by a droop in the eyelids and a slight drawl in his speech, lounged to the door of the library. Before entering, he straightened his shoulders; he did not, however, quicken his pace.

"Cornelius," said his father promptly, "I wish to send you upon an errand of some importance, but of possible inconvenience to you. I have not time to give you instructions, but you will find them in this envelope. I ask you to keep the matter and your movements strictly to yourself. May I have your word of honor that I can trust you to follow the orders to the smallest detail?"

Cornelius put on a pair of eyeglasses and held out his hand for the envelope. His manner was almost indifferent.

Mr. Woodbridge withheld the packet and spoke with decision: "I cannot allow you to look at the instructions until I have your word of honor that you will fulfill them."

"Is not that asking a good deal, sir?"

"Perhaps so," said Mr. Woodbridge, "but no more than is asked of trusted messengers every day. I will assure you that the instructions are mine and represent my wishes."

"How long will it take?" inquired Cornelius, stooping to flick an imperceptible spot of dust from his trousers.

"I do not find it necessary to tell you."

Something in his father's voice sent the languid Cornelius to an erect position and quickened his speech.

"Of course I will go," he said, but he did not speak with enthusiasm.

"And—your word of honor?"

"Certainly, sir." The hesitation before the promise was only momentary.

"Very well. I will trust you. Go to your room before opening your instructions."

And the second somewhat mystified boy went out of the library on that memorable Thursday morning to find his first order to a remote district of the city, with the direction to arrive there within three-quarters of an hour.

Out on an electric car, Cyrus was speeding to another suburb. After getting the letter from the tenth floor of the Norfolk Building, he had read:

> Take cross-town car on L Street, transfer to Louisville Avenue, and go out to Kingston Heights. Find corner West and Dwight Streets and open envelope No. 3.

Cyrus was growing more and more puzzled, but he was also getting interested. At the corner specified, he hurriedly tore open No. 3, but found, to his amazement, only the singular direction:

> Take Suburban Underground Road for Duane Street Station. From there go to *Sentinel* office and secure third edition of yesterday's paper. Open envelope No. 4.

"Well, what under the sun, moon, and stars did he send me out to Kingston Heights for?" cried Cyrus aloud. He caught the next train, thinking longingly of his broken appointment with Harold Dunning and of certain plans for the afternoon that he was beginning to fear might be thwarted if this seemingly endless and aimless excursion continued. He looked at the packet of unopened envelopes.

It would be easy to break open the whole outfit and see what this game is, he thought. *Never knew Father to do a thing like this before. If it's a joke*—his fingers felt the seal of envelope No. 4—*I might as well find it out at once. Still, Father never would joke with a fellow's promise the way he asked it of me. "My word of honor"—that's putting it pretty strong. I'll see it through, of course.*

My, but I'm getting hungry! It must be near lunchtime.

It was not; but by the time Cyrus had been ordered twice across the city and once to the top floor of a 16-story building in which the elevator service was out of order, it was past noon, and he was in a condition to find envelope No. 7 a very satisfactory one:

> Go to Café Reynaud on Westchester Square. Take a seat at table in left alcove. Ask waiter for card of Cornelius Woodbridge, Jr. Before ordering lunch, open envelope No. 8 and read the contents.

The boy lost no time in obeying this command and sank into his designated chair with a sigh of relief. He mopped his brow and drank a glass of ice water at a gulp. It was a warm October day, and the 16 flights had been somewhat trying. He asked for his father's card and then sat studying the attractive menu.

"I think I'll have—" He mused for a moment, then said with a laugh, "Well, I'm about hungry enough to eat the whole thing. Bring me the—"

Then he recollected, paused, and reluctantly pulled out envelope No. 8, and broke the seal. "Just a minute," he murmured to the waiter. Then his face turned scarlet, and he stammered under his breath, "Why—why—this can't be—"

Envelope No. 8 ought to have been bordered with black, if one may judge by the dismay caused by its order to a lecture hall to hear a famous electrician speak. But the Woodbridge blood was up now, and it was with an expression resembling that of his grandfather Cornelius under strong indignation that Cyrus stalked out of that charming place to proceed grimly to the lecture hall.

Who wants to hear a lecture on an empty stomach? he groaned. *I suppose I'll be ordered out anyway, the minute I sit down and stretch my legs. Wonder if Father can be exactly right in his mind. He doesn't believe in wasting time, but I'm wasting it today by the bucketful. Suppose he's doing this to size me up some-*

way? Well, he isn't going to tire me out so quickly as he thinks. I'll keep going till I drop.

Nevertheless, when he was ordered to leave the lecture hall and go three miles to a football field, and then was ordered away again without a sight of the game he had planned for a week to see, his disgust was intense.

All through that long, warm afternoon, he raced about the city and suburbs, growing wearier and more empty with every step. The worst of it was, the orders were beginning to assume the form of a schedule and commanded that he be here at 3:15 and there at 4:05, and so on, which forbade loitering, had he been inclined to loiter. In it all he could see no purpose, except the possible one of trying his physical endurance. He was a strong boy, or he would have been quite exhausted long before he reached envelope No. 17, which was the last but three of the packet. This read:

Reach home at 6:20 P.M. Before entering house, read No. 18.

Leaning against one of the big, white stone pillars of the porch of his home, Cyrus wearily tore open envelope No. 18, and the words fairly swam before his eyes. He had to rub them hard to make sure that he was not mistaken.

Go again to Kingston Heights, corner West and Dwight Streets, reaching there by 6:50. Read No. 19.

The boy looked up at the windows, desperately angry at last. If his pride and his idea of the meaning of the phrase "my word of honor," as the men of the Woodbridge family were in the habit of teaching it to their sons, had not both been of the strongest sort, he would have rebelled and gone defiantly and stormily in. As it was, he stood for one long minute with his hands clenched and his teeth set; then he turned and walked down the steps away from the longed-for dinner and out toward L Street and the car for Kingston Heights.

As he did so, inside the house, on the other side of the curtains, from behind which he had been anxiously peering, Cornelius Woodbridge, Sr., turned about and struck his hands together, rubbing them in a satisfied way.

"He's come—and gone," he cried softly, "and he's on time to the minute!"

Cornelius, Jr., did not so much as lift his eyes from the evening paper as he quietly answered, "Is he?" But the corners of his mouth slightly relaxed.

The car seemed to crawl to Kingston Heights. As it at last neared its terminus, a strong temptation seized the boy Cyrus. He had been on a purposeless errand to this place once that day. The corner of West and Dwight Streets lay more than half a mile from the end of the car route, and it was an almost untenanted district. His legs were very tired; his stomach ached with emptiness. Why not wait out the interval that it would take to walk to the corner and back in a little suburban station, read envelope No. 19, and spare himself? He had certainly done enough to prove that he was a faithful messenger.

Had he? Certain old and well-worn words came into his mind; they had been in his writing book in the early school days: "A chain is no stronger than its weakest link." Cyrus jumped off the car before it stopped, and started at a hot pace for the corner of West and Dwight Streets. There must be no weak places in his word of honor.

Doggedly, he went to the extreme limit of the indicated route, even taking the longest way round to make the turn. As he started back, beneath the arc light at the corner there suddenly appeared a city messenger boy. He approached Cyrus and, grinning, held out an envelope.

"Ordered to give you this," he said, "if you made connections. If you'd been later than five minutes past 7:00, I was to keep dark. You've got seven minutes and a half to spare. Strange orders, but the big railroad boss Woodbridge gave 'em to me."

Cyrus made his way back to the car with some self-congratulations that served to brace up the muscles behind his knees. This last incident showed him plainly that his father was putting him to a severe test of some sort, and he could have no doubt that it was for a purpose. His father was the sort of man who did things with a definite purpose indeed. Cyrus looked back over the day with an anxious searching of his memory to be sure that no detail of the singular service required of him had been slighted.

As he once more ascended the steps of his own home, he was so confident that his labors were now ended that he almost forgot about envelope No. 20, which he had been directed to read in the vestibule before entering the house. With his thumb on the bell button he remembered, and with a sigh he broke open the final seal.

Turn about, and go to Lenox Street Station, B. Railroad, reaching there by 8:05. Wait for messenger in west end of station.

It was a blow, but Cyrus had his second wind now. He felt like a machine—a hollow one—that could keep going indefinitely.

The Lenox Street Station was easily reached on time. The hands of the big clock were at only one minute past 8:00 when Cyrus entered. At the designated spot, the messenger met him. Cyrus recognized him as the porter on one of the trains of the road of which his grandfather and father were officers. Why, yes, he was the porter of the Woodbridge special car! He brought the boy a card that ran thus:

Give porter the letter from Norfolk Building, the card received at restaurant, the lecture coupon, yesterday evening's *Sentinel*, and the envelope received at Kingston Heights.

Cyrus silently delivered up these articles, feeling a sense of thankfulness that not one was missing. The porter went away with them but was back in three minutes.

"This way, sir," he said, and Cyrus followed, his heart beating fast. Down the track he recognized the "Fleetwing," President Woodbridge's private car. And Grandfather Cornelius he knew was just starting on a tour of his own and other roads, which included a flying trip to Mexico. Could it be possible—

In the car, his father and grandfather rose to meet him. Cornelius Woodbridge, Sr., was holding out his hand.

"Cyrus, lad," he said, his face one broad, triumphant smile, "you have stood the test, the Hezekiah Woodbridge test, sir, and you may be proud of it. Your word of honor can be depended upon. You are going with us through 19 states and Mexico. Is that reward enough for one day's hardships?"

"I think it is, sir," agreed Cyrus, his round face reflecting his grandfather's smile.

"Was it a hard pull, Cyrus?" questioned the senior Woodbridge with interest.

Cyrus looked at his father. "I don't think so—now, sir," he said.

Both men laughed.

"Are you hungry?"

"Well, just a little, Grandfather."

"Dinner will be served the moment we are off. We have only six minutes to wait. I am afraid—I am very much afraid"—the old gentleman turned to gaze searchingly out of the car window into the station—"that another boy's word of honor is not."

He stood, watch in hand. The conductor came in and remained, awaiting orders. "Two minutes more, Mr. Jefferson," he said. "One and a half . . . one . . . half a minute." He spoke sternly: "Pull out at 8:14 on the second, sir. Ah—"

The porter entered hurriedly and delivered a handful of envelopes into Grandfather Cornelius's grasp. The old gentleman scanned them at a glance.

"Yes, yes—all right!" he cried with the strongest evidences of excitement Cyrus had ever seen in his usually quiet manner. As the train made its first gentle motion of departure, a figure appeared in the doorway. Quietly, and not at all out of breath, Cornelius Woodbridge III walked into the car.

Then Grandfather Woodbridge grew impressive. He advanced and shook hands with his grandson as if he were greeting a distinguished member of the board of directors. Then he turned to his son and solemnly shook hands with him also. His eyes shone through his gold-rimmed spectacles, but his voice was grave with feeling.

"I congratulate you, Cornelius," he said, "on possessing two sons whose word of honor is above reproach. The smallest deviation from the outlined schedule would have resulted disastrously. Ten minutes' tardiness at the different points would have failed to obtain the requisite documents. Your sons did not fail. They can be depended upon. The world is in search of men built on those lines. I congratulate you, sir."

Cyrus was glad presently to escape to his stateroom with Cornelius. "Say, what did you have to do?" he asked eagerly. "Did you trot your legs off all over town?"

"Not much, I didn't!" said Cornelius grimly from the depths of a big towel. "I spent the whole day in a little hole of a room at the top of an empty building, with just 10 trips down the stairs to the ground floor to get envelopes at certain minutes. Twice, messengers met me unannounced at the top—checking up on me, I suppose, to see if I made it all the way back to that musty room. It was stifling hot there, too. I had not a crumb to eat or a thing to do, and could not even snatch a nap for fear I'd oversleep one of my dates at the bottom."

"That was worse than mine," admitted Cyrus reflectively.

"I should say it was. If you don't think so, try it."

"Dinner, boys," announced their father just outside their door—and they lost no time in responding.

It Happened on the Brooklyn Subway

Paul Deutschman

God's incredible choreography—it never ceases to amaze.

Marcel Sternberger was a methodical man of nearly 50, with bushy white hair, guileless brown eyes, and the bouncing enthusiasm of a czardas dancer of his native Hungary. He always took the 9:09 Long Island Railroad train from his suburban home to Woodside, where he caught a subway into the city.

On the morning of January 10, 1948, he boarded the 9:09 as usual. En route he suddenly decided to visit Laszlo Victor, a Hungarian friend who lived in Brooklyn and who was ill.

"I don't know why I decided to go to see him that morning," Sternberger told me some weeks afterward. "I could have done it after office hours. But I kept thinking that he could stand a little cheering up."

Accordingly, at Ozone Park, Sternberger changed to the subway for Brooklyn, went to his friend's house, and stayed until midafternoon. He then boarded a Manhattan-bound subway for his Fifth Avenue office.

"The car was crowded," Sternberger told me, "and there seemed to be no chance of a seat. But just as I entered, a man sitting by the door suddenly jumped up to leave, and I slipped into the empty place.

"I've been living in New York long enough not to start conversations with strangers. But, being a photographer, I have the peculiar habit of analyzing people's faces, and I was struck by the features of the passenger on my left. He was probably in his late thirties, and his eyes seemed to have a hurt expression in them. He was reading a Hungarian-language newspaper, and something prompted me to turn to him and say in Hungarian, 'I hope you don't mind if I glance at your paper.'

"The man seemed surprised to be addressed in his native language. But he answered politely, 'You may read it now. I'll have time later on.'

"During the half-hour ride to town, we had quite a conversation. He said his name was Paskin. A law student when the war started, he had been put into a labor battalion and sent to the Ukraine. Later he was captured by the Russians and put to work burying the German dead. After the war he covered hundreds of miles on foot, until he reached his home in Debrecen, a large city in eastern Hungary.

"I myself knew Debrecen quite well, and we talked about it for a while. Then he told me the rest of his story. When he went to the apartment once occupied by his father, mother, brothers, and sisters, he found strangers living there. Then he went upstairs to the apartment he and his wife had once had. It also was occupied by strangers. None of them had ever heard of his family.

"As he was leaving, full of sadness, a boy ran after him, calling '*Paskin bacsi! Paskin bacsi!*' That means 'Uncle Paskin.' The child was the son of some old neighbors of his. He went to the boy's home and talked to his parents. 'Your whole family is dead,' they told him. 'The Nazis took them and your wife to Auschwitz.'

"Auschwitz was one of the worst Nazi concentration camps. Paskin gave up all hope. A few days later, too heartsick to remain any longer in Hungary, which to him was a funeral land, he set out again on foot, stealing across border after border until he reached Paris. He had managed to emigrate to the United States in October 1947, just three months before I met him.

"All the time he had been talking, I kept thinking that somehow his story seemed familiar. A young woman whom I had met recently at the home of friends had also been from Debrecen; she had been sent to Auschwitz; from there she had been transferred to work in a German munitions factory. Her relatives had been killed in the gas chambers. Later she was liberated by the Americans and was brought here in the first boatload of displaced persons in 1946.

"Her story had moved me so much that I had written down her address and phone number, intending to invite her to meet my family and thus help relieve the terrible emptiness in her life.

"It seemed impossible that there could be any connection between these two people, but as I neared my station, I asked in what I hoped was a casual voice, 'Is your first name Bela?'

"He turned pale. 'Yes!' he answered. 'How did you know?'

"I fumbled anxiously in my address book. 'Was your wife's name Marya?'

"He looked as if he were about to faint. 'Yes! Yes!' he said.

"I said, 'Let's get off the train.' I took him by the arm at the next station and led him to a phone booth. He stood there like a man in a trance while I searched for the number in my address book.

"It seemed hours before Marya Paskin answered. (Later I learned her room was alongside the telephone, but she was in the habit of never answering it because she had so few friends and the calls were always for someone else. This time, however, there was no one else at home and, after letting it ring for a while, she responded.)

"When I heard her voice at last, I told her who I was and asked her to describe her husband. She seemed surprised at the question, but gave me a description. Then I asked her where she had lived in Debrecen, and she told me the address.

"Asking her to hold the wire, I turned to Paskin and said, 'Did you and your wife live on such-and-such a street?'

"'Yes!' Bela exclaimed. He was white as a sheet and trembling.

"'Try to be calm,' I urged him. 'Something miraculous is about to happen to you. Here, take this telephone and talk to your wife!'

"He nodded his head in mute bewilderment, his eyes bright with tears. He took the receiver, listened a moment to his wife's voice, then suddenly cried, 'This is Bela! This is Bela!' and began to mumble hysterically. Seeing that the poor fellow was so excited he couldn't talk coherently, I took the receiver from his shaking hands.

"'Stay where you are,' I told Marya, who also sounded hysterical. 'I am sending your husband to you. He will be there in a few minutes.'

"Bela was crying like a baby and saying over and over again, 'It is my wife. I go to my wife!'

"At first I thought I had better accompany Paskin lest the man should faint from excitement, but decided that this was a moment in which no stranger should intrude. Putting Paskin into a taxicab, I directed the driver to take him to Marya's address, paid the fare, and said good-bye.

"Bela Paskin's reunion with his wife was a moment so poignant, so electric with suddenly released emotion, that afterward neither he nor Marya could recall much about it.

"'I remember only that when I left the phone, I walked to the mirror like in a dream to see if maybe my hair had turned gray,' she said later. 'The next thing I know, a taxi stops in front of the house, and it is my husband who comes toward me. Details I cannot remember; only this I know—that I was happy for the first time in many years. . . .

"'Even now it is difficult to believe that it happened. We have both suffered so much; I have almost lost the capability to be not afraid. Each time my husband goes from the house, I say to myself, "Will anything happen to take him from me again?"'

"Her husband is confident that no horrible misfortune will ever again befall them. 'Providence has brought us together,' he says simply. 'It was meant to be.'"

Skeptical persons would no doubt attribute the events of that memorable afternoon to mere chance. But was it chance that made Sternberger suddenly decide to visit his sick friend and hence take a subway line that he had never ridden before? Was it chance that caused the man sitting by the door of the car to rush out just as Sternberger came in? Was it chance that caused Bela Paskin to be sitting beside Sternberger, reading a Hungarian newspaper?

Was it chance—or did God ride the Brooklyn subway that afternoon?

A Lesson in Forgiveness

T. Morris Longstreth

To forgive or not to forgive? Both the 14-year-old boy and the tall, haggard stranger wrestled with that question.

The Ripley brothers were as different in nearly every way as are the rapids and still pools of a mountain stream. Perhaps that is why they loved each other in a way not usually meant by "brotherly love." Will Ripley was the "still pool." He was thoughtful to the point of appearing drowsy, honest as daylight, mild-tempered, and 20. On July 7, 1863, he was up north in Pennsylvania somewhere, either alive or dead, for as you can read in the dispatches of the time, the terrible Battle of Gettysburg was just over. The Ripleys, on their farm near Washington, had not heard from him for some time.

Although Will was no soldier at heart, he had responded to Lincoln's call for more men two years before, leaving his young brother, Dan, at home to help his father and mother. Dan was now 14, a high-strung, impetuous, outspoken lad of quick actions and hasty decisions. He was the "laughing rapid." But for all his hastiness, he had a head and a heart that could be appealed to, usually.

The only thing to which he could not reconcile himself was the separation from Will. Even Will's weekly letters—which had seldom missed coming until recently, and which always sent messages of love to Dan, coupled with encouragement to stay on the farm as the best way to aid the cause—scarcely kept him from running away and hunting up his brother. Dan knew that he and his collie, Jack, were needed to look after the sheep; he knew that his father, who was little more than an invalid, must have help. But to see the soldiers marching set him wild to be off with them. In fact, Jack seemed to be the anchor that held him. Dan sometimes even thought that he loved Jack next to Will.

The summer of '63 had been unbearably hot. There had been an increasing ominous list of military disasters. Even the loyal were beginning to murmur against Lincoln's management of the war. Then Will's letters had ceased, and Mr. Ripley could get no answers from headquarters.

Dan was irritable with fatigue and his secret worry; his family was nearly sick with the heat and the tension.

The climax to this state came from an unforeseen event. Jack, crazed either by the heat or by some secret taste for blood, ran amok one night, stampeded the sheep, and did grievous damage. Farmer Ripley doubtless acted on what he considered the most merciful course, by having Jack done away with and buried before Dan got back from an errand to the city. But to Dan it seemed, in the first agony of his broken heart, an unforgivable thing. Weariness, worry, and now this knife-sharp woe changed the boy into a heartsick being who flung himself on the fresh mound behind the barn and stayed there the whole day, despite the entreaties of his mother and the commands of his father.

That evening his mother carried some food out to him. He did not touch it; he would not talk to her.

Sometime later, as the night wore on, he stole into the house, tied up some clothes into a bundle, took the food at hand, and crept out of his home. Once more he went to the grave of his slain pal. What he said there, aloud but quietly, need not be told. Sufficient it is to know that a burning resentment toward his father filled him, coupled with a sickening longing to be with his brother, Will. Ill with his hasty anger, he thought that Will was the only one in the world who loved or understood him.

In the wee hours of morning, he left the farm, forever, as he thought, and turned down the road that led to the Soldiers' Home not far away, where he hoped to find someone who could tell him how to get to Will's regiment. The sultry, starless heat of a Washington midsummer enclosed him; the wood was dark and breathless; his head throbbed. But he pushed on, high-tempered, unforgiving; he would show them all!

Suddenly, he remembered that he had not said the Lord's Prayer that night. Dan had been reared strictly. He tried saying it, walking. But that seemed sacrilegious. He knelt in the dark and tried. But when he got to "as we forgive our debtors," he stopped, for he was an honest lad. This new gulf of mental distress was too much for him; it brought tears. There in the dark by the roadside, Dan lay and bitterly cried himself into an exhausted sleep.

At the same hour another worn person, a tall, lean-faced man with eyes full of unspeakable sorrow, was pacing the chamber of the White House in the nearby city. The rebellion had reached its flood tide at Gettysburg three days before. The president had stayed the flood, bearing in tireless sympathy the weight of countless responsibilities. Now, all day long, decisions of affairs had been borne down upon him—decisions that concerned not only armies, but races; not only races, but principles of human welfare. He was grief-stricken still from his son Willie's death, and his secretary in the room downstairs, listening unconsciously to the steady march of steps overhead, read into them the pulse beats of human progress. Lincoln had given instructions that no one was to interrupt him. He was having one of his great heart battles.

Finally, shortly before dawn, the footsteps stopped, the secretary's door opened, and the gaunt, gray face looked in. "Stoddard, do you want anything more from me tonight?"

The secretary rose. "I want you in bed, sir. Mrs. Lincoln should not have gone away; you are not fair with her or us."

"Don't reproach me, Stoddard," said Lincoln kindly. "It had to be settled, and with God's help, it has been. Now I can sleep. But I must have a breath of air first. There's nothing?"

"Only the matter of those deserters, sir, and that can wait."

The president passed his hands over his deep-lined face. "Only!" he murmured. "Only! How wicked this war is! It leads us to consider lives by the dozen, by the bale, wholesale. How many in this batch, Stoddard?"

The secretary turned some papers. "Twenty-four, sir. You remember the interview with General Scanlon yesterday."

Lincoln hesitated, saying, "Twenty-four! Yes, I remember. Scanlon said that lenience to the few was injustice to the many. He is right, too." Lincoln held out his hand for the papers, then drew it back and looked up at Stoddard. "I can't decide," he said in a low voice, "not now. Stoddard, you see a weak man. But I want to thresh this out a little longer. I must walk. These cases are killing me; I must get out."

"Let me call an attendant, Mr. Lincoln."

"They're all asleep. No, I'll take my chances with God. If anybody wants to kill me, he will do it. You must go to bed, Stoddard."

The two men, each concerned for the other, shook hands good-night, and Lincoln slipped out into the dark, his long legs bearing him rapidly northward. During the heat, he usually slept at the Soldiers' Home, being escorted thither by cavalry with sabers drawn. But he hated the noise of it, and during Mrs. Lincoln's absence, was playing truant to her rules. When he neared the Home, he felt slightly refreshed and turned onto a wood road. The sky to his right began to lighten.

By the time dawn showed the ruts in the road, Lincoln realized that he was tired. "Abe, Abe," he said half aloud, "they tell me you used to be great at splitting rails, and now a five-mile stroll before breakfast— Well, what have we here?"

The exclamation was occasioned by his nearly stepping on a lone youngster lying in the road. The boy raised his head from a small bundle of clothes. The tall man stooped with tenderness, saying, "Hello, sonny. So you got old Mother Earth to make your bed for you! How's the mattress?"

Dan sat up and rubbed his eyes. "What are you doin'?" he asked.

"I appear to be waking you and making a bad job of it," said Lincoln.

"You didn't come to take me, then," exclaimed Dan, greatly relieved. "I wouldn'ta gone!" he added defiantly.

Lincoln looked at him sharply, his interest aroused by the trace of tears in the boy's eyes and the bravado in his voice. "There's a misunderstanding here," said Lincoln, "almost as bad a misunderstanding as Mamie and her mother had over Mr. Riggs, who was the undertaker back home." Here the gaunt man gave a preliminary chuckle. "Ever hear that story, sonny?"

Dan shook his head, wondering how such a homely man could sound so likable. Lincoln seated

himself on a fallen tree trunk. "Well, it was this way . . ." And he told the story.

Dan's quick, impetuous laugh might have disturbed the early-rising birds. Lincoln joined in, and for an instant Dan completely forgot dead Jack and his deserted home. For the same fleeting instant, Lincoln forgot his troubles in Dan's laugh.

The boy chuckled again. "I'll have to tell that to Fa—" He didn't finish the word, remembering with a pang that he was not going to see his father again.

Lincoln caught the swift change on his face, and it was his turn to wonder. He knew better than to ask questions. You can't fish for a boy's heart with question marks, neat little fishhooks though they be. So he said, "Our sitting here when we ought to be getting back home reminds me of another story."

"Tell me," said Dan, well won already to this man, despite the gray, lined cheeks and the sadness that colored his voice. Dan didn't know yet who he was. He had not seen the cartoons that flooded the country during the election. He was too young to go in alone to the inauguration, and the idea of the president of the United States sitting with him in the woods was too preposterous to cross his mind.

When Dan had laughed heartily over the second story, Lincoln said, "Well, sonny, I reckon we ought to be moving, don't you?" He helped the lad with his bundle.

"Are you going to the war, too?" asked Dan. "I am."

"You!" exclaimed Lincoln. "Why, you're no bigger than my own Tadpole, and he's only a wriggler yet. Does your father know?"

"I reckon he does by now," said the boy darkly. "Father's an early riser. You see, he killed my dog without my knowin', and so I left without *his* knowin'."

The hardness of the boy's voice hurt Lincoln, who said, "What's your father's name, sonny?"

"William Ripley—that is, senior. Will, that's junior, my brother, is off at the war. I'm Dan. I'm going to find my brother. I don't care if I never come back. I loved Jack better than—than—" His voice choked.

Lincoln put his hand on the boy's shoulder. He was getting the situation. "Jack was your dog?" asked the big man as gently as a mother.

"Yeah. And Father shouldn'ta killed him unbeknownst to me. I'll never forgive him that, never!"

"Quite right," said the wise man, walking with him. "Don't you ever forgive him, Dan. Or don't ever forget it—under one condition."

"What's that?" asked the boy, a trifle puzzled at the unexpected compliance of his elder with his own unforgiving mood.

"Why, that you also never forget all the kind and just things that your father has done for you. Why did he kill the dog, Dan?"

"Well—he—killed—some sheep," said the boy. He would be honest with this tall, gentle, and grave person who understood so readily.

"How old are you, Dan?"

"Fourteen, going on 15."

"That's quite a heap," said Lincoln musingly, "quite a heap! In 14 years a father can pile up a lot of good deeds. But I suppose he's done a lot of mean ones to cancel 'em off, has he?"

"No," admitted Dan.

His frankness pleased the president. "I congratulate you, Dan. You're honest. I want to be honest with you and tell you a story that isn't funny, for we're both in the same boat, as I size up this proposition—yes, both in the same boat. I am in the army in a way. At least, I'm called commander-in-chief, and occasionally they let me meddle a little in things."

"Honest?" said Dan, opening his eyes wide. He had been so absorbed in his own disasters that he had accepted this strange, friendly acquaintance without question. But now, although the forefront of his consciousness was active with the conversation, the misty background was trying to compare this man with a certain picture in the big family album, with another one pasted on the dining room cupboard door, the same loose-hung person, only this one had a living rawness—maybe it was bigness—about him that the pictures didn't give, like a tree, perhaps. But it *couldn't* be the president talking to him, Dan. If it was, what would the folks at home . . . And again his thought stopped. There were to be no more "folks at home" for him.

"Honestly, Dan. But sometimes they don't like it when I do meddle. There's a case on now. Last night I pretty nearly had 24 men shot."

"Whew!"

"But I hadn't quite decided, and that's the reason I came out here in God's own woods. And I'm glad I came, for you've helped me decide."

"I have!" said Dan, astonished. "To shoot them?"

"No! Not to. You showed me the case in a new light. Here you are, deserting home, deserting your father, bringing sorrow to him and to your mother, who have sorrowed enough with Will in danger and all; you're punishing your father because he did one deed that he couldn't very well help, just as if he'd been a mean man all his life.

"And it's like that with my 24 deserters, Dan, very much like that. They've served faithfully for years. So, can any one thing they do be so gross, so enormously bad, as to blot out all the rest, including probably a lifetime of decent living? I think not.

"Is a man to blame for having a pair of legs that play coward once? I think not, Dan.

"I tell you what I'll do, sonny." The tall man stopped in the road, a new light shining in his cavernous, sad eyes. "I'll make a bargain with you. If you'll go home and forgive your father, I'll go home and forgive my 24 deserters. Is that a bargain?"

The boy had been shaken, but it was difficult to change all at once. "It is hard to forgive," he murmured.

"Someday you'll find it hard not to," said the great man, putting out his huge palm for the boy to shake. "Isn't that a pretty good bargain, Dan? By going home, by ceasing to be a deserter yourself, you will save the lives of 24 men. Won't you be merciful? God will remember and perhaps forgive you some trespass sometime even as you forgive now."

Something of last night's horror, when he could not say that prayer, and something of the melting gentleness of the new friend before him, touched the boy. He took Lincoln's hand, saying, "All right. That's a go."

"Yes, a go home." Lincoln smiled. "I suppose I'll have to turn now."

"Where's your home?" asked the boy, knowing, yet wishing to hear the truth, to be sure, for now he *could* tell the folks at home.

"The White House," replied Lincoln, "but I wish I were going back to the farm with you."

The boy heard him vaguely, his jaw sagging. "Then you—are the president?"

Lincoln nodded, enjoying the boy's wonder. "And your servant, don't forget," added Lincoln. "You have been a help to me in a hard hour, Dan. Generals or no generals, I'll spare those men. Anytime I can do anything for you, drop in, now that you know where to find me."

The boy was still speechless with his assured elation.

"But you'd better . . . Wait." Lincoln began hunting through his pockets. "You'd better let me give you a latchkey. The man at the door is a stubborn fellow, for the folks will bother him. Here—"

And finding a card and a stub of a pencil, he wrote:

Please admit Dan'l Ripley on demand.
A. Lincoln

"How's that?"

"Thank you," said Dan proudly. "I reckon I shoulda guessed it was you, but those stories you told kinda put me off."

"That's sometimes why I tell them." Lincoln smiled again. "It's not a bad morning's work—24 lives saved before breakfast, Dan. You and I ought to be able to eat a comfortable meal. Good-bye, sonny."

And so they parted. The man strode back the way he had come; the boy stood looking, looking, and then swiftly wheeled and sped. He had been talking to the president, to Abraham Lincoln, and hearing such talk as he never had heard before—but especially the words "You have been a help to me in a hard hour, Dan." Those words trod a regular path to his brain. Dan ran, eager to get to the very home he had been so eager to leave. Forgiveness was in his heart, but chiefly there was a warm pride. He had been praised by Abraham Lincoln! Of this day he would talk to the end of his days.

Dan did not know that the major part of the day, the greatest in his life, was still to come. Certainly, the dawning of it had been beautiful.

Breathless and with eyes bright in anticipation of telling his tale, he leaped the fences, ran up to the back door, and plunged into the house. The kitchen was quiet. A misgiving ran over him. Were they all out in search of him? Would he have to postpone his triumph?

In the dining room, a half-eaten meal was cooling. He explored on, and coming out to the spacious front of the house, found them—found them in an inexplicable group around a uniformed officer. Tears were streaming down his mother's cheeks. His father, still pale from his accident, looked ashen and shriveled.

They turned at Dan's approach. He expected that this scene of anguish would turn to smiles upon his arrival. He was amazed to find that his return gave them the merest flurry of relief and alleviated their sorrow not at all.

"Danny, dear, where have you been?" asked his mother.

"The Lord must have sent you home in answer to our prayers," said his father.

Then they turned back to the officer, pleading, both talking at once, weeping. Dan felt hurt. Did his return, his forgiveness, mean so little to them? He might as well have gone on. Then he caught the officer's words: "Colonel Scott can do no more, madam. The president cannot see him, and more pardons are not to be hoped for."

Mrs. Ripley turned and threw her arm across Dan's shoulders. "Danny, Danny, you are our only son now. Will was—" She broke down completely.

"Will was found asleep while on duty, Dan," his father said grimly.

"Is he to be shot?" asked the boy. "I wonder if he was one of the 24."

They looked at him, not understanding.

"The Lord has restored you to us. If we could only pray in sufficient faith, He could restore Will," said Farmer Ripley devoutly. "Dear, let us go in and pray. We should release this gentleman to his duty. We can talk to the Father about it."

Dan realized with a sudden clearness that his brother, his beloved, was to be taken from him as Jack had been taken. It shook his brain dizzy for a moment, but he knew that he must hold on to his wits—must think. There was Abraham Lincoln, *his friend!*

"You pray," he cried to his father shrilly, "and I'll run."

"Run where, dear? Will is in Pennsylvania."

"To the White House, Mother. He said, 'Anytime I can do anything for you, drop in.' *Anything,* Mother. Surely he'll—"

"Who?" cried both his parents.

"Why, the president, Mr. Lincoln!"

"But the president is busy, dear."

"He'll see me—I know he will!" said Dan. "Look! We have a secret together, the president and I have." And the boy showed his card and poured out his story.

The mother saw a break in her gray heaven, saw the bright blue of hope.

"We must go at once," she said. "Father, you are not able to come with us, but pray here for us."

"Please take my horse and carriage," said the officer.

"Yes," said Dan, "let's hurry. Oh, I'm glad, I'm so glad!" And the joy at his luck turning back shone in his face as he helped his mother into the vehicle.

"May God help you!" said the officer.

"He does," said the boy.

It was high noon when the doorkeeper of the White House, hardened into a stony guard by the daily onslaught of Lincoln seekers, saw an impetuous youth leap from a light carriage and help a woman up the portico steps toward him.

"In which room is the president?" asked Dan.

"He's very busy," said the doorkeeper, probably for the five-hundredth time that morning. "Have you an appointment?"

"No, but he said I should drop in when I wanted to; and what's more, here's my 'latchkey.'" Dan, trembling a little with haste and pride, showed him the card "A. Lincoln" had written.

The man looked quizzically at it and at him. "In that case," he said dryly, "you'd better step into the waiting room there."

There must have been 40 or 50 people crowded into the anteroom, each on some urgent errand. Some were in uniform; all looked tired, impatient, important. Dan saw the situation and knew that Lincoln could never see them all. He whispered to his mother and showed her to a chair. Then he went up to the doorboy and asked if the president was in the next room. The boy admitted the fact but would not admit anything further.

The annoyed looks on the faces of the waiting people deepened. *Does this urchin,* said their looks, *expect to see the president today, when so many more important persons (such as we) are kept waiting?*

Dan, not caring for etiquette when his brother might be shot at any moment, slipped under the arm of the doorboy and bolted into the room.

Lincoln was standing by the window. He looked around in surprise at the noise of Dan Ripley's entry. He recognized his walking partner, made a motion for the doorboy, who had one irate hand on Dan, to withdraw, and said, "Why, Dan, I'm glad to see you so soon again. You're just in time to back me up. Let me introduce you to General Scanlon."

Dan looked into the amazed and angry eyes of a Union general who, practically ignoring the boy, went on to say, "Mr. President, I repeat that unless these men are made an example of, the army itself may be in danger. Mercy to these 24 means cruelty to nearly a million."

The president, worn not only from his sleepless night but from the incessant strain of things, looked grave, for the general spoke truth. He turned to Dan. "Did you go home, sonny?"

Dan nodded.

"Then I shall keep my half of the bargain. General, this boy and I each walked the woods half the night carrying similar troubles, trying to decide whether it was best to forgive. We decided that it was best, as the Bible says, even to 70 times seven. Dan, how did your folks take it?"

Dan spoke quickly. "It woulda killed them if I'd run off for good, for they just got word that my brother, Will—I told you about him—is to be shot for sleeping on watch. I just know he was tired out—he didn't go to sleep on purpose. I told my mother that you wouldn't let him be shot, if you knew."

Lincoln groaned audibly and turned away to the window for a moment. The general snorted.

"I brought my mother in to see you, too," said Dan, "seeing as she wouldn't quite believe what I said about our agreement."

Lincoln looked at the boy, and his sunken eyes glistened. "I agreed for 24 lives," he said, "but I don't mind throwing in an extra one for you, Dan."

And this time the general groaned.

"Stoddard," added the president, "will you see if there is a Will Ripley on file?"

The secretary left the room. Lincoln turned abruptly to the general. "You have heard me," he said. "I, with the help of God and this boy, threshed out the matter to a conclusion, and we only waste time to discuss it further. If I pardon these deserters, it surely becomes a better investment for the United

States than if I had them shot—24 live fighters in the ranks, instead of that many corpses underground. There are too many weeping widows now. Don't ask me to add to that number, *for I won't do it!*"

It was rarely that Lincoln was so stirred. There was a strange silence. Then the secretary entered with "Yes, sir, a Will Ripley is to be executed tomorrow for sleeping on duty. The case was buried in the files; it should have been brought to you earlier."

"Better for the case to be buried than the boy," said the president. "Give me the paper, Stoddard."

"Then you will!" said Dan, trembling with joy.

"I don't believe that shooting the boy will do him any good," said Lincoln as the pen traced the letters of his name beneath this message: *Will Ripley is not to be shot until further orders from me.*

Dan looked at it. "Oh, thank you!" he said. "Can I bring Mother in to see it—and to see you?" he asked.

The president looked down into the shining face and could not refuse. In a moment, Dan's mother was in the room. She was all confused; the general was red with irritation.

She read the message. It didn't seem quite clear to her. "Is that a pardon? Does that mean he won't be shot at all?"

"My dear madam," replied Lincoln kindly, "evidently you are not acquainted with me. If your son never looks on death till orders come from me to shoot him, he will live to be a great deal older than anyone else."

She stretched out both her hands, crying, "I want to thank you, sir. Oh, thank you, thank you!"

"Thank Dan here," said Lincoln. "If he had not let the warmth of forgiveness soften his heart, Will Ripley would have died. And perhaps, if I had not met him in the woods at dawn, I might have gone into eternity with the blood of these 24 men on my hands. Dan helped me.

"True, they are erring soldiers, Mrs. Ripley. But we must consider what they have done and what they will do as intently as we consider the wrong of the moment. Good-bye, Dan; we shall both remember today with easy consciences."

The waiting crowd in the anteroom could not understand, of course, why that intruder of a boy who had fairly dragged the woman in to see the president so unceremoniously should bring her out on his arm with such conscious pride. They could not understand why the tears were rolling down her cheeks at the same time that a smile glorified her face. They did not see that the boy was walking on air, on light. But the dullest of them could see that he was radiant with a great happiness.

And if they could have looked past him and pierced the door of the inner room with their wondering glances, they would have seen a reflection of Dan's joy still shining on the somber, deep-lined face of the man who had again indulged himself in mercy.

Inkspot

Louise Redfield Peattie

Of what possible value could it be, this sickly, dark blob of a kitten?

From the beginning, he wasn't wanted. Oh, of course his mother wanted him; and blind and ignorant as he was, he could feel, in the touch of her warm, eager little fingers, that Winnie wanted him. But Winnie's mother didn't, which was what really mattered. She didn't want any of them.

And they were pretty kittens at that. All, that is, except the black one, who was certainly a scrawny, rusty, unattractive little worm, weakly wriggling under the stronger crowd of his greedy brothers and sisters. So that, as they grew older and their eyes opened to milky blue innocence, they all found welcoming homes among families in the neighborhood—all but the littlest black one. There was no one to want him. Winnie found him crying his faint, plaintive cry in the woodpile, alone and hungry, and carried him in a passion of pity into the drawing room.

"It looks," said her uncle George, surveying the kitten where it stood unsteadily in the middle of the Aubusson carpet, "like a small, small blot of ink."

"And about as welcome," said his sister with a vexed laugh. "Winnie dear, we simply can't keep him." And she rang for Isaiah, the old hired houseman.

Thus, in a burlap bag with a stone tied around the top, Inkspot went to his doom. Isaiah, carrying him toward the river and shuffling along with the bag dangling forgotten from his old bony hand, never noticed when it grew a little lighter. Inkspot, standing in the dusty road, looked after him mildly, watched him hurl the loosely tied bag in a wide parabola into the river, and then, as a cart came rumbling by, scuttled into the roadside weeds. When he emerged again, the old man was already some distance down the homeward road, and Inkspot, with an anxious *mew*, trotted after him.

The family was on the veranda when Inkspot, dusty and bedraggled, wobbled up the steps. He looked at them out of his innocent and hopeful blue eyes and mewed. With a glad little cry, Winnie ran to him and gathered him up in her arms.

"Put him down, Winnie," said her mother sharply. "George, however in the world—"

"Very hard to kill a black cat," said Uncle George sagely.

But Winnie's mother was obdurate, and in the end it was Uncle George himself who carried the kitten downstairs, at arm's length, with a bottle in the other hand. There in the dungeon gloom of the basement, he found a starch box and thrust Inkspot under it; he found a rag, and saturating it with the overpowering fluid from the bottle, he thrust that too under the box.

Uncle George never told how well or ill he slept that night. But it was before breakfast that he descended to the basement. The starch box stood mutely in the middle of the floor, and he grimly took it up. Gladly crying, Inkspot dashed out and wreathed himself in happy gratitude about Uncle George's ankle.

No one heard Uncle George gasp as he mopped his brow with his silk handkerchief. Inkspot, hungry and lighthearted, bounded up the cellar stairs, and Uncle George followed, too bewildered to look twice at the starch box, where it lay overturned, showing the little knothole that had brought life all night to Inkspot's unhappy pink nose.

"I told you it couldn't be done," said Uncle George at breakfast, with an air of vindication. "Not to a cat as black as that."

Winnie's tears and entreaties broke down her mother's determination. Inkspot, reprieved, was taken into the family. It was an interlude so perfect as to constitute a cat heaven. By the glowing hearth in the drawing room there was a place for Inkspot now, where he might lie with paws softly folded under him, purring like a boiling kettle and staring at the flames with eyes holding a mystery that since time's beginning has awed humanity.

As the halcyon days passed, Inkspot's spindly legs grew stronger, his heart lighter. He took to frisking in the middle of the Aubusson carpet, chasing his tail in that delirium of fluid grace so fascinating for clumsy human beings to watch. And Winnie on the hearth rug would clap her hands and squeal in delight. Her mother, in the grownups' Olympus of proper chairs and tables, talked with a guest above the heads of the two young things.

"Old Isaiah is getting much too cranky anyway," she was saying, "and this new butler, my dear, is a marvel! English, and with the most perfect manner. He's been trained since boyhood, it seems, in the houses of the nobility."

The guest murmured appreciatively. Inkspot uncurled himself and sat up. He blinked, yawned, and began to wash his face, sitting in the middle of the hearth rug, insignificant and unobtrusive.

With a step as noiseless as Inkspot's own, the butler entered with the tray, a tall, suave figure with a lean, intelligent face sallow above his black clothes.

Inkspot stopped washing his face and stared at the newcomer.

A strangling cry broke from the butler; the tray wavered in his hands, and a cup crashed to the floor. "Take it away! Take it away!" The man's face was a sick yellow, and he stood shuddering, with the tray rattling in his hands.

"Why, what's the matter?" His mistress was on her feet. "It's the kitten! Winnie, take it away—quickly!"

Winnie jumped up, plucked the innocent Inkspot from the rug, and scurried from the room. The butler put the tray down and mopped his damp face. "Forgive me, madam. I do beg you to excuse it. It's cats, madam—I can't abide them. I'm most deeply sorry. It shan't occur again, madam—that is, if the cat keeps away."

"Very well, then, Jeffries. That's all," said his mistress hastily, and the butler stepped, a tall, quick shadow, through the heavy curtains and out of the room.

"Well!" said Winnie's mother. "Did you ever see anything so perfectly weird?"

"Oh, but it's quite well known—that horror of cats," said her guest, leaning forward animatedly. "There are people simply born that way, it seems."

That sealed Inkspot's doom. When Winnie stole up from the basement where, upon a pile of kindling, she had sat fearfully cuddling her pet, it was to hear Inkspot's banishment pronounced. She pleaded vainly, the kitten dangling limp and willing in her arms, her tears falling on his small black head so that he twitched his ears once or twice in protest. "The cat must go," decreed her mother. And Uncle George dropped him outside and closed the heavy front door upon him where he stood, mewing unhappily, in the snow that was beginning to fill the winter night.

All night the wind cried around the house, blowing the snow in drifts between the pillars, fumbling at the shutters with icy fingers. Waking in the night, Winnie heard the wind and heard, under her window, a faint and miserable mewing. She cried a little, piteously, into her pillow, there in the dark, and then went to sleep again. But Inkspot prowled still around and around the unrelenting house, his fur blown the wrong way by cruel, cold fingers of the wind.

Dawn, breaking bleakly upon a world that the wearied wind had left numb with cold, found the kitten crouched in the woodpile, in the damp straw that once had been a happy cradle. But the big sleek side that had warmed him was gone now; there was only the shut kitchen door that he watched with a forlorn stare, waiting hopefully.

When it opened, Inkspot was there in a bound, crying his thin cry joyously, looking up with beseeching round, blue eyes. Jeffries, in the doorway, sprang aside and slammed the door in the kitten's face. For a long time, Inkspot lingered, mournfully complaining, but no one came and the door never opened. After awhile, he went away forlornly, into the world to see what he could find.

So Inkspot became an outcast, an Ishmael of the alleys. He lived on pickings from ash cans and dump piles; his coat grew mangy from bad food, and his blue eyes wild and frightened. Crouching by a dustbin, licking an empty salmon can, he would bolt at a footstep, in the terror he had learned from harsh experience. He did not grow fast, poorly nourished as he was, and he became thinner daily; nothing could have been more insignificant than the superfluous black kitten that nevertheless managed to cling to life, unwanted and unhappy. Often he returned to the home of his brief happiness, for his hope was hard to kill, but always he was chased away, and once, when the sallow face of Jeffries looked down on him from the pantry window, he fled in terror.

Yet he returned once more. It was in the night, a night of black and bitter frost, with a great moon looking coldly on the world, when the old longing for remembered comfort came strongly back upon him. Over the frozen ruts of lane and alleyway he trotted, till he saw the white pillars of the house that had been home, shining and stately in the moonlight. But Inkspot did not take the box-lined path that led to them, to the big house door; he knew that door would never open to him now. Yet with its picture of the dancing fire making a dim warmness in his kitten mind, he prowled miserably and hopelessly around the side of the house, looking up with eyes that glittered in the moonlight at the blank windows.

And then, turning the corner, he stopped and stared. There was a black shadow under one of the ground-floor windows, and the window was open. He could hear the shadowy figure whispering; despite his fear, he drew alertly nearer, drawn by that open window. In it, by the moon's light, he saw the face of Jeffries. Something brightly shining—the silver tray Inkspot knew—passed through the window to the man on the ground, who stooped and put it softly in the sack at his feet.

"That's about the last of the stuff," Jeffries was softly saying. "Now I'll fetch the rope, and you can come in and tie me and gag me."

The man under the window nodded silently, and Jeffries vanished from the window. In that instant, the starved and shivering kitten ran to the window and leaped in, unseen, unsuspecting, and eager.

Despite the cold air from the open window, there was blessed warmth, and Inkspot's heart leaped within him. There was a footfall in the dark room, and a whisper, and Inkspot, who bore no grudges, who looked on all in this haven as friend, ran with a little chirp to the shadowy figure and warmly, with his whole wriggling body, caressed the approaching ankle.

A terrible, uncontrollable yell broke from the throat of Jeffries. The shadow that had been darkening the moonlit window dropped from the sill, and its footfalls sounded in noisy haste down the path. A voice called upstairs, and there were running feet. When the door opened with a flood of light, the bewildered Inkspot looked up, blinking, to see crowding figures in the doorway, as bewildered as he, staring at Jeffries where he crouched against the wall shuddering away from the small, black, anxious kitten who sat in the middle of the floor between him and escape.

The next time there were guests for dinner, a crisply aproned maid brought in the silver service. At the sight, Inkspot, sleek and fattened, rose from the hearth rug, and waving his tail with an assured and lordly mien, he strolled to the table. Winnie's mother filled a fragile saucer from the cream pitcher.

"Isn't he the dearest little creature?" she said fondly. "And do you know, he's a little hero! Let me tell you . . ."

But Inkspot, crouched greedily over the saucer, understood not a word. He only knew that somehow miraculously, he was wanted at last.

The Necklace

Guy de Maupassant

For one shining moment—
but only one—she was elegant,
beautiful, acceptable.

She was one of those pretty, charming girls born as if by a mistake of
destiny into a family of clerks. She had no dowry, no expectations,
no means of being known, appreciated, loved, married by a man
either rich or distinguished; and she allowed herself to be married to
a petty clerk at the Ministry of Education.

She was simply dressed, not being able to dress richly; but unhappy,
as one out of her class; for women have no caste or race. Their beauty,
their grace, and their charm serve them in the place of good birth and
family. Their native sensitiveness, their instinct for elegance, their
suppleness of wit, are their only aristocracy, making some daughters of
the people the equal of the greatest ladies.

She suffered incessantly, feeling herself born for every delicacy and every luxury. She suffered from the poverty of her apartment, from the shabby walls, from the worn-out chairs, from the ugliness of it all. All these things, which another woman of her station might not have noticed, tortured and angered her. The sight of the little Breton girl, who did simple housework for her, roused in her sad regrets and desperate dreams. She dreamed of quiet antechambers padded with oriental hangings and lit by bronze candelabras, and of two tall footmen in knee breeches who slept in the wide armchairs in the heavy heat of a hot-air stove. She dreamed of great reception rooms hung in old silks, of fine furniture adorned with priceless bric-a-brac, and of dainty drawing rooms, perfumed, made for 5:00 chats with one's most intimate friends, men known and sought after, whose attentions all women envied and desired.

When she seated herself for dinner—before the round table, where the tablecloth had been used three days, opposite her husband who took the lid off the soup tureen and declared with an air of enchantment, "Ah! the good old boiled beef and carrots! I don't know anything better than that!"—she would dream of elegant dinners, of glittering silverplate, of tapestries peopling the walls with figures of the days of old and with strange birds amid a fairy forest; she would dream of exquisite food served in marvelous dishes, of whispered gallantries listened to with a sphinxlike smile, all the while eating the rose-colored flesh of a trout or the wings of a grouse.

She had no fine dresses, no jewels, nothing. And she loved those things only; she felt herself made for them. She would have liked so much to please, to be envied, to be seductive, exquisite, and sought after.

She had a rich woman friend, a schoolmate of convent days, whom she did not like to visit because she suffered so much when she returned. She would weep for whole days, from sorrow, from regret, from despair, and from wretchedness.

One evening, her husband came in elatedly, holding in his hand a large envelope.

"Here," he said, "here is something for you."

She tore open the wrapper quickly and drew out a printed card that bore these words:

> The Minister of Education and Madame Georges Ramponneau ask the honor of Monsieur and Madame Loisel's company on Monday evening, the 18th of January, at the Minister's residence.

Instead of being delighted as her husband had hoped, she threw the invitation spitefully upon the table, retorting, "What do you expect me to do with that?"

"But, my dear, I thought it would make you happy. You never go out, and this is an opportunity, a fine one. I've had no end of trouble to get it. Everybody wants one; it is very exclusive, and not many invitations are given to the clerks. You'll see the whole official world there."

She looked at him angrily and declared impatiently, "What do you expect me to wear to such a thing as that?"

He hadn't thought of that. He stammered, "Why, the dress you go to the theater in. I think that's a very nice one."

He stopped speaking, stupefied, dismayed, seeing that his wife was crying. Noting two great tears slowly falling from the corners of her eyes toward the corners of her mouth, he stammered, "What's the matter? What's the matter?"

But with a violent effort, she regained her composure and answered in a calm voice, wiping her wet cheeks, "Nothing. Only I have no dress, and consequently I can't go to this reception. Give your invitation to one of your colleagues whose wife is better fitted out than I am."

In despair, he tried again. "See here, Mathilda. How much would it cost to get a suitable dress, something you could use again on other occasions, something very simple?"

She reflected a few seconds, reckoning up the cost and thinking as well of a sum that she could ask for without an immediate refusal and a frightened exclamation from the thrifty clerk.

"I can't tell exactly, but it seems to me that 400 francs ought to cover it."

He turned a little pale, for he had saved just that sum to buy a gun so that he might be able to join hunting parties next summer on the plains of Nanterre with some friends who were going to shoot at larks up there on Sundays. Nevertheless, he answered, "Very well. I'll give you 400 francs. But try to have a pretty dress."

The day of the reception approached, and Madame Loisel seemed sad, uneasy, anxious. Nevertheless, her dress was nearly ready. One evening her husband said to her, "What's the matter with you? You have acted strangely for two or three days."

And she answered, "I'm vexed at not having some jewels—not a single stone; nothing to adorn myself with. I shall look dreadfully poverty-stricken. I'd almost rather not go to this affair."

He replied, "You can wear real flowers. At this season, they look very *chic*. For 10 francs you can have two or three magnificent roses."

She was not convinced. "No. There's nothing more humiliating than to look poor among rich women."

Then her husband cried out, "How stupid we are! Go and find your friend Madame Forestier and ask her to lend you some jewels. You're well enough acquainted with her to do that."

She uttered a cry of joy. "It is true!" she said. "I hadn't thought of that."

The next day she went to her friend and related her story of distress.

Madame Forestier went to her glass-fronted wardrobe, took out a large jewel case, brought it over, opened it, and said, "Choose, my dear."

She saw at first some bracelets, then a string of pearls, then a Venetian cross of gold, and jewels of admirable workmanship. She tried on the jewels before the mirror, hesitated, but could neither decide to take them nor leave them. Then she asked, "Have you nothing else?"

"Why, yes. Look for yourself. I don't know what would please you most."

Suddenly, she discovered, in a black satin box, a superb necklace of diamonds, and her heart beat fast with intense desire. Her hands trembled as she took them up. She fastened it round her throat, against her dress, and stood in ecstasy before her reflection.

Then she asked, hesitating, full of anxiety, "Could you lend me this— nothing but this?"

"Why, yes, certainly."

She flung her arms round her friend's neck, kissed her with abandon, then fled with her treasure.

The day of the reception arrived. Madame Loisel was a great success. She was loveliest of all, elegant, gracious, smiling, and full of joy. All the men noticed her, asked her name, and wanted to be introduced to her. All the attachés of the Ministry were wanting to waltz with her. Even the minister paid attention to her.

She danced with enthusiasm, with passion, drunk with pleasure, thinking of nothing, in the triumph of her beauty, in the glory of her success, in a kind of cloud of happiness, made up of all this homage, all this admiration, all these awakened desires, this victory so complete and so sweet to the heart of woman.

She left about 4:00 in the morning. Since midnight, her husband had been asleep in one of the little salons with three other men whose wives were enjoying themselves very much.

He threw on her shoulders the wraps they had brought for the going home, modest garments of everyday wear, whose poverty clashed with the elegance of her ball dress. She felt it and wanted to flee, so as not to be seen by the other women who were wrapping themselves in rich furs.

Loisel detained her.

"Wait a minute. You'll catch cold outside. I'm going to call a cab."

But she would not listen to him and quickly ran down the staircase. When they were in the street, they found no carriage; they began to look for one, hailing the coachmen whom they saw passing in the distance.

Hopeless and shivering, they walked along toward the Seine. Finally, they found on the quay one of those old nocturnal coupés that are not seen in Paris except after nightfall, as if they were ashamed of their wretched appearance during the day.

It took them to their door in Rue des Martyrs, and they climbed wearily up to their flat. It was all over for her. And on his part, he tiredly remembered that he had to be at the Ministry by 10:00.

She removed the wraps from her shoulders before the mirror so that she could see herself once again in her glory. But suddenly she cried out. Her necklace was no longer around her neck.

Her husband, already half undressed, asked, "What's the matter with you?"

She turned to him distractedly. "I have—I have—I no longer have Madame Forestier's necklace!"

He arose, aghast. "What! How is that? It isn't possible."

And they looked in the folds of her dress, in the folds of the mantle, in the pockets, everywhere. They could not find it.

He asked, "Are you sure you still had it when you left the ball?"

"Yes. I felt it in the vestibule as we came out."

"But if you had lost it in the street, we should have heard it fall. It must be in the cab."

"Yes. That's likely. Did you take the number?"

"No. And you, did you notice what it was?"

"No."

They looked at one another, devastated. Finally, Loisel dressed himself again.

"I am going," he said, "to retrace all the walk we did on foot, to see if I can find it."

And he went. She remained in her evening dress, without strength to go to bed, collapsed in a chair, without fire, without energy, without thought.

Her husband came in about 7:00. He had found nothing.

He went to the police office, to the newspapers to offer a reward, to the companies that let out cabs for hire—everywhere, in short, where a glimmer of hope remained.

She waited all day in a state of bewilderment before this frightful disaster.

Loisel returned in the evening, his cheeks harrowed and pale. He had discovered nothing.

"It will be necessary," he said, "to write to your friend that you have broken the clasp of her diamonds and that you are having it repaired. That will give us time to explore alternatives."

She wrote as he dictated.

At the end of a week, they had lost all hope. And Loisel, now older by five years, declared, "We must take measures to replace this jewel."

The next day they took the box that had enclosed it to the jeweler whose name was inside.

After consulting his books, the jeweler said, "It is not I, madame, who sold this necklace. I only supplied the case."

Then they went from jeweler to jeweler, seeking a necklace like the other one, searching their memories, both of them ill with grief and anguish.

In a shop of the Palais-Royal, they found a chaplet of diamonds that seemed to them exactly like the one they had lost. It was valued at 40,000 francs. They could get it for 36,000.

They begged the jeweler not to sell it for three days. And they made an arrangement by which they might return it for 34,000 francs should the first string be found before the end of February.

Loisel possessed 18,000 francs inherited from his father. He would borrow the rest.

He borrowed, asking 1,000 francs from one, 500 from another, 100 francs here, 60 there. He gave promissory notes, made ruinous promises, took money from usurers and the whole race of moneylenders. He compromised all the rest of his life, risked his signature without even knowing if he could make it good or not; then, terrified and anguished by the future, by the black misery that engulfed him, and by the prospect of utter ruin, he went to get the new necklace, depositing on the merchant's counter 36,000 francs.

When Madame Loisel took back the necklace to Madame Forestier, the latter said to her in an icy tone, "You should have returned them to me sooner, for I might have needed them."

She did not open the jewel box, as her friend feared she would. If she should perceive the substitution, what would she think? What would she say? Would she take her for a thief?

Madame Loisel now experienced the horrible life of the poverty-stricken. She made her resolution to do her part, however, all at once, heroically. This frightful debt had to be paid. She would pay it. The maid was sent away; they changed their lodgings; an attic was rented up under the roofs.

She experienced the heavy work of a house, the odious work of a kitchen. She washed the dishes, wearing out her rosy nails on the greasy pots and the bottoms of saucepans. She washed the soiled linen, the chemises, and towels, and hung them out to dry on a line; she carried the rubbish down to the street every morning, and brought up the water, stopping at each landing to get her breath. And dressed like a woman of the people, she went to the grocer's and the butcher's, with her basket on her arm, shopping and haggling to the last centime of her miserable money.

Every month promissory notes had to be paid, others renewed, time asked for.

Her husband worked in the evenings, putting the books of some merchants in order, and at night he often made copies at 25 centimes a page.

And this life lasted for 10 years.

At the end of 10 years, the Loisels had paid back everything, with the usurious interest and accumulated interest as well.

Madame Loisel seemed old now. She had become a strong, hard woman, the crude woman of poor households. Her hair was badly dressed, her skirts awry, her hands red; she spoke in a loud tone, washed the floors with large pails of water. But, sometimes, when her husband was at the office, she would seat herself before the window and dream back to that evening of long ago, of that ball where she had been so beautiful and so admired. What would have happened had she not lost that necklace? Who knows? Who knows? How singular life is, how easily changed! How small a thing it takes to destroy or save you!

One Sunday, as she was taking a walk in the Champs-Élysées to relax after the toil of the week, she suddenly perceived a lady walking with a child. It was Madame Forestier, still young, still beautiful, still attractive.

Madame Loisel felt moved. Should she speak to her? Now that she had paid, she could tell her everything. Why not?

She approached her. "Good morning, Jeanne."

Her friend did not recognize her and was astonished at being addressed so familiarly by this common woman. She stammered, "But—madame! I do not know . . . You must be mistaken."

"No, I am Mathilda Loisel."

Her friend uttered a cry of astonishment. "Oh, my poor Mathilda! How you've changed!"

"Yes, I've gone through very hard days since I saw you, and some miserable ones—and all that because of you."

"Because of *me?* How is that?"

"Do you remember that necklace of diamonds you lent me to go to the ball at the Ministry."

"Yes. Well?"

"Well, I lost it."

"How is that, since you returned it to me?"

"I returned another to you exactly like it. And it has taken us 10 years to pay for it. You can understand that it wasn't easy for us, we who have nothing. But it is finished; for that I'm grateful."

Madame Forestier stopped short. She said, "You say that you bought a diamond necklace to replace mine?"

"Yes. You didn't notice it, then? They were just alike." And she smiled a smile of proud, simple joy.

Madame Forestier, deeply moved, took both her hands as she replied, "Oh, my poor Mathilda! But mine were imitation. They were not worth more than 500 francs!"

The Night of the Storm

Zona Gale

The feuding men had not spoken to each other in 10 years . . . but now— somewhere out there in a blinding snowstorm—a little girl was lost.

At one minute, the prairie had been empty and white under a low, gray sky. In the next minute, the air was filled with fine, pelting snow that drove with fury and whirled in a biting wind.

On the main road across the Lewiston Open, a man came riding. He was galloping with the wind, yet in all his haste he stopped at every one of the scattered houses on the plain and pounded on the door. The women, already busy at supper, answered the summons wondering, or the men came running from stables and cowsheds, and to these the horseman cried his message and was off before the gaping folk could stay him with questions:

"Stephen Mine's little girl's lost. She's been gone an hour. 'Nother

65

searchin' party starts as soon's enough get to Stephen's. Take your lanterns and get some rope."

With that Jake Mullet was off, on his way to Pillsbury's store in Lewiston to ring for the bucket brigade and to telephone to the few in the neighborhood who had telephones.

"Hannah Mine's girl," said the women. "Which one? Oh, not the baby. It can't be the baby!"

It went up like one cry, all over the Open, while the men made ready to leave and brought rope, and the women filled the lanterns. More than one woman gathered her skirts about her and set forth with her man, certain that Hannah Mine needed comforting and, it might be, serving, and unable to wait at home in any case. But when they reached the Mines' little house, they found that Hannah had gone with the first searching party, and their glances sweeping the three children huddled by the fire told the truth. The lost child was Hannah Mine's baby. Somewhere out in that storm, already for more than an hour, was Stephen and Hannah Mine's baby, three-year-old Lissa.

Meanwhile, Jake Mullet was riding. And when he had done what he could in Lewiston, he took the lower road back. Now he was facing the storm, and its fury was growing with the darkness. When the first farmhouse light showed through the thick white, Jake groaned. She was so little—if night came, or if in two hours they had not found her, who could hope that they would be in time?

He continued to call at the little houses and to shout his message to any whom he met lumbering through the snow. But when he came to one house, on the 40 adjoining Stephen's 40, he did not stop.

"Turn back to Mine's!" Jake shouted. "His little girl's lost. She's . . ."

Then he stopped. Here was Waldo Rowan himself, who had not spoken to Stephen and Hannah for 10 years, as all the Open knew.

"They wouldn't have my help!" Waldo flung back.

Jake pounded on, carrying coils of rope for the searchers, who were now to spread in a great circle, threading the rope, and so come drawing in. He gave not another thought to the only one on the Open who had failed to answer his appeal. Everybody was used to this feud between Mine and Waldo. Stephen would have done the same if it had been Waldo whose child was lost. But Waldo had no children to lose.

There had been a day when he and Stephen had been friends, but that was before a wrong—real or fancied—had caused that ever-widening gulf of harsh, stony anger and mutual silence. Stephen had married Hannah, and Waldo had married another girl of the village who had died, with their two-year-old baby, only a year ago. Since then he had lived alone, as dead to Stephen as Stephen was to him.

At his own line fence now, Waldo Rowan left the road and plunged into a grove of dwarf oak and on into a denser stretch of wood. It was evident that this storm was to continue 24 hours at the least, and he wanted a look at his traps. He found some empty, one dragged away, and in one something pitiful, struggling helplessly and moaning, which he dispatched and dropped in his bag. And as he did so, he thought, as he had thought before: *Declare if I wouldn't druther live on corn bread than do it. Declare if I ever set another trap.*

He plunged down into the cut, which was the short way to his cabin. There was another reason for his haste besides the weather. He had been out all day, and creeping in his veins came the giddiness and tremor that precede a chill; and with it, too, that curious lightness of head, of body, which presage a possible illness. He must get indoors, build a great fire, heat his kettle of soup, wrap up warmly, and sleep it off.

I'd ought to had the doctor give me something when I met him this noon, Waldo thought. *What was it he said? He was going 16 miles north. He won't be back tonight. I guess I can mope it out.*

The snow was of a deceiving softness and piled on the rocks of the cut as if billows of foam had rolled in, lapped, and now lay quiet. Here the wind roared through from the northeast, catching the tops of the white pines and making a furious singing. And on that wind, Waldo heard a cry.

He heard it for a little before he knew that he heard it—with that strange inner ear that catches sound too light to be measured. An animal or a way of the wind, he might have called it and thought no more; but when he was deep in the cut and before he began the rough ascent, abruptly this cry rose on a single piercing note and fell again to its quiet pulsing. He listened.

Still uncertain of what he had heard, he turned north and kept along the cut, every few steps stopping to turn his head to the wind. He was ready to face back, and then it came again. There was no mistaking now, and he broke into a run.

For all his running, he made slow progress, for there was no trail up the bottom of the cut, and the rocks were rough and huddled. He would have climbed the side and followed the trail on the west of the rim, but he had an instinct that whatever he sought cried from the bottom of the cut. He dared not halloo for fear if this were, say, a child, he should frighten it. His impulse was to run back to the road and wait for the next passerby to help him, but he dared not do that lest the faint cry be swallowed in snow and darkness. He kept on, stumbling, scrambling over waist-high rocks.

Once the faint voice ceased for so long that he told himself he had imagined the whole thing. Then it came again; there was now no mistaking what it was. Then it was silent until he heard it as a deep, sobbing breath behind him, and he had passed it.

He turned and sought on his hands and knees, calling softly, whistling, as he might to a little dog. A faint, wailing cry came from the slope just above him. He clambered toward it, his arms sweeping an arc; his hands brushed something yielding, and he was rewarded by a little scream of terror. He gathered the child in his arms.

She was very little and light. As soon as she felt herself on his chest, she

yielded to him and snuggled weakly, like a spent puppy. This was an attitude she knew, and she lay quiet, occasionally drawing a long, sobbing
breath. She was cloaked and hooded, but Waldo, feeling for her hands,
found them ice-cold, and one was bare. He unwound the scarf from his
neck and wrapped her. All the time, the fact that she was Stephen Mine's
child was barely in his consciousness. She was merely a child, terribly near
freezing, terribly near death.

To retrace his steps over the rocks with her in his arms was another thing
than forcing his own progress. Now he must move slowly and feel for each
step; he must go around the rock piles now, and not over them. He must get
back to the point where the trail crossed the cut and ascended to his cabin.
And now the darkness had fallen; the wind had its way with him; his neck
was bared to the blowing snow, and he was cutting his shoes on jagged points
and edges of the rocks. When at last he found the up trail, made the ascent
of the side, and traversed the distance to his cabin, he was shivering and chattering and hardly able to stand.

The cabin was cold, but he had left the fire ready to light. He laid the
child on a quilt before the leaping blaze, untied her hood, and chafed her
little hands. She was terribly cold and in a perilous drowsiness. Waldo
brought in his kettle of soup, hung it on the crane, dipped a little in a tin
cup and held it in the blaze. When he had forced the warm liquid between
her lips, he undressed her feet and rubbed them with snow. Her cheeks and
fingers were rosy, but he feared for the small white feet.

How'll I get word to Stephen? he thought, and in that area in which his sick
brain was working, there was no thought of anything wrong between
Stephen and him. All that had dropped away.

Stephen's little girl, he thought once, touching her hair. He had never seen
any of Stephen's children. Sitting there beside the child, hearing her soft
breathing, talking to her a little in awkward repetitions—nothing was in his
mind save deep thankfulness he had found her. Occasionally, he would

rouse her, and she would give her sleepy smile and close her eyes again. Once or twice she yawned, and he was enchanted by the little curl of her lips before she finally closed them.

The chill had now settled upon the man so that he was shaking. He drank a cupful of the soup and said that it would have to be he who would go to tell Stephen that he found her. But he could not leave her there alone, and he saw that when she was thoroughly warmed, he must wrap her up and take her home. That half mile would not matter to him now—only he must make it soon, soon, before he grew worse. When the baby was warm and rested, they would go.

He sat in his chair before the hot fire. The strong soup ran in his blood, and his weariness preyed upon him. His head sank upon his chest.

He was wakened by a sound that at first he thought came from without: a calling and a trampling. Abruptly, this impression changed, and his eyes went to the child in terror. It was she—it was her breathing. That rough, rattling sound was in her little throat, and in a moment Waldo knew. His two years of fatherhood were there to serve him, and he sprang up in that terror that all watchers upon children know.

In the same instant, the noise he had fancied to be outside was sharpened and defined. It was as he had thought—a trampling of feet. He did not see the face outside the cabin window, but there was a leap of feet onto his threshold, and Jake Mullet was there, looking like a snowman.

Jake whirled and shouted, "Stephen! Here—she's here!"

There was a rush of cold air across the floor, and Waldo sprang before the child and lifted the quilt to cover her. At the same instant, Stephen Mine leaped into the room.

"Here!" he cried out in a terrible voice. "Here?"

He strode forward, tore the quilt from Waldo's hand, and looked. The door filled with faces, with figures crusted with snow, and the cruel night air swept in and possessed the cabin. Waldo turned to the throng at the door and shook both fists in the air.

"Get in or get out!" he shouted. "Don't leave the door open on her. She's sick!"

They crowded into the room, stamping and breathing loudly, and they made way for a woman who came staggering in and threw herself beside the child. It was Hannah Mine, and she dared not touch the baby with her own stiff hands and in her wet garments. She only crouched beside her and burst into terrible dry sobs. The cabin door was sharply shut, and then the 30 and more men and women who had crowded into the room became conscious of its fearful tension.

Stephen Mine stood with his child at his feet, and he lifted his head and looked at Waldo. Stephen was a huge man. Waldo, small and shaken by his chill, began to tell how all this had come about.

"In the cut, Stephen," he said, "about a quarter mile down the cut, toward Rightseys'. I'd been to look at my traps, and I heard her cry. She was in the bottom of the cut—I found her. I've rubbed snow on her feet—but I'm afraid . . ."

Stephen Mine came close to Waldo and looked down at him.

"You expect I'm goin' to believe that?" he said.

The silence in the room was instant and terrifying.

Waldo lifted his face. The matted hair was low on his forehead—he brushed it aside, and his clear eyes met Stephen's. But his shaking hands and his shaking voice gave doubt to his hearers.

"Stephen, I swear. . ." he began, and Stephen laughed.

"I seen you sneaking past my place twice today," he said. "I know you. You found a way to get even at last, and you took it, you dog."

He stooped to the woman.

"Wrap her up, Hannah," he said.

Waldo put out his trembling hands.

"Stephen," he cried. "The child's sick—she's done. You mustn't take her out. Stay here—you're all more than welcome—and keep care of her. I've got what she needs. Don't take her out into this."

"How do I know," said Stephen Mine, "what it is you mean to give her? Hannah, wrap her up."

The woman, still breathing heavily, put her hand on her husband's knee.

"No, no, Stephen," she said. "He's right. Don't you hear her breathe? Let her stay here."

"So he can feed her no telling what? No thank you!" Stephen Mine sneered sarcastically.

Hannah seemed not to hear him.

"It's croup, Stephen," she said. "You can't take her out."

Stephen shook her off impatiently.

"I'll get out—I'll go for the doctor!" Waldo cried. "And I'll keep away. But you and Hannah stay with her here."

"Wrap her up!" said Stephen Mine.

Two or three of the neighbor women came forward now, protesting.

Jake Mullet cried out, "Look here, Mine. This ain't no time to remember old scores. You got the kid to think of."

"Wrap her up!" said Stephen Mine.

"Wait till one of us gets somewheres for a team," cried one of the men.

"Stephen—leave her here! I can wring out the hog cloths until the doctor comes. I've—I've got the stuff here that was my baby's," Waldo chattered, but now they could hardly understand him.

"Wrap her up," said Stephen coldly, and he strode to the door.

The others gave way before him and began to file out. Heavily, Hannah Mine began drawing on the child's coat, the sobs breaking through again. Some of the women gave of their own wraps, and seeing that one little mitten was missing, they put two or three pairs on the still hands.

"You carry her," said Jake Mullet to Stephen, "and I'll go to Lewiston for the doctor."

"I'll carry her—yes," said Stephen Mine, "and I'll go up yonder and telephone for the doctor. I'll not trouble any of you that'd have me leave her here."

He took the child from the mother and went out the door.

"He's beside himself," they whispered, and they understood that it was the disease of anger, or he would never have let them go away from their task that night without so much as a word of thanks.

Some lingered for a word with Waldo and would have heard more of his adventure, but all he would say was "In the cut," and again and again, "In the cut—all alone." They saw that he was a sick man, and they left him with kindly words of advice and even—though these folks are chary of expression—an outstretched hand or two. But there were some who went out muttering a half acceptance of Stephen's implication.

Alone, Waldo began moving about the cabin, mechanically folding the quilt on which the child had lain, sweeping away the snow where the trampling feet had stood, carrying the kettle back to its place in the lean-to. He felt sore, ill, and weak. He felt stunned, as if he had been flung against some great impalpable thing that had struck back at him with living hands. He could no longer save a child from death and be believed. He had turned to evil in Stephen's eyes, so that what good he did seemed evil. The wall of hate he and Stephen had built was around them, and beyond lay now more hate and evil, born of this night.

Waldo began to think . . . *If the child should die, it would serve Stephen right* . . . but he could not finish that thought. The weight of the warm little body was in his arms, the lovely curl of the child's lips as she lay before him and yawned. And her mother . . . The child must not die. She must not die.

He pictured that slow fight through the snow, the child's breathing in the thick, cold air, the heart of the mother following, the neighbors falling off one by one at their own doors and their own waiting firesides. Then Stephen would leave the child with the mother while he went to the upper road for the doctor. Would he be in time? What if the doctor was out?

Abruptly, through the blur of images in his mind, came the cheery face of the doctor whom he had met on the road that noon, "driving 16 miles north." When Waldo thought of that, it was as if his heart became a sword and smote him.

He ran to a little chest on the shelf and fumbled among its bottles. There it was, tightly corked, just as they had used it once when their baby had had such an illness, and they had pulled her through. What if Hannah happened to have nothing. . . .

He stood staring at the bottle. Then he began drawing on his mittens and his cap. His coat he had not taken off the whole time. His scarf had been bundled up and carried away with the child. He let himself out into the storm.

His chill was passing and was succeeded by the lightheadedness and the imperfect correlation of the first stages of fever. To his fancy, wavering out and seizing upon any figment, it was as if, back of the invisible drive of the snow, there were a glow of pale light. Now right, now left it shone, as if at the back of his eyes; he turned his head from side to side to find it. But there were only the cutting volleys of the snow in his face, and everywhere the siege of the wind.

Then as he stumbled on in the impeding drifts, it was again as if he were beating toward and upon that great dark wall. He kept saying to himself crazily that this was the wall he and Stephen had raised and that he must somehow get through it, beat it down, and get to the child to save her. Yet if he broke down the wall, something would rush upon him—Stephen's hatred, Stephen's hatred! And his own hatred for Stephen, for there was rage in his heart when he remembered the man's look and the man's words. But of these he did not think—he thought only of the child, and he set his teeth and charged at the wall of darkness and would not wonder what lay beyond.

In a maze of darkness and light, he went through the storm to Stephen's house.

Toward 8:00, Stephen came struggling back from the house on the upper road. He had heard what Waldo had already heard, of the doctor driving 16 miles north. And when he called Oxnard, his heart sinking at the thought of the 18 miles that lay between, there was a delay that sapped his courage—and then the word that the wires must be down, for Oxnard did not answer. He could only leave his message with the operator, for to drive the distance on such a night would mean to return too late.

Stephen came down from the upper road, and his strength and his pride were gone. Now he was empty of anger, empty of malice, empty of all save his terrible despair. It was strange to see the hate and the pride shrivel before the terrible possibility that the baby might pay the price. "If she dies," he had heard Jake Mullet say, "we'll all know who killed her."

"O God, O God!" Stephen Mine cried.

Abruptly, in the midst of the storm, he seemed to feel a lull, a silence. He went on.

It was before his gate that he stumbled over something yielding and mounded in the road. He stopped, touched the man, and with that which now at last is no decision but merely the second nature of the race, he got Waldo into his arms and to his own door.

At the sound, Hannah flung the door open, and from the darkness, wind, and snow, Stephen staggered across the threshold with Waldo in his arms.

Stephen looked down at him as he would have looked at any other man.

"How is she?" was all that his lips formed.

"Alive," said Hannah Mine.

Waldo opened his eyes, and his snow-crusted mitten tried to find its way to his pocket.

"I brought something," he said. "We had it left; give it to her."

At midnight the doctor came, the message having reached him at last. Stephen met him with a smile.

"She's safe," he said. "She's sleeping. But there's a man here—a friend of ours—sick and done for. We got him into bed. Come and have a look at him."

Up some measureless corridor, Waldo struggled at last, when many days had passed. And at its far end, it seemed to him that Stephen's face was waiting. That was odd, because it had been years since Stephen had waited for him. Yet there he was, only in back of him was still that dead wall, which neither of them could pass, and beyond it lay that old hatred and bitterness, accumulated through the years. And then there was the child—he must find the child.

One day he opened his eyes on that corridor and saw it clear. A homely room, about which Stephen and Hannah were moving, and a neighbor in homely talk beside the stove.

". . . honestly, you'll have to move out to make room for all the stuff they've brought him. The whole Open has lugged something here."

And Stephen's voice—surely Stephen's voice was saying, "That's all right. He deserves it!"

And again the neighbor's voice: "Well, I'll always be proud it was my husband who found her little red mitten down the cut."

Then a child came to hang about the doorway and to stare at the bed in which Waldo was lying. When she saw his eyes looking at her, she smiled and ran away—Stephen's child, safe, well, and smiling.

Waldo lay still. It was as if he had stood close to that dead wall of hatred he had feared, but its door had swung open, and there was nothing there.

Spring
to
Summer

Letter to Edith

Faith Baldwin

*How could toleration for the pig-tailed
little girl next door change into love?
And what if it came too late?*

Originally, the big frame house had been painted a dark, chocolate
brown. But time had softened this until it was now the color of the
candy bar a small boy carries in his pocket until it melts and takes on
bits of tweed, fluff, and general residue. And somehow there was an
undertone of pale, faded pink.

In spring, the wide front lawn was green and fresh, the lilacs and
weigelas flowered, the old apple trees in the back bent their rosy
burden of bloom. Snowball bushes and raspberry shrubs crowded
about the windows; robins and bluebirds kept house, generation
after generation, in maple and elm.

Fretwork gingerbread dripped over the big front porch, and the house wore a top hat—a square structure, the traditional Captain's Walk, although it stood many miles from the sea.

Late in May, last year, a man sat writing in the library.

It had rained earlier, and the fragrance of drenched lilacs was strong. Curtains stirred at the open windows, and a circle of yellow light fell upon an enormous kneehole desk and illuminated the face of the man sitting there—a strong profile, leaning toward harshness, square-jawed, high in the cheekbones. He sat tall, with a striking breadth of shoulder and long, solid limbs. His hair was thick and untidy, and he was intent, and sometimes smiling, as he wrote.

A clock ticked, the lilacs sighed in the wind, a drowsy bird awoke and scolded musically. The house was quiet, for it was well after midnight. It was a listening house, and if you entered it, you would have sensed life within it, of people who had lived there for many years, of people who had come briefly and recently, and gone away again. You would have thought of birth and hope, of love and grief, of fear and death.

The man laid down his pen and stretched his arms. He folded the sheets, without rereading them. He took from the desk drawer a long envelope and wrote a name on it. He wrote "Edith." He sealed the envelope and left it lying there. Then he arose and turned out the desk lamp. In the darkness, he moved to the window and looked out across the lawn at the black shapes of tree and flowering brush. He breathed in the lilacs, and whether he smiled or sighed you could not guess, or whether in the darkness his eyes were saddened or content.

After a long time, he turned and left the room, surefooted in the darkness, knowing his way so well, and went up the stairs. A light burned on the upper landing, and a stained glass window made little checkerboards of color.

On the desk, in the empty room, in the darkness, with the scent of rain-clean breeze and lilac still apparent even after the windows were closed, the letter lay waiting for tomorrow:

dith (he had written), you are to be married tomorrow—no, today, for it is very late. In the morning I will cross the lawn, jump the hedge as I have a thousand times, and walk up to the front steps to give this letter to old Hattie. I'll ask her to put it on your breakfast tray. So you will read it, lying in your bed by the windows, with the pillows behind you, I think, and your curly hair caught up with a ribbon—a blue ribbon, Edith? And when you have read it, you will laugh a little, and perhaps you will cry, only a little less because you are happy, as tears are as close as when you are sad.

Tonight I saw you briefly and, in a sense, for the last time. I shall see you differently this day. I shall see you walking down the aisle with your hand on your father's arm and a cloud of white moving about you. But I shall not be able to speak to you. I shall not be able to say good-bye to the girl I have known for two decades—I loved, I think, that long. I could not say good-bye tonight. I am not an articulate man, as indeed you must know. All I could say was, "I'll see you tomorrow." At your wedding. I wanted to say, "Stay happy, for if you are not, nothing else can compensate. Yet you will not always be happy, Edith, for life is not quite like that."

I was 10 years old when your family moved to this little town and came to live next door. We had known about you for some time. In a town of this size, the arrival of new people is of paramount importance. We hear about them from the real-estate agent, the banker, the butcher, the baker. We see the preparations, the throwing open of windows that have been closed for a long time, the women busy with scrub pails, the painters, the carpenters, the scurry and the bustle.

My mother was vastly excited, and my father also, although he pretended he was not. But good neighbors are vital in our community, and certainly to my mother, a friendly, garrulous, active woman. The right neighbors meant a cup of tea on cold winter days, a running back and forth, a borrowing and lending; they meant people to whom you turned in the time of your sorrow, people for whom you felt and did in theirs. A meat pie, a cake, a dish of scalloped potatoes—"I thought you might relish this," my mother would say to her neighbor. Or, if there was a death in the nearby house, she would go with a white cloth around her, with an offering of good food and place it quietly on the kitchen table or in the icebox. People must eat even when they grieve.

My interest was mainly—would there be boys? On the other side of us, Miss Fanny Williams lived and had her spinster being. I had friends all over the block—but would there be boys next door? At 10, a burning question. Boys with whom to play, to fight, to struggle—the struggle for leadership, for admiration, friendship, loyalty. If there was a boy my age, how much I had to show him! The place where we swam summers, with the broken diving board, the deep, brown water, still and cold, and trees bending; the place where the good fish came to the early worm.

Would he be in my grade? Did he play football and basketball? How rooted was his scorn for girls, how accurate his knowledge of the important things?

It was a bitter moment for me when you moved next door: a horrible moment, a terrible disappointment. For you had no brothers, Edith, nor sisters. Like me, you were—and still are—an only child. When your mother put your playpen in the sun and I saw you for the first time—rosy, with vigor and innocent features, a pink button for a nose, a scarlet button for a mouth, and a fluff of copper-red hair—when I saw you, fat, squat, and unsteady, when I heard you, initially your lung power, your wails of stubbornness and temper, I was outraged.

No boys. Just Edith, roaring from her playpen.

I would complain during that first summer, "That little ole baby does nothing but holler."

I liked your mother, who had a light hand with the cookie cutter; and I liked your father, who was willing, on a hushed evening with a star in the dusky sky, to permit a small boy to sit on the steps below him and talk about the vital things, the far lands he had seen as a youngster, the war in which our country recently had been involved, the Indians my grandfather had fought, the scores of baseball leagues.

But I did not like you, Edith. You frightened me.

For two years I refused to admit that you existed. This was difficult, as when you were four, you took a fancy to me. You would crawl under the hedge, stick there and yell until I came and pulled you out. You would beam at me, with the tears still wet on your cheeks and your lashes stuck into points. "Boy," you would say coaxingly, questioningly. "Boy?"

I bore with you. My mother had impressed correct conduct upon me. I was disgusted, but I was a gentleman. Now and then your mother and mine bribed me with a rare nickel, or splendid cookie, to stay with you for a time while they went down the street together to pay a call, to do an errand. On such occasions, your hired girl was busy with the wash, or perhaps she was not there at all. So I was left literally holding the baby.

I suffered agonies. You had a passion for people, for color and excitement. You still have. You wished me to mind you in full view of the passing populace. I could not coax you to the old two-seated swing in your backyard, or to the tousle of fruit trees there, adjoining our own equally untidy orchard.

No, in the front yard it must be, with you inventing the most deplorable games, and the whole town passing by to watch Doc Henderson's Jim taking care of little Edith.

The older people thought it was sweet. They congratulated my mother. But the realistic lads in my grade were highly entertained. That year they called me "Nursie." I fought on an average of twice a week. My eyes were black more often than blue.

The worst of it was that at 13 I had fallen in love. She was 16. You remember her—Rose Ann? Such a pretty girl, a cool, blonde girl, with a slim waist, a way of tossing her hair out of her eyes, and with laughter like the running of fresh water over stones. I remember the afternoon you grew tired and stickily affectionate, cookie crumbs in your hair, and the lollipop I had given you, with extreme reluctance, all over your round face and your fat hands. You were sitting on the grass by the wrought-iron urn, which bubbled with geraniums, and I beside you whittling a little boat from a stick. And you threw your arms around me, put your sticky, dirty face to mine, warm and breathing. You said, "I love you, I do."

Rose Ann went by just then, tossing the hair from her eyes and laughing. Pete Dunnage was with her. They stopped and stared on their way to drink sodas at Pop Minter's. And Rose Ann laughed until the tears ran down her cheeks. That was when I pushed you away, so hard you fell and skinned your nose.

For Rose Ann said, "Do look at Jimmy Henderson!"

And Pete, who was her age or a little older, asked, "Playing at being a mommy, Jim?"

So I left you, face down on the grass, howling your heart and lungs out, went to the fence, looked over it and demanded, "Want to make something of it?" Because I was ashamed and miserable and my world was insecure, I couldn't look at her. I said it to Pete, a few years my senior, taller than I and heavier. I was not brave, I was desperate.

It seemed curious then—but not now—that it was Pete who understood and not Rose Ann. The solidarity of the sex, perhaps. Because he pulled her away and said, "Aw, leave the kid alone."

Then they were gone, walking down the street under the dusty summer elms. I could hear her laughter, like that of a distant brook, and I could hear you screaming. So I went back, with weighted feet, and picked you up. Your nose was skinned—on a pebble, perhaps, or a little twig—and your face was scarlet. You held your breath and it frightened me. So I sat you down on your bottom and shouted, "Shut up!" and looked around to use something to distract you.

I could have murdered you, Edith. After a moment, you put your hand in mine, sticky and dirty, and warm as your cheek had been. And you looked at me, and I looked at you. Your eyes were brown—I noted them for the first time, I think.

You looked the innocence, and the love, and the trust, for I had hurt you, but you did not hold it against me. You were merely amazed to find me unkind. You said, "I am sorry." I was sorry, too.

It was after that that we became friends. By the time I was 15, I tolerated and even enjoyed you. I dug you out from under the hedge. I took you out of trees. I escorted you to my father when you had a cut thumb, a bruised foot, a bee sting. I permitted you to tag along when I went spring-exploring in the orchard and the strip of wood beyond. I killed the first snake that ever frightened you and showed you your first bird's nest. It was fun. I was a god, replete with mercy and patronage.

I could be proud. When you were seven and ill with the measles—which I regret to recall you had contracted from me—I was the only one who could coax you to take my father's medicine during your convalescence. I could be cruel: I could forbid you my august presence and watch your eyes fill with tears. I could be benevolent and cause your sun to shine again. Those were heady days, Edith. They can never come again. You'd have to be seven years to my 15.

You were adorable, if undistinguished, as a baby. You were a pretty child, with copper-red hair and pink and white skin. You were a homely little girl, going to school, the curves resolved into lankiness, your legs, scratched and brown, much too thin, your feet a little on the plump side, your teeth coming out—that was before the period of braces—and your hair, which should have saved you, merely an excuse for a nickname. "Ginger," they called you.

The grade school and high school were in the same building. I could look out and see you in the playground. You were always fighting, Edith—you had plenty of spirit. You were a terror. Your playmates came to accord you respect; your teachers gave you up as a bad job.

Now you no longer tagged at my gracious will. You just came along. And because you were growing up, and I was growing up, our relationship changed, and I became impatient again, feeling less a god than a mortal, subject to intense boredom. But you still followed me nevertheless.

Once you embarrassed me greatly. I was in the woods with Slim Waters. It began in fun, wrestling, rolling around like a couple of cubs. It turned into something else—something he did, something I said—it doesn't matter now. But you came tearing through the woods on your skinny legs, your braids flying, screaming at the top of your voice, "You stop that, Slim Waters, you just stop that!" You fell on him tooth and nail.

I still claim he was mine, that in a moment he would have surrendered without your amazonian aid. I'll never know. You bit him, Edith. You scratched his face. You kicked his shins. You pulled out his hair, and he retreated baffled and furious. Who can blame him?

He fired his parting shot. He yelled, "Jim Henderson has to get girls to fight for him!"

You were panting. You sat down on a log and dusted your hands. Your nose was bleeding a little, for it had come in contact with a hard, round head. You said triumphantly, "I fixed him."

"You needn't have bothered," I told you. I was a big, overgrown boy—but close to tears of rage. I slapped your face. I slapped it hard. I said, "I'll thank you to mind your own business," and walked away and left you sitting there openmouthed and too astonished for weeping.

You avoided me thereafter for a time. I was glad. Yet in a few weeks our relationship was on another basis, cautious, neutral, coolly friendly. You no longer tagged or followed me; when I condescended to talk to you, you answered.

Shortly before I was 18, I was graduated from high school. I was, with reluctance and surprise, valedictorian. Dry mouth, knocking knees, a voice that had nothing to do with me, spots before my eyes. Now and then the spots would clear and I could see my mother, sitting there smiling, her hands in white kid gloves straining at each other. I could see my father, his enormous bulk. I could hear him clear his throat. I could see your mother and your father, looking at me with encouragement. And I could see you, briefly, in a white dress, with your shoulder-length braids and, a recent acquisition, braces on your teeth.

That summer I worked, and in the autumn I went to the university. That changed everything. Vacations come and go; during them you are back where you belong. You discover new beauty in girls you have always known; you feel the weight of a boy's hand on your shoulder; you hear his voice in boisterous greetings; you walk down the street, and your parents' friends stop you to ask how you like college. You go to the barber's feeling very adult. This is home—yet it is different. You are growing away from it, away from these people you have always known. Your real life is back there in the echoing corridors and the classrooms, on the campus, in the places where your crowd gathers. That's life and this, a backwater where nothing ever happens.

My university was distant from this town, Edith. For the short vacations, I did not come home at all. And after the first summer, my summers were spent elsewhere. During that time, you grew up. After four years, then medical school. I remember the summer before I entered, I was home for a few weeks. Those were good weeks with my father. He talked to me so much more than he ever had, that busy man, warning me what I faced, the obstacles I would encounter, the choice I must make someday. You were—how old? Fourteen, weren't you? Going to high school. Your looks had come back, as a bright bird returns to the tree in spring. You had cut your braids, and your hair curled around your shoulders and ears. The braces were gone. There were freckles across your nose, marching like little golden soldiers. Your eyes were bigger than I remembered, and you were aloof, which amused me.

You were a kid, and I was 22 and had my first degree. I was going to be a doctor. I was a man. You were just a nice kid, Edith.

My mother said, "The boys are beginning to flock around Edith. Her mother is nearly distracted."

From my superior height and years, I was highly entertained. I saw them flock those summer nights, the gawky boys with the changing voices and the sudden loud laughter, the boys who needed haircuts or handkerchiefs, the boys whose interests lay so many years behind me.

The night before I went away, you came to dinner with your parents. Afterward, we sat on the porch. The vines screened us from the street. Was not the clematis in full bloom, Edith? I think it was—like a bridal veil falling. You and I sat in the creaky old swing, and I talked of my ambitions. I said weightily that, of course, Dad expected me to come back and take over his practice, but I wasn't sure. A city was the place. A big city, and of course, specializing.

You were not greatly interested. You remarked thoughtfully that you would never marry a doctor.

"Why not?" I asked, willing to be amused again.

You said that you had lived next door to my father for 12 years and that you were so sorry for my mother. "She never knows where he is," you told me soberly, "and he's never on time for meals. And the telephone rings all night and he has to go out in rain and heat and blizzards and high winds. I've seen him coming in mornings after being out all night, and looking so tired. I couldn't marry a man like that. I'd worry about him," you said, "all the time. I'd want to tell his patients to go away, and I'd be jealous. I'd hate them. I couldn't stand it."

After that I didn't see you for a long time. On short vacations, I went home with Winthrop Warren or Jack Elster. I became sentimental over Win's sister. She was a dark, still girl, with a slow, sultry quality. But when she announced her engagement, I wasn't as unhappy as I had feared I'd be when it was merely an eventuality.

Besides, there was my work. I liked it; it infuriated me. Sometimes I thought it would trick me, and then I fought it. The harder I fought, the better I liked it. I hated and feared my professor of surgery. I almost worshiped my professor of medicine. I learned equally from them both. I grew seemingly hard-boiled and calloused. I grew casual and profane. I walked with a swagger in my blood. Most of us did—it was the thing to do, it was protective coloration.

For in our last two years, we worked in the hospital as medical students, under direction, and we saw things. We were not just reading about them. Some of us were shocked, and most of us were frightened. We were in love and becoming lovers of the profession we had selected; but we were determined that it remain a secret and that no one should know of our passion and dedication.

My father died during my senior year. You remember, Edith? I came home, and after the services, I found myself alone. There had been a constant stream of people all that day. A man was never more loved than he. The house was heavy with the smell of flowers, the icebox overflowed with offerings. Children came, and young people and elderly people came alone or in couples, some of whom I had never seen before. Most of them wept. Everyone said, "He was so good to us."

My mother was asleep in the big bedroom, in the lonely bed in which I had been born. Doc Parker left her, with your mother sitting beside her, after he had given her a sedative, and came down to this room in which I now write, which was his retreat after office hours. Here Parker put his hand on my shoulder and said, "You'll take his place, son, very soon." And I remember saying, "Not in 50 years could I do that."

When he left, I went to the window and looked out over the snow and the long, blue shadows. The sky had that winter beauty, a clear, cold green, a star rising, a golden glowing without heat in the west. The bare limbs of the lilacs shuddered, but you could not see the swelling that was the bud.

You came in and touched my arm, Edith. I turned and looked at you. You were 18. You were more beautiful than the star rising and infinitely more compassionate. I could not recall seeing you at the service, although you were there. You had come from college 60 miles away to be there.

You asked as though we had just been talking: "Do you remember the time I went down Hellman's hill on your sled and broke my arm? You carried me here to your father. I was roaring like a bull, and you were so frightened that you were white." I remembered.

You said, "Missing him will be bad, Jimmy." I put my arm around you, and we stood there and looked at the green sky darkening and we did not speak again.

My mother came to my graduation. Somehow, I looked for your parents. I looked for you, but you were not there. Your mother had been very ill, and you had left college to help care for her, and now in the summer the three of you had gone away on a cruise.

I was lucky, Edith; I had my appointment to the big hospital, and I went to work immediately, in the unfamiliar city, with the heat and stench, the ambulance bell clanging, and the long wards furnished simply with human suffering. My mother wrote that you had not returned to college, as your mother's heart condition, while not immediately dangerous, was a constant source of anxiety. So you had stayed home to run the house and look after her.

I had two years in the hospital. My father had made that possible despite the books I found with the unpaid debts (to him) that he wrote off when he knew that he carried death with him, no farther away than arm's length.

Then we had a year together, Edith. The first strange year in which people came to me, some because of curiosity, many because of loyalty to Doc Henderson. I was young Doc Henderson. I was often discouraged.

I lost my first case. I delivered my first baby in my own bailiwick. I threw a man out of my office. I made an enemy of the next-to-the-richest woman in town. I made mistakes—and friends. I was trying. Often it seemed to me that I was getting nowhere fast, and that I would have done better to stay in the city as Dr. Merkle's assistant, learning to wear a white carnation in my lapel, to walk softly, to speak more softly still.

When my mother died in her sleep, there was nothing to hold me here, Edith, except the brass plate on the door, which had been there for some time, except my friends and the people who had learned to trust me, the remembrance of things lost—and you, Edith. You were still next door.

Before my mother died, she told me about Pete Dunnage. I had been too busy to notice. She said, "He's been in love with her for years. Of course, he's a good bit older, but he's clever and a nice man." Pete's father was president of the bank. He tided me over when I needed so much—new equipment, a car, a dozen things.

I said, "He's a swell guy. She couldn't marry a better man." Pete was in the bank, too. You'd never have to worry about him or watch him crawl out of a warm bed on cold nights, and wonder, when the blizzard struck, where he was. You'd never be troubled by patients—the pretty young women patients, the elderly, clinging patients, or those who wouldn't, or couldn't, pay their bills.

You were right for Pete and he was right for you. Yet I couldn't believe it, no matter how right you were for each other. These past two years I had seen you every day—for a minute or two, an hour, an evening, as much of it as I could manage. Your mother was my patient now, since Doc Parker had retired. I was taking care of her funny little heart, her good little heart, which would go on doing its work for a long time if I had anything to say about it.

You were my patient, too. You had that bad cold that first winter I was home, which worried me more than I told you. It was strange to go up to your room and look at you lying in the four-poster bed, with your hair tied back with a blue ribbon.

You said that morning I went to see you, "I feel ghastly, and I look it." You did. Your nose was red, your eyes were swollen, and you had a temperature. You ached all over, and you were hoarse as a crow.

I said, "You never did look like much, Edith," and sat down beside you to put the thermometer in your mouth, to hold your wrist and listen with my finger to the story of your pulse, and with my stethoscope to that of your chest. And I was frightened, because that season was a bad one for pneumonia.

It was strange for just a moment, but after that you were the little girl who howled when the bee stung her or when she bruised her bare foot on a stone. Perhaps it ceased to be strange to be there with you because it did not seem strange to you.

Yes, thinking about you and Pete Dunnage, I couldn't believe it, because you had belonged to me all these years; I had carried you in my heart, carelessly perhaps, half the time not knowing you were there, part of myself. A man doesn't think about his right arm or the air he breathes, but when one is gone he is crippled, and when he is deprived of the other, he suffocates.

The next time I saw you with Pete, there was an ache in that right arm as if it already knew itself for lost, and a choking in my throat. But I knew it was right that you were going to marry Pete someday. Everyone said so.

Once I asked you, "Are you going to marry Pete?"

You looked at me directly and answered with a question. You asked, "What would you think if I did?"

I said, "I would think it fine for both of you, Edith."

When my mother died, you came over, as you had that other time. You came into the room with me and looked at her, sleeping. You put your head down against me and cried, very bitterly. I knew you had loved her, and I knew also that you were afraid, thinking of your own mother.

I held you and wished I could cry. And I thought, *I've loved you so long, Edith, that I did not know I was in love with you. But you would never marry a doctor.*

Now we come to the year just past, with Pete coming almost every evening to your house. Nights, working in my office with the windows open, I would see the white blur of your dress, and Pete and you sitting on your front steps. You wore white a lot last summer. You were lovely in white. You needed no color, for you had your eyes, your glowing hair, and the shape of your mouth.

Was it only three months ago that the desperate girl came to my office quite late? The other parents, two or three, had gone. And here was this girl from whom fear had stripped the hardness, as a willow wand is peeled. A girl who was still pretty young. She was going to die because she wished to die; but she had repented of it. There wasn't time to get anyone. I had to do what I could.

You were walking with Pete in the garden, and you came in with Pete beside you. I couldn't leave the girl, not for a moment. There was so little time. So you were helping me, Edith, doing the hard things you had never had to do. You were white, but you didn't let me down. Pete telephoned for help, but by the time help came we'd won.

I remember looking over at you—you were standing by the window. The girl was on the couch, with blankets around her. I would put her in my car, and Miss Elie would go with me, and I would drive them to the hospital, 42 miles, for we haven't a hospital yet, although it's something my heart's set upon, as you know. (You know everything about me, don't you?) I looked at you, and at Pete, looking sicker than the patient, sweating and wiping his forehead with a shaking hand. And I thought, *It's all right. I can't lose you— even when you and Pete are married. This is what you hate, Edith, and this is what you won't ever have to face. But tonight you came through for me, because you are my friend.*

Today you will be married, Edith. This is good-bye to the baby who crawled through the hedges, the little girl who fought my battles, the child on the sled, and the 14-year-old who didn't like the smell of doctors. This is good-bye to a girl who watched a star rise, who stood beside a bed with me and looked down at a woman asleep. For never again will you be that girl, because of a ring on your finger and inarticulate pledges in the dark. You will still be there, at the core; but you will change. Life will change you. Love will, and happiness; sorrow will change you, and anxiety, the big problems and the small ones, the everyday irritations, the petty things. Birth will change you, the inevitable vigil and heartbreak, the hope and the glory. Death—but we will not think of that. Girl into woman, Edith, subtly, slowly.

Darling, good-bye.

This is a love story, Edith. It begins long ago, and it does not end. I have been your instinctive enemy. Perhaps I must be again when we meet those things upon which men and women differ so basically, and we look at each other across the chasm. I have been your sweetheart and shall so continue. Tomorrow I shall be your husband. You are not afraid, Edith? I am, I think, a little.

Good-night, darling. When you read this, it will be good-morning.

I love you very much.

Jim

The Rejected Stone

Felicia Buttz Clark

It was a huge, misshapen slab of marble stained by long years of exposure to the elements. The well-known sculptor Duccio, 40 years before, had curled his lip at it, pronouncing it worthless. Then along came a young man, poor in worldly goods but rich in dreams.

The center of old Rome was a mass of winding streets, zigzagging in and out between the tall, gloomy palaces of princes, dukes, and cardinals, and broadening occasionally into small open squares. Through a grotesque mask set in the walls, or a fountain nymph or cupid in the center of cobblestones, cool water trickled, brought over ancient aqueducts from olive-clad hills. Most of these winding ways—some of them so narrow that, by stretching out his arms, a man could touch houses on both sides—came at last to the Tiber, flowing like a huge, tawny snake to the sea at Ostia, port of the Mediterranean.

The Tiber rolled its way past the gray houses on its banks, past the island where was once the temple of Æsculapius, god of medicine; past the chattering throng of youths and maidens pacing back and forth in the late afternoon. Farther on, it flowed by orchards and meadows. Above these towered the rocks of the Aventine Hill, surmounted by a monastery. Monks in camel's-hair robes were singing the vesper song.

Bells rang out. A tall young man, about 25 years of age, wearing a shabby velvet suit much creased and powdered with white marble dust, raised his head and listened to the melodious sound of bronze on bronze. From steeple and tower the bells rang out, echoing from rock to rock, a glorious medley of discords that formed melody.

The westering sun turned the river into deep gold, such as the Etruscans had wrought into chains and bracelets before Romulus encamped with his band of shepherds upon the Palatine where later Cæsars built luxurious palaces. Now the Cæsars were gone, and in the Vatican palace lived the pope.

"Hello, Michelangelo," called a cheerful voice. "I thought I'd find you here, grubbing among the old stones. Never did I see such a fellow, working, working all the time, never stopping for any pleasure. I expect that when the rest of us are forgotten, you'll be famous."

Giorgio de Luca laughed so loudly that the sailors in a passing vessel laid aside their oars to listen. Michelangelo laughed also, but a little ruefully; one does not feel really amused at a joke on oneself.

Famous? He, a poor sculptor who scarcely knew where to find fruit, cheese, and black bread for his next meal, who had come from Florence to Rome, lured by hopes that had come to nothing? He, famous! It was, indeed, something ridiculous.

"Come on down and help," he called good-naturedly to the fellow standing above him. "In this old Marmorata, this place where the ancient Romans used to dump their spare pieces of pink, yellow, or white stones, I sometimes find a bit that serves my purpose and costs me nothing."

Daintily, Giorgio picked his way over the rough pieces of marble of all shapes. His plumed cap was stuck on the left side of his head, and a pale-yellow tea rose adorned his right ear. His green velvet mantle, worn because it was becoming and not because he needed it, was flung gracefully over one shoulder.

"Come along and have some supper, my friend. We'll find a place where there is a basin of clear water to wash your hands."

"A fountain would do." Michelangelo calmly surveyed his long, delicate fingers, fingers betokening the artist.

"Yes, but where would you find a towel?"

"Your fine embroidered kerchief would make a good towel," answered Michelangelo with a grin.

"All right. It's getting to be dusk, and if we don't hurry, the guards will shut us out for the night."

Inside the walls of the city, an occasional blazing torch lit the narrow streets. There was no moon; the two young men stumbled along until they reached an open door through which appetizing odors of fish frying in oil of the genial garlic and fragrant onion floated out into the street. There was a clamor of voices, too, ever increasing as the two pressed their way into a square room.

On one side, cooks presided over pots hanging on cranes over a blazing charcoal fire. Fowls were sizzling on iron spits whirled by a boy, sending forth such fragrance that Giorgio, conscious of his purse full of good gold and his gorgeous raiment, strode rapidly forward, and touching the plumpest fowl of all with his dapper little cane, he said, "I'll take that one. With salad—crisp, mind you—and a dash of oil and lemon and a hint of garlic."

Shouts arose from the other men:

"Michelangelo Buonarroti sups with me tonight."

"No, with me. Here's a seat, Michelangelo."

Waving his hand, the sculptor vanished into a rear room, returning immaculate as to hair and hands, his shabby suit well brushed and his worn shoes polished. He seated himself by Giorgio, now busily engaged with carving the fowl.

"Oh, I forgot to give you this letter. Your landlord said it was marked important and came from Florence." Giorgio searched his pockets, drawing out a package wrapped in oilskin.

"It's from my father." Michelangelo's hand trembled as he held the closely written sheets of parchmentlike paper. "He wants me to come home." He paused, then added dreamily, "Home to Florence."

"It's five years since you left home, isn't it?" asked his friend.

"I was 19 when Lorenzo the Magnificent died, and my hopes were high. I planned a great future. And then, you know what troubles came to Florence. I had to leave, being a friend of the hated Medici, and went first to Bologna, coming back to Florence for a time, and then to Rome in June 1496. Five long years have I spent here. I made a few pieces of sculpture, yes, and some friends. But I am as poor as when I arrived. Now that my father has lost his job, there is nobody but me to support him. My brothers do not like to work, so he urges me to return to Florence."

"And you'll be glad to?"

"Glad to go! Who would not wish to dwell in the City of Flowers? Its colors, its flowers, Giotto's Campanile rising like a lily, the churches, the sunshine—"

"Yes, I see," Giorgio said with a laugh. "But *amico mio,* how can you earn your daily bread and enough for your father and brothers?"

"With my chisel or my brush, as I always have been able to do, Giorgio. There's more in the letter. Listen: 'The other day the authorities of the Cathedral and the Woolen Guild sent word that when you came back, they want you to make a statue out of that big block of marble that was rejected as useless by the sculptor Duccio. I told them that you would see them as soon as you arrived in Florence.' Now, isn't that a job for me? I must do the work in two years. Let me see. This is April. If I set off soon, I can make my designs and begin work by autumn."

"Have you ever seen this block of marble, Michelangelo?"

"Many times. It was dug in the quarries of the Carrara, on the mountain near Pisa, facing the Mediterranean, and is of fine quality. Of course, having lain in sunshine and rain for so long, it is discolored. Also, it has been clumsily hacked until the shape is very, very curious. It will be a difficult task to bring an object of beauty out of such an ugly, misformed piece."

"I believe you can do just that," said Giorgio quietly.

"Perhaps. *Chi lo sa?* Who knows? If you have finished, Giorgio, let us go. My mind is full of plans—the form, the height. I have a feeling that, if I can work out from this old, deformed piece of marble a figure of fair design, it will be an ornament to Florence."

"And bring you fame."

"Perhaps. That is not the first object. Fame does not count much, and usually comes after we are gone; but a work of love, that is different—that lives."

"I'll go to Florence with you, my friend," Giorgio said, laying his hand, heavy with jeweled rings, on the old velvet tunic worn by the young sculptor. "I'm curious to see what you can do with a piece of rock everyone else considers hopeless."

Michelangelo whistled softly as he walked around the huge piece of marble, ivory-tinted, blackened, irregular in shape, and altogether disheartening except to a youth who loved to work and had a brain full of ideas.

"A hard problem, eh, Michelangelo?" asked Giorgio, riding up on a fiery black horse draped in scarlet and gold, with tassels dangling around its neck and a bridle clasped in gold.

Following the young Roman were several knights, the flower of Florentine chivalry. Giorgio had purchased an entire new outfit, from small velvet cap clasped with diamonds to sleeves of fine purple satin to shoes whose toes turned up six inches or more. His dark hair was cut straight across, and his hands were covered with satin gauntlets embroidered with seed pearls. Altogether, Giorgio and his fine friends were as perfect specimens of style in the year 1501 as wealth could produce.

Michelangelo, paper cap pulled over his head, white smock, none too clean, falling over a pair of leather trousers, glanced up and surveyed his friend with a gleam of laughter in his somewhat somber eyes.

"*Buon giorono,* Giorgio. Have you come to watch me work? Look out, or you'll get your new suit spoiled."

He struck so sharp a blow with his chisel that bits of marble flew about, and the high-spirited horse rose on its hind legs, pawing the air. Giorgio's velvet turban flew off, and a shout of laughter came from the delighted Florentine knights.

As the horse grew quiet, Giorgio dropped over its side, picked up the cap, placed it at the proper angle, and smiled as sweetly as one of Fra Angelico's angels frescoed on the walls of the monastery of San Marco.

Holding the bridle, he turned toward his friend, and with a new gravity, remarked, "Your labor of love promises some skill, Michelangelo. What an odd-shaped piece! Will you make a giant or a fountain? Here's a place for your ingenuity. Methinks the city council has set you at a thankless task."

Michelangelo twisted his mouth as he, too, studied the hideous, unshaped block. "They pay me gold for it," he said at last.

Giorgio laughed. "You're a strange fellow. You do not work for gold, but for the fun of making something out of nothing. The gold counts little to you."

"Perhaps, though, I need gold, my friend, being but a poor artist."

"Come on, boys," called Giorgio, springing onto his horse, "let us leave the chiseler to his work."

With a loud clatter of hooves, the party rode away, and Michelangelo began his task.

It was September 1501, a beautiful month, when soft blue haze half veiled the heights of Fiesole, when grapes hung purple and juicy upon vines festooned from tree to tree, and figs could be plucked, bursting with delicate pink meat.

Having made his measurements and his design, Michelangelo, happily whistling, bent to his task, chipping a little here, a little there, revealing beneath the discolored exterior of the rejected stone, marble of purest texture and snowiest white. The work must be finished in two years, a gigantic task, but Michelangelo had no fears; he knew that he could do it.

A high wooden wall was built around the marble block, enclosing it so that bothersome sight-seers could not distract him. From the time when the sun peeped over the rim of the mountains until it set, Michelangelo labored.

A year rolled by. Out of the shapeless marble, David was being created; his slender body standing in graceful posture, the form of his head that of a youth, the hand, and the sling. As yet, there were no features. It was as if a body were acquiring life. But the soul did not yet illuminate the face.

On a glowing October day, Michelangelo took a holiday. Long since, his friend Giorgio had returned to Rome, assuring the sculptor that when the statue sprang fully formed from the marble, he would come again to Florence. "For then you will be famous, Michelangelo *mio;* the world will ring with your praise."

"And the Medici will give me an order for statues of themselves to enhance their own glory," responded the artist, not cynically but with a touch of humor. "What is fame? It is a mist that flies away on the lightest breath of adversity. It is worth nothing. I tell you, Giorgio, that I am not working for gold, nor that my name may be spoken by men's lips, but for love—love of art and love of Florence."

"Nevertheless—mark my words—people shall come across the wide seas to gaze wonderingly at the David which you have made a creature of life out of the rejected stone."

Michelangelo laughed.

Toward Fiesole he went, alone, on this beautiful afternoon, climbing the narrow path between olive groves in whose flickering shade grazed brown sheep and over walls covered with late roses. Here were cypress hedges enclosing fair-terraced gardens, with their masses of oleander and magnolia inlaid alternately upon the blue sky, branching lightness of pale rose color and deep green breadth of shade studded with balls of budding silver. Showing through this framework of rich leaf and rubied flower were the faraway bends of the Arno beneath the olive slopes and the purple peaks of the Carrara mountains.

Michelangelo sat down on the summit, ate his supper of cheese and bread, and took from his knapsack a parchment-bound volume, black-lettered, with capitals rich in carmine and gold, wrought by monks in the monastery of Fiesole, whence had come Fra Angelico, the painter. This book was his guide in the work of creating a true figure of David, the shepherd lad.

"'And there went out a champion out of the camp of the Philistines,'" he read aloud, "'named Goliath, of Gath, and he had a helmet of brass. . . . He was armed with a coat of mail, . . . and he had greaves of brass on his legs and a brass target between his shoulders. And the staff of his spear was like a weaver's beam.'

"Well protected was Goliath," murmured Michelangelo. And he read further:

"'David rose up early in the morning, and left the sheep with a keeper. . . . And Eliab his eldest brother . . . said, "Why camest thou down hither? . . . Thou art come down that thou mightest see the battle!" . . . Saul armed David, . . . and he assayed to go. . . . And David said to Saul, "I cannot go with these." . . . And he took his staff in his hand, and chose him five smooth stones out of the brook, and put them in the shepherd's bag which he had, . . . and his sling was in his hand: and he drew near to the Philistine. . . . So David prevailed over the Philistine with a sling and a stone.'

"I've got the idea now," said Michelangelo. Rising, he put the precious book back into his knapsack, swung it over his shoulder, and walked down the hill in the moonlight, singing.

Another year passed, and the David stood perfect in form, his face eager and alive, his figure tense. The marble, the ugly stained marble, had fallen away. It was as if a shining, sparkling form that had been imprisoned had stepped forth into pulsating life.

The pompous members of the city council came in scarlet mantles and feathered hats, gazed, and pronounced it good.

Michelangelo smiled in his quiet way. Little cared he for the few pieces of gold they had promised him, nor for their commendation. In his heart he knew that the work of his hands was good. He had found a brown, unlovely block of marble; he had made it a thing of beauty to adorn the City of Flowers.

One day, early in 1504, Michelangelo wrote a letter to Giorgio, in Rome:

"The David is finished, dear friend. It is to be placed well, on the left of the entrance to the Palazzo Vecchio. If you wish to see it, come. You will not find Michelangelo Buonarroti famous, but you will find him happy. He has done the best he could."

May in Florence! Breaths of fragrance, light, warm breezes that caress the cheeks, golden sunshine, the melody of birds, and children's sweet voices.

> Across the Arno came men and women, the
> Golden Arno as it shoots away
> Through Florence's heart beneath her bridges four;
> And strikes up palace walls on either side,
> And froths the cornice out in glittering rows,
> With doors and windows multiplied.

From the hills they came, on donkey back or trudging barefoot. And out from the grim, fortresslike palaces came the great folk, all pressing toward the square where, only six years before, Savonarola had been burned. The purple, orange, pink, and green of the women's gowns mingled with the sober garb of men under the shadow of the gray building already old in the sixteenth century.

A body of horsemen, dusty and travel-stained, pushed through the crowds. Giorgio sprang down and clasped Michelangelo's hands.

"I have come to see your David," he said.

The artist, instead of answering in words, merely turned and pointed.

On the platform by the entrance stood the gigantic figure of a youth, his sling by his side, the shepherd's bag over his bare shoulder. In the sunshine, the marble from the Carrara quarries turned flesh pink. Exquisite were the features, earnest the expression. One could envision what Goliath saw: "A youth, and ruddy, and of a fair countenance. . . . Then said David to the Philistine, 'Thou comest to me with a sword . . . but I come to thee in the name of the Lord of hosts. . . .' And David put his hand in his bag, and took thence a stone, and slang it, and smote the Philistine; . . . and he fell upon his face to the earth."

Loud arose the shout: "*Evviva! Evviva* Michelangelo! Long live our Michelangelo!"

"What did I tell you?" said Giorgio, walking toward the river Arno with the sculptor. "You are at last a great man!"

"No man," answered Michelangelo, "is that. David was great only because he came to Goliath in the name of the Lord God of hosts."

For 369 years, the statue of David stood by the door of the Palazzo Vecchio. Autumnal rains fell upon it, the fogs enveloped it; upon its head the hot summer sunshine fell. Generations came and went, but people still remembered that Michelangelo had carved the splendid statue of David out of a rejected stone and brought beauty from ugliness. In 1873 it was decided to remove the original statue to the Academy of Fine Arts.

Giorgio's prophecy has really come true: "Nevertheless—mark my words—people shall come across the wide seas to gaze wonderingly at the David which you have made a creature of life out of the rejected stone."

———————— • ————————

Michelangelo Buonarroti (1475–1564) and his equally illustrious contemporary Leonardo da Vinci (1452–1519) tower over the mists of time like two titans. How strange that the two greatest artists of the last 2,000 years should have been born only a few miles from each other and have shared the same time period.

Every Moslem male expects to have journeyed to Mecca once before he dies. A saying that has become part of our Western folklore is this: "To see Paris before I die." Just so, it would seem an aborted life not to have ". . . seen Michelangelo before one dies." Be sure and see him chronologically, beginning with that colossal adolescent "David," frowning, intensely watchful, gathering his inner powers for his life-or-death meeting with Goliath. Sadly, because of security problems, you must see him cramped by Florentine museum walls, hemmed in by thousands of milling art devotees, rather than ruling free on the outdoor terrace of the Palace of the Signory, which he dominated for over three centuries. Then move on to Rome, to lie on a bench or an unoccupied piece of the Sistine Chapel floor and gaze upward, as Michelangelo did for four and a half back-breaking years, at that incredible expanse of fresco that represents the joie de vivre of Michelangelo's morning. Avoid looking at the wall, and sally out to see his "Moses" and other works in the Eternal City, saving until last his deeply moving "Pieta," aptly described as "tears in stone." Only then should you return to St. Peter's and take in "The Last Judgment," the almost horrifying Dantesque nightmare painted by an old man who had seen too much, the fresco equivalent of Shakespeare's "King Lear."

Last Day on Earth

Frances Ancker and Cynthia Hope

The brilliant scientist, in a moment of weakness, had made a terrible mistake—and now he must pay the price. But first, there was unfinished business to attend. . . .

Dr. Carlyle knew, a moment after he inserted the needle and watched the fluid drain slowly into his arm, that something had gone wrong.

It came to him, in a slow crystallization of horror, that the test tubes were not in their right order. And when he checked the numbers again, with an almost desperate precision, he saw what he had done.

He, Dr. William Roy Carlyle, at the peak of a great career in research, had injected himself with almost certain death.

He stared at the needle on the table, and while he watched, a strange light crept over it. Dawn! He raised his eyes and saw the day come through the high windows of his laboratory—gentle and golden, like a woman with her arms outstretched. His *last* dawn?

He pushed himself up from the table and crossed the room on stiff, trembling legs. The sky was flushed with a spreading light, and the east sides of all the great buildings of the city had turned gold in the rising sun. He stared at it, like an exile about to be banished from a loved country. And he knew in that bitter moment that though 43 years of his life were spent, he had never really seen the dawn before.

Too often it had merely meant a time to stop work, after some laboratory experiment carried on far into the night; a symbol that he must admit another grueling failure to find his way through the pathless forest of science.

But now, in this quickened instant, he saw the dawn for what it was: bright, gilded, promising, offering its 12 daylight hours without favor or prejudice to all on earth to do with as they pleased.

He turned away from it, passing a hand across his eyes and down over the short stubble of beard that grew along his jaw. His arm had begun to swell slowly, almost imperceptibly, in the area of the injection.

This was the way it worked—763X—slow as a drowsing rattlesnake, just as deadly when it struck. The white mice they'd tested had appeared normal for six hours after the injections. Then, just when it seemed the experiment would succeed, death had struck through both cages—violent and irrevocable.

Carlyle thrust the memory from his mind. He had tried this experiment on himself against the advice of his coworkers and his own better judgment—tried it in a moment of exhaustion, when fatigue stood at his elbow, fogging his vision, clouding his mind.

Reaching for 764X, he had accidentally taken up the old 763X, the very serum that had already been tested and proved fatal!

Now, too late, he saw what his error would cost him. There was no known antidote. He must see this day through with the cool detachment science had ingrained in him. For it would be his last experiment. His last day on earth.

He took up his pencil and began to jot the necessary data in his notebook in a quick, jerky scrawl. There was a slim chance that he could still be of some use. Science might learn through his error.

Semler came in before he'd quite finished, and with a brief nod, set about his work. It gave Carlyle a strange feeling—like a spy almost—to watch young Semler, so sure of life, frowning over his test tubes. He wanted to warn the younger man, to tell him that life was only a loan, and a brief loan at that—and that he must spend it well, spend it now!

"Semler—" he began. But the fierce discipline that the laboratory forced upon them made the words come hard. He rose restlessly and crossed the room to the window.

Spring had laid her first magic across the city in a pale web of green. Between the bricks and masonry, in empty lots and neglected backyards, the earth had come alive again, resurgent and triumphant.

"How long," Carlyle wondered aloud, "how long, Semler, since you've taken a real vacation and gotten into the country, where there's fresh earth and open sky overhead and plenty of air to fill your lungs?"

Semler was staring at him strangely through his heavy-lensed glasses. There was something about the young scientist both confused and child-like, as if he had become lost in the world of test tubes and could not find his way out again.

How gaunt he was, Carlyle thought! No color in his lean face; even his blue eyes, strained and weak from research, seemed to have faded to a paler blue than they'd been when he first came here.

"Vacation?" Semler said. "Why, not in a good while, sir. My wife went away—" he dreamed over it for a moment. "She went to Cape Cod for two weeks last summer. She told me about it—the surf and the sand dunes. I meant to get up for a weekend"—he glanced down at the glass slide in the palm of his gloved hand—"but you know how it is."

Yes, Carlyle knew. But a feeling of guilt, so poignant that it seemed almost too much to bear, seemed to take his heart and twist it. For he had never known until today that Semler had a wife. He didn't know where the man lived, where he had been born, who his parents were, what fears or doubts or dreams lived with him in his private world. He had never, in the three years they'd worked together, even asked after Semler's health.

If Semler was ill, it meant lost time on an experiment. But oh, how much he had looked past in this young assistant of his! How vulnerable Semler was—how lost and life-hungry!

"I'm arranging for you to leave for a month's vacation," Carlyle said now. "You must put your work aside and take time off. You'll come back with a fresh viewpoint, Semler. You'll see."

Semler set the slide down. His fingers in the rubber gloves trembled a bit. "But we're so close to the serum we're looking for," he protested. "Another week—another month, and we'll have it! 764X, sir, may even be the one."

Carlyle's arm had begun to throb a little, and the swelling, though still scarcely perceptible, had fanned out now in a slightly larger area. He smiled at Semler—a strange dry smile.

"Haven't we always been close to the answer, Semler? Hasn't it always been another week? Another month? Another year—while life slipped by and all the things we promised ourselves slipped by with it? Don't wait! Take your vacation while you're young and there's still time." He turned his back to conceal the emotion he knew must show in his face.

When he'd regained control of his voice again, he said evenly, "I've some business to attend. I'm taking the day off. Tomorrow"—he chose the words carefully—"tomorrow I may be called away. All my latest findings are there, Semler, if you need to refer to them. On the last page of my notebook."

He held out his hand briefly and shook Semler's gloved one. *Carry on!* his soul whispered. Then he turned and hurried down the dark, soundless corridor.

Outside, the spring sun shone warmly on his back, and as he made his way along the crowded street, the very air seemed to seduce him.

Had spring ever been so gentle, so endearing before? Had every little scene, every shop window, every face he passed ever been so wonderfully interesting? Yes, there was a time . . . he struggled to remember. And he knew suddenly when it had been . . . the year he'd fallen in love. That gave him the answer. Now that he must leave it, he had fallen in love with life.

At Sixty-second Street, he hailed a cab and gave the driver his home address. It would take a little explaining, coming home this way when he'd planned just to take a short nap in the laboratory and work the rest of the day. But he'd figure it out some way. Spring fever, he'd call it. He smiled. Life fever, that's what it came closer to being.

He stared out the cab window all the way home, pressed forward in the seat, so that when the cab stopped suddenly, he was jolted against the door. Had the forsythia bloomed this morning? Why hadn't he seen it? And the grass along the drive—it couldn't have gotten green in a single day!

Almost, it seemed, fate was mocking him. And yet he knew that was not true. His blind past was mocking this brief stretch of present.

When she heard his ring at the door, his wife came running. "Roy," she called out, "Roy, is anything wrong?"

He stood on the threshold and watched her open the door to him. Mary, his wife. Just so, she had opened her life to him 10 years ago. Mary, with her soft hair, like a wreath of golden sunlight, and her blue eyes that still could look at him as if he contained her world.

He caught her against him, soundlessly, wordlessly, and rocked her for a moment.

She struggled in his arms. "Roy, Roy," she cried, "something's gone wrong—terribly wrong! My darling, what is it?"

He felt the trembling deep inside him, the terrible trembling. For of all the bonds that held him to life, this was the strongest, the deepest.

How could he kiss her, knowing that it would be the last time?

"Nothing's wrong," he managed. "Only that it's spring, and I decided to take a day off. I promised Felice I'd take her to the park. Where's Felice?"

At the mention of her name, his little girl bounded in from the back room.

"Daddy!" she cried and flung herself upon him. "Oh, Daddy-daddy-daddy!"

Was that how it had always sounded, the funny little music of her voice, the sound of his name when she said it? Had her hair always been this way to his touch, silken and smelling of soap?

He caught her under her arms and swung her high in the air so that her starched dress fanned out behind her. "How's my big girl?" he asked, searching her dancing gray eyes. She hung around his neck, kicking and laughing, overjoyed at this surprise visit at the start of a routine day.

"We're going to the park," he announced. "Remember, Felice, I promised I'd take you—oh, a long time ago?"

Three *years* ago? Yes, three long springs ago, when Semler had first come to him to work on 124X and they'd thought they would have the answer with 125X.

"We'll buy you a balloon," he'd promised Felice, "any color you want, and we'll have lunch outside, under the big umbrellas. How will you like that?"

She'd sobbed with joy and sung that wonderful song—that wonderful, wonderful song that went, "Oh, Daddy-daddy-daddy!"

And he'd let three years slip by. 124X, 125X—like stones around his neck, they'd weighted his whole life. Why hadn't he stolen a day—an hour of all that time? He never would have missed it!

"Hurry now," he told Felice. "Put on your hat and button your pink coat. We're all three going. You and Mother and I—"

Hurry now, hurry now. Only a few more hours were left to him.

Hurry downstairs, hurry into the cab. Hurry down bright Fifth Avenue, where the sun glints on taxicab roofs, and the nursemaids push little pink-blanketed bundles with rattles swinging above them and a whole life to spend. Hurry now, hurry now. But see everything. Love everything. Taste and enjoy and exult in everything.

Oh, this is the way he should always have felt, through all the drab, weighted days when he had worried over the rent, his work, a rude word from a cabbie—when he had wasted time, time, which was life's elixir.

He took Mary's hand in his. He must remember, like a lesson he'd learned, not to press her hand too hard. Not to say anything that would let her know. She would know soon—much too soon, anyway.

They took one of the rowboats and sailed across the lagoon, Felice in one end and Mary in the other. It was so calm that all the buildings of Manhattan looked down and preened themselves in the water, and the proud white swans seemed to slip by on glass.

Felice had a lollipop, and she hung off the back of the rowboat, trailing her hand in the water, laughing and showing her starched white petticoat. Oh, it was a beautiful ride!

But the sun was climbing, climbing. And his arm had swollen so that very often now, he would have to rest the oars.

Mary moved back in the boat and put her head on his shoulder. He did not tell her that his shoulder had begun to ache, or that he felt tired.

And he did not tell Felice that the merry-go-round was a terrible effort, and when he climbed up on the child-sized black horse, he felt he had climbed a mountain.

And when 3:00 drew near, and he knew that he must go home, must make them take him home—he tried to sit straight in the cab. He tried to forget about the white mice and how they had died in their cages, and to concentrate, instead, on this day—this golden day of spring that had been the best of his whole life.

He thought he was doing well at it, even in the elevator. And then, just as Mary put her key in the lock, he heard her scream his name, and he felt his head strike the door . . . .

The lost thread of time came back to him slowly, and with it came consciousness, heavy and smothering. Something was reaching for him—black, formless, awful. He sank again. Then he saw the white blur of a room and heard someone's name being called. It was a moment before he knew it was his own name . . . Mary's voice calling him.

When he forced open his eyes, he saw Semler bending over him, breathing heavily—his eyes pale behind his thick-lensed glasses. "You're going to be all right, sir," Semler said. "They told us so—this morning."

This morning? What morning? And suddenly, startlingly, while Carlyle struggled to remember, Semler fell on his knees beside the bed. "763X," he gasped, "Dr. Carlyle, it's fatal to the test animals, but it can be used on human beings. Do you know what that means, sir? It means we're on the brink—on the brink of our great discovery!"

Carlyle endeavored to piece the words together, slowly, with a great effort. 763X! Like a key in a lock, it swung back the door of memory. The terrible moment after the injection when he realized what he'd done . . . the dawn and the way the sky had looked . . . Semler, that new Semler he had never quite known before . . . the street . . . the sweet smell of spring and life . . . Mary . . . Felice . . . the lagoon . . . and now . . . perhaps the great discovery!

He smiled a wan smile and motioned Semler closer. "Tell them—" he began, and then he shook his head and fell silent. For the world would not be interested in his greatest discovery. The one he'd made yesterday. That every day should be lived as if it were the last day—the last day on earth.

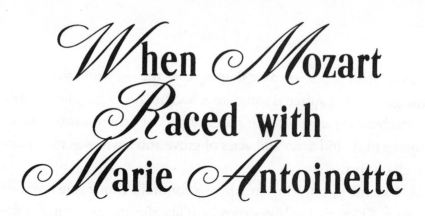

When Mozart Raced with Marie Antoinette

Katherine D. Cather

Wolfgang Amadeus Mozart, one of the greatest musical geniuses of all time, died at only 35. Lovely Marie Antoinette, born to and married to imperial grandeur, died at 38. Yet both remain as close to immortal as humanity ever gets.
But there was a time in their lives when things were much simpler, much happier—a strange time when two different worlds momentarily merged.

He was the child of a poor musician, and she was an Austrian arch-duchess, yet they played happily in the stately old garden. The fountains around the grotto splashed and murmured, their falling waters meeting below the terraces in a stream that went singing away into the pines beyond; while from a pond half hidden by reeds and rushes, a speckled trout or silver-striped bass leaped into the sunlight.

Wolfgang felt as if he had come to paradise, and it was not strange. The only garden in which he had ever played was one at his home in Salzburg, where there was just a plot of grass and a gnarled oak

115

tree, with a clump of yellow jasmine dipping over the old stone wall. It was a poor little garden that suffered sometimes because his father and mother were both too busy to care for it. But the great park at Schönbrunn, with its myriad singing birds and acres and acres of grove and lawn, was the loveliest spot in all of Austria.

"See!" he exclaimed, pointing to where a fountain threw out a veil of iridescent spray. "There is a rainbow there, just like the one we see in the sky after a shower."

Marie Antoinette nodded. To her, the gleaming colors in the spray were an everyday sight.

"Of course," she replied, "there is always a rainbow where a fountain plays. It is great fun to run through the spray. Come, I'll beat you to the aspen tree yonder."

And away they went, Marie's yellow curls flying, and merriment dancing in her wide blue eyes. For a minute, Wolfgang kept even with her. But he was younger and less accustomed to exercise, for while the royal child spent the entire summer romping in the open, he sat at piano or harp, practicing for concerts that were a large source of the family income. His father was conductor of the court orchestra at Salzburg, and orchestra directors were paid little in those days, so Wolfgang and his sister Marianne, both of whom played wonderfully well, gave exhibitions of their skill, sometimes making as much on one of these occasions as did the elder Mozart in a month. But it meant many hours of practicing, which made their bodies weaker than those of children who were free to romp and run. So Wolfgang began to fall behind, and Marie reached the goal several yards ahead of him.

"Oh," she cried merrily, "I beat you, Wolfgang Mozart! I beat you, and I am a girl!"

Wolfgang bit his lip. It was bad enough to be vanquished by a girl without being taunted about it, and he felt like running away and hiding. But it was only for a minute. Then he realized that Marie had not meant to hurt him, for he knew her kind heart, and he had not forgotten that, a few nights before, when he slipped and fell on the polished floor of the palace, instead of laughing with the others, she ran to help him up. So what did it matter if she did boast about winning? She was big-hearted and the pleasantest playmate he had ever had.

"Yes, Your Highness, you beat me at running," he answered, "but there is one kind of race in which you cannot."

Marie was alert with interest. "What is it?" she asked.

"On the harp. You may play and I will play, and we will ask the Countess of Brandweiss who does best."

The little duchess clapped her hands. "It will be splendid!" she cried. "And if you win, you may have my silver cross. But we must wait until tomorrow, for Mother will be out from Vienna then, and she will be a better judge than the countess. Let us go and practice now, so each one can do his best."

"But Your Highness," came a voice from among the trees, "do not forget that you are the daughter of an empress."

It was the Countess of Brandweiss who spoke, and Marie Antoinette shrugged her shoulders, for she knew very well what her governess meant.

Wolfgang was a boy of no rank, and but for the fact that Maria Theresa was a tender mother as well as a great empress, he would not have been at Schönbrunn. But mothers think of the happiness of their children, and sometimes royal ones allow what others would not.

So it happened that, when the Mozart children, who were on a concert tour with their father, played before the court at Vienna, and Marie Antoinette took a great fancy to the delicate-faced boy, the empress asked the musician to let his son spend a few days at Schönbrunn as the playmate of her daughter. It was an unusual honor for a lad of the people, and the Countess of Brandweiss was not at all sure that it was wise. That is why she objected to the contest. It seemed like putting them on an equality. But Marie Antoinette was too impulsive and kind to think much about such things, and she reasoned that her mother intended them to play as they wished, or she would not have invited Wolfgang to Schönbrunn.

So they went to the palace in high glee, the lad very sure of winning, and Marie almost as sure, for she had had music lessons ever since her fingers were strong enough to strum the strings, and one of the things she could do exceedingly well was to play on the harp. So both went to their practicing, and by the time that was done, Marie had a French lesson with her governess, and Wolfgang spent the remainder of the afternoon in the park alone.

The next morning, everyone about the palace was excited. The empress was coming early from Vienna, and her apartments always had to be decorated with flowers before her arrival. Marie and Wolfgang flew in and out among the workers, being really very much in the way, yet imagining they were helping. The young duchess was radiantly happy, and danced and sang. Maria Theresa was one of the world's great rulers, and affairs of state kept her so busy that she saw little of her children, especially during the summer, when they were at Schönbrunn, away from the heat and dust of the city. Throughout that time, she visited them only once a week, and for Marie Antoinette, who thought her mother was the loveliest woman in the world, the rare but joyous occasions upon which they were together were delightfully anticipated and joyfully remembered. So it was not strange that she wanted a hand in beautifying the palace for the reception of its beloved mistress.

A trumpet call from the warder at the outer gate announced the arrival of the empress, and the Countess of Brandweiss led Marie and her sister, the Archduchess Caroline, into the great hall to pay tribute to the royal mother. Wolfgang stayed back with the attendants, for the strict etiquette of the Austrian court did not permit him to be presented on such an occasion. He watched Maria Theresa embrace her daughters as lovingly as any mother who had never worn a crown, and he thought, with Marie Antoinette, that she was the most beautiful woman in the world. She was so statuesque, fair, and splendidly handsome—and the mother love gleamed tenderly in her clear blue eyes.

After the greetings were over, she moved toward her apartments, and seeing Wolfgang by the way, stooped and kissed him. Then all followed her to her reception room, and Marie told of the race.

"But Wolfgang Mozart says he can beat me on the harp," she continued, "so we are going to find out. Your Majesty and Caroline and the Countess of Brandweiss shall be judges."

Marie Theresa smiled. "It must be soon, then," she said, "for at 11:00 Baron Kaunitz comes to talk over some important matters."

"Oh!" exclaimed Marie petulantly. "It is always Kaunitz who breaks in on our good times! I wish he would go so far away that it would take him a year to get back."

For a minute, Maria Theresa looked in amazement at her daughter. Then she spoke reprovingly but gently: "My child, Baron Kaunitz is Austria's great prime minister and must be spoken of with respect by the daughter of Austria's empress."

The little duchess hung her head. She was not rude at heart, but just self-willed, and fond of having things go to suit her.

"I am sorry, Mother," she cried as she flung her arms around the empress's neck. "I know he is good and great, but why does he take you from me so often?"

"Because public affairs demand it," the mother said as she stroked the sunny curls, "and not because he is unkind. You must not fret about it, for princesses must consider many things besides their own desires. Let us be happy now and not waste time with regrets. We shall go to the hill above here—my favorite spot of all Schönbrunn. Then we shall see who plays best. Brandweiss, order the harp to be taken out, please."

The governess left the room to carry out her instructions, and Maria Theresa and the children went into the park. The wealth of flowers threw out mingled perfumes, and as they strolled along the shaded walks, among rare trees and by splashing fountains and statues (every one of which was the triumph of some great artist), Maria Theresa laughed and jested, stooping now to pick a flower or to glance over the housetops of Vienna to the Danube and the hills of the Wiener Wald.

It was good to be free from public affairs for an hour—free just like an ordinary mother, to stroll with her children and talk about books and games and pets, instead of puzzling over treaties with Frederick the Great and questions of international friendship. And as Wolfgang watched her stoop to look at a beetle or to crown Marie Antoinette with a daisy chain or laurel garland, he could hardly believe that this laughing woman was the stately ruler who presided over the destinies of the great Austrian land.

They lingered awhile at the zoological garden, and then went on past the labyrinth and the Neptune fountain to the eminence where now stands the Gloriette. A pretty rustic lodge crowned it in those days, and Maria Theresa loved the spot and spent many hours there.

Johann Michael, one of the house servants, arrived just as they did, and set the harp in its place. Then the Countess of Brandweiss came, and the empress gave word for the contest to begin.

"You play, Marie Antoinetta," she said, using the affectionate German name by which the little archduchess was called until negotiations were under way for her French marriage. For no matter how gracious the mother might be to the musician's child, the empress of Austria must observe the rules of court etiquette, one of which was that princesses must always take precedence over those of lower rank.

The girl began, and wonderfully well she played. No one knew it better than Wolfgang, and as her fingers danced along the strings, he listened in real admiration, while Maria Theresa thought with pride that few of her age could do as well. When she finished, the judges and the boy who was her competitor broke into genuine applause, and the countess smiled with gratification at her charge, very sure that, although Wolfgang had often played in public, he could not do as well.

"Now, Master Mozart," the Archduchess Caroline said, "you take the harp and see if you can do better."

Wolfgang moved to the instrument and swept his fingers across the strings. First came a few broken chords, and then an exquisite strain of melody, a folk song of old Austria still heard at eventide in the fields around Salzburg as the peasants come in from their toiling. Caroline sat with clasped hands and gleaming eyes. She had listened to that ballad many times, but never had it seemed so beautiful. The empress, very still, looked far out across the sweep of hill and plain that skirted the river, her face wonderfully tender as she listened to the gifted child. Even the punctilious countess forgot her prejudices and looked at the boy with misty eyes, for the melody took her back to the far-off time when as a child on an old estate at Salzburg, she had often sat with her mother and listened to peasant songs sweetening the twilight. Again she saw the flowers and trees of the well-remembered park, the hunting lodge, and the small wood just beyond, and heard the voice of her father, who had slept for years among Austria's honored dead.

But Wolfgang thought only of the music, and he played as seldom a child has played, something stronger and finer than his will guiding his sensitive fingers along the strings.

The melody died away, and he turned to his listeners with a question in his eyes. He was so eager to win, yet he knew the young archduchess had done remarkably well.

But Marie Antoinette did not wait for the word of the judges. She ran to him in her big-hearted, impulsive way and pinned the cross on his coat.

"You have beaten me," she said, "and the cross is yours! You have won it, Wolfgang, for I cannot play *half* as well as that!"

An attendant appeared just then and saluted the empress.

"Your Majesty," he announced, "His Excellency the Baron Kaunitz awaits your commands at the palace."

But Maria Theresa, mighty ruler of the Austrian empire, seemed not to hear. She had forgotten all about affairs of state and sat as one in a dream— a dream she would just as soon never wake from.

Beautiful Living

Mable McKee

She wanted to honor her country on Memorial Day. But what would Hilary think?

The roses in the east hedge were just budding when Mary Ruth started to rehearse the children at Newton Center for Decoration Day, as Memorial Day used to be called. Roses too were beginning to show faintly in Aunt Etta's cheeks after her long illness. The announcement that Mary Ruth was going to take charge of the memorial program made them deepen a bit more.

"It will be just like doing it myself again," Etta confided to the minister, who had come to call. "I'm telling you that Mary Ruth, though she is a college graduate and has worked almost a year on a city newspaper, has the same respect for my opinions she had before she went away to school. And the neighbors told me that sending

123

her to college would make her take on airs!"

The minister smiled. His announcement that Mary Ruth would train the children for this occasion had brought many comments from the people in his congregation. Some of the women said she would try to give a new kind of program. They were the ones not pleased with the announcement. Among them were those who had warned Aunt Etta against sending Mary Ruth to college. Others had said, "How lovely! She'll just take up her aunt's work and follow right in her footsteps. She'll be a second Etta Greer."

He kept the criticisms from Aunt Etta; the compliments he gave her. He was just getting ready to tell her some praise of the program when he saw Mary Ruth entering the room with a glass of malted milk. She was charming and did not act as if she were serving in a sick room, but rather in a modern drawing room, as a popular hostess.

Mary Ruth was slender. She was dark, too, like her Southern ancestors. Masses of midnight hair waved around her head. Her eyes were big, soft, and dusky, her mouth red and smiling most of the time. All Mary Ruth's features bespoke a nature that was generous, appreciative, and above all, rich with a sense of humor.

"I've discovered that Roy North is the monotone in the boys' chorus," she told the minister with a laugh, "and that Gracie Bennet has a nasal accent. So I've made them the pages for the pageant. They won't mind being silent when they see the gorgeous costumes I've planned for them."

Aunt Etta sat up straight on the lounge. "Mary Ruth," she exclaimed joyously, "you're repeating the pageant I gave six years ago. There were two pages in it."

Mary Ruth's arm went around her aunt's shoulders. "Yes, I am," she confessed. "There are to be a few changes to make it seem modern. Now you see why I'm insisting that you get well, so you can hear the people talking about its glories."

Half an hour later, the minister was telling his wife that he believed Mary

Ruth Davies really was happy. "Most girls would feel cramped and disagreeable if they had to do what she is now doing," he said. "But you should have seen her eyes flash when she talked about the Decoration Day entertainment."

The minister should have seen Mary Ruth's eyes at the very minute he was talking. They were still big, dusky, and soft. But in them gleamed a longing that became two big tears running down her cheeks and dropping upon her hand.

The postman had brought her a letter, and it had made her realize how homesick she was for her work, how dull and dreary this little town was, and how far away she was from the world she loved!

Mary Ruth had carried her own letters to her room up under the eaves to read. The magazine her aunt called her favorite had taken that lady's attention, so the girl had this hour for her own. An hour to dream and sob a little, to hope and plan for the future when her aunt would be well again.

"It will be a long, long time until she is well," the doctor had told her. "I'm calling her sickness rheumatism to her; but honestly, my child, I believe that homesickness for you made her worse."

There was another letter in Mary Ruth's pile that made a still deeper look of longing come into her eyes. That was from Betty Brice, who had a cozy little studio just a square and a half from Mary Ruth's newspaper office. Betty painted clever watercolor sketches that were in demand by the editors, and she was as happy and lighthearted as she was successful.

Mary Ruth tore that envelope open slowly. *I do hope she says something about Hilary,* her heart whispered softly—very, very softly, but not quite softly enough to keep a blush from spreading over her face.

Hurriedly, she glanced through the letter. Yes, near the bottom of the third page was Hilary's name. Carefully, Mary Ruth read that paragraph. Betty, her brother Fred, and Hilary were going to drive to the capital of Mary Ruth's state for a dinner on Decoration Day.

Mary Ruth's heart sang. "Oh!" she whispered. For Betty had said they were going to drive out of their way, so they would pass through Mary Ruth's village just at noon and take her to the hotel with them for dinner.

Betty remembered that Mary Ruth had been called home by her aunt's illness. She said this was the reason they said "hotel." Otherwise they would have invited themselves to Mary Ruth's home.

Mary Ruth's hands went up to her throat. Her face went a happy red. Oh, that was less than two weeks away! She would have to get the Decoration Day committee to postpone the time of the program until 3:00. Her guests would be gone then. She never could have Hilary Wright, brilliant feature writer as he was, in the audience to witness that "childish pageant."

They had met in the workaday world several months ago, and kindred interests had made them fast friends. When Mary Ruth had started home, he had taken her to the station and given her a gorgeous box of roses. One of her greatest disappointments since that day was that he did not write to her. He had seemed interested in her career; Mary Ruth had decided that his interest stopped there and that he felt she had given up her ambitions when she left the city.

But now he was coming. Mary Ruth right then began to plan the costume she would wear to the funny little old hotel. She had a new shell-pink voile. Her shoes—

A half-fretful voice from downstairs called, "Mary Ruth! Mary Ruth!"

When her aunt saw how lightheartedly the girl came downstairs, she smiled happily. The blinds of the room were drawn too low for her to see the gleam in the dusky eyes or to sense the change in the girl's whole attitude by the way she flitted through the room to her.

"Why, Lovey!" she exclaimed. "What's happened? Did you get a nice letter from Betty's studio crowd?"

"Oh, Aunt Etta!" The old musical lilt was in Mary Ruth's voice now. "Hilary Wright is coming here for Decoration Day with Betty and her brother. They asked me to go to the hotel for dinner. Isn't that lovely? I can arrange so I'll have oceans of time. The committee will postpone the program from 2:00 until 3:00, I'm sure, if I ask them."

Words giving the plan she had made for her friends' coming just tumbled from her lips. The gleam in her eyes grew more and more beautiful.

Aunt Etta saw it and thought she was making it still brighter when she announced that she was so much better that Mary Ruth could have the visitors at her own home for dinner. "I'm so sorry I am not able to do the cooking myself!" she said softly, the pain leaving her voice. "But Jane Frank will come and help you."

A little shadow crossed Mary Ruth's face, but Aunt Etta could not see it. Mary Ruth was thinking of the garrulous Jane Frank and how she would insist upon being introduced to the company she served. She would talk with them, too, while she served the dinner. Aunt Etta had always allowed that. But bravely she pushed this shadow back into the distance and reveled in the brightness of the beautiful day.

But more shadows began to come across her path just four days after she had mailed the letter to Betty, telling them to drive their car right to Aunt Etta's house, as she wanted them to eat with her in her home as she had often eaten with them in theirs.

The Decoration Day committee voted against changing the time of the entertainment. The old soldiers were to be given a supper by the Veterans of Foreign Wars. Any delay would make them late for that. Besides, the addresses to follow Mary Ruth's pageant would be long, and the delay would make some of them impossible. Her suggestion that the addresses precede the pageant was turned down by the minister himself. He knew children, he said, and they would fail to play their parts well if they had to sit and listen first.

The afternoon she heard that, Mary Ruth fairly flew down Elm Street toward home to tell Aunt Etta her troubles. From experiences with former

Decoration Day programs, Aunt Etta would be able to advise her as to whether or not the children could go through the pageant without direction. She would have to miss it now. For she never could allow brilliant Hilary Wright to hear that childish little effort. He would feel that he had far overestimated her ability when he predicted that she someday would be a great writer.

She almost burst into the living room, but stopped right there. How changed it was! A large silk flag full of bullet holes was draped over the beautiful mahogany frame of the mirror. The portraits of two fierce-looking generals hung where the sketches of the beech woods and the old river bridge had been. A blue uniform and a veteran's cap lay on the piano, and a great drum was in the place of honor on the bookcase. Other trophies of past wars in which Mary Ruth's ancestors had fought were in the room, but the great ugly drum seemed to overshadow all the rest.

Aunt Etta always brought out these family relics and decorated the house with them on Decoration Day. Mary Ruth had forgotten that in her rush of work. The old soldiers and the children of the town alike expected to see these each year. If she had thought of this, she would have asked not to have them out this time. But Jane Frank, under Aunt Etta's direction, had arranged them while Mary Ruth was gone. Now the living room, with its old walnut furniture, had lost its beauty and was almost grotesque.

Another calamity loomed, too. The town visitors would come to inspect the relics even while Betty and the two men were there. Aunt Etta would tell all the stories connected with each. Her recital of the glories of her ancestors who had settled the town and fought for it was interesting to most folks. But Mary Ruth wasn't thinking of that, but of how Hilary Wright hated boasting so much that he would not even let his men friends call him "Captain," the title he had earned in the Great War.

Of course, Mary Ruth knew he would understand Aunt Etta's motives in doing this, because she was ill. *But he'll think I'm one of the parasites who expect to win fame from the glories of their ancestors,* she told herself.

The entertainment would add to her seeming conceit. Mary Ruth knew the minister would pay tribute to her when the pageant was finished, just as he always had paid tribute to Aunt Etta. The speaker of the day might, too.

Aunt Etta told her that the children could not go on without direction. Mary Ruth's one hope was that Betty would listen to her plea not to attend the entertainment and hurry the men on to the capital. Now it seemed such a crude, pitiful small-town entertainment. Before it had seemed something beautiful, something that would teach the youngsters respect for the flag and for their country.

The whole day is going to be a miserable failure, she told herself the night before Decoration Day. She was locking the door before going to her room to retire. *A miserable, flat failure,* she tossed ironically over her shoulder to the most offending relic of all—the big drum on the bookcase.

On it her great-grandfather had beaten the call for settlers near Fort Harrison to leave their fields and rush to the defense of the fort when attacked by the Indians; on it he had sounded taps when they followed the body of some comrade from the fort to the little burying ground; and on it he had beaten a startling protest against the destruction of the burying ground when a railroad company years later had tried to lay a track across the site.

But Mary Ruth could not let herself remember a single one of these glories as she hurried up the stairs to her bedroom and indulged in a good old-fashioned cry.

Roses tumbling all over the front veranda, red roses over the trellis in the east yard, white ones covering the hedge between the flower garden and the street—Mary Ruth was sure the outside of her house had never been more beautiful than it was this Decoration Day. She was cutting some of the red ones for the tall vase on the living-room table. It was 11:00. Her company would arrive near 12:00, according to the letter Betty had written.

Everything was ready for them. Mary Ruth's pink dress was laid out on her bed. She wore a blue linen now, though Aunt Etta in her gray georgette was ready for the visitors.

Mary Ruth started to the hedge to get a few white roses to lighten up her bouquet. She had reached the north edge of it when an automobile horn sounded directly opposite her. She turned, and Betty was jumping out of the car.

"You darling!" she cried. "Why, Mary Ruth, you look good enough to eat! You surely, certainly do!"

Betty's arms held her close. Over her shoulder, Mary Ruth saw Hilary, big and broad-shouldered and smiling. Getting out of the car, he came into the yard as if he belonged there. He was shaking her hand now, his firm clasp hurting. Following her into the house and leaning over Aunt Etta, he asked gently whether she was really better.

His eyes laughed when he looked at Mary Ruth again. "I've often told little girls they were growing up," he teased, "but I must say here's one young lady who is growing back into little girlhood."

Mary Ruth thought of the pretty pink dress. *No use to don it now,* she told herself. Besides, there was more work to do in the kitchen. She had not expected them until noon, and Jane Frank simply could not finish things alone.

Out in the kitchen, she worked feverishly, listening to Betty and Fred talking about the journey. Fred had made quite a speed record, they said. Hilary's deep bass voice sounded at times when he remarked that he, too, had made a record holding on to his cap. He commented on the roses. The home, according to him, should be termed Rose Bower.

After a little, Aunt Etta was doing the talking. Mary Ruth's cheeks went red when she heard her tell how unselfish her niece was. They had not wanted her to come home when she did, because she was making such a success of her work. But Mary Ruth wouldn't let her aunt be cared for by strangers.

She talked a little lower for a time, and then her voice rose in a singsong accent that Mary Ruth instantly recognized. Aunt Etta was telling the story of the big drum and Grandfather's beating the long roll on it for his comrades to follow. Visitors came into the little house while she talked, a veteran and two little boys. They lingered a little while to listen to the story.

At dinner the story of the tattered flag was told. The guests openly praised the food. Hilary Wright ate like a small boy. As he ate, he listened to the stories. It seemed to Mary Ruth once that he looked amused. The thought that he might not be understanding Aunt Etta irritated her. She rose from her chair and went around to slip her arm around her aunt's shoulder. Softly, she said, "Grandfather isn't the only hero in the family. There is an aunt who has raised four orphaned nephews and nieces."

Aunt Etta's eyes filled with quick tears. "Why, Lovey," she said sweetly, "why, Lovey, what will our guests think? You just love me so much I seem good to you!"

Then there was the entertainment at Memorial Park. Hilary Wright and Betty went to it because Aunt Etta urged them to go and confided to them that Mary Ruth had rewritten the pageant. The minister had slipped a copy of her manuscript to Aunt Etta. It was beautiful, she said. Fred stayed at the house with Aunt Etta to rest, so that he would be ready to make another speed record when they started on to the capital.

The next hour was a dream to Mary Ruth. Children recited their lines just as she had taught them, singing more beautifully than ever before; veterans in blue wiped tears from their eyes when boys representing them marched away to war. Mary Ruth had not forgotten one of them in the pageant.

Then the final curtain rose, and a little girl came upon the platform, carrying a wreath to put on a great tombstone. It was a tribute from the veterans of the Civil War to the boys who had fallen in the last fight for their country, the Great War.

Mary Ruth saw Hilary Wright wiping his eyes. A little later, her hand was clasped in his.

"It was beautiful, Mary Ruth," he said almost reverently. "Simple and beautiful and sincere. These children will remember it all their lives. They will be better citizens for it."

Somehow, she found herself alone with Hilary, walking toward a secluded spot in Memorial Park. Betty had slipped away, wisely reading the look of longing in Hilary's eyes.

"Mary Ruth," he said softly when they were under the beautiful sycamore trees close to the river, "I didn't think there were any girls like you left, girls who would leave their career and come home to their aunt to nurse her and try to take her place in the community so she wouldn't be unhappy. I knew that you could write beautifully, but I didn't know you could live so beautifully, too.

"Your aunt told about your grandfather beating the long roll for his comrades. That touched me as few stories do. But not half so much as this afternoon when you, too, paid tribute to the men who were now your comrades and beat the long roll for the people in this town to follow."

His hands closed over her slender ones. "I'm coming back," he promised, "while the roses are still in bloom, Mary Ruth, dear. I may not be half big enough or good enough for you, but I hope I can make you care for me. I'm going to try."

Dusk again settled over the rose-covered cottage on Elm Street. The last of the schoolchildren had inspected the relics—the tattered flag, the portraits of the soldiers, and even the great drum. Aunt Etta was lying back in her invalid's chair, tired but happy.

Jane Frank rattled the dishes in the kitchen as she sang in her nasal tone, "Mine Eyes Have Seen the Glory."

A slender girl in a beautiful pink dress, with dusky eyes shining like stars, lovingly touched the flag, the uniform on the piano, the two fierce portraits, and then lingered longest of all before the big drum.

Kneeling beside her aunt, she said, "Oh, it's been a beautiful day, Aunt Etta! And I owe it all to you."

The invalid's fingers strayed through Mary Ruth's midnight hair. "Lovey, Lovey," she whispered softly, "it *has* been a wonderful Decoration Day!"

The Captive Outfielder

Leonard Wibberley

What possible connection could there be between Johann Sebastian Bach and Grasshopper Smith?

The boy was filled with anxiety that seemed to concentrate in his stomach, giving him a sense of tightness there, as if knotted up into a ball that would never come undone again. He had his violin under his chin, and before him was the music stand. On the walls of the studio, the pictures of the great musicians were frowning upon him in massive disapproval. Right behind him was a portrait of Paganini, who positively glowered down at the boy, full of malevolence and impatience.

That, said the boy to himself, *is because he could really play the violin and I can't and never will be able to. And he knows it and thinks I'm a fool.*

Below Paganini was a portrait of Mozart in profile. He had a white wig tied neatly at the back with a bow of black ribbon. Mozart should have been looking straight ahead, but his left eye, which was the only one visible, seemed to be turned a little watching the boy. The look was one of disapproval. When Mozart was the boy's age—that is, 10—he had already composed several pieces and could play the violin and the organ. Mozart didn't like the boy either.

On the other side of the Paganini portrait was the blocky face of Johann Sebastian Bach. It was a grim face, bleak with disappointment. Whenever the boy was playing, it seemed to him that Johann Sebastian Bach was shaking his head in resigned disapproval of his efforts. There were other portraits around the studio—Beethoven, Brahms, Chopin. Not one of them was smiling. They were all in agreement that this boy was certainly the poorest kind of musician and never would learn his instrument, and it was painful to them to have to listen to him while he had his lesson.

Of all these great men of music who surrounded him, the boy hated Johann Sebastian Bach the most. This was because his teacher, Mr. Olinsky, kept talking about Bach as if without Bach there never would have been any music. Bach was like a god to Mr. Olinsky, and he was a god the boy could never hope to please.

"All right," said Mr. Olinsky, who was at the grand piano. "The Arioso. And you will kindly remember the time. Without time no one can play the music of Johann Sebastian Bach." Mr. Olinsky exchanged glances with the portrait of Bach, and the two seemed in perfect agreement with each other. The boy was quite sure they carried on disheartened conversations about him after his lesson.

There was a chord from the piano. The boy put the bow to the string and started. But it was no good. At the end of the second bar, Mr. Olinsky took his hands from the piano and covered his face with them and shook his head, bending over the keyboard. Bach shook his head, too. In the awful silence, all the portraits around the studio expressed their disapproval, and the boy felt more wretched than ever and not too far removed from tears.

"The *time,*" said Mr. Olinsky eventually. "The time. Take that first bar. What is the value of the first note?"

"A quarter note," said the boy.

"And the next note?"

"A sixteenth."

"Good. So you have one quarter note and four sixteenth notes making a bar of two quarters. Not so?"

"Yes."

"But the first quarter note is tied to the first sixteenth note. They are the same note. So the first note, which is *C* sharp, is held for five sixteenths, and then the other three sixteenths follow. Not so?"

"Yes," said the boy.

"THEN WHY DON'T YOU PLAY IT THAT WAY?"

To this the boy made no reply. The reason he didn't play it that way was that he couldn't play it that way. It wasn't fair to have a quarter note and then tie it to a sixteenth note. It was just a dirty trick like Grasshopper Smith pulled when he was pitching in the Little League. Grasshopper Smith was on the Giants, and the boy was on the Yankees. The Grasshopper always retained the ball for just a second after he seemed to have thrown it and struck the boy out. Every time. Every single time. The boy got a hit every now and again from other pitchers. Once he got a two-base hit. The ball went joyously through the air, bounced and went over the center-field fence. A clear, good two-base hit. But it was a relief pitcher. And whenever Grasshopper Smith was in the box, the boy struck out. He and Johann Sebastian Bach—they were full of dirty tricks. They were pretty stuck-up, too. He hated them both.

Meanwhile, he had not replied to Mr. Olinsky's question, and Mr. Olinsky got up from the piano and stood beside him, looking at him, and saw that the boy's eyes were bright with frustration and disappointment because he was no good at baseball and no good at music either.

"Come and sit down a minute, boy," said Mr. Olinsky, and he led him over to a little wickerwork sofa.

Mr. Olinsky was in his sixties, and from the time he was this boy's age, he had given all his life to music. He loved the boy, though he had known him for only a year. He was a good boy, and he had a good ear. He wanted him to get excited about music, and the boy was not excited about it. He didn't practice properly. He didn't apply himself. There was something lacking, and it was up to him, Mr. Olinsky, to supply whatever it was that was lacking so that the boy would really enter into the magic world of music.

How to get to him then? How to make real contact with this American boy when he himself was, though a citizen, foreign-born?

He started to talk about his own youth. It had been a grim youth in Petrograd. His parents were poor. His father had died when he was young, and his mother had, by a great struggle, got him into the conservatory. She had enough money for his tuition only. Eating was a problem. He could afford only one good meal a day at the conservatory cafeteria so that he was almost always hungry and cold. But he remembered how the great Glazunov had come to the cafeteria one day and had seen him with a bowl of soup and a piece of bread.

"This boy is thin," Glazunov had said. "From now on, he is to have two bowls of soup, and they are to be big bowls. I will pay the cost."

There had been help like that for him—occasional help coming quite unexpectedly—in those long, grinding, lonely years at the conservatory. But there were other terrible times. There was the time when he had reached such an age that he could no longer be boarded at the conservatory. He had to give up his bed to a smaller boy and find lodgings somewhere in the city.

He had enough money for lodging, but not enough for food. Always food. That was the great problem. To get money for food, he had taken a room in a house where the family had consumption. They rented him a room cheaply because nobody wanted to board with them. He would listen to the members of the family coughing at nighttime—the thin, shallow, persistent cough of the consumptive. He was terribly afraid—afraid that he would contract consumption himself, which was incurable in those days, and die. The thought of death frightened him. But he was equally frightened of disappointing his mother, for if he died he would not graduate, and all her efforts to make him a musician would be wasted.

Then there was the time he had had to leave Russia after the revolution. The awful standing in line to get a visa and then to get assigned to a train had taken seven months. And the train to Riga—what an ordeal that had been. Normally, it took 18 hours. But this train took three weeks. Three weeks in cattle cars in midwinter, jammed up against his fellow passengers, desperately trying to save his violin from being crushed. A baby had died in the cattle car, and the mother kept pretending it was only asleep. They had had to take it from her by force eventually and bury it beside the tracks out in the howling loneliness of the countryside.

And out of all this, he had gotten music. He had become a musician. Not a concert violinist, but a great orchestral violinist, devoted to his art.

He told the boy about this, hoping to get him to understand what he himself had gone through in order to become a musician. But when he was finished, he knew he had not reached the boy.

That is because he is an American boy, Mr. Olinsky thought. *He thinks all these things happened to me because I am a foreigner, and these things don't happen in America. And maybe they don't. But can't he understand that if he made all these efforts to achieve music—to be able to play the works of Johann Sebastian Bach as Bach wrote them—it is surely worth a little effort on his part?*

But it was no good. The boy, he knew, sympathized with him. But he had not made real contact with him. He hadn't found the missing something that separated this boy from him and the boy from music.

He tried again. "Tell me," he said, "what do you do with your day?"

"I go to school," said the boy flatly.

"But after that? Life is not all school."

"I play ball."

"What kind of ball?" asked Mr. Olinsky. "Bouncing a ball against a wall?"

"No," said the boy. "Baseball."

"Ah," said Mr. Olinsky. "Baseball." And he sighed. He had been more than 30 years in the United States, and he didn't know anything about baseball. It was an activity beneath his notice. When he had any spare time, he went to a concert. Or sometimes he played chess. "And how do you do at baseball?" he said.

"Oh—not very good. That Grasshopper Smith. He always strikes me out."

"You have a big match coming up soon perhaps?"

"A game. Yes. Tomorrow. The Giants against the Yankees. I'm on the Yankees. It's the play-off. We are both tied for first place." For a moment he seemed excited, and then he caught a glimpse of the great musicians around the wall and the bleak stare of Johann Sebastian Bach, and his voice went dull again. "It doesn't matter," he said. "I'll be struck out."

"But that is not the way to think about it," said Mr. Olinsky. "Is it inevitable that you be struck out? Surely that cannot be so. When I was a boy—" Then he stopped, because when he was a boy, he had never played anything remotely approaching baseball, and so he had nothing to offer the boy to encourage him.

Here was the missing part then—the thing that was missing between him and the boy and the thing that was missing between the boy and Johann Sebastian Bach. Baseball. It was just something they didn't have in common, and so they couldn't communicate with each other.

"When is this game?" said Mr. Olinsky.

"Three in the afternoon," said the boy.

"And this Grasshopper Smith is your bête noire—your black beast, huh?"

"Yeah," said the boy. "And he'll be pitching. They've been saving him for this game."

Mr. Olinsky sighed. This was a long way from the Arioso. "Well," he said, "we will consider the lesson over. Do your practice and we will try again next week."

The boy left, conscious that all the musicians were watching him. When he had gone, Mr. Olinsky stood before the portrait of Johann Sebastian Bach.

"Baseball, maestro," he said. "Baseball. That is what stands between him and you and him and me. You had 20 children and I had none. But I am positive that neither of us knows anything about baseball."

He thought about this for a moment. Then he said, "Twenty children—many of them boys. Is it possible, maestro—is it just possible that with 20 children and many of them boys . . . ? You will forgive the thought, but is it just possible that you may have played something like baseball with them sometimes? And perhaps one of those boys always being—what did he say?—struck out?"

He looked hard at the blocky features of Johann Sebastian Bach, and it seemed to him that in one corner of the grim mouth there was a touch of a smile.

Mr. Olinsky was late getting to the Clark Recreation Park for the play-off between the Giants and the Yankees because he had spent the morning transposing the Arioso from *A* major into *C* major to make it simpler for the boy. Indeed, when he got there the game was in the sixth and last inning, and the score was three to nothing in favor of the Giants.

The Yankees were at bat, and it seemed that a moment of crisis had been reached.

"What's happening?" Mr. Olinsky asked a man seated next to him who was eating a hot dog in ferocious bites.

"You blind or something?" asked the man. "Bases loaded, two away, and if they don't get a hitter to bring those three home, it's good-bye for the Yankees. And look who's coming up to bat. That dodo!"

Mr. Olinsky looked and saw the boy walking to the plate.

Outside the studio and in his baseball uniform, he looked very small. He also looked frightened, and Mr. Olinsky looked savagely at the man who had called the boy a dodo and was eating the hot dog, and he said the only American expression of contempt he had learned in all his years in the United States. "You don't know nothing from nothing," Mr. Olinsky snapped.

"That so?" said the hot-dog man. "Well, you watch. Three straight pitches and Grasshopper will have him out. I think I'll go home. I got a pain."

But he didn't go home. He stayed there while Grasshopper looked carefully around the bases and then, leaning forward with the ball clasped before him, he glared intently at the boy. He pumped twice and threw the ball. The boy swung at it and missed, and the umpire yelled, "Strike one."

"Two more like that, Grasshopper," yelled somebody. "Just two more and it's in the bag."

The boy turned around to look at the crowd and passed his tongue over his lips. He looked directly at where Mr. Olinsky was sitting, but the music teacher was sure the boy had not seen him. His face was white and his eyes glazed so that he didn't seem to be seeing anybody.

Mr. Olinsky knew that look. He had seen it often enough in the studio when the boy had made an error and knew that however much he tried, he would make the same error over and over again. It was a look of pure misery—a fervent desire to get an ordeal over with.

The boy turned again, and Grasshopper threw suddenly and savagely to third base. But the runner got back on the sack in time, and there was a sigh of relief from the crowd.

Again came the cool examination of the bases and the calculated stare at the boy at the plate. And again the pitch with the curious whip of the arm and the release of the ball one second later. Once more the boy swung and missed, and the umpire called, "Strike two." There was a groan from the crowd.

"Oh and two the count," said the scorekeeper, but Mr. Olinsky had got up from the bench and, pushing his way between the people on the bleachers before him, he went to the backstop fence.

"You," he shouted to the umpire. "I want to talk to that boy there."

The boy heard his voice and turned and looked at him aghast. "Please, Mr. Olinsky," he said. "I can't talk to you now."

"Get away from the back fence," snapped the umpire.

"I insist on talking to that boy," said Mr. Olinsky. "It is very important. It is about Johann Sebastian Bach."

"Please go away," said the boy, and he was close to tears. The umpire called for time-out while he got rid of this madman, and the boy went to the netting of the backstop.

"You are forgetting about the Arioso!" said Mr. Olinsky urgently. "Now you listen to me, because I know what I am talking about. You are thinking of a quarter note, and it should be five sixteenths. It is a quarter note—C sharp—held for one sixteenth more. *Then* strike. You are too early. It must be exactly on time."

"What the heck's he talking about?" asked the coach, who had just come up.

The boy didn't answer right away. He was looking at Mr. Olinsky as if he had realized for the first time something very important that he had been told over and over again, but had not grasped previously.

"He's talking about Johann Sebastian Bach," he said to the coach. "Five sixteenths. Not a quarter note."

"Bach had 20 children," said Mr. Olinsky to the coach. "Many of them were boys. He would know about these things."

"For land's sake, let's get on with the game," said the coach.

Mr. Olinsky did not go back to the bleachers. He remained behind the backstop and waited for the ceremony of the base inspection and the hard stare by the pitcher. He saw Grasshopper pump twice, saw his hand go back behind his head, saw the curiously delayed flick of the ball, watched it speed to the boy, and then he heard a sound that afterward he thought was among the most beautiful and satisfying he had heard in all music.

It was a clean, sharp *click,* sweet as birdsong.

The ball soared higher and higher into the air in a graceful parabola. It was 15 feet over the center fielder's head, and it cleared the fence by a good four feet.

Pandemonium broke loose. People were running all over the field, and the boy was chased around the bases by half his teammates, and when he got to home plate he was thumped upon the back and his hair ruffled, and in all this Mr. Olinsky caught one glimpse of the boy's face, laughing and yet with tears pouring down his cheeks.

A week later, the boy turned up at Mr. Olinsky's studio for his violin lesson. He looked around at all the great musicians on the wall, and they no longer seemed to be disapproving and disappointed in him.

Paganini was almost kindly. There was a suggestion of a chuckle on the noble profile of Mozart, and Beethoven no longer looked so forbidding. The boy looked at the portrait of Johann Sebastian Bach last.

He looked for a long time at the picture, and then he said two words out loud—words that brought lasting happiness to Mr. Olinsky. The words were: "Thanks, Coach."

The Arioso went excellently from then on.

Two Courageous Missionary Brides

John T. Faris

They traded the safety of New York for the wilds of the Oregon Territory.

"Narcissa, would you be willing to go with me across the mountains?"

The question was asked eagerly by stalwart Marcus Whitman, who had just returned to his home in Rushville, New York, after a venturesome exploring trip through the West to the mountains of the Oregon country. It was in 1833, when Oregon was a no-man's-land longed for by Great Britain and despised by the United States.

But Dr. Marcus Whitman had learned enough about the new country to see that the nation that secured title to it would be fortunate. He wanted to be one of the pioneers to make a home there. It was his purpose to go out prepared to teach the Indians and to guide the settlers—whom he was sure would follow—into a self-respecting, God-fearing life.

However, he did not want to go alone. He felt that no better object lesson could be given to the Indians than a Christian home. So he sought Narcissa Prentice, who had already promised to be his bride, and asked her if she would be willing to be his partner in making the venturesome journey and in setting up a pioneer home among the Indians.

He told her he knew what he was asking. The way was long and rough. It had been only six years since the building of the first railroad in America. Where they were going they would have to use canoes or horses; many times they would have to walk. Indians would be all about them, and Indians who had learned to dread the white man might prove dangerous neighbors.

Narcissa Prentice laughed off his fears and said of course she would go with him. But she would be lonely if there was not another woman in the party. So the marriage was postponed till Dr. Whitman could find a husband and wife willing to go with them.

For a while, the search was in vain. Then he heard of Dr. H. H. Spalding and his young bride, who were about to leave as missionaries to the Osage Indians on their reservation in northern New York. He tried to reach them but learned that they had already started for their new home.

Whitman jumped into his sleigh and started off to track them down. After a long pursuit, he joined up with them during a blinding snowstorm. There was no time for a lengthy introduction, so he shouted, "Ship ahoy! You are wanted for Oregon!"

The surprised travelers drew rein, and Whitman explained his strange words. But the day was cold, so they agreed to drive on side by side to the little inn in the village of Howard, New York, not far away. Before the log fire at the inn, numerous questions were asked and answered.

"I have promised to go back this spring," Whitman explained. "I am to be married as soon as I return home. Then we are to go out to Missouri, where we are to join the fur traders till we are met by the Nez Percés, among whom we are to live. They will show us the way to our new home. We'll live on buffalo and venison, we'll travel on horseback, and we'll spend the nights in tents or rolled in blankets on the ground. Will you go with us?"

Dr. Spalding wanted to say yes, but he feared for his wife's health. She had recently recovered from a long sickness. So he said to her: "It is not your duty to go. Your health forbids it, so I shall leave it to you."

Mrs. Spalding went off by herself to decide the question of her duty. Ten minutes later, she returned, her face shining, and said, "I have made up my mind for Oregon."

Her husband asked her if she really understood what her decision meant. He reminded her of the perils of the 3,000-mile journey and the loneliness of the faraway home; but she was firm.

The wedding of Narcissa Prentice and Dr. Whitman followed the agreement. Then began one of the strangest wedding journeys ever taken—by rivers, across plains, and over mountains to the mysterious land "where rolls the Oregon."

All went well till the Missouri River was reached, at the point where the fur traders who had invited the missionaries to join them said they would wait. Four days before the arrival of the party, when the traders heard that there were women with the missionaries, they decided to push on alone. They thought they had enough to attend to in protecting themselves from the Indians. They little knew the spirit of Mrs. Whitman and Mrs. Spalding.

Dr. Spalding said that the Whitmans should decide whether or not to go on alone, as clearly they must return home. Brave Mrs. Spalding carried the day by her determined words, however: "I have started for Oregon, and to Oregon I will go or leave my body on the plains."

So the missionary party hurried on their way alone, hoping to overtake the fur traders within a week or 10 days. Mrs. Spalding and Mrs. Whitman were the life of the company, encouraging the men where obstacles hindered them and spurring them on when Dr. Whitman was tempted to say, "Let's go back." He didn't say this often, but when he was kicked by a mule; shaken by the ague; stripped by a tornado, not only of his tent, but his blankets; and crowded off the ferryboat by an awkward, uncivilized frontier cow, it is not strange that he was discouraged.

Dr. Whitman had provided a spring wagon for the two brides, but Mrs. Whitman preferred to ride on horseback by the side of her husband, leaving the wagon to Mrs. Spalding, who was not yet strong. On other horses rode the husbands and Mr. W. H. Gray, who was to be the business agent of the mission station; following them came two teamsters, in charge of the wagons bearing the supplies.

At last the fur traders were overtaken. The men were sorry to see the women, but Mrs. Whitman and Mrs. Spalding soon won all hearts. Before long they were looked on as a positive addition to the company, in spite of the dangers from Indians. For protection, there were more than 200 men, but the attention of many of these had to be given to the 600 animals taken along for food. The animals tempted the Indians, and it was necessary each night to camp with the stock in the center, around these the tents and wagons, and about the whole encampment a company of vigilant sentinels.

The experienced plainsmen shook their heads when they saw the wagons, and they told Dr. Whitman that it would be impossible to take them across the mountains. But he insisted they must go. He was not thinking merely of the comfort of those who would use them, but more of the great importance of proving to the world that a wagon could be taken to Oregon. He was looking forward to the day when there would be in that country more white people than Indians. Yet men and women would be prevented from making the journey by the statement that it was impossible to colonize Oregon by wagon. An English editor had said that American wagons could not make it to the Columbia River, and Americans were believing it. It was Dr. Whitman's purpose to show that they were wrong.

The traders shrugged their shoulders when Whitman said his wagon, if not the others, must go through. They said, "I told you so," when one night, in a bit of rough country, he fell behind with his beloved wagon and came into camp late, warm and puffing—but cheery, too, for he had had only one upset.

The Indians were fascinated by the first wheeled vehicle they had ever seen. They put into jerky syllables the sounds it made as it rose and fell and stopped in the soft grass and among the rocks, and called it *Chick-chick-shani-le-kai-kash.*

Pronounce those syllables and see if they do not remind you of the creaking of a wagon.

Through canyons, along creek beds, up rocky precipices, the wagon was pushed and hauled. Many times it was overturned, but still the doctor would not listen to those who urged him to abandon it. At last, when the way became too rough for four wheels, he made the wagon into a cart, added the extra wheels to the load, and pushed on. Further on the cart was left, but only for a little while. Then it was taken the rest of the way to the mission station. Dr. Whitman had triumphed, and those who said colonists could never go to Oregon were effectively answered. Historians have said that the journey of the wagon almost from coast to coast was a more important event for the country than the building of the 1,200 miles of railway during the same year.

For many weeks of their journey, the travelers had an abundance of food. In the buffalo country, where a single herd sometimes covered 1,000 acres, the hunters could slaughter the noble animals at will. In anticipation of later days when game would be scarce, the caravan paused to jerk, or dry, the buffalo meat. The jerked meat did not seem very appetizing so long as fresh, juicy buffalo steak was to be had, but when the herds vanished, all were glad to use it. Yet how they longed for a little bread to go with it!

Once Mrs. Whitman wrote: "Oh, for a few crusts of mother's bread! Girls, don't waste bread in the old home."

That is the nearest to a complaint the brave woman came during all that arduous journey, in spite of scorching sun, the clouds of alkaline dust that stung the eye and throat, the impure water they were compelled to use, and the myriad of mosquitoes and buffalo gnats.

When, on July 4, 1836, the missionaries were at last over the crest of the Rockies, 2,500 miles from home, they paused, spread their blankets, unfurled the American flag, and knelt in a prayer of dedication to God of the Oregon country. The act meant more than the missionaries knew. One historian of Oregon said that it went far toward giving to the United States 6,000 miles of Pacific coast.

Soon after, hardy frontiersmen were met, who had not seen a white woman for years. They looked reverently on the faces of the two brides. Years later, one of them said, "From that day when I took again the hand of a civilized woman, I was a better man." And the trapper said, "There is something the royal Hudson Bay Company and its masters can't drive out of Oregon." He knew that the coming of women meant the dawn of civilization.

Dr. Whitman picked his location on the banks of the Walla Walla. Dr. Spalding went 100 miles farther, to a spot on the banks of the Clearwater. On these two sites the men, assisted by the Indians, built roomy log cabins. Then they sent for the brides.

Just in time for the Christmas of 1837, Mrs. Whitman reached her new home after a trip of 250 miles. The wolves in the thickets that fringed the banks of the Walla Walla were howling dolorous greetings. The brave woman, smiling as she thought of the snug shelter prepared for her, pushed on to the blazing fire in the home.

She was too weary that night to inspect the place where she was to spend a few happy, busy years. She was content to wait for the revelations of the next day. She did not fear them, for she knew that her husband, with the two teamsters who had come with him across the mountain, and two other men whom he had secured elsewhere, had been busy clearing the land of underbrush and building a house. She was content to think that they had done their best.

Six weeks the men had toiled. They had enclosed a house of one large room, whose open fireplace was ready to glow with welcoming heat for the visitor or, first of all, for the wife, without whom the house would never be anything more than a house. But when Mrs. Whitman entered through the door, the house became a home.

And what a home it was—chairs rudely made, with skins stretched across them; a table made of four posts covered with boards sawed by hand; stools made of logs sawed of proper length; pegs along the walls upon which to hang the clothing, nails being too expensive a luxury; beds fastened to the walls and filled with dried grass and leaves.

Mrs. Whitman's gratitude for these blessings was so great that she found her journal, which had been her companion on the journey from New York, and wrote: "We reached our new home December 10; found a house reared and the lean-to enclosed, a good chimney and fireplace, and the fire laid; but no windows or doors except blankets. My heart truly leaped for joy as I alighted from my horse, entered, and seated myself before a pleasant fire; for it was night and the air was chilly."

Mrs. Spalding was just as happy in the cabin her husband had built for her, and she set to work at once to make it homelike. Then she began to gather the children of the Indians about her for instruction. At first the Indians were suspicious, but it was not long till she found her way to the hearts of all.

Mrs. Whitman, too, gathered the Indians into her home for instruction. Her teaching and Dr. Whitman's training worked many changes for the Indians.

For 10 years, they lived quietly in the lonely place they had chosen. Once during those years, Mrs. Whitman was left alone, month after lonely month, wondering if her husband was dead or alive. In the annals of human history there are few feats to compare with Dr. Whitman's epic journey 3,500 miles in the dead of winter to Washington, D.C. He reached there just in time to save the Oregon country for America.

When Dr. Whitman finally returned, he found that everything was in fine condition, owing largely to Mrs. Whitman's careful management during his absence. There, for several years more, husband and wife worked together, spending themselves unselfishly for the Indians.

Their work was brought to a tragic close in 1846. There was an epidemic among the Indians. Medicine men, who were jealous of the influence of the white teachers, whispered that they were responsible for the sickness. The suspicious Indians believed the stories. They fell upon the home on the banks of the Walla Walla and put to death not only Dr. and Mrs. Whitman but a number of friends who were with them.

The Indians who lived about the home of the Spaldings became restless as they heard of the bloody deed done by their kinsmen. On Sunday morning, when Dr. Spalding was away from home, friendly Indians urged Mrs. Spalding to flee with them to their camp.

Mrs. Spalding longed to go. Her heart yearned for her children, but she stopped to think that it was Sunday. For years she had been teaching the Indians to keep the day holy. What impression would be made on their minds if she should be seen moving to the camp on that day? Her resolution was taken promptly. So she replied firmly, "I will not flee on this day."

But early on Monday the Indians friends were back again. This time she went with them. And she was just in time. The aroused Indians rushed upon her house but found it empty. In their anger at the escape of Mrs. Spalding, they carried away many articles and destroyed many others.

As Dr. Spalding returned, he feared the worst; but when he found his loved ones safe at the Nez Percés camp, his heart overflowed with joy. The reunited family returned to their home, only to be driven from it once more when the Cayuse war, brought on by the Whitman massacre, broke up the mission stations in the region. Then, under guard of 40 faithful Indians, Dr. Spalding took his family to Fort Walla Walla. It was his joy to return to his work after many years' absence, but Mrs. Spalding died four years later. Her most lasting monument was built in the hearts of the Indians.

Mrs. Whitman's monument stands on the site of the home to which she went as a bride. And in the town of Walla Walla, only a few miles away, admirers have built to her memory and the memory of her husband, Whitman College, where young men and women are trained to follow their courageous example.

At the Eleventh Hour

Eunice Creager

Both Milly and Gertrude desperately wanted that teaching job. There wasn't much Milly wouldn't do to get it. . . . . Then came the unexpected opportunity— the great temptation.

"Mrs. Miller said the choice of the school board lies between you and Gertrude Dosch, Milly. Of course it was told confidentially. You must not repeat this."

Milly looked up from the big dictionary she was studying. Her effort at a smile was rather pitiful. "Well, that's an advantage, anyway, isn't it, Mother?" she said, laughing cheerfully. "A race with only one."

"In my judgment, it is not much of a race, Milly. Gertrude's work has been brilliant, but careless; you have built on solid foundations. You are by far the better student and more deserving of it."

"Oh, Mother! How can you say that?" objected Milly nervously,

155

trying to keep a sob out of her voice. "I see so many questions in these old teachers' examinations that I do not know! To think of Gertrude always having help like this! She must know all the answers. How I wish I could have had them a month or two ago!"

"She probably never looked at them much. It was good of her to lend them to you, though."

"She couldn't help it," remarked Milly dryly. "I asked her for them."

"And the dictionary—did she lend you that?"

"No. She has one, but she would never have offered it. Besides, she would need it for her own reference work. Philip Brooks insisted on bringing me his this afternoon. You were uptown. He said it would be helpful, and it certainly is."

The telephone rang suddenly, insistently. "I'll answer it, Mother. I think it is one of the girls. Hello!"

Gertrude's voice at the other end of the line answered happily. "Hello! Are you going tonight?"

"No, I'm not going, Gertrude."

"Now what's the matter, Milly? Studying, I'll warrant you! Catch me poring over my books! Well, I'll have to get on my new dress. Oh, it is a perfect dream of yellow and white. I am wild about it."

Milly hung up the receiver and met the questioning eyes of her mother.

"What is it, Milly? Was there a party tonight? Why aren't you going?" Then an understanding look crept into the mother's tired, faded eyes. "I feel sure I could have made the blue silk presentable if you had told me in time."

"It wasn't that altogether, Mother," Milly said truthfully. "I felt that while I had the back numbers of these teachers' magazines, I should make use of them and lose no time. It is only two days now until the teachers' examination." Then, as she noticed her mother's drawn face, she cried out: "Oh, do put up your sewing and go to bed, Mother! You look so tired. You have done enough for two persons today. Do put it up," she coaxed, bending over her mother's chair, "and, oh, Mumsie, pray for me tonight!"

Mrs. Benton gave her daughter a quick look and held out her arms. Milly jumped into them. "There, there! You are all nervous and unstrung. Pray for you? I have prayed for you, child, every night since you entered the world. That's what mothers are for. I think you will get the place; but if you don't, it will be only a matter of time. Don't worry, Milly. We will pull through some way. Good night, and don't sit up too late."

Milly sat down at the library table littered with teachers' magazines and the big dictionary with a firm determination to keep her mind on her study.

On the day of the teachers' examination, Milly walked briskly toward the courthouse, in which the examination was to be held. Strangely enough, her former nervousness had vanished, and in its place was a calm confidence, the result, probably, of a good night's sleep. The night of the party, Milly had read questions and answers until her brain whirled; then, with a remnant of sanity remaining, she had closed the books and put them out of sight. "I will not look at them another time," she declared. "'Tis true I haven't a library or help like these magazines, but all my life I have been a better student than Gertrude. Why should I cloud my brain by cramming at the last? I will not look up another thing!"

As the result of this wisdom, Milly's brain was never clearer than when she took her seat and began work. A glance at the morning subjects sent a thrill of exultation through her. Gertrude, across the aisle, was writing rapidly and confidently. Milly began what she knew would be good work.

The morning passed quickly, and 12:00 came. As the papers were handed in, Milly stopped at Gertrude's desk. "Are you ready to go now, Gertrude?" she inquired pleasantly.

"I am not going home for dinner. I am going across the street to Aunt Linda's," answered Gertrude, avoiding Milly's eyes and making no effort to rise.

Milly, with a puzzled look, passed out of the room. At the door, Mr.

Baxter, the county superintendent, held out a cordial hand. "I must congratulate you, Miss Benton, on your good work this morning. I have been looking over your paper."

"Oh, thank you, Mr. Baxter. But I may meet my Waterloo this afternoon. History is what I fear."

"You have cause," the superintendent answered quickly. "It is the stiffest examination I have ever known."

Milly went slowly down the courthouse steps, her high spirits a little dampened by this news. A crowd of girls, school aspirants, flocked down the steps ahead of her, their voices floating back.

"Oh, we can't hope to get the place at the main building if we do pass. That lies between Gertrude Dosch and Milly Benton. All we can hope for is a country school. They say it is hard for the school board to choose between them, and that they are waiting to see who passes the better examination before they decide."

"Won't Gertrude splurge if she gets it? She said she wanted it because then she could buy more pretty clothes."

"Whew-who-ah! Whew-who-ah!" Will Martin's peculiar and familiar whistle rang out. Milly smiled and waited. "Say, have pity on a fellow, will you? I've been trying to catch up ever since you left the courthouse. Guess what I have in my pocket."

"Couldn't guess," said Milly, dimpling.

Will's laughter was always infectious. "The examination questions, Milly—none other."

Milly gave a startled exclamation.

"Baxter gave them to my business college last night. Of course they gave them to me with the understanding that I let no one see them, but mum's the word, Milly. I know how you dread history, and it's a hard one, too, I'll tell you. Here, take them! No one will ever know."

Will held out the papers, and for one brief moment that seemed like years,

Milly wavered. She thought of the three hard years since her father's death; how her mother had struggled, baking, sewing, ironing, working beyond her strength to get her through school; of her mother's physical breakdown in the last few months. She must have that school. It not only meant bread and butter, but also medical attention for her mother.

On the other hand, this thing she was contemplating meant the upheaval of all her years of training. She remembered her mother's face and the look in her eyes when she said, "Pray for you? Why, child, I have prayed for you every night since you entered the world."

"I can't do it, Will," she said, quietly. "Thanks, but I can't do it."

"Oh, come! You don't mean it," coaxed Will, a quizzical expression in his eyes.

Milly turned away with an air of finality. "Yes, I am in earnest."

"Well, good-bye, then! Good luck to you. Not many would have turned down that offer, Milly."

Milly thought so herself as she watched Will, with the coveted history questions, swing jauntily down the street.

The history examination more than justified the rumor of "stiff." Milly's heart sank as she looked at the questions; but pushing them in the background of her mind, she went to work on the other subjects and soon had finished them to her satisfaction.

Across the aisle, Gertrude took her history questions and calmly wrote "History" at the top of her paper. Ah, she was ready, too!

Milly sat in her seat and chewed her pencil in a vain effort to answer question number one. Gertrude wrote calmly and confidently on. Indeed, the steady scribble of Gertrude's pencil began to get on Milly's nerves. How did it come that Gertrude found the questions so easy to answer? She had always been weaker in history than Milly.

At last, hot and exasperated, Milly was forced to hand in her paper with two questions unanswered. Sick at heart, she turned her steps homeward.

Gertrude, calm and cool in her green linen, had left the courthouse an hour before. Milly walked on, a sense of utter failure weighting her limbs. She felt suddenly old and tired. A lump rose in her throat. History had spoiled everything for her. Even if she answered the other questions correctly, she could not hope for anything higher than 80 percent.

Mrs. Benton was not at home, for which Milly was truly thankful; it gave her an opportunity to indulge in a good cry.

A few days later, Milly was returning from town when Lulu Thaxter overtook her. "Milly," she began anxiously, "have you put in your application for a country school?"

Milly smiled ruefully. "Yes, I did, the day after the teachers' examination."

"Look here, Milly, there's something odd about that," said Lulu, lowering her voice.

"Gertrude answered every question in the examination correctly. What do you know about that? I went to Uncle William's to look up a reference in their library. You know he is on the school board. There were voices in the other room. I did not pay any attention until your name was mentioned. Before I realized what I was doing, I had heard a lot that was not intended for me. They all agreed that your papers were better, but two of the history questions were blank. Did you forget them, honey?"

"No," groaned Milly. "I simply didn't know them, Lulu."

"Well, Mr. Baxter met with the board, and he was strong for you. He said, aside from the two questions left blank, yours were the finest set of papers he had ever examined; and although your grade was lower than Gertrude's, he recommended you to the school board. Well, they disagreed. Uncle William Miller stood firm for you, while Mr. Wells and Mr. Thompson wanted to give the place to Gertrude. You know it's all mixed up with politics some way. Unfortunately, Mr. Baxter couldn't vote, and the majority ruled, and the school went to Gertrude. Oh, Milly, I could just cry! But don't mind, for Mr. Baxter said the county trustee would give you the best school he had if you wanted it."

The best country school he had! Milly turned this over in her mind as she left Lulu and walked slowly homeward. Even the best, with board taken out, was a pitifully small amount of money. It meant another year of hard work for her mother, who was at the breaking point now. It was a bitter disappointment.

"Well, Mother, I guess it's a sure thing I shall be a country schoolma'am," remarked Milly that night, smiling at her mother, although tears were fighting for mastery; and she repeated the story to her mother.

Mrs. Benton's pale face whitened, but that was the only sign. "Never mind, Milly. It will be only a question of time. Have patience, dear. You are so young; the country school will give you experience."

"Experience, yes, but not much money. We need the money so, Mother. I had thought . . ." Milly's voice trailed off pitifully.

"Never mind, darling. Don't lose your fine sense of values. I know we are poor and need money badly, but all the money in the world would not satisfy me if you were weak and shallow like some girls. I thank God every night for the strength of character of my dear girl. As long as I have this knowledge and the knowledge of our love for each other, I can work hard with a light heart, for I have something better than money."

"Oh, Mother, how could anyone be very bad and live with you? But does it always pay to do right, I wonder?"

"Always. What a strange question for you to ask, Milly. What is it?"

"Nothing, only—oh, sometimes it seems that the one who does wrong gets the best of everything."

"Not for long," declared Mrs. Benton gravely. "The one who does right wins in the end."

On the morning of the day the assignments were to be published, Milly was uptown trying to match some braid for her mother. She was thinking of Gertrude and what joy the day would bring her, and wondering, too, why she had not seen her lately. Glancing out of the window, she saw

Gertrude and Will Martin coming out of Dr. Miller's office. Will looked red and excited, and Gertrude was weeping bitterly.

Milly's heart gave a quick throb of pity. *Mrs. Dosch is worse,* she thought quickly. Gertrude's mother had not been well all summer. *Here I was, half envying her, and perhaps she is in terrible trouble.* After a vain attempt to overtake them, Milly decided she would telephone and ask about Gertrude's mother; but when she got home, her own mother was so ill from a severe headache that it drove the incident from her mind.

By afternoon Mrs. Benton was suffering so much that Milly started to Dr. Miller's office to get medicine. The old man looked up as she entered and grunted a good afternoon. "How's the schoolma'am?" he said teasingly.

"All right—if I am one. But Mother needs some more medicine for her head, Doctor."

The old man rose stiffly and went behind the counter. He often filled his own prescriptions. Milly leaned over the counter. "Tell me which school I got," she coaxed. "Will you, Dr. Miller? Do you know?"

The doctor set the big glass jar down on the counter and regarded her with jovial eyes. He winked. "Milly, did you ever meet Old Nick on the street in broad daylight?" he asked; and then, as if in answer to the amazement in Milly's eyes, he went on, his little eyes twinkling: "On the street, in the guise of a friend with a—well, let's say examination questions in his pocket?"

Watching Milly closely and observing the look of understanding leap to her eyes, the fat old man laughed out loud. "But Will, unlike Old Nick, doesn't know how to keep a still tongue. He talks too much," chuckled the doctor. "I got a whiff of the news and brought him in here, but he wouldn't talk, not he—stubborn as an old mule. Then I went for Gertrude; that brings them to time."

"Gertrude?" gasped Milly. "What has she to do with it?"

"Hoity-toity!" jeered the old man, thoroughly enjoying himself. "Don't think you're the only one! You're second choice, Milly. Gertrude was first choice, and she fell for them. Guess his conscience got to hurting him some, so he had to offer them to you, too. Well, I got them both in here. Will blustered and Gertrude cried, but I got the truth out of them all right. Thought it was odd she came out with such flying colors. Talk about many a slip 'twixt cup and lip! Why, the girl had that school.

"Well, I did some quick work. That school board was here in a jiffy, and I stated my case. It was easy sailing after that. The tide turned, as I knew it would, and you have the place at the main building. Gertrude hasn't any. I tell you, we had to hustle, though, to get those names changed at the *Herald* office. We were just in time."

During the recital, Milly had run the gamut of emotions. "Pinch me," she said finally. "I must be dreaming."

The doctor's eyes softened. "It is no dream, child. Here are the powders. Run home and tell your mother. I know what it means to you." Waving aside her thanks, he hurried the bewildered girl out of his office.

Once outside, Milly almost ran along the street, so eager was she to get home with the glad news. As she sped past Brooks's store, Philip Brooks ran out, waving a paper. "Wait a minute! Congratulations, Milly."

"Oh, Philip, is that tonight's *Herald?* Let me see it."

Smiling at Milly's eagerness, Philip handed her the paper. There it was in big headlines: "Miss Benton Gets Place at Main Building." Milly read it with dancing eyes and cheeks aglow.

"Wait while I get my hat," said Philip, "and I'll take you home in the car; it's about supper time anyway."

In a moment, they were spinning rapidly down the street and were soon at Milly's home. Milly danced happily up the steps and into her mother's room. "Oh, Mother, you were right! You are always right," she cried joyously. "I've won! I've won!"

God Never Forgets

Florence C. Kantz

Her husband was away, and her children were too young to solve the crisis. Was she doomed to die?

Two long weeks, then one day of bliss, then two more long weeks! Muriel's head dropped to a broad, receptive shoulder as Bob's arm tightened gently around her.

"Sometimes I almost wish we had never come out here on this old prairie," she said. "I feel as if I am all alone in a big, silent world."

Once more on the western prairie ranges of South Dakota, the annual season of haymaking had arrived. To the homesteader, these seasons were as inevitable as the proverbial blue Monday washday to the housewife, and equally as necessary. For though the miles of rolling stretches, dotted with half-wild range cattle, were now covered with an abundance of grass, a few months hence they would become a vast bleached ocean, coldly unresponsive to the gnawing hunger of its wandering inhabitants.

In the immediate vicinity surrounding the Harding homestead, there was no grass suitable for cutting and storing. This necessitated securing it from a section 15 miles to the east. It was hard for Bob to leave his young wife and two small children for four weeks of isolation in this sparsely settled region included in the Cheyenne Indian Reservation. True, he usually came home for the weekend once during the time. But the hours spent with his loved ones for just one day seemed literally to fly in contrast with the slow rate at which they dragged as soon as he bade his family good-bye and returned to his task in the hayfield.

But Muriel was a real partner and tried to make things as easy as possible by keeping a smiling face, though underneath her cheerful manner she was constantly striving to keep back the tears. Four weeks of longing and loneliness! This time it seemed that she could not keep the gray from filtering through.

As she hid her face on his shoulder and cried, there was a long moment of silence; then smoothing aside the soft brown hair that lay against his cheek, Bob gently raised her chin until her brown eyes were looking full into his own. "Dearie!" His lips formed only the one word, but what she saw in his eyes made her throw her arms around his neck in a quick burst of penitence for her momentary childishness.

"Bob, dear, I'm sorry. I know it is harder for you than for us, and after all, why try to cross a bridge when it is very improbable that there is even a place where one could be built? I know you *must* go, and of course Robert, Marjory, and I shall finish both of those quilts that I began a year ago; I shall take the opportunity to make that wildflower collection that Robert has been planning on for two months; and then we shall do the whole place up in fine shape for your homecoming. I have been waiting for a chance to dispose of the accumulated sticks and stones and dead man's bones around the house and yard for a long time, and now it has come."

Bob smiled happily at her sudden voluble endeavor to turn the silver lining of her cloud broadside to the sun of his smile. Somehow she could never remain troubled for long in the assuring presence of this handsome, bronze-faced man to whom she had entrusted her all, and with whom she had come "out West" to make a home. And a cozy home it was, though the logs that formed the sides and the front of the two-room structure were rough-hewn and not too straight. The rear was but the side of a hill cut out, and into this space the remainder of the house fitted, having the appearance of just emerging from a tunnel. The dainty white ruffled curtains that covered the square windows seemed to belong to the picture, as did the pink and white morning-glory vines Muriel had coaxed and cajoled into climbing the posts that supported the veranda. Even in these rude surroundings, one could recognize in countless little ways the magic touch that distinguished this simple home from most of the rude cabins scattered here and there over the wide, windswept prairie. It was the kind of home in which one would naturally expect to find a "heap o' livin'."

"Muriel, you will never cease to be a marvel to me," smiled Bob. "Could a man ever find a more lovely, inviting pool in which to bathe his innermost soul than your own understanding companionship?" he added with unstudied simplicity. Then, remembering that he must be on his way, he released her, and catching up little curly-haired Marjory in his arms, he swung her to a place on his broad shoulders, took Robert's small hand in his own, and led the way out to the wagon.

"I wish that telephone line about which we have heard so much would materialize," he exclaimed. "But if wishes were horses—"

"You mean telephones, don't you, Daddy?" corrected Robert.

"Well, I guess it makes little difference what you call them; they are still just wishes anyway, my little man. By the way, dear, when you go on your wildflower excursion, be careful about snakes. There seems to be an unusual number around this summer. With the nearest doctor 95 miles away, and the nearest neighbor 15, you must take no chances. I shall count the days until I can be with you again, even if it will be for only a day. But remember, 'this, too, shall pass away,' and soon I shall have finished my work and will come 'marching home.'"

"Bob, you are the champion gloomicide of the world! Already I am planning the reception banquet for your homecoming."

He smiled as he kissed her and the children and drove away. At the top of "Last Look," a small hill over which the road led, he turned as usual and waved to his loved ones, who always regarded this moment as the final good-bye.

"There's water on 'oo cheek, Muvver. Did it sprinkle?" inquired little Marjory, looking up at Muriel.

"No, darling," she answered, hastily brushing away the telltale tear. "That's not rain; it's just a drop of water that escaped from the spring of love. Sometimes it gets so full, it just *has* to run over."

The day passed rapidly for the children, and by the time the summer sun had bowed itself out from the presence of the glamorous day, they were ready for a good night's rest. When supper and prayers were over, Muriel tucked them quickly into bed and sat down beside them for the bedtime talk they always had together. It was the final applause of the day's symphony.

"Mother, will Daddy be afraid all by himself tonight?" questioned Robert, who was a thoughtful boy of six years.

"No, dear, he will not. You know the verse in the Bible that tell us angels will watch over him and keep him from harm?"

"Say it, Muvver," interrupted little Marjory, who dearly loved to hear Muriel "say the Bible."

"All right, dear. Will you say it with me?" As they repeated the words with which they were so familiar, little Marjory joined in on each word that she could remember. "He shall give His angels charge over thee, to keep thee in all thy ways. They shall bear thee up in their hands, lest thou dash thy foot against a stone."

As they finished, Robert was silent for a moment as if meditating; then with a questioning look, he asked, "Does God *ever* forget to tell the angels to watch over us?"

"No, son, God *never* forgets. Why do you ask?"

"Well, you know that time when I was running to catch Bingo, and I stubbed my toe on that sharp stone that was sticking out of the ground and hurt me so bad? Well, I think God must have forgotten *that* time." Then, hopefully, "I guess God didn't forget, but maybe the angels weren't watching very good."

Muriel looked into the upturned face of her little son as she answered, "Have you ever run into that stone again, Robert?"

"Why, no, Mother, of course not. I always go *around* it. And I am careful not to run into other stones either."

Muriel took his little hand in hers—the little hand that held so much of the happiness of this home within its unconscious grasp—and, brushing aside the brown hair, looked into his innocent gray eyes, so like his father's, and said quietly, "Life is full of sharp stones, dear, and sometimes the angels have to let us stub our toes on one before we will be careful to go around them whenever we come to them. But you remember how tenderly Daddy picked you up and carried you into the house, and how we washed the blood off and wrapped your foot all up carefully. And each day Daddy watched while I dressed it until it was all well again. Not once did we forget."

"Yes, I remember," Robert assented. "And Daddy felt so sorry. No, I guess God doesn't forget."

An hour or so later as Muriel blew out the light and laid her head on her pillow, she softly repeated to herself, "God never forgets."

The old-fashioned clock on the mantel, which had come down to Bob as a family heirloom, struck the hour of midnight. Its slow, sonorous tones shattered the uncanny stillness of the sultry night. As it lapsed back into silence, save for a measured ticktock, ticktock, a coyote on a distant hilltop gave a long, drawn-out call to its mate, which answered from the crest of another ridge. Muriel stirred uneasily and became dimly conscious that someone was calling to her.

"Muvver, Muvver." Yes, it was Marjory's voice that had initially roused her to consciousness. "Muvver, I'm thirsty," came the little voice through the darkness.

"All right, dear; Mother will get you a drink," answered Muriel as she sat up in bed and laid back the covers. When she stepped onto the floor, her foot came into contact with a cold moving mass, and she knew, even before she felt the hot sting of the poisoned fangs in her heel, that she had stepped on the coiled body of a rattlesnake. The buzzing whir of the rattles accompanied her terrified scream as she leaped aside in the darkness.

With a bound, she was through the door and into the adjoining room, searching for a match. She lit the lamp and looked frantically for something with which to kill the snake. With only a glance at her lacerated foot, she seized the ax by the wood box and returned to the bedroom. The thought of the children's danger brought disregard for her own. Calling to little Marjory, who had begun to cry with fright, she told her to lie still while she killed the snake. She looked desperately for it, but it had vanished. Thinking that perhaps it had crawled out of the house again through the same hole somewhere between the logs by which it had entered, she at last gave up her search and turned her attention to the wound on her heel.

Already her heel was beginning to swell, and streaks of red were slowly running upward from the wound. What could she do? In desperation, she squeezed and pressed it as best she could; then she bathed it in kerosene and bandaged it tightly. But she realized as the pain increased with the swelling that she was fighting a losing battle. Quieting the frightened children, she at last succeeded in getting them back to sleep. How thankful she was that they did not realize the real situation; it would be easier for her to carry out her plans.

"Oh, if Bob were only here," she repeated over and over again. Lifting her heart to God in an agonized prayer for help, she pleaded, "O God, send someone. I cannot leave my little ones here all alone!"

Suddenly, the words of the evening before came to her almost as if a voice had spoken them: "God never forgets. He shall give His angels charge over thee." The words seemed to quiet her tortured mind, and she repeated to herself the promise God made to the apostle Paul: "My grace is sufficient for thee."

She had given her heart to God when she was a young girl and had often felt His keeping power. She knew what it was to trust Him, and she was not afraid of death if such was His plan for her. But the horror of the situation was not in what was to befall her. It was August, and the heat was intense. It would in all probability be but a matter of three or four days until the poison had finished its deadly work. She thought of what the children would do without her during those nine or 10 days that must elapse before Bob would return, and the thought was maddening.

By the time morning came, she had formulated her plans. She would first write a letter to leave for Bob. She sat down, placed her now greatly swollen leg on another chair, and began to write. Again and again tears blinded her eyes, but she struggled on at her heartbreaking task.

The morning sun just peeking over "Last Look" sent a radiant beam through the window and touched Robert on the eyelids with a warm kiss, awakening him. Sitting up in bed, he turned to look for his mother just as she said, "Good morning, darling." But the greeting that always came back with a smile froze on his lips, and a look of horror came into his eyes as he cried, "Oh, Mother! There's that snake under your chair."

Disregarding her crippled leg, Muriel leaped from the chair, and her horrified gaze revealed a large rattler coiled on the floor beneath it. Seizing the ax and the broom, she succeeded in killing it, thus eliminating the terrible menace to the children, and sank limply into a chair.

Now came the hardest part of all. She must prepare them for the awful experience that was ahead of them. Choking back the tears, she tried to appear as calm as possible. She told Robert just what and how to do until his father should return. Passing over the specter of death as lightly as possible, she dwelt at length on how they were to conduct themselves after she should "go to sleep." Marjory was too small to understand just what it was all about, but she knew that something was wrong, and that "Muvver" felt bad. She saw the evidence of tears, and coming over to Muriel, she patted her face, saying, "Don't ky, Muvver. God will charge His angels over 'oo."

"Yes, and you know, Mother dear, God never forgets; you told me He doesn't," comforted Robert.

All day Muriel worked as best she could with the terrible pain in her leg, which was swelled to her hip now and was turning dark purple. She baked all that she could and placed things where the children would have access to them. Sick, weak, and racked with pain, she struggled for self-control. The long hours of the night ahead haunted her. If only she could see Bob just once more. "God never forgets—I must not doubt," she assured herself again and again.

The rays of the afternoon sun were lengthening as an old, double-seated buggy drawn by two small Indian ponies jogged slowly along the bare prairie road. The drooping heads and the unsteady gait as the ponies dropped into a walk told the story of fatigue. Their sides were wet with sweat, and as the rickety old buggy creaked along over the heat-surfeited ground, their lagging hoofs stirred up clouds of restless dust and sent the grasshoppers catapulting into the rusty-bladed grass. The loosened spokes of the wobbly wheels clattered a noisy protest as the merciless sun seemed to enfold everything in a thick blanket of heat. Even the prairie dogs sat quiet and motionless on the mounds of their humble domiciles, quite in contrast to their usual vociferous barkings at any stranger who dared to pass their thickly populated villages.

The occupants of the dust-covered vehicle rode in silence; it was too hot for conversation, save for an occasional remark offered without invitation to respond. The man was a white man, while the woman who sat beside him was a full-blooded Indian. At length, in answer to a sudden animated remark by the squaw, the squaw man—for such are the white men called who marry Indian women—looked at his watch and shook his head.

"We haven't got time to stop today. Some other time we will."

"Go see white squaw. Must see white squaw," answered the woman.

"But if we drive over past there, we'll have to stay all night, as the horses are too tired to go the extra distance," remonstrated the man not unkindly.

"Go see white squaw. See white squaw *now,*" insisted the woman, sitting up resolutely.

Rather reluctantly, the man yielded and turned the horses into the side road that led away to the Harding homestead. He worked among the Indians as a minister and had stopped to call on the friendly Hardings once before while making the rounds of the reservation. Covering the two intervening miles, they at last reached the top of "Last Look."

Robert, who was in the yard, spied them, and with only a momentary look, he rushed into the house, crying, "Mother, there is someone coming down the road."

"Thank God," exclaimed Muriel, and she burst into sobbing. *God had remembered.* Then quickly controlling herself, she waited with beating heart.

"It's a man and an Indian woman," reported Robert from the window.

He watched the squaw alight. Then he ran to the door and opened it as she reached the threshold. Muriel greeted her with as much of a smile as she could gather together on her drawn and swollen face. But before she could speak, the squaw, who had stopped just inside the door, gave one horrified look, then she threw up her hands and cried, "Ugh, snake," and ran wildly from the house.

Muriel was dumb with fear. Was the poor superstitious Indian running away to leave her to die without help? Oh, it could not be! She called after her, but the squaw did not heed. Out to the buggy she ran and spoke excitedly to the man; then she hastened out over the prairie, seemingly in search of something.

Alighting from the buggy, the man hurriedly entered the house. He approached Muriel and assured her that his wife would be back shortly and listened while she explained to him what had happened.

Soon the squaw returned with her arms full of roots that she had dug up with her bare hands. She was chewing some of them, dirt and all. Hurrying to Muriel's side, she hastily tore off the bandage, and taking the chewed paste from her mouth, she put it on the wound. Then turning to the man, she spoke rapidly to him in the Indian language. He went out quickly, and she returned to her task of chewing more roots. As fast as she had a mouthful prepared, she took the plaster off the wound and replaced it with a fresh one.

Soon the man returned with an armful of the roots. These the squaw hastily put into a pan and set him to pounding them into a pulp. This relieved her of the task of chewing them, but not before the membrane had been burned off the inside of her mouth. This root, which goes by the name of snakeroot among the Indians, has an acid juice when crushed and is irritating to tender membranes.

Muriel's leg was swelled clear to her body as large as the skin would permit and had turned a purplish black. The pain was almost unbearable. Rapidly and constantly the squaw worked, aided by the efforts of her husband, until, after hours of suspense, the pain lessened and the inflammation seemed to be coming under control. All night the ministration continued, and by morning there was a marked improvement.

As soon as arrangements could be made, Muriel and the children were packed into the old buggy. After leaving a letter for Bob telling him where they were, they started for the Cheyenne Indian Reservation Agency, where the government doctor lived.

Upon their arrival, the doctor, after a careful examination, announced that the crisis was past and that, owing to the Indian squaw's faithfulness in treatment, Muriel would recover.

For some reason he could not explain, Bob felt impressed to leave his work and go home that weekend instead of waiting until the next. It was a long trip to make for just one day, but he could not seem to resist the urge to go. Accordingly, he arrived home just at sundown.

As he approached the house, it seemed strangely quiet. With an uneasy feeling, he turned the knob and stepped in. Finding the note Muriel had left for him on the table, he quickly read it. His face paled as he turned rapidly and went out, locking the door after him. Unhitching the horses from the wagon, he turned them into the pasture, and hurriedly catching one of the saddle ponies, he was soon riding furiously away in the direction of the agency.

It was a very pale but happy Muriel who smiled up at him as he bent over and kissed her. "Thank God you are safe, and I still have you with me," he said with a voice choked with emotion.

That night as Muriel turned on her pillow and closed her eyes, she repeated softly, "God never forgets."

Summer to Autumn

Purple and Fine Linen

Anna Brownell Dunaway

The world was divided between the haves and the have-nots, between those born for the purple and those born for poverty—at least that's what Pauline thought. And then came the train ride.

There was a 15-minute wait at the little transfer station at Junction City. Pauline begrudged every second of it. The wedding ceremony of her friend was set for 8:00. That would barely give her time to greet the family and slip into her peach taffeta bridesmaid's gown.

She moved restlessly about the dingy little waiting room, nibbling a chocolate bar. There would be no time to snatch even a bite after she got there. The candy would have to sustain her until the wedding ceremony was over. The dinky little local she was about to board did not have a diner. That was what one got for traveling to out-of-the-way places like Weeping Water. Pauline smiled disdainfully as she repeated the name half aloud. What a teary sound it

179

had, suggestive of funeral wreaths and weeping willows rather than a wedding.

Pauline was an Easterner and city-bred to the core. She had never lived away from the rumble of streetcars and the noise of traffic. She had a hazy idea that country folk and small-town dwellers spent their days milking cows and gathering eggs. The stares of the loungers and the sights and sounds of a village depot grated upon her sensibilities. She moved impatiently to the window and laid down her purse, ticket, and gloves for a moment, while she powdered her nose before the lid of her pigskin case.

"Excuse me"—it was a low voice at her elbow—"but is this your glove? I picked it up under one of the seats."

Pauline snatched it with an annoyed gesture. "Why, yes, I believe it is mine, thank you." She was proverbially careless, perhaps because things came to her so easily that they gave her no sense of responsibility. Now reminded of her shortcomings, she took a hasty inventory of her belongings. Bag, silk umbrella, gloves, ticket, fitted traveling case—all at hand. Would the train never come? It was already overdue. She tapped the floor impatiently with her foot, clad in its immaculate mole oxford.

"I believe I hear the local whistling now." It was the same friendly voice. Pauline turned and observed the girl to whom it belonged. Then she looked away with an almost imperceptible lift of her eyebrows. These familiar people in wayside stations, always trying to essay conversation! Evidently, a little native on her way to "weekend" with somebody, as the local newspapers would put it. Her plain blue serge suit had a homemade look to Pauline's fastidious eye, and although it was the first day of September, the girl wore a straw hat.

If there was anything in which Pauline was not careless, it was the purple line of convention that marked the times and seasons of wearing apparel. She was smugly conscious of the becoming lines of her twill suit of mole brown, with its hat of velour to match. Pauline was an unconscious snob in the matter of dress. She was wont to measure people by a certain rigid standard, which meant for her purple and fine linen.

She picked up her traveling case. People were hurrying out of the station. Pauline, anxious to get a seat in the train where Pullman accommodations were not to be had for love or money, followed in their wake, counting over her belongings as she went. Yes, she had them all: traveling case, gloves, handbag, umbrella—

"Where to, miss?"

"Weeping Water," said Pauline haughtily. She made her way down the aisle and dropped into what she mentally termed a "stuffy" red plush seat. Well, anyway, there was the consolation that it wouldn't be long now. A few hours' ride and then her destination, and all the fascinating excitement of a wedding.

If it was a small-town wedding, it was to be complete in every detail. Joan Markham, her roommate at college, had not spent four years at Smith for nothing. There were to be guests from everywhere, with ushers, brides-maids, and all the modern paraphernalia of a fashionable wedding. It was even to be something paradoxical—so old-fashioned as to be ultra-new. Joan would wear a quaint old-fashioned gown of satin that had been her mother's, with a court train of crepe chiffon.

Pauline's artistic mind reveled in the thought of her peach taffeta gown, with its tight-fitting bodice and full skirt. The other bridesmaid would wear green taffeta, and the maid of honor, lavender. They would carry old-fash-ioned nosegays of garden flowers and wear long, black-lace mitts. Pauline felt a little hurt that Joan had not asked her to be her maid of honor. But prob-ably Joan had felt bound to ask the groom's sister.

She gazed out unseeingly at the golden wheat fields, visioning, instead of them, the scene of the wedding. The house would no doubt be a bower of asters and smilax. She pictured the bridal party descending the old-fash-ioned staircase. Joan insisted on a home wedding. In some ways, Joan was

just a bit old-fashioned in spite of her Smith training. But it was a house that lent itself to just such a wedding, rambling and roomy. Pauline had spent several vacations there.

It was all in perfect keeping, if Weeping Water was a mere blur on the map. And Joan's people were real gentlefolk. Her father had given up a career as a surgeon in a big city to stay on in the little town and carry on the practice that his father had had before him. Pauline felt that she could safely approve of Joan's family. Not that Joan could dress as she did—not on a country doctor's salary—but she felt she could make much of nothing. She had an air that placed her in the purple-and-fine-linen class. Joan would look like a duchess in her wedding gown. Her thoughts switched to her own peach taffeta—peach, green, and lavender. What delicate shades—a regular rainbow wedding.

"Excuse me"—the deprecating voice again, with its friendly intonation—"is this your handkerchief? I found it in the aisle."

"Why, I believe it is. Thank you." Pauline took it frigidly. The shabby little girl at the junction waiting room again. She seemed to be a veritable Nemesis, popping up everywhere with lost articles. Pauline was annoyed that the girl still hesitated in the aisle, swaying with the jerking motion of the train.

"I looked about for you in the car," she was saying, "and did not notice until now that you were sitting just across from me. They're losing time right along. I hope we won't be late. This train usually runs behind schedule."

"Yes?" murmured Pauline coldly. Her eyes were fixed stonily on the window. She wasn't in the habit of picking up chance acquaintances, especially those who did not adhere to the purple line. And how disquieting the girl's words were. What if the train were too late for the wedding? Then what? Not to be there to be Joan's bridesmaid—to wear the quaint taffeta gown—

"Your ticket, madam."

Pauline recalled her eyes from the window with a start. The girl had taken her seat. The conductor stood there waiting. She had forgotten all about the ticket. Mechanically, she reached into her handbag. The ticket was not there.

The conductor cleared his throat impatiently. Pauline turned out the contents of her bag in a heterogeneous heap: handkerchiefs, powder puff, cards, small change——but no tiny square of cardboard. She went through the various pockets frantically, even though she knew, with the calmness of conviction, that her ticket reposed on the window sill in the waiting room at Junction City. Now that she was miles away from it, she saw it as clearly as when she laid it there. Slowly, she returned the things to her bag.

"I—haven't my ticket," she said composedly, opening her purse. "I remember now that I left it in the waiting room at Junction City."

The conductor eyed her coldly. "The fare," he said, making a note in his book, "is three dollars and 87 cents. You will get your refund of the agent at Weeping Water."

"Refund?" repeated Pauline, as a parrot might. At that moment, the word "refund" was the farthest from her thoughts, for she had just made another amazing discovery. The small change in her bag counted up to exactly 57 cents. There was no roll of bills in her purse. And she remembered with a sickening consciousness that she had neglected to stop at the bank to cash a check before leaving home. She had felt all along that there was something she had forgotten. So this was it. The few bills she had had were spent before she reached Junction. There were the tips, the meals—

"Three eighty-seven," repeated the conductor sharply.

Pauline made an effort to retain her poise and to speak calmly. "I—have not that amount with me. I came off in such a rush that I neglected to cash a check. Will you take a check? I have my checkbook—"

"Can't take a check," snapped the conductor, now obviously put out. "If you haven't your ticket or its equivalent, you will have to get off at the next stop."

"But you don't know who I am," gasped Pauline. "My father is William J. Sherman, of the Sherman Trust Company—"

"Can't help it." The conductor was moving down the aisle. He pulled the bell cord. "Next stop's Pender. You get off there."

Pauline started after him, her face flaming. A few around her were watching her with curiosity. She noted covert smiles. So they didn't believe her. They thought her a common sponger—a deadbeat. The train was already slowing down. She looked out of the window with a feeling of panic. What she saw was a low, red depot, a mill in the distance, an elevator, and a watering tank. With the calmness of despair, she read on the weather-beaten station "Pender." To think of being set off here—in these wilds, where trains stopped but once a day! A bridesmaid with no money and the wedding taking place without her—

"Pender—Pender—Pender-r-r!"

The brakeman passed down the aisle, calling the name raucously. He stopped and lifted her traveling case. The train came to a standstill.

Gloweringly, the conductor waited on the platform. Pauline walked uncertainly down the aisle, her eyes blurred with tears. She felt the eyes of the whole car upon her.

"Too bad," sympathized the brakeman as he assisted her down the steps. "Common thing. Happens every day. Mebbe you can get someone to drive you over to where you were going."

So she might. She hadn't thought of that. Pauline took fresh hope. But another thought! Whom could she hire for 57 cents? No, it was hopeless—relentless—

"Wait a minute." It was the fresh, sweet voice of the girl of the waiting room. She stood on the top step holding a blue silk parasol with ivory tips. "Isn't this yours? I was deep in a book and only just saw you getting off. Is this your station? I thought you were going to Weeping Water."

"Conductor put 'er off," explained the brakeman laconically. "Lost her ticket—no money—"

"You lost your ticket?" cried the girl incredulously. "I remember seeing it in the window of the waiting room at Junction City."

"All aboard," called the conductor. The brakeman doffed his cap.

"Time's up," he said apologetically. "We don't stop here but a few minutes."

"Could I—" began Pauline, desperately making a plunge forward. "Could I—" A thousand wild schemes had darted into her mind. If she could borrow—beg; if she could telegraph her father; but the train was moving. She dropped her suitcase and fumbled blindly for her handkerchief.

"Wait!" cried a ringing voice. "Stop!" It held an authoritative note. "Put her back on. I have money. I will pay her fare. Why, it's an outrage, putting a girl off like this!" The girl reached down her hand to Pauline, who was keeping pace with the barely creeping train. The brakeman, grinning, swept her up, suitcase and all. Pauline clung to the girl's hand as if to a lifesaver. Curiously enough, at this moment she had the sensation of being beyond her depth in a river, and that someone was holding water wings to her.

The girl loosened her hand and tendered a crisp bill to the conductor. He handed her back the change with an impervious smile.

"This way," said the girl, leading Pauline through the rear of the car behind them. "It's a smoker, but we don't care. Everybody will be craning their necks in that other one. We'll just sit here."

"But you don't know me," cried Pauline, finding her voice, and regarding the other in amazement. "How can you trust me like this—a perfect stranger? And I was so horrid!"

"I grew up on the prairies," the girl said with a smile, "where everything is open and frank like the plains themselves. No jungles, or swamps, or hidden ugly things. And I always know intuitively whom I can trust." She took out another crisp bill and laid it in Pauline's hand. "You'll need it before you get home," she insisted.

"Your name then, and address," said Pauline with the suspicion of a choke in her voice.

"Nellie Newton, Herington, Kansas."

"Street and number?"

"Only that," Nellie said with a laugh. "Oh, we don't have to be labeled out West."

Pauline scribbled rapidly. After all, she must have been mistaken in her vision of water wings. It must have been an angel instead. She said earnestly, "I'll make this up to you—oh, I will!"

"Of course," murmured the girl simply. She turned to the window with an involuntary exclamation. "Oh, see! The sun is setting over there in the west. Isn't it beautiful?"

Pauline followed her gaze. Used as she was to city spires and skyscrapers, she was rather disappointed to see only fleecy, airy clouds tinged with blue, green, and purple, like myriads of rainbows. But there was something about its quiet beauty that held her.

"Few things," spoke up Nellie suddenly, "can equal a prairie sunset."

"Unless it be," said Pauline with sincere homage, "a daughter of the prairies."

The girl laughed.

"They're stopping again," she said, looking out. "This is Wayne. We can slip back to our own seats quietly, while the crowd is getting on and off. If I don't see you again, good luck and—good-bye."

"Good-bye," returned Pauline. She was thinking that the girl was a little thoroughbred. Now that she had established the best kind of credentials for friendliness, she was not taking advantage of it. Her eyes followed the erect figure. To think that she had ever thought her commonplace and ordinary— just because her suit wasn't in the latest extreme style!

"She might wear the purple robes of royalty," she said to herself humbly. Back in the other car, she found her seat had been taken, and she was forced to content herself with one that she shared with a sleepy old gentleman who wore a black skullcap. But she minded nothing now, for she had not been left behind at Pender. And that was not all. There was something in her heart that sang.

The train thundered into the little station 35 minutes behind time. Pauline scrambled into a bus—she had written Joan not to meet her, as she had been undecided about her time of leaving. The house was in a bustle of preparation, and so she went straight to her room, stopping only for a hurried peek at the bride.

When she had slipped into the peach taffeta and had joined the wedding party at the head of the stairs, the strains of Lohengrin's Wedding March were floating up to them from below. Pauline fell into step beside the brides-maid in green. Then she gave such an undignified jump as to slow for a moment the stately procession. For there, marching ahead of the bride, very erect and very sweet in her gown of lavender taffeta, was the maid of honor, and she was no other than the little traveling companion who had paid her fare!

Their eyes met in recognition. The bridesmaid in green intercepted the look.

"Isn't Joan's cousin a dear?" she whispered. "And doesn't she wear lavender well?"

Pauline nodded absently, for she was thinking of something she had wrested from the prairies that was the nicest thing she had ever put in her memory box. It was that better far than outward apparel is the purple and fine linen of the heart and mind.

The Boy
on the
Running Board

—·—

Annie Hamilton Donnell

Martin Folsom was a stern father who ruled his family by fear. And then, on the way to Damascus . . .

Everything was wrong with Martin Folsom. Everything—not just this and that and t'other. But of course the apex of wrongness had come with the discovery that his son, Ross, had lied to him. That was one of the things he would not have believed.

"No, sir," Ross had said when it ought to have been "Yes, sir." For afterward, following a subjection by his father to the third degree, the boy had sobbed out his confession.

Sobbed—that was another thing. A man-child had no business sobbing. Martin told Caroline as much.

"I'm 53 and I've never cried in my life!" he stormed to his gentle little wife.

She was used enough to his storming, but this time the very soul of her wrapped itself about the son she had borne, in an anguish of sheltering.

"You frightened him, Martin. Rossie's only 10."

"Frightened! What business has a boy being frightened! You make too much of him."

"Someone shall 'make of' him! He shall never be afraid of his mother anyway!"

There had been many such scenes between Martin Folsom and his two sons. Forrest, the 11-year-old son, had come in for his full share. But a man should bring up his own boys, shouldn't he? Well?

"Where's that tax bill? It was among the papers in this clip. If Ellen's been meddling here again—"

"I'll find it, Martin. It must be there somewhere."

"It isn't in the clip where I put it. I've got to pay my taxes today or I'll lose my discount. If I'm going to Damascus at all, I'll have to start sometime! It wouldn't be the first time that child has played with my things."

"Not *things*—just the 'Ducky Clip,' as she's named it. She does love to open and shut its bill. Here's the paper, Martin."

"Well, it's lucky you found it. Where's Ellen? Ellen!"

"Don't, Martin! She is so little and—thin. Don't scold Ellie!"

"Well, somebody ought to teach her something. *I* never was allowed to meddle with my father's things."

"Perhaps he didn't have any Ducky Clip. Martin, aren't you going to let Ellie ride to town with you! I told her I'd ask you."

"Why doesn't she ask me herself? Scared to?"

Ah, that was it! Ellie was scared to. But she did so want to go!

"It does her good to ride, Martin. Keeps her out of doors—"

"Well, can't she 'keep' outdoors without going to Damascus with me? No, she can't go today, tell her. I'm going alone. Tell her that when she stops meddling with my things I'll take her along."

The mother's slender hand shot out and picked up the clip in the shape of a duck's head, with its broad yellow bill that might start quacking any moment. She opened and shut the bill, a tender little smile on her face.

"Look, Martin—look! It *is* funny! If you were only six—"

"Where's my other hat! I never can find it where I left it! Remember to tell Ross to hoe that corn every minute till I get back. No shirking now! I'll know exactly how much has been done. By good rights he should be punished more than that for lying to me."

"Oh, but, Martin—" She hesitated to provoke her husband further, but she needed to say it.

"Well, now what?"

"The sun will be terrible out there in the middle of the day, Martin!"

"He lied to me in the middle of the day, didn't he? How about that's being terrible!"

Oh, that—that was terrible, too. But if he hadn't been afraid—isn't it terrible for a son to be afraid of his father? A little son—Rossie was still so little.

"Martin, didn't—didn't you ever lie when you were 10? Just—once?"

But the man was, or pretended to be, too intent upon his memorandum list, over which he was poring, to heed her last words. He was not, indeed, much in the way of heeding. It was to be heeded that Martin Folsom required.

He pounded heavily out through the long hall, but above the noise of his steps, a piping sound came to his ears. The sound of a child crying.

One child a liar, another a baby! Time for Forrest to get to his work now. "Where's Forrest, Caroline?"

"Forrie?" Oh, she did not want to tell him where Forrie was! Life to poor Caroline Folsom was chiefly a succession of eager defenses of her brood. Her soul felt battered sometimes, as now.

"You might as well out with it. One o' these days I'm going to burn that boy's storybooks up! Worthless stuff, all of them! Has he done his stint at the woodpile?"

Oh, must she tell him Forrie had not done his stint?

The bustling town of Damascus was six good miles away. On hot days like this, they were six bad miles. Martin Folsom, in his chugging little car, was in no mood to enjoy any kind of miles. He was out of tune with the pleasant country scenery, out of tune with his family, his errand—life generally. He needed someone along with him to scold at.

In this mood, he came perilously close to letting the small car drive itself. Small wonder it did not do something much worse than it did.

For a dreadful instant, the man's heart lost its beat. The child's cry in his ears struck horror to his very soul. He had scarcely strength to clamber out from behind the wheel.

It sounded almost like Ellie's voice.

"Oh! Oh! *OH!*"

He must not shut his eyes. He must—look.

"Oh, you've run over Henry Ward Beecher! Oh, he's killed dead!"

Another voice now. Someone came padding briskly on bare feet. This voice was almost a Forrest voice, but actually laughing.

"Stop taking on, Celie Grant! Don't you see we haven't got to kill him now? Thank you, mister! See, the wheel went right across his neck—now we'll take him in to Mother to be roasted!"

The pair of them, sister and brother, were brown and freckled. The boy's laughing face was eager with explanations.

"We drew lots to see which 'd catch him an' which 'd cut off his head. Celia was catching him. We picked out Henry Ward Beecher because he was the biggest. Mother said nothing was too big for Father!"

"Father's coming home!"

"Yes, go ahead, Celia. You can tell the rest."

"Today he's coming! Mother keeps singing every minute, doesn't she, Jeddie?"

"Well, I guess any mother'd sing when she hadn't seen a father for four whole months. Father's a drummer, but he doesn't hardly ever drum so long at a time. He hasn't seen—"

"Shh! Let me tell—I want to tell!"

The boy swept a low bow. "Ladies first!" he said with a smile. "It's a present we've got for Father this time!"

"It's the baby!" chanted the child who might have been Ellie. "We're going to give him a present of the baby! She's almost a month old, isn't she, Jeddie? Mother's did her all up."

"She means," explained the boy, "her clothes. Mother's done those up starchy's anything! You see, we never wrote a word to Father when the baby came. Mother said we'd surprise him; she said wasn't it fine the baby came so nice and early, so's to be a *little* grown up when Father got home. She doesn't make anywhere near such faces now."

"We've swept everything and dusted everything and cleared up everything and—and—"

"Killed the rooster!" The boy laughed.

"And Jeddie drew the lot to go to town, didn't you, Jeddie? To meet Father."

On his way again, Martin Folsom found himself a little more in tune with his surroundings. He noticed how lush and green the grass fields were after the long rain, how the grain was growing, how everything pointed to a good harvest. He remembered things, too—the boy's freckles and the excited chatter about "Father." Must like Father pretty well, those kids.

"Hello, mister! I'm on your running board!" The small befreckled, laughing face of Jeddie appeared at his elbow. "I'll get off if you'd rather, but riding's nicer than walking."

Martin put out a hand and opened a door.

"Get in," he said.

"Oh my! Honest? This is fine! You see, Father's train isn't till after dinner, but I thought I'd go real early so's not to miss it. And—and there was your running board—" He broke into soft chuckles. "I didn't want to waste a running board! Besides, I'd shaken all the rugs and done all the things Mother wanted me to, so I just came," he finished simply.

He was ridiculously small, there on the seat beside Martin. Yet the joy effervescing within him and escaping in wrigglings and little spurts of whistled tunes made him far from a negligible companion on the road to Damascus. To save his life Martin could not keep his eyes from the boy. What on earth was he doing now?

Jeddie was doubling and undoubling his short arm and regarding the doubled aspect of it with pride.

"I guess he'll think that's some muscle! Father'll like that! And I can pitch ball better now; I'll give him some good ones, all right! We take turns pitching. Father's a southpaw. The Grant family team's some team! Only, now that the baby's come, I don't know about Mother's being first base—"

"Mother?"

"Yes, she's a good first-bagger! You ought to see her catch! Of course it isn't a real 'nine,' but we manage. Celia's going to make a regular player. I don't suppose you're on a team, are you?"

"On—a team?"

"Yes. Home team, you know, like us. If you haven't got any boys—"

Martin Folsom looked straight ahead over his wheel. He was thinking of Forrest and Ross. He found it exceedingly difficult to imagine them on a "team" with himself and Caroline and little Ellen. He found it hardest of all to imagine himself on that team.

"You can't very well play ball without *any* boys!" Jeddie said with a laugh. "Father says it's lucky there's two men in our family. We're pals, me and Father."

Here was a still more difficult thought to entertain, this thought of pals. Martin Folsom could not compass it. The happy voice beside him ran on unweariedly.

"When Father retires—that means doesn't *drum* anymore—we're going to have the best time! Of course we'll have to work like fun on the farm. That's it, like fun! When we hoe now, Father and me, we run races to the end of the row! Sometimes I beat him. And when Mother comes out and brings us something to drink, she kisses Father when I am not looking, and kisses me when Father isn't looking, but we always kind of see!" Here for lack of breath the running chronicle paused.

Suddenly, Martin swung about. "Did you ever lie to him?" he demanded.

"To Father? Oh! Oh, I wish you hadn't asked! Right now—today, I mean. It—it sort of spoils the—the way I was feeling." But the boy was game. "Yes, once," he said very low.

"Because you were afraid of him?"

"Of Father—*afraid?* You couldn't be afraid of Father. No, I just—lied. 'Riginal sin, Mother said, was the matter with me. But I've never had it since. You don't catch me being a mean skunk twice! We—we both cried, me and Father. Then Father held out his hand and said, 'Put it there,' and I put it there, and that was our contract. Like signing the pledge, Father said."

The little chugging engine had the stage to itself for a space then. And presently it chugged into the busy little streets of Damascus. Martin's face was curiously thoughtful. He was thinking long thoughts. To his own surprise, he took the boy to a restaurant with him for luncheon. And looking across the small round table he found himself remembering that never in his life had he so lunched with a son. What would Forrie or Rossie have thought to be there, experience little thrills of adventure like this stranger boy, another father's son? What would he himself have thought?

"This is fun, ain't it? I have something to tell Celie. If you don't mind, I guess I'll carry her my pie. I can wrap it in a paper napkin—it's a nice dry pie. She'll like it because it came from here. We'll play rest'rant with it!"

Another strange thing did Martin Folsom do, after his errands were finished. He went to the railroad station when "Father's" train was due. Of course it was to see if the duplicate parts of his mower had come, but to tell the truth, he knew the letter ordering them had barely had time to reach the factory. Transparent, very transparent, why Martin went to the station. But there he found himself a few moments before that train time. To further deceive or attempt to deceive himself, he even started in the direction of the freight house, but he never got there. A small boy came catapulting down upon him.

"It's on time! You couldn't make Father's train late. He'd get out and push!" A clear little cackle of mirth rose above the subdued stir of the busy place. "There's only nine minutes more now. I just looked. Pete says I'll wear the clock all out! Pete's the man that hollers the trains. He knows Father. Most everybody knows Father," he said with quiet pride.

"Say, mister, what'll you bet he'll get out of the front car? He always does. He says he isn't going to waste a whole train length of time!"

Suddenly, the boy stiffened, listening intently.

"Wait! Can't you hear? There's Father whis'lin'!"

In another moment, the train was in sight, a puff of white smoke around a curve. It drew into the station, Jeddie running along beside it, abreast of the foremost car. Martin Folsom saw no more.

"Too soon for those mower parts to get here," he muttered, and he turned away. He did not want, after all, to see the meeting between that father and that son.

He had half intended to wait and offer the two a ride home, but an entirely new thought presently banished everything else. A startling thought, distinctly terrifying as he neared his car and got an uninterrupted view out into the country. Some men were gazing and talking.

"Must be a fire out there—odd, isn't it, how plain smoke shows up on clear days like this? Likely as not that fire's six or eight miles away."

"Likely as not six miles."

"Well, a little fire makes a terrible lot of smoke sometimes. *I* don't live out that way anyhow!"

"Nor I," said the other laughing comfortably.

But Martin Folsom lived out that way.

He cranked his car in a little panic of haste. Once out on the straight high-way, he stepped hard on the accelerator. The farther he got, the more exactly that smudge of thick smoke seemed to hang over his buildings—over Caroline and his children. The man was not reasonable in his dread; he conjured up most unlikely things. It was broad daylight. Warned in plenty of time, people did not burn to death in their houses. Not in houses with all those outside doors—one, two, four chances to get out, to say nothing of windows.

Ellie sometimes played up in the attic.

He drove faster. He did not even see the little Grant house, halfway, with its air of impatient waiting for Father. The child, Celia, waved to him from its front porch, but he was not looking at her. He was thinking of another little child, Ellie.

"Henry Ward Beecher's most done!" called Celia. "You can smell him roasting!" but it was smoke that Martin Folsom smelled.

Curiously, as he got quite near, the smudge faded out appreciably. Did that mean it was nearly over? Was he too late?

In another minute he would swing around into full sight.

The house was standing there, untouched—*untouched!* All the buildings were there. And suddenly it came to Martin Folsom that they were the most beautiful buildings he had ever seen, the dearest. He looked at them through a mist; he had to brush it away.

"Caroline—Carrie! Ellie!" he called as he climbed out from behind his wheel. "Forrie! Rossie!" None of them answered. He called again.

"Carrie! Carrie!"

The house was empty; he went from room to room. He could find no one in the shed or barns. Out in the cornfield, no short figure labored with a hoe. No one anywhere. And now new and unreasonable dread.

The smoke was lessening rapidly. It appeared to be over the woodlot. And, as Martin gazed, a small procession came into sight—a bedraggled, smudgy procession. Caroline carried pails and walked wearily. Little Ellie trailed behind. He noted that only Ross was missing in the procession.

It came nearer still. Then Martin saw the smoke stains on his wife's tired face—on Ellie's and Forrie's faces. It came to him that they were the most beautiful faces he had ever seen.

Even in that flash of space, he had time to remember the light in that boy Jeddie's face and in the little girl's. He had time to miss the light here, in these faces.

"Where's Rossie?"

It is strange how in our moments of deepest feeling we can think of only the ordinary things to say.

"He's waiting to make sure," Caroline Folsom said.

"He's afraid you'll think he set it," explained Forrest with a boy's bluntness. "But he didn't."

"He didn't do anything but put it out," the mother said quietly. "We don't have any idea how it started, Martin. Rossie just looked up from hoeing and there it was. Seems odd, after all the rain we've had—but it was *there*. Maybe somebody was having a picnic and built a fire. Martin, we tried so hard to stop it!"

"We did, too, stop it!" shrilled Ellie. "Mother and me and the boys! They beat and beat and beat, didn't you, Forrie? And Mother and me watered and watered."

"Yes," said the dear smudged face that looked down at the child, smiling encouragingly. "Only a little of the lot was burned after all. But we're sorry any of it did. We're—we're tired," Mother said. "Ellie's almost too tired to walk, Martin."

He swung the child to his shoulder and walked beside them. All the things he wanted to say, that came thronging to his lips, he could not say. He could not tell Caroline he loved her. He could not reach up and squeeze the little limp hand or rub his cheek against the little warm body of Ellie. The habit of *not* saying, not rubbing or squeezing, shackled him like a heavy chain.

Was it too late?

He set the child down and went across the fields to Rossie. Perhaps, remembering that other boy and "Father," it might be easier with Rossie.

The boy was unbelievably smoked and smudged. He leaped to his feet from his lounge under a tree, at sight of his father.

"It's out," he said. "All of it's out. I waited." His bare toes scuffed in the dirt; Rossie did not look at Martin. "I never set it," he muttered. "You can call it lyin' if you want to."

It was then that the shackling chain snapped. An immense shame for himself, and pity for his sullen young son, caught at Martin Folsom's throat. But he could speak. He could lay his arm across the boy's straight little shoulders.

"Come on home, son."

Son—he could say it.

"We'll have some supper and then, you know what we're going to do? Get ready to go fishing! Get the hooks and lines out—you and me and Forrie. We'll celebrate putting out the fire! Yes, sir, make a regular camp-out of it. We'll borrow Nathan Tuttle's tent. We can string up a curtain for Mother and Ellie."

"Mother and—Ellie?"

"Sure, they're going, too. We'll stay overnight and we won't set fire to any woods with our fires either! The one who catches the biggest fish will get a prize." This last, being the inspiration of the moment, filled Martin with pride. In the gentle glow of it, the pair of them swung home together.

Martin's arm remained across the boy's shoulders. They were keeping step. He had never kept step with a son before. There was something splendid and at the same time rather heartbreaking in the thought. It meant so much lost time.

"My!" the boy kept mumbling. Rossie, too, suffered from an inability to say the things, all the things, that came thronging to his lips. They dammed up in his throat and choked him. But Rossie's face—

Martin Folsom caught a glimpse of his son's face. It was lit like the face of that other son of that other "Father."

"My!" mumbled Rossie, too full for utterance. He did not understand the miracle of this new father that strode beside him, keeping step, holding him with that pleasant weight of his arm. How could Rossie know that Martin, like Paul in the Holy Book, had seen a great light on the road to Damascus?

Overnight Guest

Hartley F. Dailey

Why did the nervous young man drive off in the wrong direction?

Greenbriar Valley lay almost hidden by the low-hanging clouds that spilled intermittent showers. As I plodded through the muddy barn-yard preparing to do my afternoon chores, I glanced at the road that led past our place and wound on through the valley. There was a car parked at the side of the road a little way beyond the pasture corner.

The car was obviously in distress. Otherwise, no man so well-dressed would have been out in the pouring rain, tinkering with it. I watched him as I went about my chores. It was evident that the man was no mechanic—desperately plodding from the raised hood back to the car seat to try the starter, then back to the hood again.

When I finished my chores and closed the barn, it was almost

201

dark. The car was still there. So I took a flashlight and walked down the road. The man was sort of startled and disturbed when I came up to him, but he seemed anxious enough for my help. It was a small car, the same make as my own but somewhat newer. It took only a few minutes for me to spot the trouble.

"It's your coil," I told him.

"But it couldn't be that!" he blurted. "I just had a new one, only about a month ago." He was a young fellow, hardly more than a boy—I should have guessed 21, at most. He sounded almost in tears.

"You see, mister," he almost sobbed, "I'm a long ways from home. It's raining. And I've just got to get it started. I just *got* to!"

"Well, it's like this," I said. "Coils are pretty touchy. Sometimes they'll last for years. Then again sometimes they'll go out in a matter of hours. Suppose I get a horse and pull the car up into the barn. Then we'll see what we can do for it. We'll try the coil from my car. If that works, I know a fellow down at the corner who'll sell you one."

I was right. With the coil from my car in place, the motor started right off, and it purred like a new one. "Nothing to it," I grinned. "We'll just go see Bill David down the road. He'll sell you a new coil, and you can be on your way. Just wait a minute while I tell my wife, Jane, where I'm going."

I thought he acted odd when we got down to David's store. He parked in the dark behind the store and wouldn't get out. "I'm wet and cold," he excused himself. "Here's 10 dollars. Would you mind very much going in and getting it for me?"

We had just finished changing the coil when my little daughter, Linda, came out to the barn. "Mother says supper's ready," she announced. Then turning to the strange young man, she said, "She says you're to come in and eat, too."

"Oh, but I couldn't," he protested. "I couldn't let you folks feed me. I've got to get going anyway. No, no, I just can't stay."

"Don't be ridiculous," I said. "After all, how long will it take you to eat? Besides, no one comes to Jane's house at mealtime and leaves without eating. You wouldn't want her to lie down in mud in front of your car, would you?"

Still protesting, he allowed himself to be led off to the house. But it seemed to me as if there was something more in his protests than just mere politeness.

He sat quietly enough while I said the blessing. But during the meal he seemed fidgety. He just barely picked at his food, which was almost an insult to Jane, who is one of the best cooks in the state and proud of it.

Once the meal was over, he got quickly to his feet, announcing that he must be on his way. But he had reckoned without Jane.

"Now, look here," she said, and she glanced at me for support. "It's still pouring rain out there. Your clothes are all wet, and you can't help being cold. I'll bet you're tired, too; you must have driven far today. Stay with us tonight. Tomorrow you can start out warm and dry and all rested."

I nodded slightly at her. It isn't always advisable to take in strangers that way. Unfortunately, there are many who cannot be trusted. But I liked this young man. I felt sure he would be all right.

He reluctantly agreed to stay the night. Jane made him go to bed and hung his clothes to dry by the fire. Next morning she pressed them and gave him a nice breakfast. This meal he ate with relish. It seemed he was more settled that morning, not so restless as he had been. He thanked us profusely before he left.

But when he started away, an odd thing happened. He had been headed down the valley toward the city the night before. But when he left, he headed back north, toward Roseville, the county seat. We wondered a great deal about that, but decided he had just been confused and made a wrong turn.

Time went by, and we never heard from the young man. We had not expected to, really. The days flowed into months, and the months into years.

The Depression ended and drifted into war. In time, the war ended, too. Linda grew up and established a home of her own. Things on the farm were quite different from those early days of struggle. Jane and I lived comfortably and quietly, surrounded by lovely Greenbriar Valley.

Just the other day I got a letter from Chicago. A personal letter, it was, on nice expensive stationery. "Now who in the world," I wondered, "can be writing me from Chicago?" I opened it and read:

Dear Mr. McDonald:

I don't suppose you remember the young man you helped, years ago, when his car broke down. It has been a long time, and I imagine you've helped many others. But I doubt if you have helped anyone else quite the way you helped me.

You see, I was running away that night. I had in my car a very large sum of money, which I had stolen from my employer. I want you to know, sir, that I had good Christian parents. But I had forgotten their teaching and had got in with the wrong crowd. I knew I had made a terrible mistake.

But you and your wife were so nice to me. That night in your home, I began to see where I was wrong. Before morning, I made a decision. Next day, I turned back. I went back to my employer and made a clean breast of it. I gave back all the money and threw myself on his mercy.

He could have prosecuted me and sent me to prison for many years. But he is a good man. He took me back in my old job, and I have never strayed again. I'm married now, with a lovely wife and two fine children. I have worked my way to a very good position with my company. I am not wealthy, but I am comfortably well off.

I could reward you handsomely for what you did for me that night. But I don't believe that is what you'd want. So I have established a fund to help others who have made the same mistake I did. In this way, I hope I may pay for what I have done.

God bless you, sir, and your good wife, who helped me more than you knew.

Robert Fane

I walked into the house, and handed the letter to Jane. As she read it, I could see the tears begin to fill her eyes. With the strangest look on her face, she laid the letter aside.

"For I was a Stranger, and ye took Me in," she quoted. "I was hungered, and ye fed Me; I was in prison, and ye visited Me."

Little Johnny Slept Here

C. M. Williams

The marriage was dead, the old house was deserted, and the sun was sizzling overhead. What answers could possibly be found here?

John pulled the car off the narrow country road in front of an old deserted farmhouse. The cloud of dust that had been following us caught up and enveloped us. I grabbed the folded road map and fanned myself in exasperation. The sun blazed down.

"Well," John said, "this is it. Let's go view the ruins."

"It's too hot. You go. I'll wait."

"Come on," he urged. "I'll show you where I used to hang my sock for old Santa."

"Sail on!" I said impatiently. "Go ahead and get it over with."

John waded through the knee-high grass to the old house alone. While he was exploring the past, I sweltered and seethed in the present.

We were on our way home from a month-long argument to California. The trip had been a sort of last-ditch attempt to save our disintegrating marriage, with the unspoken understanding that if harmony wasn't restored before we reached home, we'd go our separate ways. We had not so much as touched each other, even once, in the last three weeks, and we rode in the car like strangers—he in his corner, I in mine.

John had set his goal in life and worked hard to reach it. When his success was assured at last, I began to feel left out, neglected. I thrive on affection and being needed. Without them, I was desolate.

"Come on in," he called from a broken window. "I just saw Grandpa's ghost come down the stairs. No telling who you might see here." He was trying to be jocular. I pretended not to hear.

When John finally came back to the car he was carrying a No Trespassing sign that had fallen over in the grass.

"You're not going to take that thing home, I hope," I said.

He didn't answer but took a pencil and printed on the sign "LITTLE JOHNNY SLEPT HERE." Then he went back, set it up in front of the old house, and again disappeared inside.

"Why?" I thought. "What's in there?" I was broiling in the car. I got out and made my way through the tall, dusty grass.

When I entered the house, John was just standing there, amid dust and cobwebs and bits of broken plaster fallen from the ceiling. This was the parlor that was also a bedroom when company came, he said. A bed had stood in the corner, with a headboard as high as his grandfather. The pillows always stood up and were covered by square pillow shams with peacocks in bright-colored cross-stitch.

We went to the kitchen. He showed me where the old cookstove used to stand, and the wood box he'd filled for Grandma so many times. And the kitchen table. "It was covered with oilcloth," he said, "oilcloth with pansies on it. The prettiest pansies I ever saw."

Upstairs, we entered a big, forlorn-looking room with one tall window. "I used to lie on the bed here and imagine that the window reached right up into the sky."

"I understand now why you wanted to come back here," I said. "It was home to you, wasn't it?"

"No. Not home. Just a here-today-gone-tomorrow sort of place. I was too much for the old folks. I'd be here a few weeks, then an aunt or uncle would take me over for a while. Wherever I happened to be, my suitcase was always under the bed, waiting to go when they tired of me. I probably was a nuisance.

"One time I was visiting my cousins. There was a row of clothes hooks on the wall, just our height. Each one had a name under it, and no one dared to use another's hook. If only, I thought, I had a hook all my own like my cousins had! I finally found one and asked Aunt Millie, 'Could I please put my name under that empty one?'

"'Oh, you won't need it,' she told me. 'You won't even be here next week.'

"I ran out on the porch and howled and howled until she made me stop it.

"Another time, my cousin Curt hurt himself. Aunt Millie gathered him up in her lap to bandage his toe, and held him for a while to stop his crying. I remember standing by the screen door watching; it seemed to me the most wonderful thing in the world to have a mother hold you close while she bandaged your toe, and say, 'Never mind. Everything's going to be all right.'

"I guess that's what I've really wanted, all my life. Someone to hold me when I was hurt or lonely; a place to live that was *my* home, this week and next week and always; and my own hook to hang my coat on."

John sat on the dusty windowsill and pulled me down beside him. He was almost casual as he related his story, but the vivid picture that came through tore at my emotions and wrenched me out of that cocoon of self-pity I had been weaving around myself. I was watching a lonely, motherless six-year-old, in this very room, a long time ago. Suddenly that boy was very dear to me.

I could hear the winter winds rattling the windows of the old farmhouse, just as he had then, and, peering out through the frosted panes, I could see the moon. It gave the lonely little fellow the only comforting light in the dark, shivery room and seemed his only friend.

That evening Grandpa had said to Aunt Alice, "We'll bring the boy over in the morning. He's big enough to fetch in the wood for you. I'll come for that calf next week."

So he'd been traded off, he assumed, for a calf. He'd never again get to sit for hours in Grandpa's beautiful black buggy and pretend he was driving a team of prancing black horses. The buggy would still have its own special place, there between the corn bin and the horse stall. *It* had a home. Only little boys were traded like calves.

Almost lost in his grown uncle's nightshirt, the boy crawled out of bed and tiptoed over the cold floor to the window. He stuck his forefinger in his mouth to make it warm and wet, then rubbed it against the frosted pane to clear a spot through which to see. He looked up at the moon, and his small body shivered. "Please, Mr. Man-in-the-Moon," he pleaded, "don't let Grandpa trade me off. *Please* let me stay."

"I bawled myself to sleep that night," the man beside me said, and chuckled as if it were funny.

When he finally stopped talking, I found that my hand had somehow stolen into his, and I was grasping it tightly. But it was not just the hand of my husband that I was holding so protectively; it was also the hand of a very small, very frightened, heartbroken little boy.

Never again was I able to look at John without seeing, too, a reflection of the little fellow who wanted only a hook to hang his coat on, a place to call home—and someone to reassure him when he stubbed his toe. Now I realized that I had no monopoly on the need for affection and reassurance. And, with a new serenity, I could understand his *intention,* and that this was what really counted.

Now when he said, "Get your war paint on. Let's go for a ride," I knew it was his way of saying, *I love you. Come share the big outdoors with me.* Or when we'd planned to visit friends for the evening, and he suddenly said, "Let's just sit here on the porch instead and listen to the rain on the roof," I knew he meant, *I'd rather be at home alone with you than anyplace else in the world.*

As John and I rode down that dusty country road away from the old house, we turned a corner into a different life. In the years that followed, there grew a nearness and dearness between us. When irritation tempted me to be impatient, or when I knew things were going wrong for him, I'd quietly slip my hand in his. *Never mind. Everything will be all right.* No matter how tense the situation, his response was always the same—a tightening of his hand on mine.

And then one day, John suffered a severe cerebral thrombosis, after which he did not move again and seemed to be in a coma. As I rode beside him in the ambulance on the way to the hospital, I clasped his hand firmly in mine and spoke clearly, "Never mind, dear. Everything will be all right."

His staring eyes focused on my face for one brief instant, and I felt a perceptible tightening of his hand.

Was it a split second of awareness or just a reflex response? I do not know. But I like to believe that in that moment, he knew, if ever so briefly, fulfillment of his lifetime need for love and reassurance.

Birthdays Are Lovely

Author Unknown

Polly had never heard of birthdays before . . . so when one finally came, she didn't really know what people did with them.

Polly was a dear girl who lived on a large farm with plenty of chickens, cows, and horses; but Polly never thought much about how nice all these were, for her father and mother were always hard at work. The two brothers worked with their father; her sister helped her mother in the house; and Polly washed the dishes, scoured the knives, fed the chickens, and ran errands for the family, and for all the summer boarders besides.

One of the boarders, Miss Cary, was watching Polly shell peas one morning and thinking that she did a great deal of work for such a little girl. Finally, she asked, "How old are you, Polly?"

"Eight," Polly answered.

213

"You're almost nine," said her mother.

"When is her birthday?" asked Miss Cary.

"Why, let me see; it's this month sometime—the seventeenth of July. I declare, I'd have forgotten all about it if you hadn't spoken." And Mrs. Jones went on with her work again.

"What's a birthday?" Polly asked shyly.

"Why, Polly," exclaimed Miss Cary, "don't you know? It's the anniversary of the day you were born. Didn't you ever have a birthday present, Polly?"

"No," said Polly, looking puzzled.

"We never have much time for these things," Polly's mother said. "It's about all I can do to remember Christmas."

"Yes, I know," Miss Cary said, but she resolved that Polly should have a birthday.

When she came down to breakfast the morning of the seventeenth, Miss Cary met Polly in the hall and, putting a little purse into her hand, said kindly, "Here, Polly, is something for you to buy birthday presents with."

Polly opened the little bag and found in it nine bright silver quarters. She ran as fast as she could to tell her mother.

"Why, child!" her mother said, "that's too much money for you to spend. Better save it. It will help buy you a pair of shoes and a warm dress next winter."

Almost any girl would have cried at this, and Polly's eyes did fill with tears; but as her mother wanted her to help "put the breakfast on," she took the plate of muffins into the dining room.

Miss Cary noticed the wet lashes and said, "Mrs. Jones, please let Polly go down to the stores today and spend her birthday money."

Mrs. Jones could not refuse this request. So after she had put the baby to sleep, Polly was allowed to go down to the village, which was a good two miles away, all by herself. The happy girl would have willingly walked five miles to spend her precious money.

It was late in the afternoon when she came back. The boarders were lounging about, waiting for the supper bell to ring. They all smiled at the little figure toiling up the road, with her arms full of bundles.

Polly smiled back radiantly through the dust that covered her round little face as she called to Miss Cary, "Oh, I've got lots of things! Please come into the kitchen and see."

"No, it's too warm there," Miss Cary said. "Come into the living room, where it's cool, and we can all see."

So they went into the house, and Polly began to unwrap her packages and exhibit her purchases.

"There," she said as she tore the paper from an odd-shaped bundle. "This is for Mother"—she held up an eggbeater—"'cause it takes so long to beat eggs with a fork."

The boarders looked at each other in surprise, but Polly was too busy to notice.

She fairly beamed as she held up a green glass necktie pin for inspection. "Isn't it lovely?" she said. "It's for Father."

"This isn't much," she continued, opening a small bundle, "only a rattle for Baby. It cost five cents."

The boarders looked on in silence as the busy little fingers untied strings. No one knew whether to laugh or feel sorry.

It was wonderful what nine quarters would buy, and not strange that the little girl had spent a whole half day shopping. There was a blue tie for brother Dan, and a pink one for Tim; a yellow hair ribbon for sister Linda; some hairpins for Grandma; and a small bottle of cologne for Jake, the "hired man." Then there was but one package left. Polly patted this lovingly as she opened it.

"This is the nicest of all, and it's for you," she said as she handed Miss Cary a box of pink writing paper. "It seemed too bad that you only had plain white paper to write on, when you write so lovely. So I got you this. Isn't it pretty?"

"Why, it's beautiful, Polly dear," Miss Cary said, "but what have you bought for your birthday present?"

"Why, these," said Polly, "these are all my presents. Presents are something we give away, aren't they?" And Polly looked around, wondering why all were so still.

"It is more blessed to give than to receive," said one of the boarders softly, and Miss Cary put her arms around Polly and kissed the hot, dusty little face again and again.

"It's been a lovely day," Polly said. "I never had any presents to give away before, and I think birthdays are just lovely."

The next month, after Miss Cary returned to the city, *she* had a birthday; and there came to Polly a most wonderful doll, with beautiful clothes, and a card saying, "For Polly, on my birthday, from Lena Cary," which, by the way, immediately became the doll's name.

Miss Cary was not the only one who caught Polly's idea of a birthday. The rest of the boarders remembered, and through the year, as each one's birthday came, Polly received a gift to delight her generous little heart.

When the seventeenth of July came around again, Miss Cary was not on the farm, but she sent Polly a little silk bag with 10 silver quarters in it—and Polly still thinks "birthdays are lovely."

Monty Price's Nightingale

Zane Grey

He was the best cowboy on the range—until his nightingale began to sing. . . . But then came a plume of smoke.

Around campfires, they cursed him in hearty cowboy fashion and laid upon him the ban of their ill will. They said that Monty Price had no friend—that no foreman or rancher ever trusted him—that he never spent a dollar—that he could not keep a job—that there must be something crooked about a fellow who bunked and worked alone, who quit every few months to ride away, no one knew where, and who returned to the ranges, haggard and thin and shaky, hunting for another place.

He had been drunk somewhere, and the wonder of it was that no one in the Tonto Forest Ranges had ever seen him drink a drop. Red Lake, Gallatin, and Bellville knew him, but no more of him than the

217

ranges. He went farther afield, they said, and they hinted at darker things than a fling at faro or a fondness for red liquor.

But there was no ranger, no cowboy from one end of the vast range country to another, who did not admit Monty Price's preeminence in those peculiar attributes of his calling. He was a magnificent rider; he had an iron and cruel hand with a horse, yet he never killed or crippled his mount; he possessed the Indian's instinct for direction; he never failed on the trail of lost stock; he could ride an outlaw and brand a wild steer and shoe a vicious mustang as bragging cowboys swore they could, and—supreme test of all—he would endure, without complaint, long toilsome hours in the piercing wind, freezing sleet, and blistering sun.

"I'll tell you what," said old Abe Somers, "I've ranched from the Little Big Horn to the Pecos, an' I've seen a sight of cowpunchers in my day. But Monty Price's got 'em all skinned. It shore is too bad he's unreliable—packin' off the way he does, jest when he's the boy most needed. Some mystery about Monty."

The extra duty, the hard task, the problem with stock or tools or harness—these always fell to Monty. His most famous trick was to offer to take a comrade's night shift.

So it often happened that while the cowboys lolled round their campfire, Monty Price, after a hard day's riding, would stand out the night guard, in rain and snow. But he always made a bargain. He sold his service. And the boys were wont to say that he put his services high.

Still they would never have grumbled at that if Monty had ever spent a dollar. He saved his money. He never bought any fancy boots or spurs or bridles or scarves or chaps; his cheap jeans and saddles were the jest of his companions.

Nevertheless, in spite of Monty's shortcomings, he rode in the Tonto on and off for five years before he made an enemy.

There was a cowboy named Bart Muncie who had risen to be a foreman and who eventually went to ranching on a small scale. He acquired a range up in the forest country where grassy valleys and parks lay between the wooded hills, and here in a wild spot among the pines, he built a cabin for his wife and baby.

It came about that Monty went to work for Muncie and rode for him for six months. Then, in a dry season, with Muncie short of help and with long drives to make, Monty quit in his inexplicable way and left the rancher in dire need. Muncie lost a good deal of stock that fall, and he always blamed Monty for it.

Some weeks later, it chanced that Muncie was in Bellville the very day Monty returned from his latest mysterious absence. And the two met in a crowded store.

Monty appeared vastly different from the lean-jawed, keen-eyed, hard-riding cowboy of a month back. He was haggard, thin, shaky, spiritless, and somber.

"See here, Monty Price," said Muncie with stinging scorn, "I reckon you'll spare me a minute of your precious time."

"I reckon so," replied Monty.

Muncie used up more than the allotted minute in calling Monty every bad name known to the range.

"An' the worst of all you are is that you're a liar!" concluded the rancher passionately. "I relied on you an' you failed me. You lost me a herd of stock. Put me back a year! An' for what? God only knows what! We ain't got you figgered here—not that way. But after this trick you turned me, we all know you're not square. An' I go on record callin' you as you deserve. You're no good. You've got a streak of yellow, an' you sneak off now an' then to indulge it. An' most of all, you're a liar! Now, if it ain't all so—flash your gun!"

But Monty Price did not draw. The scorn and abuse of the cowboys might never have been, for all the effect it had on Monty. He did not see it or feel it. He found employment with a rancher named Wentworth and went at his work in the old, inimitable manner that was at once the admiration and despair of his fellows. He rolled out of his blankets in the gray dawn, and he was the last to roll in at night.

In a week all traces of his weakened condition had vanished, and he grew strong, dark, and hard, once more like iron. And then again he was up to his old tricks, more intense than ever, eager and gruff at bargaining his time, obsessed by the one idea—to make money.

To Monty, the long, hot, dusty, blasting days of summer were as moments. Time flew for him. The odd jobs; the rough trails; the rides without water or food; the long stands in the cold rain; the electric storms when the lightning played around and crackled in his horse's mane, and the uneasy herd bawled and milled—torment of his comrades were as nothing to Monty Price.

And when the first payday came and Monty tucked away a little roll of greenbacks inside his vest, and kept adding to it as one by one his comrades paid him for some bargained service—then in Monty Price's heart began the low, insistent, and sweetly alluring call of the thing that had ruined him. Thereafter, sleeping or waking, he lived in a dream, with that music in his heart, and the hours were fleeting.

On the mountain trails, in the noonday heat of the dusty ranges, in the dark, sultry nights with their thunderous atmosphere, he was always listening to that song of his nightingale. To his comrades, he seemed a silent, morose, greedy cowboy, a demon for work, with no desire for friendship, no thought of home or kin, no love of a woman or a horse or anything, except money. To Monty himself, his whole inner life grew rosier, mellower, and richer as day by day his nightingale sang sweeter and louder.

And that song was a song of secret revel—far away—where he gave up to this wind of flame that burned within him—where a passionate and irresistible strain in his blood found its outlet—where wanton red lips whispered, and wanton eyes, wine dark and seductive, lured him, and wanton arms twined around him.

The rains failed to come that summer. The grass bleached on the open ranges and turned yellow up in the parks. But there was plenty of grass and water to last out the fall. It was fire the ranchers feared. And it came.

One morning above the low, gray-stoned, black-fringed mountain range rose clouds of thick, creamy smoke. There was fire on the other side of the mountain. But unless the wind changed and drew fire in over the pass, there was no danger on that score. The wind was right; it seldom changed at that season, though sometimes it blew a gale. Still the ranchers grew more anxious. The smoke clouds rolled up and spread and hid the top of the mountain, and then lifted slow, majestic columns of white and yellow toward the sky.

On the day that Wentworth, along with other alarmed ranchers, sent men up to fight the fire in the pass, Monty Price quit his job and rode away. He did not tell anybody. He just took his little pack and his horse, and in the confusion of the hour he rode away. For days he had felt that his call might come at any moment, and finally it had come. It did not occur to him that he was quitting Wentworth at a most critical time. It would not have made any difference to him if it had occurred to him. He rode away with bells in his heart. He felt like a boy at the prospect of a wonderful adventure. He felt like a man who had toiled and slaved, whose ambition had been supreme, and who had reached the pinnacle where his longing would be gratified.

His road led to the right, away from the higher ground and the timber. To his left, the other road wound down the ridge to the valley below and stretched on through straggling pines and clumps of cedar toward the slopes and the forests. Monty had ridden that road a thousand times. For it led to Muncie's range. And as Monty's keen eye swept over the parks and the thin wedges of pine to the black mass of timber beyond, he saw something that made him draw up with a start.

Clearly defined against the blueblack swelling slope was a white-and-yellow cloud of smoke. It was moving. At 30 miles distance, that it could be seen to move at all was proof of the great speed with which it was traveling.

"She's caught!" he cried. "Way down on this side. An' she'll burn over. Nothin' can save the range!"

He watched, and those keen, practiced eyes made out the changing, swelling columns of smoke, the widening path, the creeping dim red.

"Reckon that'll surprise Wentworth's outfit," soliloquized Monty thoughtfully. "It doesn't surprise me none. An' Muncie, too. His cabin's up there in the valley."

It struck Monty suddenly that the wind blew hard in his face. It was sweeping straight down the valley toward him. It was bringing that fire. Swift on the wind!

"One of them sudden changes of wind!" he said. "Veered right around! An' Muncie's range will go. An' his cabin!"

Straightway Monty grew darkly thoughtful. He had remembered seeing Muncie with Wentworth's men on the way to the pass. In fact, Muncie was the leader of this fire-fighting brigade.

"Sure he's fetched down his wife an' the baby," he muttered. "I didn't see them. But sure he must have."

Monty's sharp gaze sought the road for tracks. No fresh track showed! Muncie must have taken his family over the shortcut trail. Certainly he must have! Monty remembered Muncie's wife and child. The woman had hated him. But little Del with her dancing golden curls and her blue eyes— she had always had a ready smile for him.

It came to Monty suddenly, strangely, that little Del would have loved him if he had let her. Where was she now? Safe at Wentworth's, without a doubt. But then she might not be. Muncie had certainly no fears of fire in the direction of home, not with the wind in the north and no prospect of change. It was quite possible—it was probable that the rancher had left his family at home that morning.

Monty experienced a singular shock. It had occurred to him to ride down to Muncie's cabin and see if the woman and child had been left. And whether or not he found them there, the matter of getting back was a long chance. That wind was strong—that fire was sweeping down. How murky, red, sinister that slow-moving cloud!

"I ain't got a lot of time to decide," he said. His face turned pale and beads of sweat came out upon his brow.

That sweet, little golden-haired Del, with her blue eyes and her wistful smile! Monty saw her as if she had been there. Then like lightning flashed back the thought that he was on his way to his revel. And the fires of hell burst in his veins. And more deadly sweet than any siren music rang the song of his nightingale in his heart. Neither honor nor manliness had ever stood between him and his fatal passion.

He was in a swift, golden dream, with the thick fragrance of wine, and the dark, mocking, luring eyes on him. All this that was more than life to him—to give it up—to risk it—to put it off an hour! He felt the wrenching pang of something hidden deep in his soul, beating its way up, torturing him. But it was strange and mighty.

In that terrible moment, it decided for him, and the smile of a child was stronger than the unquenchable and blasting fire of his heart.

Monty untied his saddle pack and threw it aside. Then with a tightly shut jaw, he rode down the steep descent to the level valley. His horse was big, strong, and fast. He was fresh, too, and in superb condition.

Once down on the hard-packed road, he broke into a run, and it took an iron arm to hold him from extending himself. Monty calculated on saving his horse for the run back. He had no doubt that would be a race with fire. And he had been in forest fires more than once.

Muncie's cabin was a structure of logs and clapboards, standing in a little clearing, with the great pines towering all around. Monty saw the child, little Del, playing in the yard with a dog. He called. The child heard and, being frightened, ran into the cabin. The dog came barking toward Monty. He was a big, savage animal, a trained watchdog. But he recognized Monty.

Hurrying forward, Monty went to the open door and called Mrs. Muncie. There was no response. He called again. And while he stood there waiting, listening, above the roar of the wind he heard a low, dull, thundering sound, like a waterfall in a flooded river. It sent the blood rushing back to his heart, leaving him cold. He had not a single instant to lose.

"Mrs. Muncie," he called louder. "Come out! Bring the child! It's Monty Price. There's a forest fire! Hurry!"

He stepped into the cabin. There was no one in the big room—or the kitchen. He grew hurried now. The child was hiding. Finally, he found her in the clothespress, and he pulled her out. She was frightened. She did not recognize him.

"Del, is your mother home?" he asked.

The child shook her head.

With that Monty picked her up, along with a heavy shawl he saw, and, hurrying out, he ran down to the corral. Muncie's horses were badly frightened now. Monty sat little Del down, threw the shawl into a watering trough, and then he let down the bars of the gate.

The horses pounded out in a cloud of dust. Monty's horse was frightened, too, and almost broke away. There was now a growing roar on the wind. It seemed right upon him. Yet he could not see any fire or smoke. The dog came to him, whining and sniffing.

With swift hands, Monty soaked the shawl thoroughly in the water, and then wrapping it round little Del and holding her tight, he mounted. The horse plunged and broke and plunged again—then leaped out straight and fast down the road. And Monty's ears seemed pierced and filled by a terrible, thundering roar.

He had to race with fire. He had to beat the wind of flame to the open parks. Ten miles of dry forest, like powder! Though he had never seen it, he knew fire backed by heavy wind could rage through dry pine faster than a horse could run.

Yet something in Monty Price welcomed this race. He goaded the horse. Then he looked back.

Through the aisles of the forest, he saw a strange, streaky, murky some-thing, moving, alive, shifting up and down, never an instant the same. It must have been the wind, the heat before the fire. He seemed to see through it, but there was nothing beyond, only opaque, dim, mustering clouds.

Ahead of him, down the road, low under the spreading trees, floated swiftly some kind of a medium, like a transparent veil. It was neither smoke nor air. It carried pinpoints of light, sparks, that resembled atoms of dust floating in sunlight. It was a wave of heat propelled before the storm of fire. Monty did not feel pain, but he seemed to be drying up, parching. All was so strange and unreal—the swift flight between the pines, now growing ghostly in the dimming light—the sense of rushing, overpowering force—and yet absolute silence. But that light burden against his breast—the child—was not unreal.

He must have been insane, he thought, not to be overcome in spirit. But he was not. He felt loss of something, some kind of sensation he ought to have had. But he rode that race keener and better than any race he had ever before ridden. He had but to keep his saddle—to dodge the snags of the trees—to guide the maddened horse. No horse ever in the world had run so magnificent a race.

He was outracing wind and fire. But he was running in terror. For miles he held that long, swift, tremendous stride without a break. He was running to his death whether he distanced the fire or not. For nothing could stop him now except a bursting heart. Already he was blind, Monty thought. And then, it appeared to Monty, although his steed kept fleeing on faster and faster, that the wind of flame was gaining. The air was too thick to breathe. It seemed ponderous—not from above, but from behind. It had irresistible weight. It pushed Monty and his horse onward in their flight—straws on the crest of a cyclone.

Ahead there was light through the forest. He made out a white, open space of grass. A park! And the horse, like a demon, hurtled onward, with his smoothness of action gone, beginning to break.

A wave of wind, blasting in its heat, like a blanket of fire, rolled over Monty. He saw the lashing tongues of flame above him in the pines. The storm had caught him. It forged ahead. He was riding under a canopy of fire. Burning pine cones, like torches, dropped all around him, upon him.

A terrible blank sense of weight, of agony, of suffocation—of the air turning to fire! He was drooping, withering, when he flashed from the pines into an open park. The horse broke and plunged and went down, reeking, white, in convulsions, killed on his feet. There was fire in his mane. Monty fell with him and lay in the grass, the child in his arms.

Fire in the grass—fire at his legs roused him. He got up. The park was burning over. It was enveloped in a pall of smoke. But he could see. Drawing back a fold of the wet shawl, he looked at the child. She appeared unharmed. Then he set off running away from the edge of the forest. It was a big park, miles wide. Near the middle there was bare ground. He recognized the place, got his bearings, and made for the point where a deep ravine headed out of the park.

Beyond the bare circle there was more fire, burning sage and grass. His feet were blistered through his boots, and then it seemed he walked on red-hot coals. His clothes caught fire, and he beat it out with bare hands.

Then he stumbled into the rocky ravine. Smoke and blaze above him— the rocks hot—the air suffocating—it was all unendurable. But he kept on. He knew that his strength failed as the conditions bettered. He plunged down, always saving the child when he fell. His sight grew red. Then it grew dark. All was black, or else night had come. He was losing all pain, all sense when he stumbled into water. That saved him. He stayed there. A long time passed till it was light again. His eyes had a thick film over them. Sometimes he could not see at all.

But when he could, he kept on walking, on and on. He knew when he got out of the ravine. He knew where he ought to be. But the smoky gloom obscured everything. He traveled the way he thought he ought to go, and went on and on, endlessly. He did not suffer anymore. The weight of the child bore him down. He rested, went on, rested again, went on again till all sense, except a dim sight, failed him. Through that, as in a dream, he saw moving figures, men looming up in the gray fog, hurrying to him.

Far south of the Tonto Forest Ranges, under the purple shadows of the Peloncillos, there lived a big-hearted rancher with whom Monty Price found a home. He did little odd jobs about the ranch that by courtesy might have been called work. He would never ride a horse again. Monty's legs were warped, his feet hobbled. He did not have free use of his hands. And seldom or never in the presence of anyone did he remove his sombrero. For there was not a hair on his head. His face was dark, almost black, with

terrible scars. A burned-out, hobble-footed wreck of a cowboy! But strangely, there were those at the ranch who learned to love him. They knew his story.

The Breakwater on Elk Creek

———— • ————

G. E. Wallace

*"Really," he added, "you didn't hire
me to do a day's work. You hired
me to do a job."*

While Mr. Gordon, senior partner of the firm of Gordon and
Sterrett, wholesale merchants, in the city of Dutton, was scowling at
a list of names, and thinking of the qualifications of this one and that
one listed there, it was raining up at Summitt.

"Well?" Mr. Sterrett, the junior partner, questioned when the
silence had grown oppressive.

"I don't think," Mr. Gordon finally said, "that one of these young
fellows," he nodded at the names on the list, "is qualified for the
position. I really don't!"

And then he went on to give his reasons. And after that the two
partners were back to where they had been a week before. There was

a position open, not an especially important one, but one that would lead to an important promotion later. And the young fellow who was to be hired to fill that position must have certain qualifications—and one, at least, was rather uncommon. They had been racking their brains to find a young man for that position.

"Well," Mr. Sterrett said with a deep sigh, "we can let the matter drop, for the time being. Maybe later we shall find the young fellow we want."

"Maybe," Mr. Gordon said, but he said it doubtfully. There was one qualification the young fellow *must* have!

And then he looked outside, and saw the raindrops on the window, and said, "That reminds me!"

And the rain did remind him that up at Summitt, which was a hamlet in the hills, he had a summer home, and Elk Creek ran through his land, and something had to be done about Elk Creek.

When in flood, Elk Creek roared down out of a steep gully, gathering force as it went, and then swept in a half circle across a flat, a level flat that was really a lawn, set out with shrubs and bedecked with trees. Mr. Gordon was proud of that flat. His summer home was on it.

Outside, the rain was pattering against the windowpane. And in Summitt, if he could read weather signs, there was even more rain. Mr. Gordon wondered how that creek was behaving. He was worried, for during the last few months it had been exceptionally high and had gone on a rampage, and was threatening to cut a new channel across that flat.

So Mr. Gordon frowned at the raindrops and thought, *That reminds me! When I get up to Summitt this weekend, I must hunt up someone and hire him to fix that creek!* For it would not do to allow it to wash the land away.

And thus it is that George Jennings comes into the story.

Fate, most folks thought, had played a rather scurvy trick on George Jennings. He was a fine fellow, 18, a high school graduate—and there you were. There was nothing more to say. He was honest, industrious, a smart young fellow, and if he had been born in a different community, he might have made something of himself. For instance, he could have gone on to school or entered some big industrial plant. But in Summitt there were no schools higher than the little local high school. And in Summitt there were no industries. In Summitt there was nothing, save woods and hills and pure air and pure water. Opportunity knocks, the proverb has it, at everybody's door. Well, maybe—! But what opportunity was there in Summitt? Except, of course, to remain and plow the rocky fields of the small farms and do the manual tasks that sometimes came your way.

No one in Summitt ever had a chance. There was this one and that one, as proof. They were just where they had been five years before. They had had no chance to advance.

And so it would be with George. Everyone knew that. He was smart; he was likable; but he was in Summitt. "He be a nice boy," said old Mr. Taber, who had had occasion to hire him. "He be obliging, and always does a little more than you expect."

Now George was out plowing one of the stoniest fields in the whole township on the Friday that Mr. Gordon, slipping away from the city and his business cares, drove over to see him.

George let his horses stand in the furrow while he walked down to the edge of the field and to the road where Mr. Gordon's car stood.

And George listened to what Mr. Gordon had to say.

"You understand?" Mr. Gordon asked, after he had explained what he wanted.

George nodded.

"I want you to plow or scrape the old channel deeper—it's filled up with gravel—and then I want you to build a breakwater where the creek's trying to cut a new channel."

And then Mr. Gordon was gone.

One good day's work, and one good day's pay—four dollars! If that were opportunity, opportunity was well disguised. One day's work—digging out a creek!

Still, George was thankful. Money did not grow on bushes—not in Summitt. He could use the four dollars, all right. And he proved he was glad to get the job by arriving at Mr. Gordon's place bright and early the next day.

He plowed out the creek bed. He used a scoop and drew the gravel over to where it would do the most good in protecting the bank that was being threatened. It took skill to guide the horses and to keep the bay steady. He was just a colt and wanted to work himself into a lather.

Mr. Gordon came down about noon and watched him for a while.

"Is it hard work?" he asked.

"No, not very," George said. It wasn't. It was easier than he had expected.

And that afternoon he began building the breakwater. He shaped stakes and drove them down into the creek bed, he nailed planks to those stakes, and then he tied the whole breakwater to other stakes up on the bank.

"It's a pretty good job!" Mr. Gordon said. "I think it will hold."

George did not answer, although he thought so, too. He suddenly thought of something, a better idea than he had had, although it meant more work. What if he had cut into the bank and sunk wooden wings to the breakwater so that if the stream did begin to eat behind it, the creek would be foiled?

"And here's your pay," Mr. Gordon said.

And that ought to have taken George Jennings completely out of the story. He had been hired to do a good day's work. He had done it, and he was tired. And he had his pay for his work.

But he drove home through the dusk, stabled the team, and sat by the kitchen window looking out across the hills. He couldn't put the breakwater out of his mind.

If—well—if that wooden breakwater were protected by a living breakwater set in front of it, it would be doubly secure!

The trouble with breakwaters, he thought, *is water gets in behind them.*

Still, he had built his with wings, sloping back and into the bank, and that ought to hold. He had done all he had been paid to do. Why worry?

But if water did get behind breakwaters, they were gone. In fact, they could be worse than nothing at all and just hold the creek against the bank from which they were supposed to keep it.

Jim Wilson, George thought, *has fought a creek all his life.*

Which was true. Jim Wilson, an old bachelor, had a house on the edge of a creek, and the creek had stubbornly tried to eat away the land on which Jim Wilson's house stood. It had failed. Mr. Wilson had been as stubborn as the creek. He could have moved his house, but he had made up his mind he wouldn't, and he hadn't. Year after year he had fought that creek, and licked it.

I guess I'll go over and see Mr. Wilson, George thought.

He tramped a good three miles that evening, and Mr. Wilson talked with eloquence about a subject in which he was learned. He compared the value of elms and willows when it came to holding banks, and he showed George just how a patch of willows "that I put in six years ago" had held the bank of the creek. "Those willows are sort of pushing the creek over where it belongs," Jim Wilson said with glee. He knew creeks.

"Do you mind," George asked, "if I cut a few of the willow shoots?"

"Cut all you want!" Mr. Wilson was generous.

The stars came out and twinkled. George kept on cutting. A thin sliver of a moon drifted over the treetops, seemingly so close it was going to snag. George went on cutting.

"You just stick those willow shoots in the ground, and they will root and grow," Mr. Wilson said, coming to the door of his house about 9:30. George was through cutting by then and turned toward his home, loaded down with the slender willow shoots he had cut.

Early Monday morning, George went back to the breakwater he had built and was busy planting the willow shoots when Mr. Gordon walked out of his house. He came down and over to where George was working, and stood there frowning.

"I just thought I'd put in a few willows," George said.

He explained all about willows, and how they rooted, and how their roots held the land, and how their trunks caught silt and sediment and built up the land.

"If they are given a chance to grow," he said, "they'll hold the bank and protect the breakwater behind them. Of course the water may get back of them when it gets high sometimes, but at least they'll give added protection."

Mr. Gordon nodded. "But—" he said.

And there you were. The contract had called for a day's work, at a day's pay. And George was putting in more time.

"That's all right," George said. "I just thought I'd add a little something extra, to make sure the bank will hold." He smiled. "Really," he added, "you didn't hire me to do a day's work. You hired me to do a job."

Mr. Gordon knew he ought to go back to the city, and yet he stood and stared at George.

"By the way," he finally asked, "what education have you had?"

"I was graduated from high school," George answered.

"You had no special business training, then?"

"None," George admitted, and he sighed wistfully to himself as he said it. He surely would have liked to have business training! In fact, if he could secure it, he'd take up the work now. But there were no schools near Summitt.

Opportunity, you see, was lacking in Summitt. Absolutely.

"Hmm!" Mr. Gordon said.

He watched George, and continued watching him until George had put in the last of the willow shoots that in time would become a living breakwater.

"There," George said with satisfaction, "that's done!"

And then he tramped home, while Mr. Gordon went on down to the city.

In Summitt there were jumbled hills, and rocks, and small farms, and also Elk Creek.

Of course, there were fine fellows there, too, fellows like George Jennings, presentable young fellows, but what chance would they ever have? Opportunity just did not exist in Summitt, where Elk Creek flowed, where Elk Creek went on rampages in high water.

"I say," Mr. Gordon said to Mr. Sterrett when he had arrived in the city, "you remember last Friday we were talking about that job in the shipping department, the one that will lead in time to superintendent of shipping?"

"Yes," Mr. Sterrett said and sighed audibly.

"Well," Mr. Gordon said, "you don't need to worry about that position any longer!"

"What!" Mr. Sterrett exclaimed. "Did you find someone qualified?"

"I did," Mr. Gordon said. "I found a fellow, a young fellow, who was hired to do a certain thing, and then went on and did a little extra."

"Of his own accord?" Mr. Sterrett asked.

"Of his own accord," Mr. Gordon said.

They sat and smiled happily at each other.

And thus it was that opportunity came to Summitt—and to one who was ready to seize opportunity.

The Rebellion of Pa

J. L. Harbour

Two bosses in the same house are one too many.

A little old man stood before the sink in Maria Denny's kitchen washing dishes. He had a gingham apron tied around his waist. The soft breeze brought a scent of lilac bloom into the kitchen. The old man gave a little sniff. "Them laylocks smell sweeter'n common. Hetty was allus so fond of 'em. I remember the spring her and me set them bushes out. God bless her. She's with Him now in the Garden of Paradise. I often wish that."

"Pa!"

"Yes, M'ria."

"You got them dishes done yet?"

"Just about, but I've got the skillets to wash yet."

237

"Seems to me you're turrible puttery this morning."

"There was more dishes to wash than common, M'ria."

"Well, finish them up as soon as you can and then mop up the kitchen floor. We must start in on regular house cleanin' next week."

A suggestion of a frown came into the old man's ruddy face. His aversion to house cleaning amounted to real loathing. Maria prided herself on her thoroughness, and her husband and their four noisy children had invaded the old man's home. Maria had even suggested that it would be well for her father to transfer his possessions to her in return for being taken care of.

But gentle and yielding as he was, he refused to consider this proposition. "No, no, daughter, I can't do that; not even if you are my only child, and it will all be yours sometime. The old place must be mine as long as I live."

From the day of Maria's arrival in his home, Pa's authority had been set aside. "Silas will take charge of the farm, Pa, and you can just take it kind of easy around the house."

No one ever took it easy under the same roof with Maria Denny. A woman of tireless energy and phenomenal physical strength, she conceded nothing to the possible weakness of others, or to their disinclination to be at work every waking moment. Pa soon found that the conducting of his farm had been less laborious than taking it easy around the house under the direction of Maria. She even proposed that her father should have some knitting work on hand for the long winter evenings.

"Grandfather Dennis knit all his own socks," she said in defense of her plan. Pa made no reply, but when Maria brought him the stocking she had set up for him, he took the balls of coarse gray yarn and the shining knitting needles and calmly lifted a lid of the red-hot stove and dropped them onto the glowing coals. When Maria turned like fury upon him, he stood erect and said in a terrible voice: "Silence, woman, this house is still mine. Speak, and you go out of it to return no more while I live."

Maria was less domineering for several days after that, and then she lapsed

into her old petty tyranny. One day a telegram came, telling Silas of the death of his father, and he and Maria departed to attend the funeral. Silas was an only child, and when he came home, he brought his mother with him. She had felt that it would be better for her to remain in her own home, as she was but 65 and in excellent health. But Silas protested that it would be better for her to make her home with him. It would be cheaper, for her farm could be rented and she could save up the money and thus increase the amount Silas would receive at her death.

Lucinda Denny had her regular duties assigned her. "And when you ain't got anything else to do, Mother, you can sail in on the carpet I've set up in the loom," said Maria. "Some of the neighbors want carpets woven and will pay, so you can always have some weaving on hand for pickup work."

Pa's sympathy went out to Lucinda Denny the moment he knew she was to be an inmate of her son's house. Before a week had passed, Lucinda had come to the conclusion that it was a burning shame the way Pa had to work for his daughter. Naturally enough, the old couple began to give voice to their sympathy for each other. Pa sought to lighten Lucinda's burdens, and sometimes when Maria was out of the way, he would help her at the loom and they would talk over their grievances. Thus a year passed, and Maria grew more tyrannical than ever.

Lucinda bore her unhappy lot in silence. Pa was her only confidant, and to him she sometimes said, "Seems as if I can't stand it another day. I didn't have to work half so hard in my own home as I do here. There's no place for old folks like a home of their own. They never should try to mix in with their children."

"No, their children shouldn't try to mix in with them," replied Pa.

One day Silas and Maria announced their intention of taking their children and driving a few miles distant to spend a few days with a cousin of Maria's.

"I reckon, Mother, that you and Pa could do for yourselves a few days, couldn't you?"

"I should think likely," said Pa before Lucinda could reply. "Of course, we're poor, weak critters who can't do much but crawl to our woodpile and carpet loom, but I reckon we might skeer up strength enough to skirmish around and git a bite to eat, feeble and worthless though we be."

Almost numberless were the commands given to Lucinda and Pa by Maria and Silas on the morning of their departure. The moment the wagon containing Silas and Maria started, a humorous twinkle came into the face of Pa, and he shook his fist after the retreating family and said, "Scat!" Then he turned to Lucinda and said, "When the cat's away, the mice will play. Not a single thing they told me to do am I going to do while they are away. Never felt so young and giddy in my life." He held out the skirt of his shabby old coat between his thumb and finger and began to dance a hornpipe.

"Why, Pa Allen," exclaimed Lucinda, with the first smile her face had known for months, "how you do act!"

"I act as I feel. Come, let's skip around a little just to prove to ourselves that we've got a little life left in us yet."

He caught her by the hands and pulled her to her feet. They clasped hands and whirled around like a pair of children. They gasped for breath, then loosened their grasp, and Lucinda dropped into a chair with her hands pressed to her sides, but she laughed gleefully.

"Now, Lucinda, I'll tell you what I'll do. I'll run down one of the spring pullets, and we'll fry it for dinner. Maria is too close ever to fry a pullet she can sell for 25 cents a pound. But we'll fry one every day she's gone. I guess they're my pullets as much as they are hers. And we'll take our pick and choice of anything we find in the preserve closet. I guess it's made from my fruit. Let's fix up the best dinner ever cooked in the house since Maria came here to live. Whoopla! When the cat's away, the mice will play."

They were like a pair of children freed from irksome restraint. The summer sunshine had flooded the room. Lucinda had gathered a little bouquet of pink and white asters and had put them in a little vase in the corner of the table.

"Robert and I allus had a few flowers on our table," she said.

"So did me and Hetty. It looks like old times to see that cheery little bunch of posies on the table. This is great, Lucinda; I feel as if I was about 20 years old. I reckon if Maria and Silas could see us now they'd cause to worry about us not bein' able to git a bite to eat. Another cup of tea, please. Ain't tasted such good tea in a coon's age. Maria thinks tea should be boiled about a half an hour or some of the strength will be lost. Turrible savin', Maria is. She'd faint if she saw this table with two kinds of preserves and plum sauce and three kinds of jelly, and fried pullet, and two kinds of pie, Lucindy. Never et anything to beat this apple pie, and these buttermilk biscuits are more like the biscuits Hetty used to make than any biscuits I ever et. Yum, yum." He smacked his lips greedily, and his merriment increased.

Suddenly, he jumped to his feet and said, "Oh, say!"

"Why, what is it, Pa Allen?"

"This, Lucindy. Why can't we keep this up right along? This house is mine, mine! I spent the best years of my life to earn it. It is wrong that you should have been made to give up your own home. Lucindy, you have lived for more than a year in this house with me. You wouldn't be afraid to trust your happiness into my keeping, would you, Lucindy?"

"No, I wouldn't."

"Nor would I be afraid to trust my happiness to you after what I've seen of your kind and gentle ways. Lucindy, we're not such old people after all. We may have years of life before us, and we have the right to make them happy, peaceful years. They never can be under the rule of our children, who have no right to rule over us. Marry me, Lucindy, marry me this very day."

"I—I—why, it don't seem as if I could, Pa Allen."

"Yes, you can. You got to. My lands, maybe you'd better do it to save our reputations. If it gets out that we're livin' here alone three or four days, some idle gossip will take hold and talk about it. Come, Lucindy, let's give ourselves the right to live alone here the rest of our lives. Thanks be, I've held on to my place and my bank account. And I'm ready to share 'em with you."

An hour later, Lucinda came out to where Pa was waiting for her in the buggy. She wore a neat brown silk gown and a becoming little bonnet with a wreath of white on it.

"You look as purty as a brand-new hearse," said Pa gallantly. "Say, Lucindy, you've dropped 15 years of your age behind you since this morning."

"Well, you're a regular boy again."

"It's as much fun as elopements. Kinder wish I'd histed a ladder to your winder and tuck you that way. But there ain't no one to pursue us like there is in novels."

"There would be if Silas and Maria knew of it."

"Well, I must guess. Won't their eyes bulge when they get back? But we've got the law on our side—thanks be."

The bridal couple were standing at the gate when Silas and his family returned. The moment the wagon came to a standstill, Pa said without a tremor in his voice:

"You needn't get out, any of you. You'll find everything you brought here in your own house down the road. They ought never to have been brought here in the first place. This house and all that's in it is mine—mine and Lucindy's, and—silence, Maria! We have no reproaches to offer; we have no hard feelin's even. We're too happy for that. We're just as happy as a bride and bridegroom should be.

"Yes, we're bride and bridegroom. It mixes up the relationship dreadful, and Lucindy and I have nearly got nervous prostration tryin' to figure out just what relationship you and your children bear to us. Mebbe you can figure it out as you drive along to your home. Come along, Lucindy. Seems to me I smell the biscuits burning that you put in the oven. We'd better hurry on home now, for it looks real showery."

Autumn to Winter

God's Rooster

Author Unknown

Johnny didn't believe in going to church, but a deal was still a deal.

One morning last spring a young man of 30 stood in his barnyard and looked at the threatening skies. It was the latest season Ontario had ever known, and now that the land was finally ready for seeding, the heavens refused to dry up.

"If I only had some help, I might get the back 20 seeded before the rain breaks again," he complained to himself. "But there's not a man to be had anywhere. . . . Oh, well, I might start on it anyhow."

When he came out of the stable with a team of horses, a car was turning in the lane. "That new preacher they got down at Stumptown," he mumbled. "He ought to know better than to bother farmers at a time like this! I don't go to church anyhow."

The reverend gentleman got out of his car. He was a young man himself. "You're Johnny Bond," he said offering his hand. "Glad to know you. I'm the new preacher. Sparks is my name."

"Glad to know you, Reverend."

"But you are very busy right now trying to get some seed in before it rains again, and you'd be glad if I'd get on my way," the preacher said and smiled. "Look here, do you need some help? I need some exercise. Have you another team needing the same thing?"

"You bet I have," Johnny said and headed for the stable.

The preacher caught him by the arm. "There's a catch in it. My church needs pew-warmers. If I work for you this morning, I want you to come to church next Sunday."

Johnny thought the matter over. "Never did work overtime at going to church," he said, "and I never aimed to, but then I never aimed to see a preacher running a planter either. Okay, it's a deal."

At noon when they came up to the house from the fields, Johnny was puzzled. "What in the world could make a fellow decide to wear his collar backwards?" he asked.

"Why not?" The preacher cracked an egg into the frying pan.

"That always seemed to me to be a job for a guy with white hands and an artificial smile," Johnny told him frankly. "I never did bank on religion much anyhow."

"Don't believe in it?"

"I believe God helps them that help themselves, and as far as the rest is concerned, it's just a bunch of fairy tales to keep old women calm."

The preacher went on slicing potatoes into the frying pan. "What makes you think like that, Johnny?"

"Never had reason to think anything else. You pray over your vittles before you eat, but does it make them taste any better? And some folks, like my friend Holtom across the road, have been to church since God made little apples, and does it make him any better? Right now he's entering a suit against me because my line fence runs five feet over on his farm, and I've cut down some of his trees. Look, Sparks, you seem a sensible chap. You really don't believe all that church stuff, do you?"

"Yes, I do, Johnny. If you would give yourself a chance to prove this thing, you'd understand why. You think a preacher's a sort of social figurehead, an accessory to go well with a wedding or a funeral, don't you, Johnny?"

"It's just like when you go to a fortune teller," Johnny said. "She tells you anything you want to know about the future, but you know very well that if she could foretell the future she wouldn't be living in a tent and dressed in rags. You can bless our seed grain, but if you really believed it was going to make it grow any better, you would probably do a little farming yourself to help out with that missionary work. You take—"

The Reverend Sparks suddenly sang out, "I've got it, Johnny!" He went to the door. "Sorry I have to go now, but I've got to get on this idea you've given me."

"What idea?"

"Come to church Sunday morning and you'll see."

Johnny Bond was at church the next Sunday, and so were a great many others who hadn't seen the inside of a church since the last chicken supper. There was a buzz of small talk in the pews.

"At the suggestion of one of our friends," announced the preacher, "this church is going into the farming business. Today no collection will be taken. The collection plates have been piled with dollar bills. Each of you is invited to take five dollars. This money is to invest for the church in any way you see fit.

"The last Sunday of October you will be asked to put back onto the plate the earnings of your investment. We are leaving the accounting to you. No one is going to ask how much you bring back in October, or whether or not you have kept your accounts straight.

"Some of you may think me very foolish and unbusinesslike, but I see no better way to propagate the faith than to put it to an actual everyday test. There is not a doubt in my mind but that our faith will be amply rewarded."

After the service, Johnny went up to the preacher and drew him aside. "Where did you get that money?"

"It was my own."

"I think you are crazy as a loon."

"You don't know faith."

"I know Stumptown. I'd like to bet you you never see half of that money again."

"Are you investing too?"

"Well, I didn't have five dollars worth of faith, but I did take three."

"Fine. This was your idea, you know. I was disappointed to see some of our people refuse to take the money."

"I noticed my neighbor Holtom was one of those who wouldn't bite," said Johnny. "Now listen, Reverend, I know what you stand to lose, but I'm going to be strictly honest about this, and if I don't earn a cent on the investment I'm not going to take something out of my pocket just to make it look nice. And if I go in the hole I'm going to tell you about it. You need to come down to earth, and I'll be hanged if I don't think this fool idea might be the very thing to make you do it."

That night Johnny dug out the farm magazine and began looking over the advertisements. "Guess I'll get the Lord a setting of eggs with that money," he said. "But I can't have just ordinary stuff, or I'd get it mixed up with what's in the barnyard already." And before he went to bed Johnny had written to one of Canada's leading poultry farms for a setting of eggs from their very best prizewinning stock.

A week later the eggs came, and Johnny promptly put them under the best clucker he had. Three weeks later, out of the setting of 15 eggs, came three bedraggled-looking chicks.

Aha! Johnny thought. *I'd like to know what the preacher is going to say 'bout this.*

Before the day was over, two of the three chicks had given up the ghost. And the old hen, apparently disgusted, refused to acknowledge the other as her own.

"Well, Skeezix," said Johnny, holding the remaining little fluff ball up to the lamplight, "you're going to have to lay an awful lot of eggs between now and the last day of October if you're to pay the Lord back that three dollars."

But a week or so later it became evident that Skeezix would never lay any eggs. Skeezix had decided to become a rooster.

Skeezix went to bed every night for the next month with Johnny. Johnny put him in a little box on the chair at the head of the bed, and he left the lamp burning all night to keep him warm. And Johnny began his accounting with the following entry for the debit side:

Extra coal oil, 10 cents

When Skeezix was a month old he had grown too large for the box. Johnny tried leaving him out with the other chickens during the night, but Skeezix didn't fit in. As soon as the screen door was opened Skeezix made a dash for the house, and when Johnny would chase after him he would invariably flutter upstairs. When Skeezix was two months old, he decided to learn how to fly. This he did so well that the chicken fence was no more than a low hurdle to him, and Johnny would no sooner reach the fields in the morning than he would find Skeezix trotting along behind him picking up stray crickets.

"If he ain't the beat of any bird I ever saw!" said Johnny with a note of affection.

But there came a day when Johnny wasn't so affectionate. Skeezix was strutting around the back porch and belligerently pecking at a saucer of milk assigned for the cat. Suddenly Skeezix rose straight into the air like a helicopter and descended into the half can of cream.

"I ought to drown you in it!" Johnny exploded. "I'll have to throw that cream to the pigs now, and by hang, I'm charging the damages to your account."

Two days later, the same cat and the same rooster had an argument outside the parlor window, and in the ensuing fracas the rooster flew straight through a pane of fancy red and blue glass. And a week later when Johnny backed the car out, Skeezix got one leg under a wheel.

"If you were my own I'd wring your neck," Johnny said, holding the dangling leg. "But seeing as how you're the Lord's, I suppose this calls for special attention." Johnny put the bird in the car with him and drove into town. At the preacher's he asked for some advice.

"Reverend," he said, "this is the last of the three bucks I invested for the church. His leg's busted. To date he's cost me a broken window, half a can of cream, the coal oil it took to keep him warm when he was a chick, besides what it took to keep him in bed and board. Now are you willing for me to throw him in the frying pan, or do you want me to go on with this fool idea?"

The preacher smiled. "Don't wring his neck yet. Patch up his leg and go on with the game."

A few minutes later Johnny drove into the veterinarian's yard. The doctor laughed, and Johnny got a little peeved.

"Aw, patch this leg like I told you! If you must know, this is the Lord's rooster—the only one I got left, so make it good!"

"Oh," said the vet. "That's different. You know I got dragged in on that deal, too."

"What are you raising?"

"Bought me a pair of rabbits. They had two litters already, and I'll be hanged if the price didn't go up three cents a pound last week. I wish I'd bought them on my own."

When Skeezix returned to the barnyard with the splint on his leg, Johnny built a special little pen for him on top of the duck house, and to that refuge Skeezix returned whenever danger threatened. But this elevated abode gave

Skeezix a landing field, which made it easy for him to reach the windowsill of his master's bedroom. Each morning the first glint of dawn would find Skeezix perched there and crowing like an alarm clock.

But one morning Skeezix wasn't there. Johnny went to the little pen atop the duck house. "Wind blew the door shut," he muttered. "Poor little beggar couldn't get in last night. Wonder where he went." And although there was no end of important jobs, Johnny spent two hours looking for Skeezix.

Johnny was ashamed of himself for letting it worry him so much. "Nothing but a bit of a rooster with a broken leg," he kept telling himself, but still he kept on searching. Finally he heard the peculiar crow that could belong only to Skeezix coming from the Holtom barnyard.

"That fool bird would pick a place like that for his vacation!" Johnny muttered between his teeth. "I've got a good notion to let him stay there." But in a few minutes he was shuffling up the Holtom lane, dredging for words to say when he should meet Holtom.

But it wasn't Holtom he saw at first. It was a girl. And when he had taken a second look at her, Johnny suddenly forgot all about the rooster and every-thing else. The girl was very pretty.

"Good morning," Johnny gulped.

"Good morning," she smiled. "Were you looking for my uncle, Mr. Holtom?"

"Oh, no," said Johnny. "I'm looking for a Leghorn rooster with one leg in a splint. Seen him?"

She laughed again. "I guess we did see him. We were eating breakfast when he came strutting into the kitchen as important as the king's nephew. Perched on the back of a chair and scolded us until we fed him. My, but he's cute."

Johnny was thinking, *And so are you*, but he said instead, "And may I ask who you are and why you are up here in this neck of the woods?"

"Oh, I'm just a city slicker doing a little farming for my uncle. Name's Ellen. By the way, who could you be?"

Johnny told her, and he took a long time doing it.

But the excursion to the Holtom farm was not to be entirely pleasant. On the way down the lane he met Holtom himself. The two men glared at each other.

"Decided to pay me that 50 bucks for them trees, or do I sue you?" Holtom demanded.

"Go ahead and sue!" Johnny told him.

The fact that Ellen's uncle and he were at war gave an unpleasant tinge to a morning that would otherwise have been very pleasant, and the next day he dropped in to see a lawyer.

"If the line fence is over on his side, Holtom is in the right, and you'll have to pay for the trees you cut down. There's nothing I can do to help you," the lawyer told him bluntly.

But that night Johnny shut Skeezix out of his pen on purpose. The next morning he again visited the Holtom farm. By the end of the week Johnny was getting along quite well without the rooster's help. It was scarcely a month later when Johnny asked the inevitable question.

"Oh, Johnny," she answered, "that just couldn't be. Not yet anyhow."

"You mean your uncle?"

"He's furious enough, as it is. It would be terrible if he found out that we were talking of marriage."

"Ah, I'll pay him the 50 bucks and shut the old boy up."

"It would take a great deal more than that, I'm afraid." She gave him a kiss. "Just be patient."

Johnny was peeved when he went to bed that night. Ellen wasn't the kind of girl you felt like waiting for. You wanted her now.

He finally rolled off into sleep. But then he was wide awake, and there Skeezix was at the bedroom window. And it wasn't morning. It was just past midnight. Johnny fumbled across to the window, and as he heaved it up he became aware of a commotion in the duck pen. A minute later, still in his nightshirt and armed with shotgun and flashlight, Johnny crept up to the door of the pen and threw it open. The beam of light revealed the startled faces of two boys whom Johnny at once recognized as two of Stumptown's less civilized characters.

"What's in the bag?" Johnny demanded, grabbing one of the boys by the collar. No answer.

"Two big ducks for two boys? Where's the rest of your gang?" No answer. "I asked you where the rest of your gang was!"

"They're over at Holtom's trying to get a turkey."

Johnny took them into the house and grabbed the phone. "Holtom!" he bellowed. "Grab your gun and get out to the turkey shed. You have visitors!"

Half an hour later Johnny was over at the Holtom farm, and his two captives were still with him. "Did you get them?" Johnny asked.

"Too fast for me. But they didn't get none of my turkeys. I counted 'em." Holtom looked at the boys. "Going to call the cops or take them in?"

That wasn't Johnny's idea at all. "What these guys need is to fork a few thousand sheaves." He turned to the boys. "If you rascals want to work on the farm till harvest is over, we'll keep quiet. Otherwise—"

The boys suddenly became very enthusiastic about farm life.

"Okay," said Johnny. "Use us right and we'll use you right. Which do you take, Holtom?"

"I've been doing all right without one so far."

"Maybe so, but you're going to lose your niece pretty soon. I'm going to marry her." Johnny figured there would never be a better time to tell him.

Holtom didn't know what to say, so Johnny went back home and took both boys with him. Early next morning Holtom was at his back door.

"Been thinking it over some," he said, "and I figure I better take one of those boys." He kicked at the doorsill awkwardly. "Guess that was a pretty decent thing for you to call me up last night. Saved me some money, and seeing as how we're going to be related soon, I guess there's no use arguing anymore. Could we shake hands?"

Johnny grabbed his hand eagerly. "By the way, I found out you were right about those trees. I'll be paying you that 50 bucks one of these days soon."

"Aw, forget it. You can have that to pay for the hired man you caught me. Or a wedding present."

Sometime in September the Reverend Mr. Sparks once again came out to Johnny's for a bit of exercise, and when they went in to dinner Johnny said, "Won't have to be batching like this for long, you know. Guess we'll be calling you in for the hitching next week."

Then after dinner he took down the calendar and showed the preacher the account. This is the way he had it figured:

Debit

Coal oil	$ .10
Half can cream all shot	3.25
Pane of glass busted	1.29
Veterinary bill	1.00
Feed (estimated)	.32
TOTAL	$ 5.96

Credit

Two ducks saved	$ 3.50
Lawsuit headed off	50.00
One hired man corralled (Priceless)	
Wife located (Even more priceless)	

"It's a good thing you can't put a price tag on those last two items," Johnny said, "but even the way it is it looks like I'll be putting $47.54 on that plate next month."

"But you haven't finished your calculation yet," the preacher insisted. "You still have the rooster. You've got to add on whatever he brings."

"But I'm not selling him. There isn't enough money in Stumptown to buy that bird."

"It's still the Lord's rooster, and if you want him you'll have to pay the plate whatever he would bring."

"Guess that's right. Well, he's probably worth about 30 cents a pound. Okay. I'll weigh him up and put it in the plate, but I'm not parting with him."

As the preacher wheeled his car around and headed down the lane, he found a big car blocking the way.

"Do you own this place?" the stranger asked.

"No. Just a godfather." The preacher called Johnny out.

Sitting atop the gate post, and eyeing the pompous stranger with an air that was just as pompous, was Skeezix. And the pompous man was looking at Skeezix.

"I want to buy that rooster," the man told Johnny. "Brown Leghorns are a hobby of mine. That's very fine bird you have there."

"Yes," Johnny explained. "I sent away for the eggs. He's—"

"Don't tell me!" the man interrupted. "You can't tell me anything about a Brown Leghorn. His leg's a little crooked but it won't hurt him for breeding. I'll give you 15 dollars for him."

"Oh!" Johnny groaned miserably.

"Whether you take it or not, it's still 15 dollars more for the plate," said the preacher merrily.

"Well, I'll make it 20, then," said the big man impatiently. "But he's not worth any more. Here." He took the green stuff out of a fat wallet.

"Oh no," Johnny groaned again. "I really couldn't take that. You see—"

"Look," yelled the big man. "Here's 25. But that's as high as I'll go."

Johnny finally found his tongue. "I can't sell him and don't offer me any more!" he said violently. "He's a pet. Money won't buy him. And please don't waste any more time here. You make me nervous!"

But when Johnny got to the house he was laughing about it.

When the last Sunday in October came around, and while his charming wife sat beside him in the pew and held the plate, Johnny forked out $72.54.

And he smiled as he did it.

Hector and Rudolph

Linda Harrington Steinke

Too often we take for granted the special people in our lives.

"This is such a sad place today, but someday . . . someday this is going to be the happiest place on earth!"

Theresa spoke these comforting words as we stood apart from the mourning crowd, in the shade of a lone pine, at the graveside service of our beloved Rudolph—her great-uncle and my friend.

I could not bring myself to look at the casket poised above the gaping vault just yet. The ground seemed to be a less painful place to look. Yes, a very good place; nothing there to cause a cascade of tears. Ever so slowly my eyes drifted forward until they unintentionally crossed paths with another gravesite. No lush grass covered its hideous outline. Just plain old packed dirt adorned with a few scattered clumps of quackgrass.

Hector . . .

The tears I had determined to hold in check broke away and flowed unbridled down my face. Unashamedly, I let them pour. Only later would I wonder why I had tried to stifle them . . . they were so soothing.

Hector and Rudolph. Death took them both within a year and two months of each other.

Theresa's gentle voice interrupted my reverie. "Just think, Linda, the very next thing Uncle Rudolph will see is his angel's face and Jesus coming for him."

I smiled wistfully at the thought—envisioning the happy moment—and braved a look at her face. It was radiant, imbued with the promise of victory by the One who carries the keys to the grave and death.

Yes, there would indeed be victory over the grave for Rudolph and Hector. Let them rest from their struggles and pain now.

I thought of how fortunate I was to have known them. I first met both men in church:

The day hadn't started out well. My handsome Canadian husband and I had sneaked into the back pew of the church. Our first day there as newlyweds, and we were late! What would people think! I blushed at the thought.

We arrived at the end of song service. As I sat observing my fellow parishioners, I was forced to look time and time again at one fellow. He was sitting two seats ahead of us, singing his heart out in a loud, (and I do mean LOUD—he had his volume set two notches above the rest of us combined!), hillbilly sort of way. He was not keeping up with the pianist either—he was singing too slowly for that! If he noticed that he was off beat, dragging dreadfully and at times discordant, he didn't show it. He didn't seem to mind at all! His eyes were shut; his face was the picture of blissful peace.

I leaned over to Ken and whispered, "Who's that fellow up there singing . . . the one who looks like Burl Ives?"

"Oh, that's Hector," Ken replied with a knowing smile. "He teaches the lesson, too! We'll stay here for his class."

As soon as Hector finished opening prayer for the class study, he jumped right into the lesson with no preliminary introductions. It soon became obvious that Hector could moderate his way through heavy discussion with ease. I really enjoyed the lesson—the people weren't afraid to get into heavy-duty debating! However, I remained silent, mouselike, sizing up the people and their attitudes.

"Well, what does Hosea 14:4 have to say about that? We don't have to guess. The Bible gives us the answer!" Hector had decided to end the rut we had been in for the past few minutes. The text wasn't in the lesson quarterly; he had pulled it from the inner recesses of his memory. His eyes scanned the class, looking for some hapless victim. When they got to Ken and me, they stopped.

No, not us! I thought as I shook my head in a "don't you dare" fashion.

Ken nudged me with his elbow. "You answer!" he whispered with a smile.

"What are you poking me for?" I hissed as loudly as I dared. "You know these people—YOU answer!"

The teacher settled this playful dispute.

"Well, Linda . . . That is your name, isn't it?" Twenty pairs of eyes turned to face me as I cowered in the back pew. At least the people were all smiling!

I noticed, too, the twinkle in Hector's eye. I'd seen one like that before . . . in my brother's eyes, just before he'd tease the living daylights out of me.

Cautiously and with a blush, I answered his question. "Yes, that's my name."

"Well, Linda, we're happy to have you here with us today. So how 'bout YOU answer the question for us. How does Hosea 14:4 answer our question? You do know that text, don't you?" He smiled as a teacher would while patiently putting up with a floundering student . . . or perhaps a cat that has cornered a mouse.

I cleared my throat and smiled back. "Well, Hector . . . That is your name, is it not?" (He and the rest of the class seemed amused with this rather audacious beginning.) "I'm happy to be here, too, but sorry to say I don't know that text. I'll be happy to look it up for you, if you like."

"You go right ahead and do that. We'll wait!" Hector's massive 275 pound, five-foot-six frame started shaking as he tried to contain a laugh.

I scrambled through the clingy pages of the minor prophets for the text that was supposed to be on the tip of my tongue. *Did I just gain an older brother?* I asked myself.

It turned out that I had indeed. This was the beginning of a friendship that was filled with fun and its share of sibling disagreements, which we both took with a grain of salt. The pesty older brother and the snot-nosed kid sister—that about describes Hector's and my friendship.

Over the years, I came to appreciate his knowledge of God's Word. We swapped books and matched wits as he'd throw out to the class statements that begged to be disagreed with, even if it meant playing devil's advocate. Hector refused to spoon-feed us the pablum of the Word. He plowed right into hard-to-answer questions and made us think.

He was a seeker of ever-unfolding truth. His personal studies sometimes took him into uncharted theological territory. In the parking lot after church, we'd take five minutes to share what God had taught us the previous week. He'd try out his new insights—some seemed ingenious, others half-baked and even borderline heretical!

But the one thing I appreciated the most about him was that he never graced the inside of the church with his unusual ideas. He never abused his position of teacher to take unfair advantage of the captive class, forcing his personal offbeat views as the "Gospel truth" on all present. I wish there were more teachers like him.

Whereas Hector was a bachelor and somewhat unrefined in manners, speech, and dress, Rudolph gave the impression of being an elder statesman. Genteel, refined, and over six feet tall, he spoke with quiet dignity.

"You are Ken's wife?" he asked with a soft German accent as he clasped my hand in greeting that first morning after church. "We love Ken. He's such a good man. We love you, too!"

His wife, who stood smiling at his side, added, "I sorry, my English not so goot!" Her smile conveyed what her words could not: It was full of warmth and genuine affection. It meant so much to have such unconditional acceptance showered on me: a new bride—a freshly transplanted Yankee— thousands of miles away from family and friends. It was the beginning of a friendship that would become more like family as the years progressed.

I loved watching Rudolph and his wife together. It's wonderful to see a marriage like theirs—a team, each for the other and both for the Lord—in youth, but it is especially beautiful in old age. They shared a great love of fishing; and in the process of trying to outfish each other, they ended up with trophies galore, his and hers. Because they tried to outlove each other, too, it was easy to understand why it was so hard on him when she passed away.

"At least she didn't suffer. It was quick! That's the way I hope to go," he comforted himself and me a few weeks after her funeral.

He grieved, though you wouldn't know by his words, for he never complained. But if you looked closely at his eyes, you could see it: pain, haunting pain. Then, as if he weren't in enough pain, arthritis began its savage assault on his hands and knees.

"Mr. Zotzman! Good morning! How are you today?" I chirped as I shook his huge hand before church one morning.

"Fine as ever and so happy to see you today," he gently replied with quiet cheerfulness. But his grip did not have its usual strength.

The arthritis must be flaring up again, I thought. Knowing his tendency to put it off as long as possible, I ventured a daughterly question out of concern: "Did you take your medicine today?"

"No," he said shaking his head slowly. "It's not helping . . . but . . . why should I complain when I have so much to be thankful for."

He did not say this to play the saint. He truly was a heroic person. His early years of suffering had taught him such gallantry.

Over the years, he had shared some of his stories with me: stories of his family's deportation to Siberia during World War I, when he was 10, and of the long, hard journey back to Poland after the war, when he was 14. The family had walked much of the way with no shelter from the elements. With no food available, they were forced, at one point, to boil tree bark and eat it to curb their gnawing hunger pains. As a result, Rudolph was left blind for five days.

"It was awful." He spoke with a guarded hush as he relived the horror of it. "I thought I would be blind forever!"

On the last leg of the journey, they were able to travel by train. Some food was available: brown bread soaked in boiling water.

He continued, "Once, when our train stopped, I got off and waited in line an hour for water for my family. I didn't even get to the front of the water line before the train started moving again. I ran back to our car as fast as I could, but it was no use: The train was moving too fast. I caught the next boxcar, but the people on board wouldn't let me on. They just pushed me off. I guess they figured I was trying to steal a ride.

"I want you to know, if it hadn't been for my dad, I wouldn't be here today. He'd been watching the whole time. When he saw that I'd missed the boxcar, too, he saved my life. My father saved my life!" He was 14 again, reliving the absolute panic of being separated from his family (possibly forever) in a chaotic world of fleeing refugees. But then came the sweet relief: the sight of his father jumping off the train. Rudolph's eyes filled with tears. The thought of that moment, some 70 years before, still left him profoundly moved and grateful for his father's immense demonstration of love and concern for his son's welfare.

His voice broke as he continued, "If Dad hadn't jumped, they [I didn't ask who] would have shot me. Young men traveling alone were shot, no questions asked. We were lucky, though: We caught a ride on a military train, and in three days, we caught up with the rest of the family. God took care of us! So much could have happened that didn't."

He showed me photo albums that chronicled his life. One picture showed a studious-looking man sitting outside on a lawn chair with an open Bible in his sturdy hands. I looked questioningly at Rudolph.

"Yes," he answered thoughtfully, "that's me. I was raised a Baptist, and I have always loved God." It would be this mutual love relationship that would be his solid rock for the series of Job-like crises to fall upon him.

One by one, his cherished freedoms and independence were taken from him. It was fortunate that no one was hurt when he had his car accident; but after that experience, it was decided that he'd have to give up his driver's license and sell his car. His weakening health forced the selling of his home and a move into the local adult care facility. He agreed to all of this, knowing it was the right thing to do, but detesting it just the same. All of his life, he had been an independent and proud man. This loss of independence was almost more than he could bear.

One day, at church, Hector pulled me aside and confided, "Well, I had to go out and buy a boat to take Old Man Zotzman out fishin'. You know how he loves to fish! Well, what are you goin' to do with a guy like that . . . sittin' around feeling so down in the dumps. I guess I'll have to haul him and the boat out to the lake tomorrow morning."

A stranger overhearing this would have thought by the tone in Hector's voice that this was a tremendously great imposition on him. But his gruff talk was all bluff.

"Hector," I said with admiration, "that's one of the nicest things I've ever heard of one friend doing for another."

He grinned. It was a two-way street, though: I found out later that Mr. Zotzman would be supplying all the fishing gear.

Had Hector been able to order the manner of his passing, it would have been while fishing with his friend Rudolph. And that is where his great heart failed him—on that fishing expedition.

Mr. Zotzman never really recovered from the loss of Hector. He found it hard to explain why: "Why Hector, and not me?" he'd ask when I visited him after his friend's heart attack. "Hector was just in his fifties, and me, I'm an old man in my eighties. I've lived a good, full life; Hector still had many years ahead of him. Why?" The whole time he spoke, his gaze was focused on an unoccupied spot some three feet ahead.

For a week or so, each time I'd visit, he'd ask the same question, staring in the same manner. I could give him no answer, and I knew that he wasn't really expecting one from me. He didn't want a sermon or medical facts. He just needed someone to listen as he tried to come to terms with something that was horrible and shocking to his soul.

Eventually, he said, "I don't know why Hector died and I lived—that's in God's hands." Upon his face played a fatigued smile. "I'll just trust God. He knows best, and someday He'll tell me!"

Each time I visited him, during the weeks and months that followed, Rudolph was visibly weaker. When not able to get away to visit, I'd send him encouraging notes.

He would glow with appreciation for each short visit and each card. Once he leaned back, with a faraway look in his eyes and said, "What good does money or power or a fancy house do me now, lying here in this bed? What would I do without my family and friends?" What indeed!

He was not a hard person to visit. Why, even the nurses picked flowers from the hospital flowerbeds to give to him. That alone speaks volumes as to what kind of man he was—loving and kind.

Over a period of weeks, I could tell by different things he said that he had gone from fighting the thought of dying . . . to resigning himself to his death . . . to looking forward to it. When he reached that last point, I knew it wouldn't be long.

On our last visit, he had become so weak that his hushed voice kept cutting out on him and he was unable to lift his head from the pillow. I purposely kept our visit short. Somehow I sensed that this would be our last visit.

After our usual good-bye prayer and kiss, he gazed up at me with sad, sunken eyes and whispered, "Inasmuch as you have done it unto the least of these . . ." He didn't finish the sentence but continued to hold my gaze.

Up till this point, I had been able to keep a stiff upper lip. After all, I was there to comfort and cheer him, not vice versa. But these kindly words caught me off guard. I was overwhelmed and felt so undeserving, even a bit embarrassed at the implication, for those intentions had never crossed my mind: I was there to visit my friend, period! But deeper yet, I was affected by his tender and humble attitude. I was in the presence of a man who deeply loved God, and you could sense the spirit of God in the room.

"Mr. Zotzman!" I cried. "Don't you ever consider yourself 'the least'!" The tears brimmed over. I had to look away to compose myself. My throat ached as it tightened. Never had it felt so tight!

When I again faced him, I took his hand in mine and found that I could barely speak above a whisper. "Mr. Zotzman, don't you know that it is you who have given me courage and strength for the hard times?" I sobbed. "Your life has been a living picture of Jesus to me all these years, but especially now! I'm just so glad that we've gotten to know each other and that you're my friend! I think of you as the Christian father I never had!" There, I'd finally given voice to the feelings I'd carried around all those years.

With a trembling hand, he wiped a tear from his eye. I knew then that the feeling was mutual: I was his "adopted" daughter.

Soon after, Rudolph slipped into a coma. On a Sunday afternoon, he quietly entered his rest.

At his funeral, testimony after testimony spoke of the special friendship he and his Lord enjoyed and of how "he did no man harm—only good all his life." There was not a doubt in anyone's mind that we'd be reunited with him when Jesus comes again.

My two friends: Hector and Rudolph, lying asleep in Jesus in that little country cemetery. To them, their sleep will seem but a moment. To the rest of us who knew and loved them, the thought of their resurrection fills us with joy.

A Day's Pleasure

Hamlin Garland

She was trapped in a hardscrabble life of all work and no joy. Then someone noticed . . .

When Sam Markham came in from shoveling his last wagonload of corn into the crib, he found that his wife, Delia, had put the children to bed and was kneading a batch of dough with the dogged action of a tired and sullen woman.

He slipped his soggy boots off his feet and, having laid a piece of wood on top of the stove, put his heels on it comfortably. His chair squeaked as he leaned back on its hind legs, but he paid no attention; he was used to it, exactly as he was used to his wife's lameness and ceaseless toil.

"That closes up my corn," he said after a silence. "I guess I'll go to town tomorrow to git my horses shod."

"I guess I'll git ready and go along," said his wife in a sorry attempt to be firm and confident of tone.

"What do you want to go to town fer?" he grumbled.

"What does anybody want to go to town fer?" she burst out, facing him. "I ain't been out o' this house fer six months, while you go an' go!"

"Oh, it ain't six months. You went down that day I got the mower."

"When was that? The tenth of July, and you know it."

"Well, mebbe 'twas. I didn't think it was so long ago. I ain't no objection to your goin', only I'm goin' to take a load of wheat."

"Well, just leave off a sack, an' that'll balance me an' the baby," she said spiritedly.

"All right," he replied good-naturedly, seeing she was roused. "Only that wheat ought to be put up tonight if you're goin'. You won't have any time to hold sacks for me in the morning with them young ones to get off to school."

"Well, let's go do it then," she said sullenly resolute.

"I hate to go out agin, but I s'pose we'd better."

He yawned dismally and began pulling his boots on again, stamping his swollen feet into them with grunts of pain. She put on a coat and one of the boys' caps, and they went out to the granary. The night was cold and clear.

"Don't look so much like snow as it did last night," said Sam. "It may turn warm."

Laying out the sacks in the light of the lantern, they sorted out those that were whole. Sam climbed into the bin with a tin pail in his hand, and the work began.

He was a sturdy fellow, and he worked desperately fast; the shining tin pail dived deep into the cold wheat and dragged heavily on the woman's tired hands as it came to the mouth of the sack. She trembled with fatigue, but held on and dragged the sacks away when filled, and brought others, till at last Sam climbed out, puffing and wheezing, to tie them up.

"I guess I'll load 'em in the morning," he said. "You needn't wait fer me. I'll tie 'em up alone."

"Oh, I don't mind," she replied, feeling a little touched by his unexpectedly easy acquiescence to her request. When they went back to the house, the moon had risen.

It had scarcely set when they were wakened by the crowing roosters. The man rolled stiffly out of bed and began rattling at the stove in the dark, cold kitchen.

His wife arose lamer and stiffer than usual and began twisting her thin hair into a knot.

Sam did not stop to wash, but went out to the barn. The woman, however, hastily rinsed her face with the hard limestone water at the sink and put the kettle on. Then she called the children. She knew it was early, and they would need several callings. She pushed breakfast forward, running over in her mind the things she must have: two spools of thread, six yards of cotton flannel, a can of coffee, and mittens for Kitty. These she must have—there were oceans of things she needed.

The children soon came scudding down out of the darkness of the upstairs to dress tumultuously at the kitchen stove. They humped and shivered, holding up their bare feet from the cold floor, like chickens in new-fallen snow. They were irritable, and snarled and snapped and struck like cats and dogs. Mrs. Markham stood it for a while with mere commands to "hush up," but at last her patience gave out, and she charged down on the struggling mob and cuffed them right and left.

They ate their breakfast by lamplight, and when Sam went back to his work around the barnyard, it was scarcely dawn. The children, left alone with their mother, began to tease her to let them go to town also.

"No, sir—nobody goes but the baby. Your father's goin' to take a load of wheat."

She was weak with the worry of it all when she had sent the older children away to school, and the kitchen work was finished. She went into the cold bedroom off the little sitting room and put on her best dress. It had never been a good fit, and now she was getting so thin, it hung in wrinkled folds everywhere about the shoulders and waist. She lay down on the bed a moment to ease the dull pain in her back. She had a moment's distaste for going out at all. The thought of sleep was more alluring. Then the thought of the long, long day, and the sickening sameness of her life, swept over her again, and she rose and prepared the baby for the journey.

It was a little after sunrise when Sam drove out into the road and started for Belleplain. His wife sat perched upon the wheat sacks behind him, holding the baby in her lap, a cotton quilt under her, and a cotton horse blanket over her knees.

Sam was disposed to be good-natured, and he talked back at her occasionally, though she could only understand him when he turned his face toward her. The baby stared at the passing fence posts and wiggled his hands out of his mittens at every opportunity. He was merry at least.

It grew warmer as they went on, and a strong south wind arose. The dust settled upon the woman's shawl and hat. Her hair loosened and blew unkemptly about her face. The road, which led across the high, level prairie, was quite smooth and dry, but still it jolted her, and the pain in her back increased. She had nothing to lean against, and the weight of the child grew greater, till she was forced to place him on the sacks beside her, though she could not loose her hold for a moment.

The town drew in sight—a cluster of small frame houses and stores on the dry prairie beside a railway station. There were no trees yet that could be called shade trees. The pitilessly severe light of the sun flooded everything. A few teams were hitched about, and in the lee of the stores a few men could be seen seated comfortably, their broad hat rims flopping up and down, their faces brown as leather.

Markham put his wife out at one of the grocery stores and drove down toward the elevators to sell his wheat.

The grocer greeted Mrs. Markham in a perfunctorily kind manner and offered her a chair, which she took gratefully. She sat for a quarter of an hour almost without moving, leaning against the back of the high chair. At last the child began to get restless and troublesome, and she spent half an hour helping him amuse himself around the nail kegs.

At length she rose and went out on the walk, carrying the baby. She went into the dry-goods store and took a seat on one of the little revolving stools. A woman was buying some woolen goods for a dress. It was worth 27 cents a yard, the clerk said, but he would knock off two cents if she took 10 yards. It looked warm, and Mrs. Markham wished she could afford it for Mary.

A pretty young girl came in, and laughed and chatted with the clerk, and bought a pair of gloves. She was the daughter of the grocer. Her happiness made the wife and mother sad. When Sam came back, she asked him for some money.

"What you want to do with it?" he asked.

"I want to spend it," she said.

She was not to be trifled with, so he gave her a dollar.

"I need a dollar more."

"Well, I've got to go take up that note at the bank."

"Well, the children's got to have some new underclothes," she said.

He handed her a two-dollar bill and then went out to pay his note.

She bought her cotton flannel, mittens, and thread, and then sat leaning against the counter. It was noon, and she was hungry. She went out to the wagon, got the lunch she had brought, and took it into the grocery to eat it—where she could get a drink of water.

The grocer gave the baby a stick of candy and handed the mother an apple.

"It'll kind o' go down with your doughnuts," he said.

After eating her lunch, she got up and went out. She felt ashamed to sit there any longer. She entered another dry-goods store, but when the clerk came toward her saying, "Anything today, ma'am?" she answered, "No, I guess not," and turned away with foolish face.

She walked up and down the street, desolately homeless. She did not know what to do with herself. She knew no one except the grocer. She grew bitter as she saw a couple of ladies pass, dressed in the latest city fashion. Another woman went by pushing a baby carriage, in which sat a child just about as big as her own. It was bouncing itself up and down on the long slender springs and laughing and shouting. Its clean round face glowed from its pretty fringed hood. She looked down at the dusty clothes and grimy face of her own little one and walked on savagely.

She went into the drugstore where the soda fountain was, but it made her thirsty to sit there, and she went out on the street again. She heard Sam laugh and saw him in a group of men over by the blacksmith shop. He was having a good time and had forgotten her.

Her back ached so intolerably that she concluded to go in and rest once more in the grocer's chair. The baby was growing cross and fretful. She bought five cents' worth of candy to take home to the children and gave the baby a little piece to keep him quiet. She wished Sam would come. It must be getting late. The grocer said it was not much after one. Time seemed terribly long. She felt that she ought to do something while she was in town. She ran over her purchases—yes, that was all she had planned to buy. She fell to figuring on the things she needed. It was terrible. It ran up into 20 or 30 dollars at the least. Sam, as well as she, needed underwear for the cold winter, but they would have to wear the old ones, even if they were thin and ragged. She would not need a dress, she thought bitterly, because she never went anywhere. She rose and went out on the street once more, and wandered up and down, looking at everything in the hope of enjoying something.

A man from Boon Creek backed a load of apples up to the sidewalk, and as he stood waiting for the grocer, he noticed Mrs. Markham and the baby, and gave the baby an apple. This was a pleasure. He had such a hearty way about him. He on his part saw an ordinary farmer's wife with dusty dress, unkempt hair, and tired face. He did not know exactly why she appealed to him, but he tried to cheer her up.

The grocer was familiar with these bedraggled and weary wives. He was accustomed to see them sit for hours in his big wooden chair and nurse tired and fretful children. Their forlorn, aimless, pathetic wandering up and down the street was a daily occurrence and had never possessed any special meaning to him.

In a cottage around the corner from the grocery store, two men and a woman were finishing a dainty luncheon. The woman was dressed in cool, white garments, and she seemed to make the day one of perfect comfort.

The home of the Honorable Mr. Hall was by no means the costliest in town, but his wife made it the most attractive. He was one of the leading lawyers of the county and a man of culture and progressive views. He was entertaining a friend who had lectured the night before in the Congregational church.

They were not in serious discussion. The talk was rather frivolous. Hall had the ability to caricature men with a few gestures and attitudes, and he was giving his eastern friend some descriptions of the old-fashioned western lawyers he had met in his practice. He was very amusing, and his guest laughed heartily for a time.

But suddenly Hall became aware that Otis was not listening. Then he perceived that he was peering out of the window at someone, and that a look of bitter sadness was falling on his face.

Hall stopped. "What do you see, Otis?"

Otis replied, "I see a forlorn, weary woman." Mrs. Hall rose and went to the window. Mrs. Markham was walking by the house, her baby in her arms. Savage anger and weeping were in her eyes and on her lips, and there was hopeless tragedy in her shambling walk and weak back.

In the silence, Otis went on. "I saw the poor, dejected creature twice this morning. I couldn't forget her."

"Who is she?" asked Mrs. Hall softly.

"Her name is Markham; she's Sam Markham's wife," said Hall.

The young wife led the way into the sitting room, and the men took seats and lit their cigars. Hall was meditating a diversion when Otis resumed suddenly: "That woman came to town today to get a change, to have a little play spell, and she's wandering around like a starved and weary cat. I wonder if there is a woman in this town with sympathy enough and courage enough to go out and help that woman? The saloon-keepers, the politicians, and the grocers make it pleasant for the man—so pleasant that he forgets his wife. But the wife is left without a word."

Mrs. Hall's work dropped, and on her pretty face was a look of pain. The man's harsh words had wounded her—and wakened her. She took up her hat and hurried out on the walk.

The men looked at each other, and then the husband said, "It's going to be a little heated for the men around these diggings. Suppose we go out for a walk."

Delia felt a hand on her arm as she stood at the corner.

"You look tired, Mrs. Markham. Won't you come in a little while? I'm Mrs. Hall."

Mrs. Markham turned with a scowl on her face and a biting word on her tongue, but something in the sweet, round little face of the other woman silenced her, and her brow smoothed out.

"Thank you kindly, but it's 'most time to go home. I'm looking fer Mr. Markham now."

"Oh, come in a little while. The baby is cross and tired out. Please do."

Mrs. Markham yielded to the friendly voice, and together the two women reached the gate just as two men hurriedly turned the other corner.

"Let me relieve you," said Mrs. Hall.

The mother hesitated. "He's so dusty."

"Oh, that won't matter. Oh, what a big fellow he is! I haven't any of my own," said Mrs. Hall. A look passed like an electric spark between the two women, and Delia was her willing guest from that moment.

They went into the little sitting room, so dainty and lovely to the farmer's wife, and as she sank into an easy chair, she was faint and drowsy with the pleasure of it. She submitted to being pampered. She gave the baby into the hands of the Swedish girl, who washed his face and hands and sang him to sleep, while his mother sipped some tea. Through it all she lay back in her easy chair, not speaking a word, while the ache passed out of her back and her hot, swollen head ceased to throb.

But she saw everything—the piano, the pictures, the curtains, the wall-paper, the little tea stand. They were almost as welcome to her as the food and fragrant tea. Such housekeeping as this she had never seen. Her mother had worn her kitchen floor thin as brown paper in keeping a speckless house, and she had been in houses that were larger and costlier; but something of the charm of her hostess was in the arrangement of vases, chairs, and pictures. It was tasteful.

Mrs. Hall did not ask about her affairs. She talked to her about the sturdy little baby and about the things upon which Delia's eyes dwelt. If she seemed interested in a vase, she was told what it was and where it was made. She was shown all the pictures and books. Mrs. Hall seemed to read her visitor's mind. She kept as far from the farm and her guest's affairs as possible, and at last she opened the piano and sang to her—not slow-moving hymns, but catchy love songs full of sentiment. Then she played some simple melodies, knowing that Mrs. Markham's eyes were studying her hands, her rings, and the flash of her fingers on the keys—seeing more than she heard—and through it all Mrs. Hall conveyed the impression that she, too, was having a good time.

The rattle of the wagon outside roused them both. Sam was at the gate for her. Mrs. Markham rose hastily. "Oh, it's almost sundown!" she gasped in astonishment as she looked out of the window.

"Oh, that won't kill anybody," replied her hostess. "Don't hurry. Carrie, take the baby out to the wagon for Mrs. Markham while I help her with her things."

"Oh, I've had such a good time," Mrs. Markham said as they went down the little walk.

"So have I," replied Mrs. Hall. She took the baby a moment as her guest climbed in. "Oh, you big, fat fellow!" she cried as she gave him a squeeze. "You must bring your wife in more often, Mr. Markham," she said as she handed the baby up.

Sam was staring with amazement.

"Thank you, I will," he finally managed to say.

"Good night," said Mrs. Markham.

"Good night, dear," called Mrs. Hall, and the wagon began to rattle off.

The tenderness and sympathy in her voice brought tears to Delia's eyes— not hot nor bitter tears, but tears that cooled her eyes and cleared her mind.

The wind had gone down, and the red sunlight fell mistily over the world of corn and stubble. The crickets were still chirping, and the feeding cattle were drifting toward the farmyards. The day had been made beautiful by human sympathy.

How Patty Earned Her Salt

W. L. Colby

**Things aren't always what they seem—
and neither are people.**

"She doesn't even earn her own salt," Patty had heard her mother say
that morning in an impatient tone. "If she were only a boy, now, she
might run errands or do something to get a little money, and we
need every cent we can get, with the interest money to be paid, and
land knows what else!"

"Tut, tut, child!" replied the good old Quaker grandmother. "Thee
must remember, Sophia, that the little one's a mere chick yet and can
only pick up the bits the mother hen scratches for." And Mrs.
Drake, without saying more, had gone about her work, all unconscious that her words had been heard by the little girl beneath the
window.

Poor Patty! How those words kept repeating themselves in her ears! Was it true that she did not earn her salt? And she was so fond of salt. Her father often laughingly remarked that Patty would probably want to salt her coffee when she grew to be a woman.

How she wished she were a boy! Then, as her mother had said, she might earn some money by doing errands. Only the day before, the boy who came to deliver the groceries had told Patty's mother that old Miss Hunter wanted a boy to run errands for her. "But," he added, "she's so awful stingy with her money that none of the boys will go near her."

Perhaps, though, thought Patty, *she would be willing to give salt for pay.* And couldn't she run errands just as well as any boy? Her feet were good and strong, and didn't she walk three quarters of a mile each day to school and back?

Patty resolved, in spite of all the stories she had heard about the stingy old woman, that she would go and ask Miss Hunter to let her do the errands for her; although her little heart beat like a triphammer at the very thought of so bold an undertaking.

Miss Hunter lived in an old-fashioned mansion, only a short distance from the unpretentious farmhouse of the Drakes. Her brother had been a much-respected squire in the quiet town and was supposed to have been wealthy. But when he died, leaving his place to his only sister, Miss Hunter immediately dismissed two of the servants, retaining only one old man, who was lame and very deaf, to do the chores, while she occupied one room and seemed determined to have nothing to do with anyone.

The only time she was to be seen on the street was on Sundays, when she drove to church in the strange old chaise behind the dismal-looking horse, which won for itself the title of "Old Calamity." She never went to the store herself, and if a peddler were so bold as to call at her door, he was ordered away at once with the remark, "Don't come near me with your trash; I can't afford it!"

Patty had seen her in church—sitting always in the same position, never moving a muscle of her face until the sermon was over—when she would take her spectacles off, put them into their case, and walk out in a slow, dignified manner, speaking to no one and looking neither to the right nor the left.

Such was the woman Patty had determined to serve. Was it any wonder her heart failed her? But as often as she felt like giving up her enterprise, her mother's words "She doesn't even earn her salt" would ring in her ears, giving her fresh determination.

Accordingly the next day, on her way home from school, Patty walked bravely up the weed-grown path and knocked on the front door with the great brass knocker, which represented a lion holding a ring in his mouth. If the lion's head had been a live one, Patty would scarcely have stood more in fear of it.

It seemed to her hours before she heard any sound, and not daring to knock again, she made up her mind to give up the attempt and go home, when she heard a scraping sound as of a huge bolt being slid, and the door was opened a little.

"No, we don't want anything today," exclaimed a squeaky voice, "we've got all the pins and needles we want, and—"

"If you please, ma'am, I don't want to sell anything," answered Patty, breaking in on the old lady's speech, fearful lest the door would be closed before she could make known her errand. "I'm Patty Drake, who lives in the house just a little way down the road, and I've come to ask you—"

"You needn't come here begging," began the old lady in a sharp tone of voice. "We have enough to do to take care of ourselves without—"

"But, if you please, ma'am, I don't want to beg for anything, either," again broke in Patty. "Only I heard the other day that you wanted a boy to do errands for you, and so I thought—that maybe—perhaps—I could do them for you."

"But you are not a boy," answered the old lady, opening the door a little wider.

"No'm, but I can walk just as well as a boy, and teacher says I've got a good mem'ry, and you'd only have to pay me in salt," replied Patty.

"Pay you in salt, child! What do you mean?" exclaimed the old lady, opening the door still wider to get a view of her visitor.

"Why, you see, ma'am, Mother said yesterday that I didn't even earn my salt, and I do like it so much, and I thought maybe you would let me do your errands for you and pay me in salt, and you could hang a towel from the window whenever you wanted me, just as Mother does when she wants the baker to stop, and I could do all the errands you would want done before and after school," answered the little girl almost in one breath, anxious to cover all possible objections at once.

"Well, well! I never!" muttered Miss Hunter. "How old are you, pray tell?"

"If you please, ma'am, I'm nine years old, going on 10."

"And do you think you could keep your own counsel, child?"

"If you please, what is it to keep your own counsel?" asked Patty.

"Why, it means that you mustn't tell people all that you see and hear in other folks' houses."

"Oh, I never do that!" exclaimed Patty. "Mother doesn't allow me to tell what I hear folks say, 'cause she says it's telling tales out of school, and I'm sure, if you would only let me do your errands for you, I would never tell anybody what I heard."

"Humph!" muttered Miss Hunter. "Your mother is more sensible than most people, and I guess," she continued, half-musing, "that this little girl is just the one I want; she's big enough to do small errands, and Jake can do all the large ones—which aren't many—and," turning to Patty, "so you would be willing to take pay in salt, would you?"

"Oh, yes'm, indeed I would!" she cried. "Will you—oh, will you let me?" Her eyes fairly danced at the prospect.

"Well, if Mother is willing, and you will be sure to do your work in good shape. You will have to watch sharp for the cloth I hang out when I want you. Mind, it won't do for you to be off playing every time I want you; and you know, above all, you are to keep your own counsel. Can you do an errand for me this afternoon?"

"I suppose," faltered Patty, "I ought to ask Mother first; but I know she will let me, and I will be right back." And suiting the action to her words, she sped away as fast as her feet could carry her.

Her mother was not at home, but in answer to Patty's breathless request that she might go and do something for Miss Hunter, the dear old grandmother, half-dozing in her chair, said "Yes." Patty scampered back, scarcely able to contain herself, and thinking all the time how pleased her mother would be when she would hear that her little girl was actually "earning her own salt."

Miss Hunter answered her knock, and handing her a covered basket, told her to take it to old Mrs. Brown, a poor, lame widow living at the end of a crossroad that ran between Patty's home and Miss Hunter's. "But mind," she added, "you are not to say anything about it to anybody." Patty assented, carrying the basket as she was bidden.

It did not take her long to do her errand. Then, as Miss Hunter said there was nothing else to do that day, she hurried home, eager to tell her mother the good news.

But she was doomed to disappointment. Her mother was indignant and declared that Patty should not be allowed to do any such thing. "The idea!" she exclaimed, "pay you in salt, indeed! No, she shan't, not if I know it."

But here the grandmother interposed. "And why not let the child do as she wishes, Sophia? Did not thee say but yesterday that Patty was good for naught at home, and if she does as the old lady desires she will not be doing mischief. She surely can do no harm, and who knows," she added, "but the little one's innocent ways may have a good effect on the old woman?" And at length Mrs. Drake yielded, as she always did, sooner or later, to her mother's calm reasoning.

So Patty entered regularly upon her duties as errand girl. To be sure, she did not have very much to do for the old lady, but then she was doing something and was no longer a useless being.

As time wore on, there grew a strange attachment between the old lady and Patty, and after a while it became quite an ordinary affair for Patty to stop at Miss Hunter's on her way home from school, even when the cloth was not hanging from the window. She delighted to step in and wash the dishes on a Saturday and to help Miss Hunter dust the rooms on sweeping day.

People wondered much at it, but Patty, true to her word, kept "her own counsel" and did not tell what she often longed to have others know: Oh! she did want so much, sometimes, to tell people that what they took for miserly actions were only self-denying for the sake of others. For Patty could have told of many a basket of needed things that went into the little cottage at the end of the lane. Many a time she had carried jellies and dainty dishes to the houses of sick, poor people, but always with instructions that the receiver must tell no one whence they came. Miss Hunter told Patty confidentially that if the townspeople knew about it, they would send every beggar who came along to her, and she despised beggars.

Strange as it may seem, for once, the village gossip was baffled; those who received favors from the old lady respected her whims and "kept their own counsel." True, some wag in the village jokingly remarked "that the old miser," pointing to Miss Hunter's house, "had grown so greedy that she sent a basket to collect the rent from some of her tenants," but no one knew the real facts of the case.

Patty might have told, too, about the weekly letter she carried to the post office containing money to pay the board of an old feeble-minded uncle in a distant, private hospital, simply because this same uncle had taken care of Miss Hunter when she was a little girl. She had resolved that as long as she lived, he should not want for a single comfort. This had been her principal reason for the economy of the fortune left her by the squire, which was far from being as large as people supposed.

Misjudged by others, the old lady kept on in her way, taking great comfort in her newfound friend, for such Patty proved to be. Patty, on her part, began to love the one who denied herself luxuries for the sake of others.

The summer wore away, and winter came on cold and severe. Patty's father met with several losses in succession. First, the barn burned down, then his two best cows died of a prevalent disease, and things began to look unusually discouraging. Worst of all, the interest on the mortgage would soon be due again.

Mrs. Drake complained bitterly of their "poor luck," and Patty, young as she was, shared the feeling of gloom and despair that hung over them, for no one knew what they would do, or where they would go, if they lost their home.

One morning, as Patty was starting to school, her father called her to him. "Are you going to stop at Miss Hunter's?" he asked.

"No, sir, but I'd just as soon; I shall have time enough."

"Well, I wish you would take this letter to her," and he added, "you might stop on your way home for an answer."

Patty took the letter and carried it as she was bidden, wondering much what it could be about, for her father did not often write a letter. What could he be writing to Miss Hunter for—was it something about her?

All day long her mind kept reverting to the letter, and she could hardly wait for school to be dismissed, so anxious was she to see Miss Hunter, in hopes that she might find out something about it.

When Miss Hunter opened the letter Patty left that morning and read it, she found just a few simple sentences, stating that the writer, George Drake, having met with severe losses, would be unable to pay the interest on the mortgage that was held by her, and asking for time to obtain the necessary money.

Although the day seemed very long to Patty, school at length came to a close, and she hastened as fast as possible to the old lady's house.

Miss Hunter answered her knock and invited her to come in. As it was very cold, the woman insisted that Patty should sit down by the fire and warm herself. For a little while they sat in silence, and then the old lady said, "Patty, do you remember the day you came and asked me to let you do my errands?"

"Yes'm."

"Have you forgotten what you told me you wanted for pay?"

"No'm."

"Why haven't you asked me for your pay?"

"Because I thought you would give it to me when you wanted to."

"Well, I've been thinking today," replied the old lady, "that it is about time you received some of your wages. You have been a good girl and have earned your salt well." So saying, she handed Patty a tin pail, which she said was full of salt.

"Be careful not to spill any, and be sure you bring back the pail, as I cannot spare it long," she admonished.

"Thank you ever so much," exclaimed Patty, thinking how pleased her mother would be when she should show her that she had really earned something.

"Oh!" suddenly remembering her errand, "I was to call for an answer to the letter I left this morning."

"Never mind the answer tonight," replied Miss Hunter.

It seemed to Patty that the old lady had a beautiful expression on her face that she had never seen before, as she bade her good night.

She hurried home with her pail of salt, feeling very happy at the thought that it was all her own. But Mrs. Drake shared no such feeling; her indignation began, as usual, to rise, and it was an effort for her to control herself and keep from saying harsh things, which would have spoiled Patty's pleasure. What was a little pail of salt, compared with what Patty had done!

The tears sprang to her eyes. "And she even wants you to bring back the pail, doesn't she? The sting—" but a look from Patty made her pause. "Well, no matter, I'll empty it right away, and you can carry the pail back tomorrow morning. We are almost out of salt anyway—that's one comfort."

So saying, she carried the salt into the pantry.

In a moment they heard her utter an exclamation of surprise. "Mother! Patty!" she called. "Come here quick!"

They hurried into the pantry to see what could be the matter, and Mr. Drake, who was just bringing in the milk, joined them.

On the table was a pan into which Mrs. Drake had just poured the salt. But what was that glittering here and there in the pan? Gold; yes, gold coins—eagles, half-eagles, a number of smaller coins—all bright and shining, as if happy at the thought of the good they might do. And in an envelope was a gift of the mortgage on the house, presented to Patty Drake, from her friend Adeline Hunter, with these words: "You have earned your salt."

The Widened Hearth

Fannie H. Kilbourne

A widow and her teenage daughters decide to reinvent Thanksgiving Day.

"Wouldn't you think they would be invited *somewhere?*" Kathleen demanded. "Wouldn't you think even boarders would like to go out to dinner on *Thanksgiving?*"

"Couldn't we tell them that we don't serve meals on holidays?" Lois suggested.

Their mother shook her head. "It's never done. All boardinghouses have a big dinner on holidays."

"Oh, Mother," Lois protested, "please don't call this a boarding-house! Having four paying guests doesn't make a place a boarding-house."

"That which we call a rose—" Kathleen quoted lightly.

"Whatever you call it," their practical mother said, "it seems to bring its responsibilities."

"It isn't fair that being poor should keep us from having a home," said Lois. "It's bad enough having all the extra work, but it's having boarders around all the time that I mind. Home isn't home when it's full of strangers."

"It's bad enough to have boarders any time," Kathleen said, taking up the plaint, "but it does seem as if they might go away on holidays!"

Their four "paying guests" had been with the Martins for three months. Taking them had seemed the inevitable sequel to the Consolidated failure. During the long years of Mrs. Martin's widowhood, the check from the Consolidated had been one of the rocks of assurance on which her life was built.

Then the Consolidated failed, and the check stopped coming. It all happened with a suddenness and unexpectedness that stunned the Martins. For days Mrs. Martin was more bewildered and incredulous than she was frightened. But the fright followed soon enough. Never could she forget the terror of the hot July evening when she had finally accepted the fact that the Consolidated check would come no more and had taken account of her resources.

There was "home," an attractive 10-room stone house. Chestnut Avenue had been on the outskirts of town when Mrs. Martin had gone to the stone house as a bride 20 years ago. During the 20 years, the city had slowly crept up—a store building here, an apartment house there. Electric cars thundered up and down the next block, hotels and bakeries appeared on the cross streets; the neighborhood was only a few minutes' walk from the busiest part of the city—yet Chestnut Avenue stood alone, a shady, restful island of homes in the restless sea of traffic.

Besides home, the assets were few; the tiny income that was still coming would scarcely pay the coal bill and the taxes. Then there were the girls, Lois aged 17, Kathleen aged 15, still in high school, two lovable liabilities. Home was in a desirable part of the town, near business yet quiet. "Paying guests" offered the only solution to the problem.

"Well, if we've sunk to where we have to take boarders, we'll take them," Lois had said grimly. "We'll give them comfortable rooms and good food, but we won't—"

"Won't be clubby with them," Kathleen suggested.

"No, we won't," Lois had agreed. "They'll have their own lives, and we'll have ours. We won't let their being here spoil our home life."

The four boarders had been able to pay good prices for their large sunny rooms and appetizing meals; they knew nothing of the planning and penny-pinching behind the fruit salad. The Martins kept to themselves as much as possible, striving to maintain their means of livelihood on a formal, businesslike basis.

"We could fool ourselves all right before," Lois went on almost tearfully, "pretending keeping boarders didn't make any difference. But on holidays it shows up. We can't have people we'd like here for dinner with four strangers, and we can't go anywhere ourselves because we have to stay and get dinner for them."

"I thought surely Miss Dunn would be invited somewhere," Kathleen said. "Didn't you, Mother?"

"She expected to go home," Mrs. Martin explained, "and then, just last week, the schools decided to stay open Friday, so she can't go."

"I heard her refuse an invitation over the telephone just before she found out," said Lois.

"I suppose we ought to have a turkey," mused Mrs. Martin. "And turkey is 55 cents a pound. I wonder if we'll have to have soup?"

"We had five courses last year," Lois reminded them wistfully. "We won't have to bother with cheese, crackers, and candied orange peel and things like that this year, anyway. Isn't it funny how much more work it seems to be to get up a dinner for people you don't want than for people you do? I never think of the trouble of clearing up after a party, but the idea of washing the dishes after this dinner—well, I just wish Thanksgiving were over!"

"Girls!" cried Kathleen, suddenly straightening up and looking from one to the other with bright eyes. Kathleen always addressed her mother and sister in that collective way, which secretly delighted her quiet, practical mother. "Girls, let's make it a party. As long as we've lost our home anyway, let's get some fun out of it. Let's pretend we're giving a dinner party and have place cards and flowers and—well, maybe not flowers, but everything that is spiffy and cheap and—"

She paused enthusiastically, but her enthusiasm was not reflected in the faces of the other two.

"Getting up a big dinner is about all the work I want," sighed her mother.

"Oh, we'll do all the party part of it, won't we, Lois?" said Kathleen. "Oh, come on; it would be lots of fun. We haven't had a party since the Consolidated failed. Come on, please! It would be great fun!"

"I suppose I could paint the place cards myself," said Lois.

"We could send them invitations," Kathleen went on eagerly. "Of course, they'd come anyhow, but it would let them know that it was a party. We—"

"We'll use the gorgeous stationery Aunt Kate gave me for my birthday," said Lois.

"We can have alligator-pear salad," said Mrs. Martin, "if Uncle Will's box from Florida gets here in time. That is always considered as quite a delicacy."

"We'll have a fire in the grate," said Lois.

"And serve the coffee in front of it!" said Kathleen, suddenly inspired.

Enthusiasm had begun its leavening; already Thanksgiving dinner had begun to be a "party."

Tuesday evening a large square envelope lay at each boarder's place.

"Mrs. Anne Upland Martin and her daughters, Miss Lois and Miss Kathleen Martin, would be pleased to have you take dinner with them at 2:00 Thanksgiving Day and spend the afternoon, if there is nothing else that you want to do."

The message was of Kathleen's composing and was written in Lois's pretty hand. The four boarders read the missives through and then looked up.

"Well, I'll be tickled to death," said pretty little Miss Dunn. "I was so disappointed about not being able to go home that I had decided to stay in my room and cry all day."

"You can count on me," said Mr. Willis. He worked on the *Tribune* and had planned to hurry away after dinner and attend the football game with two or three other young newspapermen. But for the last month or so it had been growing upon Mr. Willis just how pretty and sweet little Miss Dunn was, and this seemed a splendid chance to get better acquainted with her.

"Well, I haven't anywhere else to go, so I guess *I'll* be here all right," said Miss Dempsey. Plain, blunt, middle-aged Miss Dempsey was a secretary in one of the flour mills.

"It's most kind of you to ask me," said the fourth boarder with the slow, gentle courtesy that fitted so well with his white hair and frock coat, "but I am afraid that unless . . ." He hesitated. "My nephew is to be in town for Thanksgiving Day. I just received word this morning, and I wondered if it would be a great imposition—"

"We'd be glad to have him come, too," Mrs. Martin said cordially.

Mr. Thompson beamed.

"He would be happy to come," he said.

"Kathleen," her mother protested when the three Martins were in the kitchen, washing the dinner dishes, "I wish you had let me see those invitations first. What on earth did you ask them all to spend the afternoon for? It was all right to make the dinner a party, but an ill-assorted group like that will be as restless as witches before the day is over."

"Why, Mother!" Kathleen's dish towel paused reproachfully in mid-air. "Who ever heard of people's leaving a party the minute dinner is over! They're not a bit more ill-assorted than most of our family parties."

"Besides," said Lois, coming to her sister's support, "we said, 'if there is nothing else that you want to do.' If they think they're going to be bored they needn't stay."

"Well, there's no helping it now, anyway," said Mrs. Martin philosophically. She paused a moment. "I wonder what Mr. Thompson's nephew is like?"

"I'll bet he's a fashionable young bachelor," said Lois. "Mr. Thompson has quite a lot of money and—"

"I'll bet he wears spats," was Kathleen's contribution. "I'm glad we thought of having coffee in front of the fire. He'll see that we're not so slow ourselves."

Thanksgiving breakfast was a light, hasty meal.

"We wouldn't eat anything, anyhow," said Mr. Willis. "We don't want to cramp our style for dinner."

The party was bringing an element of personality into the pleasant formality that had been the atmosphere of the house.

"Oh, I *hope* it will snow!" said Kathleen, scanning the cloudy sky. "It would seem so much more Thanksgiving-y."

"We nearly always had sleighing for Thanksgiving at home in New Hampshire," said Miss Dempsey.

After breakfast Mr. Willis departed for the office. Mr. Thompson left for the station to meet his nephew, and the two women went upstairs to their rooms. Then the folding doors between the dining room and the living room were closed, and from that time on in the back part of the house preparation ruled supreme.

Mrs. Martin moved briskly from table to refrigerator, from sink to stove. At 10:00 she put the turkey into the oven. Lois deftly made butter balls, washed lettuce, and chopped nuts. But it was Kathleen who kept up the spirit of the party.

"Oh, girls! Look!" she called, watching with rapt eyes the few feathery flakes that were sifting down upon the hard brown ground. "There!" she said. "Now just come and see if this table doesn't look lovely."

At either end, hollowed pumpkins were filled with shining apples and oranges, grapes, and bananas. The place cards, yellow chrysanthemums painted by Lois, waved from the tops of the tall slender glasses. And scattered about the table in holders of cardboard and gilded walnut shells were dozens of little candles waiting to be lighted.

"Why, Kathie, it's lovely!"

"And cheap!" Kathleen said eagerly. "It didn't cost a penny except for the candles. The walnut shells came from the nuts in the mincemeat; the pumpkins the boarders will eat later in pies that Mother will make of them."

"Mother," she protested later in the day, "you're not going to wear *that* dress! Why, don't you know, Mother, this is a *party!*"

Just at noon the doorbell rang, causing great excitement. It proved to be a box of flowers from one of Miss Dunn's admirers.

"Girls, look at these!" said Kathleen, coming back to the kitchen with her arms full of American Beauties. "Miss Dunn says we can have them for the dining room." She placed the two tall vases on the buffet. "There! That gives the whole thing tone. The nephew with the spats will give one glance at those, and he'll know this is no husking bee."

A little before 2:00, the nephew arrived. Lois was the first to see him. She clutched Kathleen, and the two peered through the crack in the double door. He was a tall, awkward, freckle-faced boy of 16 or so. The girls stared for a moment, then retreated to the kitchen for a hysterical outburst.

"A fashionable bachelor!" gasped Lois.

"Did you notice any sp-spats?" said Kathleen.

At quarter past two the dining-room curtains were drawn, the three dozen little yellow candles lighted, and the doors flung open. There was a delighted gasp from the five guests.

It was a most successful party. The boarders had put on their holiday moods with their holiday clothes. In a soft blue silk dress, Miss Dempsey did not seem half so much the brusque, reserved business woman. And little Miss

Dunn, in her straight black velvet dress with its lace collar, with her wide blue eyes and her yellow hair, curling softly against her creamy neck, made a picture from which Mr. Willis could hardly take his eyes. He told funny stories of newspaper life and bandied jokes with Mr. Thompson with a geniality that would have made any party "go." Mr. Thompson watched Bobby Smith at first, eager for his sister's boy to have a good time and appear to advantage. He soon dropped all responsibility there, however, when he found him stealing almonds from Kathleen's cup and telling Lois about a football game.

With one exception, they were the same people that gathered at the same table twice a day. Now instead of a businesslike boardinghouse dinner prepared for pay, was the gracious atmosphere of a feast prepared for love. It showed in Mrs. Martin's "best" dress, that gracious spirit, in the alligator-pear salad and in the candied orange peel; it twinkled in the tiny yellow candles and chuckled in the silly little conundrums written on the backs of the place cards. It was the spirit of hospitality that brings forth its best for guests.

When they had eaten the last bit of mince pie and the last little candle had flickered out, it was after 4:00. According to plan, they all went into the living room to drink their coffee round the snapping wood fire.

"I'm glad we saved all these berry boxes from canning time," said Kathleen, putting on another armful. "They burn up in a minute, but don't they make the most thrilling fire!"

The feathery snowflakes had changed to a cold autumn rain that blew against the windows. Twilight fell early; the firelight flickered, leaving shadowy corners in the living room. After a bit, words came fitfully; there were little periods of silence.

Kathleen, in her place on the floor beside the fire, ceased poking idly at the wood. Sensitive, responsive, she had caught the strange, wistful solemnity that so often steals down on holiday evenings. She leaned back against her mother's knee.

"It seems sort of—sort of ghostly, doesn't it?" she said in a hushed tone.

Then the ghosts stole in, the ghosts of other and different Thanksgivings.

"How well I remember the first Thanksgiving after we came west," said Mr. Thompson. "It was the year after the Indian trouble. Minneapolis was St. Anthony Falls then."

It was a story of pioneer days that he told, of raw country, of hardships and successes. Then Miss Dunn told of the first year that she had taught school in the New Hampshire hills and of their having been snowed in the day before Thanksgiving and having to stay until Friday morning with nothing to eat but what was left in the children's luncheon baskets. Mrs. Martin told of a Thanksgiving when, as a bride and fledgling housekeeper, she had had to entertain wealthy friends of her husband's.

When the clock struck eight, it was like a signal summoning them from the past. Miss Dunn straightened up suddenly.

"Please, Mrs. Martin," she said, "we've recovered from our feasting. Please let us all help do the dishes."

"Oh, no, we'll do them after—" Mrs. Martin began.

"After we've gone home, you were going to say," Miss Dunn accused her. "But we're already at home, you see; so there's no chance of our going. Please!"

Mr. Willis was already on his way to the dining room.

"This is a heaven-sent opportunity," he said. "I've always wondered whether all this newfangled domestic science amounted to anything. We have a domestic science teacher at our mercy, and we'll see if she really knows how to wash dishes."

The Martin kitchen that night was a hilarious place. At the sink, Mr. Willis, with a gingham apron tied about his neck, washed dishes. Kathleen presided over another pan on the table; Lois and Bobby Smith raced to see who should wipe each plate and cup as it came from the hot rinsing water. Miss Dunn wiped the dishes that Mr. Willis washed, and, judging from her occasional laughter and blushes, acquaintance was progressing quite as fast as well. There was much rivalry between the two teams, much good-natured bandying back and forth that ended with Mr. Willis's seizing Lois and depositing her high and dry upon the top of the refrigerator, where he left her until he and Miss Dunn had caught up with the rival team.

At last they all went back to the living room for a little music. Miss Dunn played, and Lois and Kathleen went out to the cabinet in the hall in search of some old books of music. They stole a moment for congratulations. Kathleen seized her sister about the waist.

"Honestly, hasn't this been the nicest holiday party we've ever had!"

"Everybody has been so nice," said Lois. "Wasn't it dandy of Mr. Thompson to invite us all to the theater tomorrow night in honor of his nephew? I haven't been to the theater in a decent seat since the Consolidated failed."

"They were all so nice," said Kathleen. "The idea of Miss Dunn's saying she'd just love to help me make over my pink dress! I like even Miss Dempsey. Do you know," she went on eagerly, "I believe it was because we were pretending we really wanted them here that they seemed so nice. We didn't keep kind of—kind of resenting them all the time."

"But the funny part is," Lois admitted in a whisper, "it wasn't pretending at all after the first. Why, when we were all fooling in the kitchen, I suddenly thought how glad I was that it wasn't going to end like most parties—everybody go home, and it's over with a bang—that they'd all be here for breakfast in the morning and for dinner tomorrow night and right on."

"I know it," said Kathleen eagerly. "Of course, it's a lot more work, and home isn't the same, but I think it's going to be real fun having them here."

"They probably won't always seem quite so nice as they do tonight," said Lois sagely. "They're at their best today. But then—"

There was a little pause in the music; then from the living room came soft, familiar notes:

Mid pleasures and palaces though we may roam,

Be it ever so humble, there's no place like home.

One voice after another took up the old tune, Mr. Thompson's a bit quavery, Miss Dempsey's a bit off key.

In the shadowy hall Kathleen's arm tightened round her sister. Where the light from the living room fell, she could see the rug over which they had all walked so many happy days, the corner of the case where their favorite books were kept; she knew what was in the shadowy corner—the hat rack with their mother's coat and umbrella, the clock that had ticked so loud in the stillness the night their father died, the window seat where their mother stopped to wave good-bye to them when they started off for school. It all seemed suddenly, poignantly sweet. Perhaps some Thanksgiving—

The plaintive melody went on. Kathleen's eyes suddenly filled with impulsive tears.

"Think of their singing that anywhere but home!" she said, with her voice choking a little.

"I know it," said Lois. "I was just thinking that, too. I'm—oh, I don't care if the Consolidated did fail—I'm so glad we've got the house and each other!"

"And honestly," said Kathleen, laughing shakily, "I'm thankful that we've got the boarders. If we can somehow manage to make it seem like home to them, too—"

The last flicker had died out in the fireplace; the little, old-fashioned grate with its narrow hearthstone was black and dead. But the spirit that kindles all home fires was burning bright. And in the magic of that Thanksgiving night, the hearth where only three had gathered had suddenly grown wide.

Joseph's Coat

Author Unknown

Aunt Caroline sent Joseph a coat—a warm coat. But it had a flaw, and the minister's son found it.

It was nipping cold for November. Winter had arrived before schedule.

"My, this coat feels good!" Joseph gave a little flying leap to express how good it felt. His thin legs seemed to lose themselves upward, his happy face, mounted on a thin little neck, to lose itself downward in the huge new coat.

Mother was happy today, too, as she watched him down the road.

"Nobody will look at his back," she thought. "They'll just look at his face, and say, 'My, that boy's warm, I know!'"

But somebody looked at his back. At the junction of the roads, a little way on, the minister's boy and his particular friends swung in behind Joseph. They were all warm, too. The minister's boy's coat was

301

new, too, but a different "new" from Joseph's. It had a fur collar that turned up—up—about his ears, and it was exactly broad enough and long enough.

All at once somebody shouted. It was the minister's boy.

"Oh, look! Joseph's coat—Joseph's coat o' many colors!" Then the others took it up. "Joseph's coat o' many colors! Looker there! Looker there!"

Suddenly Joseph was no longer warm; a nipping cold struck through to his small vitals.

"Joseph's coat! Joseph's coat!"

He knew there was something the matter with it, and it must be with the— the behind of it, for that was all those boys could see. All the leap had come out of Joseph's thin little legs, all the joy out of his heart. He went on because you couldn't get to school without going on. But that was all—just went on.

At the schoolhouse he waited around, instinctively facing front to folks, until they had all gone in. Then he took off his "new" coat, and looked at the behind. Then he knew.

There was a long straight seam in the middle, and on each side of it the thick cloth had faded to a different shade, a distinctly different shade. Two

colors really, one on each side of that long straight seam—a cruel little trick of the sun. Joseph was only eight, but he saw at once why they had called it Joseph's coat of many colors. It *was* Joseph's coat of many colors.

The next day Joseph waited behind a wall at the junction of roads until the minister's boy and his particular friends had come and gone. Then he slipped out and followed them. That helped a little—he tried to think it helped a little. But there were recesses and noon-ings—of course he might stay in recesses and noonings; you don't have to wear an overcoat when you stay in.

Joseph stayed in. Through the window he could see the minister's boy's new coat having a splendid time. The third day he saw something else. He saw the minister's boy in *his* coat—the one Aunt Caroline sent—strutting about the yard amid the others' shouts of delight. Some of the others tried it on and strutted. Joseph just sat in his seat and looked at them.

The next day he turned Aunt Caroline's coat inside out, and wore it so. He waited till he got nearly to the fork in the road, and then turned it; he wasn't going to make Mother feel bad too. She had lined the coat anew with shiny black cotton stuff all of one color. Joseph felt a little better; this would help.

But it only made things worse. The minister's boy and his particular friends instantly saw the ridiculousness of that inside-out little coat. "Look at it! Look at it—inside out! *Wearin' it* inside out!" The joke was just too good!

There was just one other thing to do, and Joseph did it the next day. The place where the roads forked was about halfway from Joseph's home to the schoolhouse; so he went warm halfway the next day. The other half he shiv-ered along, very small indeed, and very cold indeed, outside of the Aunt Caroline coat. For he had left Aunt Caroline's coat folded up behind a stone wall. Going home that afternoon, he was warm the last half of his way, anyway. It helped to be half warm.

For a day or two the sun and the wind conspired together to befriend little Joseph. But the fourth day the wind blew and the sun rested. There was snow, too, in fine steely flakes, and Joseph's teeth chattered, and he ran on stiff little legs, and blew on stiff little fingers. He kept looking ahead to the last half of going home. He wished he had pushed the Aunt Caroline coat farther in under the stones out of the way of the snow.

"Joseph Merriam," called the teacher on the day after the snowstorm. She had her roll book and pencil waiting, but she got no answer. It was strange for Joseph Merriam not to answer the roll call; he was one of her little steadies.

"Joseph is not here, I see; can anyone tell me if he is sick? He must be sick."

"Yes'm, he is. He's got the pneumonia dreadfully," someone answered. "There were lights in his house all night, my father said."

For many nights there were lights, and for many mornings the doctor's sleigh. Joseph lay in his bed, saying wild, mixed-up words in a weak little voice.

"I'm most to the stone wall; then I'll be warm!"

"Joseph's coat o' many colors—Joseph's coat o' many colors!"

"I don't want Mother to know they laughed; don't anybody tell Mother."

The minister's boy heard of those wild little words, and pieced them together into a story. He remembered who had cried, "Joseph's coat o' many colors!" tauntingly, cruelly. And now—oh, now he remembered that Joseph had not worn any overcoat at all those last days that he went to school! *No coat.* The heart of the minister's boy contracted with an awful fear. He took to haunting Joseph's house in all his free minutes—waiting at the gate for the doctor to come out, and shivering with something besides cold at his brief answers. The answers grew worse and worse.

There came a day when the answer struck the minister's boy like a blow in the face, and a night when lights shone all over Joseph's house, in every room. The day and the night were Thanksgiving day and night. *Thanksgiving!* It had always been such a beautiful day at the minister's house, and for weeks the minister's boy had looked forward to it. But now everything was different. The day that usually hurried away in leaps when you wanted it to creep, crept today. Would it always be Thanksgiving day? The minister's boy was glad—*glad*—when the cousins drove off at night-fall. He was glad to go to bed and try to forget.

But going to bed was not going to sleep. He lay in his own bed, remembering that other little bed of Joseph's. When remembering was too great a torture, the minister's boy crept out of bed and dressed himself. Out into the clear, cold starlight, down the frozen road, he crept toward Joseph's lighted windows. He was not sensible of being cold anywhere but in his soul—he shivered there.

A long time he stood waiting for he knew not what. Then someone came out of the house. It was not the doctor; it was the minister. The boy could not see his face, but you don't have to see your own father's face. They went back down the dim night road together, and together into the minister's study.

"I've killed him," the boy said. "I've killed Joseph. I did it."

The minister's face was curiously lighted in spite of this awful confession of his son. The light persisted.

"Sit down, Philip," he said, for the boy was shaking like a leaf. "Now tell me."

All the story, piece by piece—the boy told it all.

"So it was I—I killed him. I—I didn't *expect* to—"

Silence for a little. Then:

"Did you think Joseph was dead, Philip? He came very close indeed to it; but the crisis is past, and he will get well. I waited to know."

"You mean—I—*haven't?*"

"I mean you haven't, thank God. Kneel down with me and thank Him." Father and son knelt together, their hearts overflowing with glad Thanksgiving praises.

When, after a long while, the boy was slipping away, the minister called to him gently.

"Come back a moment, Philip."

"Yes, I'm back, Father. I know what you're thinking of. Father, may I— punish myself this time—for making fun of a boy—a *little* boy? It needs a good deal o' punishin', but I'll do it—please let me do it, Father! Please— please *try* me, anyway."

And because the minister was a wise minister, he nodded his head.

When little Joseph got well, he wore to school a beautiful warm coat with a soft furry collar that went up—up—around his ears. It was very thick and warm and handsome, and all of a color. Joseph wore it all the way.

The rest of the winter the minister's boy wore to school an Aunt Caroline coat of many colors.

The Thankful Book

Helen Peck

*One mother's legacy said
volumes to her offspring.*

A little group of men and women with smiling lips and sadly sober
eyes talked together fitfully in a country living room. When silences
dropped, like snuffers on a candle, someone was sure to start with
guilty haste and reopen the conversation, which flourished for a
while, only to die once more.

They turned with quick relief to greet the entrance of the home-
keeping sister. She held a little package, and her eyes smiled, as well
as her lips. She had learned the lesson.

"Come near, dears," she said with the motherly accent of the eldest
of many kindred. They gathered close, and she showed them words
written in a delicate script upon the wrapping.

"To the dear children who will be coming together on Thanksgiving Day," they read in silence.

"She told me she knew you would come, for the sake of the past days," went on the quiet voice.

The hush with which they listened answered, "Of course," as they watched the unwrapping of their gift. It was an old-fashioned little leather-bound book that emerged, limp and bent with much handling. Upon the cover in gilt letters was printed the little-girl name that tightened throats as they read "Her Book."

A letter dropped from between the covers with superscription similar to that upon the wrapper. The big sister broke the seal and read to them the message with a voice whose clearness never dimmed.

Dear Children:

My grandmother gave me this book many years ago, when I complained bitterly that everything seemed to go wrong. She asked me to promise to write in it some reason for thankfulness contained in every event in my life. I began it when not more than a child, and have kept my promise to that dear saint.

I was about to destroy it today, when the thought came to me that it might perhaps be to you a guiding message upon the coming Thanksgiving Day. So I give it to you, my very dears, with my prayer that to you also may come the knowledge its keeping has taught me.

The reader laid aside the sheet to open with tender, caressing fingers the little book; and they gathered still closer. The pages were closely written in a hand that showed steady growth from childish scrawl to clear-cut script of the well-poised woman. Some pages bore telltale spots as of tears. Some were torn as by a hasty hand that would have snatched them from their place, and then repented.

"Shall I read, dears?" asked the calmly gentle voice. They begged her to begin, and leaned still more closely, not to miss a syllable—men and women turned children again as they sat once more at the feet of her who had written with no thought of their reading.

The flyleaf bore the same explanation as that contained in the letter, with the frank addition, "It seems rather silly to me. How could there be a thankful to everything? But it is a nice book, and I like to write in it: so I shall. Besides, I promised Grandma. I wonder, could there be any thankful to that promising?"

The first chronicle was dated the very next day. "I thought it would be very easy to write I was thankful Rebecca Corning gave me a tart this afternoon. Then all of a sudden, it gave me an awful stomachache. How could a child be thankful for a pain? I'll have to ask Grandma. I did, and she said to think it out. So I've been thinking since. I s'pose it's because now I know that tarts with such rich stuffing are not good for me between meals. Oh, dear, I do like them!"

"Poor baby," smiled the reading sister.

"Something dreadful has happened," she read on. "It took me two whole days to think up a thankful to it. My darling Prince is dead. He has lived in this house ever since I got born, and even before. And he was still a real good dog, only blind and lame. I just cried and cried, and said I wasn't thankful one bit. Then Grandma told me stories about how he used to run and take care of me when I was a baby, and all of a sudden I got dreadful sorry for his not doing it anymore—because he couldn't. So I guess I am thankful he needn't limp around any more and bump into things. But I don't want any other dog ever."

"Rebecca and me got mad at each other," began one entry during those early days, "and it was all my fault. I said a horrid thing about her dog just because mine was dead and I didn't have it anymore. We didn't speak for two whole hours. Then I suddenly got ashamed, and we made up. I got ashamed, because how could I write down in this book I was thankful to be mad at Rebecca? That would be ridiculous. So I just had to ask her forgiveness. So now I am thankful we got glad again. Not just for writing, but because it's much nicer to be friends again. I wish I didn't speak so quick."

"Poor lamb," smiled the reading sister.

"I have the very beautifulest thankful in the whole world to write down," began one burst of pure joy. "I got out of bed to write it. Mother came upstairs a while ago and sat on my quilt and hugged me tight, and said I had been a specially good girl for a whole week, and called me her blessing. She said she had watched me trying to keep my temper. I am very thankful to have an understanding mother. It is lovely to get called a blessing."

The girlish philosophy groped more and more surely, as the pages turned, and the child merged into the maiden.

"I am going to boarding school," she wrote. "At first it was hard to feel thankful. I love to live here with my family, but I suppose there are many things to be learned at such a place, and I am thankful I am smart enough to learn some of them. I might have been simpleminded like that boy at the poorhouse who shakes a shaving all the time. It would be awful to be like that. And, anyway, I shall probably have a very pleasant time when I get used to it."

They listened to descriptions of early school days, to the tightening grip of the girl upon the facts of life learned by contact with her fellows.

"I have a sad thing to write," began one record. "I have failed in history. It took quite a long time to think out a thankful for that, but this is it: I am thankful that I know it was my own fault. I hate history and didn't pay proper attention to it. I am thankful that I know better for next term. It is quite hard to pay much attention to things you hate, but you have to if you want good marks, which I do."

Even the good times brought their lessons, big or little. Vacation time was ushered in with one of them.

"Never did I expect to write I was thankful for slapping somebody, but just the same I am. It was at Rebecca's party, walking on the piazza between dances, that a boy (I shan't write down his name because I think it would be mean, and anyhow I don't expect to ever see him again; he doesn't live here)—well, anyway, the first thing I knew, he'd grabbed me around the waist and kissed me. And that was the slapping part. Grandma mourns my quick temper, but that time I think she would have been thankful for it, too. Anyhow, I am."

"Dear book," began another page, tear-spotted, "I thought I could never tell you I was thankful darling Grandma has passed away, but I can now. The last time I came home for vacation, she didn't know who I was. It frightened me dreadfully, but Mother explained that she was so old; it sometimes happens to people like that. So now, I am truly thankful she won't have to grow any more forgetful. And I shall never, never forget to write in this book, because she asked me to."

"Bless her heart," whispered the reading sister.

The end of school days brought with it a thanksgiving without a flaw. "I am thankful that I got a prize in history at graduation, for two reasons: because Father was so proud, and because it was what I hated once and had to work at hardest. It is really not bad at all, even interesting in spots, except the dates. I don't believe even Grandma would have expected me to be thankful for dates."

Then with the coming of a sweetheart, the girl became with one breath a woman.

"Dear, darling book," they read, "I am so thankful I have you to talk to! I couldn't say it out loud, even to Mother, and I do need someone to tell how wonderful the world is since John came, and I know he loves me. It isn't hard to think of thankfulnesses for that. I am thankful for every littlest thing about him, the way he looks and talks and acts, because he is tall and not too good-looking, because he thinks me prettier than I really am, because he is so sweet to Mother, because Father thinks he is so smart, because he has a good position, because his name is John, and a hundred other reasons. I was just going to write, because he hasn't any relatives, but I am thankful I was ashamed of it in time. What would I do without mine, I'd like to know! I would be thankful for whole crowds to be nice to for his sake."

The entries in the little book thereafter sang so pure a song of love and thankfulness as to bring the first tremble to the voice of the reading woman, who knew not that of which they spoke.

Then on a torn and spotted page, they read: "I haven't written for a long time. I couldn't. I couldn't think of one thing to be thankful for when Mother and Father were both lost in that awful boat. I have been almost stunned, and even began to feel there weren't any thankfulnesses anywhere. Then I remembered that Grandma and Mother had both said they knew there was one in everything, and I had promised to try to find it. So I began trying, rather rebelliously and doubtingly, to think of one, and John helped. It was having him that brought it at last. And now I *am* thankful that they went together, which I see now is as it should be, and quite wonderful that after a long and exceptional life of understanding together here they should give up life together, with never an hour of separation. The going was a shock to me; but what a happiness to them to have been together at the last! And I wonder, after all, if their going at any other time and in any other manner would not have been just as great a shock to me. I doubt that, no matter how peaceful the earthly end of those we love, it finds us prepared; it must ever be a shock to us. And so at last I am thankful for those two dears whose spiritual understanding was so perfect that they had to but touch the things of this plane to make them glow with the light of their great love. John and I are going to be married right away, and for this I am thankful."

After a slight pause the quiet voice continued. "The thankfulnesses are very thick just now, for the dear wonder of it all. It seems to me this material world is scarce big enough to hold all the beauty and all the marvelous sweetness that have been unfolded to me in this new life. The vision of the possibilities of the future is very dazzling, as seen by these blessed months John and I have had together. Like a fair piece of tapestry into which is woven threads of many colors, I see the golden thread of our love running in and out the length and breadth of the cloth, ever lending its dominant note of light to brighten the pattern where the somber colors largely form the pattern. This vision helps to lighten the practical side of the homemaking; and I am very thankful that the guidance of a wise mother fitted me for that."

Then came the first little rift.

"I shall make myself write it down for punishment. Oh, my miserable temper! Am I never to get the best of it? It has run away with me again. I blew up at my poor, dear, hard-working boy about some foolish thing, and he looked so surprised and hurt. I don't know whether I ought to be thankful that he didn't answer back, or not. I was ashamed in one second, and I am thankful for that. Perhaps the remembrance of his face will be better than a scolding. I think perhaps I may be thankful for a patient husband. I don't know why people are so horrid to those they love best. I do mean never to be so again."

"I haven't been able to catch my breath long enough to write lately," began the next entry. "John's lost position and illness came so suddenly that every-

thing has been topsy-turvy. But now I may stop a minute to think. How
can I be thankful for my poor lad's trouble and bad heart? I don't think
anybody could say that; but I am thankful for some of the consequences,
for the opportunity to shoulder my end of the load, for a strong constitu-
tion and good spirits. I am thankful, too, that we never sold the old homestead that Grandmother left me, and have had that to fly to for refuge. I am
thankful for the quiet and the greenness, for the birds and the smell of the
ground. John is better already, and eager to begin being a gentleman farmer.
Oh, I am thankful for that, and that our coming darling may breathe fresh
air and roll on real grass! Nobody can know how thankful I am that I could
help when the need came."

"Bless her," whispered the reader to those whose murmur of assent
answered "Amen." They knew how she had always helped.

Then came a cry of rapture almost beyond expression.

"I may write but a word, but that one I must add quickly to my dear book
of thankfulness, if I can. With what words of gold shall a woman speak of
her firstborn child? It needs a greater skill than mine. I may only say that I
am thankful to God for every hour of waiting, for every task, for every pang
that has wrought this miracle of perfect love."

They read more of the first days of country homemaking, of the little
makeshifts to piece out a slender income, and the statement wrung many
times from difficult experience that she who wrote was thankful things were
not too easy. "It was hardness that drew us closer."

Then more babies came, and the mother heart almost burst with thankfulness for each new soul to tend and shape. Many an entry was but a
hurried scrap of anecdote concerning childish doings, all important to the
mother who rejoiced in the clasping arms of "dear, dirty darlings" and who
yearned for more time to chronicle their growth and development.

"I am thankful I had a temper," was one confession. "The memory of that
helps to keep me patient now, when the children show traces of it."

Smiles and tears struggled for mastery upon the faces of those who listened to the tale of those hard, work-filled days.

Then came a long period wherein there had been no entry, after which, on a separate page, came this:

"It has taken many, many months for me to learn wherein lay the thankfulness in John's going from me. When they brought him home to me, and during the long, painful months that followed, it would have been impossible for me to write a line in this little book; but I have learned many lessons since that day. I know now that only through much suffering—by going down to the very depths of despair—do we learn to know the realities. They may be told to us, preached to us all our earthly lives, but until everything material has been swept from beneath our feet here and now on this earthly plane, until nothing is left for us to hold to, until all light has disappeared and we are completely enveloped in earthly darkness, and are groping for light, does the white light of the divine Spirit begin to illumine the darkness for us and grow in brilliancy as our understanding unfolds, until, ere we are conscious of it, our whole being is vibrant with its rays. And for this light, for this divine understanding, I am so truly thankful.

"The long, weary months of nursing, of witnessing the suffering of one's best beloved, the agony of helplessness at such a time, the failure of all financial affairs, John's end, and then the months of my own illness and complete prostration—it took all this, and more, to open my inner eyes; for until I had passed through the very gates of hell, I was not to know regeneration. But now I know, now I see, and never before did I live. All the dear years John and I were together, I was existing on the surface, with merely the intuition of holy things; but at last I have entered the holy of holies and am conscious of my oneness with the divine Spirit—oneness with the whole universe, animate and inanimate. Now for the first time do I feel my oneness with all humanity and know that all beings are my brothers, and for this, dear God, I am thankful; and thankful, too, that in those long months of his suffering, John, too, learned some of this. We both learned the patience, tolerance, and forbearance so necessary to the larger understanding and love. And now the material things of life sink into insignificance and appear as they are, petty and trivial by comparison, taking their rightful place in the scheme of things.

"I know now that nothing ever happens out of time or place; therefore, as it was given unto me to minister to my dear love when the need called, so has it been shown through him the way for a larger ministering by me to our brothers. Therefore, dear little book, I am very thankful and at last can feel that I have been privileged in much suffering, for only to those who are strong enough to overcome in the struggle is the trust granted."

The entries that followed, though only hurried snatches, told of work and sometimes of weariness of the flesh. But they were always filled with gladness of spirit, of pride in the growth and success of the little flock she shepherded alone, and never failing to recognize the bright spot on the ofttimes heavy horizon.

The voice of the reading sister whispered into the quiet of the dusky room. Then, after a moment's hush, came another, a man's it was, deep with the emotion of which his manhood was not ashamed.

"Let us finish it, brother and sisters. May I write it? Let us say just this, in simple words like hers:

"We, her children, are thankful, proudly thankful, for the brave heart that was, and still is, our mother."

Grandmother's Quilt

Annie E. S. Beard

It was a thing of rare beauty—made entirely from pieces of wedding dresses over the years—destined for the first granddaughter when she married. Then came the sound of cannons . . . and the quilt went to war.

Grandmother Barkin's cottage was in one of the side streets, in the outskirts of the city. A real, old-fashioned cottage it was even then, and that was more than 20 years ago. It was painted brown and had a gabled roof and latticed windows, with a large, covered porch over the doorway. The inside was divided into several small rooms, all filled with heavy, old-fashioned furniture, of which Grandmother was very proud.

The most curious thing in the house, however, and that which the old lady valued most, was a large quilt made by her own hands, and which was really a marvelous piece of workmanship. It consisted of a heterogeneous collection of pieces of any kind and every kind of material that ever by any possibility went into the composition of a woman's dress.

But the particular feature and crowning glory of the whole was that every single piece in it was actually a portion of somebody's wedding dress. High and low, rich and poor alike had contributed to this wonderful quilt, with fragments of silk, satin, and velvet and sections of chintz, brocade, muslin, and even calico. The center piece was of pale blue silk from Grandmother's own wedding dress, and on it was worked in rose-colored silk the words "Love One Another." Many an interesting story was connected with those once brightly colored pieces, some of them now fading from age. Time had often passed unheeded as Grandmother, with an eager audience gathered around her, told of people and things suggested by the various sections. Of necessity, from the character, it had been many years in process of manufacture, and consequently most of the weddings associated with it dated some scores of years back.

Having no daughter of her own, Grandmother had long ago destined this quilt for a gift to the granddaughter that was first married.

Mary Barkin, who, being an orphan, lived with her grandmother, was the only prospective claimant. As there was another married son, however, still living, who might at any time become father to another female Barkin, Mary's prospects of obtaining the quilt were liable at any day to suffer impairment. A remote contingency, certainly, but then stranger things have been known to happen prior to this stage of the world's history. Knowing these facts, Mary's friends were wont sometimes to say, laughingly, "Hurry up, Mary, you will lose the quilt!"

Mary Barkin, however, did not seem to avail herself of the friendly suggestions. She was now 25, and, although more than one opportunity had offered itself, still Mary remained unmarried, and Grandmother's quilt was still in its maker's possession. The truth was that she was one of those girls who are more particular as to the kind of a man they marry than about getting married. So night and morning Mary wended her way back and forth to the store where she was employed, content that both she and the quilt could wait until the rightness of things and people became manifest.

Nevertheless, the monotony of the said walks was greatly relieved when, occasionally, Leonard Wynn walked in the same direction and beguiled the time with pleasant talk. And when, in the fall of 1861, he told her one night that he had enlisted and was going to start immediately for the seat of the War Between the States, she suddenly realized that life was not as bright as it had seemed. Often during the lonely journeyings of that winter did she recall that last week and the farewell clasp of the hand, and then her cheeks would pale and a dread foreboding fill her heart lest, indeed, he should never come back again.

Amid all Cleveland's busy workers during wartimes there was none more earnest and untiring than Mary Barkin. Like many another woman, she worked the harder for all soldiers for the sake of the one she could not help.

The enthusiasm and patriotic spirit of the women of Cleveland reached through all ranks and infused themselves into the hearts of everyone, both young and old. Nor was Grandmother Barkin an exception. The only son left to her had gone to fight for his country, and henceforth nothing that she could give was too good for the soldiers. Freely and abundantly did she send supplies from her stores, but the crowning sacrifice was yet to be made.

Early one bright winter morning, a carriage rolled up to Grandmother's door, and from it stepped two eager young ladies. It did not take long to tell their mission. "What can you give us for the new hospital, Mrs. Barkin?" was the question, and to its answer Grandmother gave some moments of anxious thought. Then, slowly rising from her chair, the old lady left the room and proceeded to her store closet. Out from the chest that had treasured it so long she drew the beautiful quilt enveloped in its wrapping of white, and fragrant with the perfume of lavender.

Then, calling her granddaughter, she said: "Mary, they need quilts at the hospital. I have no others ready-made. Are you willing to give up this one?"

And Mary, to whom it now brought only suggestions of possible sorrow, gave glad assent, feeling that every gift added one more chance of comfort for her absent friend.

So Grandmother's quilt adorned one of the cots in the hospital and gave warmth and pleasure to many a poor sufferer, while serving a purpose far other than that to which originally destined by its owner.

The weeks passed by, and Christmas came at length—came, alas, to an earth not ready for its blessing of peace—to a country where good will to men was, even then, buried in the flood tides of the fierce hate and rancor of civil strife. O Christmas! Merry Christmas! Your chimes rang out merrily that year, for, to many an aching heart, they woke memories like funeral bells of vacant places, never to be filled again by the old familiar faces, while the burden of anxiety that lay on other hearts shut out all realization of Christmas merriment. Nevertheless, those who missed the joyousness of the season for themselves did their utmost to bring to the soldiers within reach all the pleasure possible.

On Christmas morning, Mary Barkin joined a group of ladies who were busily engaged in preparing comforts for the hospital inmates. If it was not within their power to restore limbs that were lost or maimed in the service of their country, or to bring back the glow of health and manly vigor to those wasted by disease, yet they could and did give unexpected pleasure by their bountiful supplies of good things. For a time, at least, the various woes were forgotten, or at most, the sense of them partly obliterated by the comfort and satisfaction of a good dinner. And in seeing the pleasure they gave, the hearts of the givers were lightened of their own burdens.

Mary Barkin even forgot for a time her anxiety as to the fate of Leonard Wynn, in watching the eager looks of the poor fellows, as she passed from cot to cot in the long rooms, distributing oranges and grapes. Then, having emptied her basket, she went to assist in feeding those who were unable to help themselves. Taking a plate of jelly in her hand, she stepped to the side of one of the cots, noticing as she did so that Grandmother's quilt—the treasured quilt so willingly given to the service of the country's defenders—lay upon the bed. The sight of it brought a rush of tender memories, filling her eyes with tears so that, for a moment, she did not see the face upon the pillow.

Then, with a start, she recognized Leonard Wynn. Was it indeed the same who had left her more than a year ago, strong and well, in all the blooming vigor of young manhood, now stretched upon this bed of pain, with white wan face and large sunken eyes? Yes, there was no doubt about it, for the first words she heard were these: "Ah, Mary, I have been watching and waiting for you."

"Why did you not call me or send a message for me?" she asked.

"I felt sure you would come sometime," he answered. "The sight of this," touching the quilt, "made me feel sure of it."

"It is not often I get here, only sometimes on Sunday to read to the patients and write letters for them."

"Will you come next Sunday?" he asked wistfully.

"Yes, if you wish it."

He was not strong enough to talk much, and, seeing this, Mary insisted on his silence. As she fed him with the jelly she had brought, she talked busily of all the news she thought he would care to hear. Then, promising to come again on Sunday, she went away.

Once more, in the presence of this old friend, she realized that absence had done for her what, in all probability, it had failed to do for him—giving a visionary significance to the friendship of the past and peopling the future with dreams that had no foundation in fact. For the present, the gladness of seeing him again overpowered the bitterness of this conviction. Rejoicing in the knowledge that war, with all its terrors, had not yet had power to rob her of this friend, she ignored, for the time being, all consciousness of that which might have been—a state of feeling that speedily deserted her, however, when, after a few weeks, he rejoined his regiment.

On her first visit to the hospital after his departure, Mary noticed that her grandmother's quilt had vanished from its accustomed place. Somewhat surprised, she asked one of the nurses one day what had become of it.

"That pretty quilt, ma'am, with the motto on it? That was taken away by one of the boys whose bed it covered during his stay here. He asked the ladies if he might have it, and sent another in place of it. He said it was made by an old friend of his. This is the one he sent, ma'am." The nurse showed Mary a new quilt covered in scarlet merino, which lay on the bed.

And so the Christmas of 1862 had come and gone—come, bringing to Mary Barkin a joyous surprise, a lifting of the burden of anxiety, some happy days spent in the joy of a renewed friendship, given back, as it were, from the very jaws of death; and gone, taking a hope dearer than life itself—and Grandmother's quilt, full of tender memories.

So the days and months, and even a year, sped on, bringing victory and defeat, joy and sorrow, into the hearts and lives of thousands. Once again Christmas dawned upon the earth, and though the wings of the dove of peace were not yet outspread over the land, the mourning hearts were yet more numerous than a year before, yet the hope of final victory grew stronger day by day. Many hearts and homes were preparing joyful welcomes for the boys in blue who were coming home on veteran furlough. The festivities held in their honor were numerous, and during their stay the city celebrated.

Mary Barkin was as busy as ever during those days, first serving on one committee of arrangements and then on another. Time flew by and she had small leisure for rest or thought. Personally, she was not interested in the daily arrivals from the seat of war, for Leonard, she knew, did not belong to either of the regiments expected in Cleveland. Tired out, she stood, at the close of the second day's proceedings, leaning wearily against a pile of boxes in the passageway leading from the rooms of the Sanitary Commission. It was fast growing dark, and for a few minutes she closed her eyes to snatch, if possible, a brief interval of much needed repose.

Was she dreaming, or was that really Leonard Wynn's voice? How long had she been asleep, and what was this that lay under her head? She was positive nothing had been there when she shut her eyes. The rest she was so enjoying was so delightful that she was in no hurry to disturb it, but curiosity compelled her to raise her head sufficiently to examine her novel pillow.

One glance sufficed to reveal Grandmother's quilt. How did it get there?

The thought roused her at once, and she strove to rise, but before she could do so, two strong arms imprisoned her, and looking into the face bent above her, her eyes met those of Leonard Wynn.

"I've come for my Christmas gift, Mary," he said, and drawing the quilt toward himself with one hand, he pointed to the inscription, "Love One Another," in its center. "I wanted it a year ago, but decided that I would not ask you to take, in return, a maimed, sick soldier. I kept the quilt in memory of you. See, I fixed it so that it should come back to you if anything happened to me," and he showed her a label fastened securely to the quilt: "To be sent to Miss Mary Barkin, Cleveland, Ohio."

Then he told her how one cold winter's day, it had saved his life. While sitting close to the fire, by which he and some comrades were trying to warm themselves and to cook some potatoes, a stray ball from the enemy's batteries came whistling through the air, taking a straight course toward him. Being chilled through by protracted exposure to the inclemency of the weather, he had wrapped the quilt around himself in double folds in the old shirt with which he always kept it covered. The ball struck him, but in consequence of the thickness of the quilt, got no further than his coat. The holes that marked its passage through the quilt remained as tokens of its protective qualities.

So Grandmother's quilt went back to its original owner, and Mary's right to it as a wedding gift was in fair way established.

Yet another year went by and still another Christmas dawned upon a country racked by civil war. It brought no relief to the sick and wounded that filled the hospitals to overflowing.

Once again, among the number was found Leonard Wynn. Fighting days were over for him, for, this time, the left arm was gone. Mary, of course, was his constant attendant, and one of her first acts was to fetch Grandmother's quilt and lay it over his cot. And whenever he would try to charge Mary to give him up and not sacrifice herself to a one-armed man, she would only point to the old inscription. She would tell him that as long as that command remained, she proposed to obey its dictates as unflinchingly as he had done those of his country, adding, "You forget, Len, that I am proud to be the wife of a man who bears such convincing proof of his loyalty and self-sacrifice."

The Red-Haired Doll

Ella Enslow, with Alvin F. Harlow

The little mountain girl had only one request—but it was nearly impossible to fulfill.

Henry Cavin is one of the kindliest, most upright men in Shady Cove—true salt of the earth—but distressingly poor. Like most of the others, his family is too large. Two years ago last Christmas, when Cavin's wife—but first let me tell something about our Christmases.

When I came into the Cove, the notion of Christmas as a celebration of Christ's birthday had almost faded from public consciousness. The Christmas tree, a German tradition first seen in New York City less than a century ago, was unknown among our people. Their English-Scotch-Irish ancestors had already settled in the mountains at that time and had never since been in contact with urban customs.

Santa Claus, another Germanic myth, they had heard of and seen pictured, but they had never witnessed an impersonation of the genial saint. Gift-giving had become an obsolete custom among a people too poor to give.

Christmas, in fact, had been established as a day on which to eat a little more than usual, to fire off guns at sunrise and—for men and youths—to get drunk. Even men who drank little or none at other times drank on Christmas. Seemingly, it was something that you just had to do then, in order to avoid being classed as eccentric.

Hoping that I might in some degree be able to change this conception, I began staging in the schoolhouse Christmas celebrations such as town folk are familiar with, but which were great novelties to our people. Our best singers were taught carols, and the Christmas spirit was inculcated through the children.

On my second Christmas, we gave a rather elaborate affair. I had crossed all my friends off my gift list so that I might give to Shady Cove; and I begged my friends to give, not to me, but money and goods for my people. I wrote to acquaintances in the North for help; I begged from the merchants in Teviston. The Depression was beginning to pinch us pretty hard by that Christmas of 1931, and there were children starting the winter with no shoes. I succeeded in getting a few pairs and gave these and other practical things to widows and widows' children.

I had borrowed costumes from the schools and churches in the larger towns of the county and contrived a few more out of cheap materials. For our entertainment, we had carols, drills, three short playlets, and a tableau representing the birth of Jesus, with older pupils impersonating the Holy Family, the Wise Men, and the shepherds, and the Star of Bethlehem glittering rather gaudily in the background. It was crude and amateurish, of course, but to the proud parents who saw their children actually appearing as public entertainers, singing, acting, putting on a dramatic program, it was perfect. The tableau in the stable at Bethlehem, with which we closed the evening, actually brought tears to some leathery masculine cheeks where tears had not been seen in years.

For our next Christmas, we had a tree, more carols and skits, and a Santa Claus. There were the usual little treats of candy and oranges for everybody at these affairs—paid for out of the teachers' slender salaries, of course—and there was a present for every woman in the Cove: curtains, aprons, towels, table scarfs, and other things, all made of carefully washed flour and grain sacks by my girls in the afternoon sewing classes, and all with bits of colored embroidery on them.

A heavy snowstorm—an unusual event for our part of the country—came just before our celebration, so that it was like the Christmas of the legends. Drifts were blown almost up to cabin roofs in some places, the creek was ice-locked, and the road was deep in snow. But nothing could stop these people from coming to the party. They came on foot, on horseback, and in wagons, many carrying barefoot children wrapped in tattered blankets or quilts. Even the elders came, many with their feet wrapped in gunnysacks; some very old folks hobbled in with canes or long staves. Everyone's pleasure in the affair was hearty and satisfying.

But alas, there were a few who just had to miss the party. Henry Cavin's eldest boy, Charlie, aged 13, couldn't come because he hadn't even a fragment of a shoe and nothing that he could substitute so that he might walk through the snow. Our party was to be on Wednesday evening, four days before Christmas. On the Friday before, Cavin came to my house and asked if there wasn't some sort of work he could do, just any kind of work, to earn a pair of shoes for Charlie.

Cavin was one of the most willing of those who worked to pay for relief given them. His farm was so poor, and he could find so little to do to bring him any real cash, that much of his time was spent thus in warding off charity. He was touchingly grateful for the aid frequently extended to his family, and bobbed up at my house every little while, asking whether there wasn't something more he could do for aid already given; he didn't yet feel that it had been fully paid for.

I knew of no secondhand shoes that could be found for Charlie, so my sister and I drove to Teviston and bought a pair for him, then skirmished around and found some sort of job whereby the father might pay for them. I knew that Mrs. Cavin was expecting another baby at any moment; and sure enough, at 2:00 the next morning her husband woke me and told me his wife was in convulsions. He had walked the three miles from home to Dawyer to phone for a doctor and could get none to come, so of course he fell back on me. Whether he could ever pay the bill, if I assumed it, was a grave question; but we just couldn't let that mother die and leave several little children orphans, so I started calling physicians. I tried those in Teviston, Gibbsville, Grimshaw, and Saylesboro, 12 miles to the south of us. There was an influenza epidemic on then, and one doctor himself was ill; others were out on cases or were so worn out that they wouldn't come.

Finally, when I had called the seventh man, I won a promise to attend; but it was long afterward—after dawn, in fact—when he arrived, and by that time the baby had been born three hours since and was lying in a chair, wrapped in a tattered fragment of quilt (they had nothing else in which to clothe it), and the mother was still in convulsions. The bed was almost bare of coverings, but my mother walked all the way to the cabin that morning, carrying a pair of sheets, a pillowcase, towels, and cloths. Meanwhile, I was begging Miss Merrion for some baby clothes, and that kind soul succeeded in finding them for me. In the end, we saved both mother and child—which may or may not have been fortunate for either. Human beings, old or young, born and reared under such conditions, seem as tough as the greenbriers that creep over our hillsides.

Several months later, I came home from the funeral service of a former pupil one morning and found my mother anxiously awaiting me.

"One of Henry Cavin's children has just brought word," she told me, "that his little girl 'Melia's hand has been cut off"—a child seven years old—"and they want you to come. They must have a doctor, too."

That, of course, was the major reason why poor Cavin had sent for me. They not only wanted Teacher there to comfort them, but they wanted Teacher to stand sponsor for them financially. I called up Dyatt and assumed the bill, urging him, as usual, to make it as easy for us as he could—which the good old scout would have done anyhow, without my asking him. He rushed down from Gibbsville; I jumped into his car and we went as far as we could down the Cove, then walked another mile to the Cavin home. I wish I could convey on this page even a bare outline of the picture of poverty, woe, and suffering that greeted us when we entered the cabin.

Cavin himself had been absent, working on some little job he had been able to procure, and four of his children had been helpfully trying, in his absence, to add to the stock of firewood. Two of the girls were working on a log with a crosscut saw, while a small boy and 'Melia were helping. Exactly how it happened it is hard to say; but with edged tools in the hands of children anything is likely to occur. 'Melia was trying to roll away a block that had just been sawed off when the boy made a stroke at the log with an ax. Her first and second fingers were almost entirely severed and the third and fourth were frightfully cut, nearer to the tips.

The one-room plank cabin in which they lived—not nearly so warm as a log house—was a scene of abject poverty. Only one bed and two chairs for a father, mother, and flock of children. A fireplace for heating and cooking, a long box (reminding me of a coffin) for general storage, and an auxiliary seat. One of the chairs was a rocker; but its right arm and rocker were missing, and to replace the rocker that side of the chair had been suspended by a wire from the ceiling.

In this chair, 'Melia was sitting when we arrived, with her father and mother by turns pathetically trying to hold the remains of her fingers together. In the two hours and more that had dragged by since the accident, she had screamed and wept with pain until she was hoarse. Her dress was soaked with blood, as were her parents' hands and clothing and the chair—in fact, the whole room was in shambles. Some of the other children were crying, too; the boy who had struck the ghastly blow was particularly grief-stricken. The father's hands shook, and perspiration streamed down his face, which was almost as deeply contorted with agony as his little child's.

Dr. Dyatt rushed in, gave one glance at the injured hand, dropped his bag, threw off his coat, turned up his shirtsleeves, and said briskly, "Now, just let me have a pan of water to wash my hands in."

Mrs. Cavin's gaze at him, though weary and dulled by suffering, yet had something of astonishment and reproach in it. "We hain't got no washpan, Doctor," she told him.

"Oh, it doesn't matter; a stewpan—any kind of pan'll do."

The poor woman's eyes moved dazedly about the little room as if trying to remember something she knew did not exist. The truth of the matter was that they had not a tin or enameled pan or kettle of any sort. The only cooking vessels they owned were a skillet and an iron pot in which beans had been cooked that day, and which still stood in the dead ashes of the fireplace with a remnant of the beans in it, forgotten in the great trouble that had come upon the household. A lard pail held a gallon or so of water brought from a distant spring, but some of that water must be saved for other purposes.

Finally, they remembered Cavin's dinner bucket, in which he had carried his lunch when he was working in the mines at Coaldale two years and more ago. We poured a little water into that, and the doctor washed his hands—and then there was no towel! A rag was all that the harassed housewife could produce, and it was none too clean. One could have wept over such dire poverty if it would have done any good.

Meanwhile, I had been starting a fire on the hearth, and when the doctor was done with the dinner bucket, I put a little water in it to heat. Then the trouble began. Maddened by torture and fear, 'Melia struggled with super-childish strength against us, and the parents were too near collapse, too horrified by the sight of the doctor's instruments, to aid us. I was trying to hold down her legs and the uninjured arm; Dr. Dyatt, with one hand clutched about her wrist while she fought to free it, had only the other hand to work with. After two or three minutes of this, our nerves were beginning to be frayed—at least I know mine were.

"Dr. Dyatt," I said, "let's stop a moment. We aren't getting anywhere, and we won't if we keep on this way. Let me talk to 'Melia a bit."

He paused, and I looked into 'Melia's eyes, trying to be as hypnotic and soothing as I could. "Now, listen, honey," I said. "Dr. Dyatt has to hurt you to make your hand well. He's going to hurt you a lot more yet, but if you don't be quiet and help us, your hand won't get well, and maybe you won't have any fingers at all. Now, just think for a moment; think what you'd like to have best of anything in the world, and then if you'll be very, very still and let Dr. Dyatt tend to your hand, I'll get it for you."

She didn't have to ponder that long. Still half-sobbing, she gasped, "Oh, Miss Enslow, I'd like to have a doll!"

"You shall have it," I promised. I knew that when she got it, it would be the only real doll in Shady Cove. In our sewing classes, we had dressed up some bottles and tin cans and rude images of wood, but no one had ever possessed a doll such as one saw in the stores when one went to town.

With her right hand, 'Melia clutched the wire that held up that side of the chair and, still whimpering a little, held up her left to the doctor. To own a doll, she was willing to go through hell.

Dr. Dyatt had just begun again to fit one of the mutilated fingers back into place as nearly as it could be done, when in a half-whisper, so dreadful was her pain, she made one further request—not a stipulation, but a petition in all humility: "Miss Enslow—can't the doll have red hair?"

"I'll try, darling," said I. "If they make them with red hair, you shall have one."

That was enough. With her good hand clutching the wire with a death-like grip, she sat with eyes closed most of the time while tears stole out from under the lids, sweat ran down her face, and blood appeared on her lower lip where her teeth were biting it. Dr. Dyatt trimmed away shreds of flesh, sewed the fingers back in place, and put the hand in splint bandages. Then we hurried back to his car.

At home, I ran out my own little bus, and Sister Jessie and I rushed up to Teviston to find a doll. But the offerings there were poor. Apparently, Teviston really stocks up on dolls only around Christmastime. A few minutes sufficed to show that the ones on hand in the two or three stores that handled them were few in number, and none of them had red hair.

"Well, we'll have to try Southmont," I said. "I can't fail 'Melia when she's been such a little heroine."

We hopped into the car, went back past Dawyer lickety-split, and 40 miles farther on to Southmont, the only real city in our area. Hastily parking my bus at a curb, we began our high-pressure search.

Dolls were numerous, but none with red hair. At each place, I would plead, "But haven't you more in your stockroom? I must have one with red hair."

Section managers and floor men were somewhat annoyed by my persistence, but when I told them why I wanted a particular doll, that put a new face on the matter, and they dug into their reserve stock with a will. But store after store failed us. "I don't believe they make 'em with red hair," said more than one manager. But we pressed on.

Luckily, some of the stores there keep open until 6:00. And finally, just a few minutes before closing time, down in a basement stockroom—eureka!—there she was: a big, beautiful doll with auburn-red tresses, one of the sort that go to sleep when you lay them down.

"I'll take it!" I exclaimed, and the man put the lid on the box. Then sober sense returned to me.

"Wait a moment," I said. "What's the price?"

"Five dollars and 98 cents," he replied.

Five dollars and 98 cents! I stood appalled. That's a lot of money to a person drawing only 50 dollars a month salary and putting most of it back into her business. The salesman waited, looking at me inquiringly. It was only a price tag to him—"$5.98"—but to me it was six dollars. Through my mind flitted thoughts of what I could do with six dollars for my school and my people; six dollars' worth of schoolbooks, six dollars on our piano, six dollars' worth of boys' overalls, girls' cheap print dresses, cod liver oil—and here I was thinking of spending it all on a doll!

"I've got to have it," I murmured weakly.

"Let's take it," said Jessie. "I'll pay half of it." And so the thing was settled. With the precious cargo carefully stowed on the rear seat, we dashed back to the hills, stopping at my home only a moment to let my family know what I was doing, then rushing down into the Cove. I had promised to deliver the doll before I slept, and deliver it I must!

Darkness had fallen long before we arrived, and we had to stumble that last mile over the rough trail by starlight. Nightfall is bedtime for such folk as these, for their days are hard and they cannot afford oil for lamplight; but I knew that the Cavins would be up and waiting for me. I try never to fail in a promise to my people if it is humanly possible to keep it. I knew that if Cavin, one of the most faithful of them all, had made such a promise to me, he would have fulfilled it even though he had to do it on hands and knees at midnight.

Sure enough, when we came in sight of the cabin we saw a faint flicker of fire-light through its one window. With the exception of two or three of the younger children who hadn't been able to stand the strain, they were all still awake, listening eagerly for my footsteps, conjecturing what the doll would be like.

But evidently even their wildest dreams had never approached the reality of the beautiful vision that burst upon them when I laid the box down before the fire, took the lid off, and tilted it slightly so that the light would fall upon the doll. One chorused gasp of amazement and admiration arose; they were momentarily stricken dumb by the splendor of the gift. If I had laid the crown jewels of England down in their midst, they would have been but little more dazzled.

"And it's got red hair," whispered 'Melia.

She will never have a good hand again, the poor dear. Dr. Dyatt did what he could under the circumstances, and by a miracle of skill and good luck got the wounds healed without infection. But the first two fingers are stiff, and the third and fourth are none too good. Still, to most people, those two fingers are only minor aids anyhow. It was her left hand that received the blow, but the curiously unfortunate circumstance was that 'Melia was born left-handed, and now she has had to learn to do things with her right.

But that doll! It was the chief wonder of Shady Cove. Other girls came for miles to see it, and as a special favor they were sometimes permitted to hold the box in their arms. For although 'Melia has owned the doll for two years as this is written, it has never been taken out of the box in which it came. It is too fine, too precious. No one is even allowed to touch it—no one, that is, save 'Melia herself, its "mother," and she ventures to touch its painted face, its hair, its frilly dress, reverently, only with her fingertips. Unless some accident happens to it, I fancy she will still have that doll when she reaches womanhood. But oh, the pathetic yearning, the heartburning among other little girls as they look at it!

"Miss Enslow," said one of them to me earnestly, "if I could have a doll like that, I'd be willing to have my hand cut off."

"Meditation" in a Minor Key

Joseph Leininger Wheeler

Can a person's life be dominated by a single piece of music? Two people's lives?

"Eight minutes until curtain time, Mr. Devereaux."

"How's it looking?"

"Full house. No. *More* than full house—they're already turning away those who'll accept Standing Room Only tickets."

"Frankly, I'm a bit surprised, Mr. Schobel. My last concert here was not much of a success."

"I remember, sir. The house was barely a third full."

"Hmm. I wonder . . . uh . . . what do you suppose has made the difference?"

"Well, for one thing, sir, it's your first-ever Christmas concert. . . . For another, people are regaining interest—that Deutsche Gramophone recording has all Europe talking. But pardon me, sir. I'd better let you get ready. Good luck, sir."

And he was gone.

No question about it, he mused as he bowed to acknowledge the applause, the venerable Opera House was indeed full. As always, his eyes scanned the sea of faces as he vainly searched for the one who never came—had not in 10 long years. He had so hoped tonight would be different. That package . . . it hadn't done the job after all.

Ten years ago tonight, it was. Right here in Old Vienna. It was to have been the happiest Christmas Eve in his life: Was Ginevra not to become his bride the next day?

What a fairy tale courtship that had been. It had all started at the Salzburg Music Festival, where he was the center of attention—not only of the city but of the world. Had he not stunned concert goers by his incredible coup: the first pianist to ever win grand piano's Triple Crown: the Van Cliburn, the Queen Elizabeth, and the Tchaikovsky competitions?

Fame had built steadily for him as one after another of the great prizes had fallen to him. Now, as reporters, interviewers, and cameramen followed his every move, he grew drunk on the wine of adulation.

It had happened as he leaned over the parapet of Salzburg Castle, watching the morning sun gild the rooftops of the city below. He had risen early in order to hike up the hill to the castle and watch the sunrise. A cool alpine breeze ruffled the trees just above, but it also displaced a few strands of raven black hair only a few feet to his left. Their glances met—and they both glanced away, only to blush as they glanced back. She was the most beautiful girl he had ever seen. But beautiful in more than mere appearance: beautiful in poise and grace as well. Later, he would gradually discover her beauty of soul.

With uncharacteristic shyness, he introduced himself to her. And then she withdrew in confusion as she tied the name to the cover stories. Disarming her with a smile, he quickly changed the subject: What was *she* doing in Salzburg?

As it turned out, she was in Europe for a summer-long study tour—and how his heart leaped when she admitted that her study group was staying in Salzburg the entire week. He made the most of it: Before her bus had moved on he had pried from her not very reluctant fingers a copy of the tour itinerary.

And like Jean Valjean's inexorable nemesis, Javert, he pursued her all over Europe, driving his concert manager into towering rages. Had he forgotten that there was the long and arduous fall schedule to prepare for? Had he forgotten the time it took to memorize a new repertoire? . . . No, he hadn't forgotten: The truth of the matter was that his priorities had suddenly changed. Every midweek, in around-the-clock marathons, he'd given his practicing its due— then he'd escape in order to be with Ginevra for the weekend.

They were instant soul mates: They both loved the mountains and the sea, dawn and dusk, Tolstoy and Twain, snow and sand, hiking and skiing, gothic cathedrals and medieval castles, sidewalk cafés and old bookstores. But they were not clones. In art, she loved Georges de la Tour and Caravaggio, whereas his patron saints were Durer and Hieronymus Bosch. In music, he preferred Mozart and Prokofiev, whereas she reveled in Chopin and Liszt.

He knew the day he met her that, for him, there would never be another woman. He was that rarity: a man who out of the whole world will choose but one—and if that one be denied him . . .

But he wasn't denied. It was on the last day of her stay, just hours before she boarded her plane for home, that he asked her to climb with him the zigzagging inner staircases of the bell tower of Votivkirche, that great neo-gothic cathedral of Vienna, paling in comparison only with its legendary ancestor, St. Stephens.

Far up in the tower, breathing hard for more than one reason, his voice shook as he took both her hands captive . . . and looked through her honest eyes into her heart—his, he knew, even without asking. She never actually said yes, for the adorable curl of her lips, coupled with the candlelit road to heaven in her eyes, was her undoing.

The rapture that followed comes only once in a lifetime, when it comes at all.

. . . Then the scene changed . . . and he stiffened as if receiving a mortal blow . . . for but four months later, in that self-same bell tower, his world had come to an end. That terrible, terrible night when his nuptial dreams were slain by a violin.

Ginevra drew her heavy coat tighter around her as the airport limousine disappeared into the night. Inside the Opera House she made her way to the ticket counter to pick up her pre-reserved ticket.

From the other side of the doors she heard Bach's "Italian Concerto" being reborn. . . . She listened intently. She had not been mistaken after all; a change *had* taken place.

Leaning against a pillar, she let the distant notes wash over her while she took the scroll of her life and unrolled a third of it. How vividly she remembered that memorable fall. Michael's letters came as regularly as night following day: long letters most of the time, short messages when his hectic schedule precluded more. Her pattern was unvarying. She would walk up the mountain road to the mailbox, out of the day's mail search for that precious envelope, then carry it unopened on top of the rest back to the chalet, perched high on a promontory point 1,600 feet above the Denver plain. Then she'd walk out onto the upper deck and seat herself. Off to her right were the Flatirons massed above the city of Boulder, front-center below was the skyline of Denver—at night a fairyland of twinkling lights —and to the left the mountains stair-stepped up to 14,255-foot Longs Peak and Rocky Mountain National Park. Then she'd listen for the pines—oh! those heavenly pines! They would be soughing their haunting song . . . and *then* she would open his letter.

So full of romance were her starlit eyes that weeks passed before she realized there was a hairline crack in her heart—and Michael was the cause of it. She hadn't realized it during that idyllic summer as the two of them had spent so much time exploring gothic cathedrals, gazing transfixed as light transformed stained glass into heart-stopping glory, sitting on transepts as organists opened their stops and called on their pipes to dare the red zone of reverberating sound.

She finally, in a long letter, asked him point-blank whether or not he believed in God. His response was a masterpiece of subterfuge and fence-straddling, for well he knew how central the Lord was to her. . . . As women have ever since the dawn of time, she rationalized that if he just loved *her* enough—and surely he *did*—then of course he would come to love God as much as she.

So it was that she put her reservations and premonitions aside, and deflected her parents' concerns in that respect as well. Michael had decided he wanted to be married in the same cathedral where he had proposed to her—and as it was large enough to accommodate family as well as key figures of the music world, she had reluctantly acquiesced. Personally, she would have much rather been married in the small Boulder church high up on Mapleton Avenue. A Christmas wedding there, in the church she so loved . . . but it was not to be.

Deciding to make the best of it, she and her family drove down the mountain, took the freeway to Stapleton Airport, boarded the plane, and found their seats. As the big United jet roared off the runway, she looked out the window at Denver and her beloved Colorado receding below her. She wondered: Could Michael's European world ever really take its place?

It was cold that memorable Christmas Eve, and the snow lay several feet deep on Viennese streets. Ginevra, ever the romantic, shyly asked Michael if he would make a special pilgrimage with her.

"Where to?" queried Michael. "It's mighty cold outside."

"The bell tower of Votivkirche."

He grinned that boyish grin she loved. "I really *am* marrying a sentimentalist, aren't I? . . . Oh, well," he complained good-naturedly, "I guess I'd better get used to it. Let's find our coats."

An unearthly quiet came over the great city as they once again climbed the winding staircases of Votivkirche. She caught her breath at the beauty of it all when they at last reached their eyrie and looked down at the frosted rooftops and streets below. Michael, however, much preferred the vision she represented, in her flame-colored dress and sable coat.

Then it was . . . faintly and far away . . . that they heard it. They never did trace its origin exactly; it might have wafted its way up the tower from below, or it might have come from an apartment across the way. Ordinarily, in the cacophony of the city, they could not possibly have heard it, but tonight, with snow deadening the street sounds, they could distinctly pick up every note. Whoever the violinist was . . . was a master.

Ginevra listened, transfixed. Michael, noting her tear-stained cheeks, shattered the moment with an ill-timed laugh. "Why, you old crybaby . . . it's nothing but a song! . . . I've heard it somewhere before. . . . I don't remember who wrote it, but it's certainly nothing to cry over."

He checked as he saw her recoil as if he had slashed her face with a whip. Her face blanched, and she struggled for control. After a long pause, she said in a toneless voice: "It is not a song . . . it is 'Meditation' by Massenet."

"Well, that's fine with me," quipped Michael. "I'll just meditate about *you.*"

There was a long silence, and now, quite ill at ease, he shuffled his feet and tried to pass it all off as a joke.

But in that, he failed abysmally. "You . . . you don't hear it at all," she cried. "You just don't. . . . I never hear that melody without tears . . . or without soaring to heaven on the notes. Massenet had to have been a Christian! . . . . And, furthermore, whoever plays it like we just heard it played has to be a Christian too!"

"Oh, come now, Ginevra . . . aren't you getting carried away by a simple little ditty? *Anyone* who really knows how to play the violin could play it just as well. . . *I* certainly could—and I don't even believe in . . . in God." He stopped, vainly trying to slam his lips on the words in time, but perversely they slipped out of their own accord.

Deep within the citadel of her innermost being, Ginevra felt her heart shudder as if seized by two powerful opposing forces. Where the hairline split in her heart once was, there was an awful crack, and a yawning fault took its place.

The look of agony on her face brought him to his senses at last—but it was too late. She looked at him with glaciered cheeks and with eyes so frozen that he could barely discern the tiny flickering that had, only moments ago, almost overpowered him with the glow of a thousand love-lit candles.

She turned, slipped something that had once been on her finger into his coat pocket, and was gone. So quickly was the act done that at first he failed to realize she was no longer there. Then he called after her and ran blindly down the stairs. Ginevra, however, with the instinct of a wounded animal, found an unlocked stairwell door and hid inside until he had raced down the tower and into the street. Much later, she silently made her way out into a world made glad by midnight bells. But there was no Christmas gladness in her heart.

She determined never to see him again. Neither his calls nor his letters nor his telegrams would she answer; writing him only once: "Please do not EVER try to contact me in any way again."

And he—his pride in shreds—never had.

Never would he forget that awful Christmas when—alone—he had to face the several thousand wedding guests and the importunate press with the news that it was all off. No, he could give them no reasons—and then he had fled.

Since he had planned on an extended honeymoon, he had no more concerts scheduled until the next fall. That winter and spring he spent much time in solitude, moping and feeling sorry for himself. By late spring, he was stir-crazy, so he fled to the South Pacific, to Asia, to Africa, to South America—anywhere to get away from himself and his memories.

Somehow, by midsummer, he began to regain control; he returned to Europe and quickly mastered his fall repertoire. That fall, most of his reviews were of the rave variety, for he dazzled with his virtuosity and technique.

For several years, his successes continued, and audiences filled concert halls wherever he performed. But there came a day when that was no longer true, when he realized that most dreaded of performing-world truths: that he had peaked. Here he was, his career hardly begun, and his star was already setting. But why?

Reviewers and concertgoers alike tried vainly to diagnose the ailment and prescribe medicinal cures, but nothing worked. More and more the tenor of the reviews began to sound like the following:

> How sad it is that Devereaux—once thought to be the rising star of our age, the worthy successor to Horowitz—has been revealed as but human clay after all. It is as if he represents a case of arrested development. Normally, as a pianist lives and ages, the roots sink deeper and the storm-battered trunk and branches develop seasoning and rugged strength. Not so with Devereaux. It's as if all growth ceased some time ago. No one can match him where it comes to razzle-dazzle and special effects . . . but one gets a bit tired of these when there is no offsetting depth.

Like a baseball slugger in a prolonged batting slump, Michael tried everything. He dabbled in every philosophy or mysticism he came across. Like a drunken bee, he reeled from hive to hive without any real sense of direction.

And "Meditation" had gradually become an obsession with him; he just couldn't seem to get it out of his consciousness. He determined to prove to her that you didn't have to be religious in order to play it well. But as much as he tried, as much as he applied his vaunted techniques and interpretive virtuosity to it . . . it yet remained as flat, stale, and unmoving as three-hour-old coffee.

He even went to the trouble of researching the tune's origins, feeling confident that it, like much concert music, would have no religious connections whatsoever. In his research, he discovered that "Meditation" came from Massenet's opera *Thais,* which he knew had to do with a dissolute courtesan. Aha! He had her! But then, he dug deeper and discovered, to his chagrin, that although it was true that Thais had a dissolute sexual past, as was true with Mary Magdalene, she was redeemed—and "Meditation" represents the intermezzo bridge between the pagan past of the first two acts and the oneness with God in the third act.

So he had to acknowledge defeat here too.

As for Ginevra, she was never far from his thoughts. But not once would his pride permit him to ask anyone about her, her career, or whether or not she had ever married.

He just existed, measuring his life by concerts and hotel rooms.

Ginevra, too, after the long numbness and shock had at last weathered into a reluctant peace, belatedly realized that life had to go on. But just what should she do with her life?

It was during a freak spring blizzard that the answer came. She had been sitting in the conversation pit of the three-story-high massive moss rock fireplace, gazing dreamily into the fire . . . when suddenly, the mood came upon her to write. She reached for a piece of paper, picked up her Pilot pen, and began a poem about pain, disillusion, and heartbreak. The next day, she mailed it off to a magazine. Not long after, it was published.

She decided to do graduate work in the humanities and in education. She completed, along the way, a master's, and later a Ph.D., becoming in the process the world's foremost authority on the life and times of a woman writer of the American heartland. She also continued, as her busy schedule permitted, to write poems, essays, short stories, inspirational literature, and longer works of fiction.

So it was that Ginevra became a teacher of writing, of literature—and life. Each class was a microcosm of life itself; in each class were souls crying out to be ministered to, to be appreciated, to be loved.

Because of her charm, vivacity, and sense of humor, she became ever more popular and beloved with the passing of the years. She attracted suitors like children to a toy store—yet, though some of these friendships got to the threshold of love, none of them got any further. It was as if not one of them could match what she had left behind in Vienna.

The good Lord saw her through. He shored up her frailties and helped to mend the brokenness.

Meanwhile, she did find time to keep up with Michael's life and career. In doing so, she bought all his recordings, playing them often. Yet, she was vaguely dissatisfied; she too noted the lack of growth—and wondered.

One balmy day in late November during the seventh year after the breakup, as she was walking down the ridge to her home, she stopped to listen to her two favorite sounds: the cascading creek cavorting its way down to the Front Range plain, and the sibilant whispering of the pines. Leaning against a large rock, she looked up at that incredibly blue sky of the Colorado high country.

As always, her thoughts refused to stay in their neat little cages. She had tried all kinds of locks during those seven years, but not one of them worked. And now, when she had thought them safely locked in, here came all her truant thoughts, bounding up to her like a rag-tag litter of exuberant puppies, overjoyed at finding her hiding place.

And every last one of the little mutts was yelping Michael's name.

What would he be doing this Christmas? It bothered her—had bothered her for almost seven years now—that her own judge had refused to acquit her for her Michael-related words and actions. Periodically, during these years, she had submitted her case to the judge in the courthouse of her mind; every last time, after listening to the evidence, the judge had looked at her stern-faced. She would bang the gavel on the judicial bench and intone severely: "Insufficient evidence on which to absolve you. . . . Next case?"

She couldn't get out of her head an article she had read several months before—an article about Michael Devereaux. The writer, who had interviewed her subject in depth, had done her homework well. The individual revealed in the character sketch was both the Michael Ginevra knew and a Michael she would rather not know. The interviewer pointed out that Michael was a rather bitter man for one so young in years. So skittish had the interviewee been, whenever approached on the subject of women in his life, that the writer postulated that somewhere along the way Devereaux had been terribly hurt by someone he loved deeply. . . . Ginevra winced. The writer concluded her character portrait with a disturbing synthesis: "Devereaux, his concert career floundering, appears to be searching for answers. But he's not looking in the direction of God. Like many, if not most, Europeans of our time, he appears to be almost totally secular; thus he has nowhere but within himself from which to draw strength and inspiration. Sadly, his inner wells appear to retain only shallow reservoirs from which to draw. . . . A pity."

A nagging thought returned to tug at her heartstrings: What had she done—what had she ever done—to show Michael a better way? . . . "But," she retorted, "I don't want him to become a Christian just for me!"

But this time that oft-used cop-out didn't suffice; she kept seeing that stern-faced judge within. In the long, long silence that followed was born a plan of action. If it worked, if he responded as she hoped he might . . . sooner or later . . . she would *know!* For inescapably, the secret would "out" through his music.

She determined to implement her plan of action that very day.

Several weeks after Ginevra's decision, Michael had returned to his hotel after a concert, a particularly unsatisfactory one—and it seemed these days that there were more and more of this kind. Even the crowd had been smaller than any he could remember in years. He was convinced that his career and life were both failures—and that there was little reason to remain living. He went to bed and vainly tried to sleep. After an hour or two of thrashing around, he got up, turned on the light, and looked for the last packet of mail forwarded to him by his agent. There was something in it that intrigued him. Ah! Here it was.

A small registered package had arrived Air Mail from New York—there was no return address, and he didn't recognize the handwriting on the mailer. Inside was a slim, evidently long-out-of-print book titled *The Other Wise Man* by an author he had never heard of: Henry Van Dyke. Well, it looked like a quick read, and he couldn't sleep anyhow.

A quick read it was not: He found himself re-reading certain passages several times. It was after 3 A.M. before he finally put it down. He was moved in spite of himself. Then, he retired, this time to sleep.

During that Christmas season, he reread it twice more—and each time he read it he wondered what had motivated that unknown person to send it.

Three months later came another registered packet from New York. It too was obviously a book—and, to his joy, another old one. To his relief—for he had an intense fear of God and religion—it did not appear to be a religious book. The author and title were alike unknown to him: Myrtle Reed's *The Master's Violin*. The exquisite metallic lamination of this turn-of-the-century first edition quite took his breath away. Someone had spent some money on this gift!

He read it that night, and it seemed, in some respects, that the joy and pain he vicariously experienced in the reading mirrored his own. And the violin! It brought back memories of the melody, the melody which just would not let him go, the melody that represented the high tide of his life.

It was mid-June, three months later, when the next registered package arrived from New York. This time, his hands were actually trembling as he opened the package. Another book by yet another author he had never heard of: Harold Bell Wright. Kind of a strange title it had: *That Printer of Udel's.* But it was old and had a tipped-in cover. The combination was irresistible. He dropped everything and started to read.

He was not able to put it down. In it he saw depicted a portrait of Christian living unlike any he had ever seen before, a way of life that had to do not just with sterile doctrine but with a living, loving outreach to one's fellow man. He finished the book late that night. A month later, he read it again.

By late September, he had been watching his mail with great anticipation for some time; what would it be this time? Then it came: another book, first published in 1907, by the same author, with the intriguing title *The Calling of Dan Matthews.* It made the same impact upon him that its predecessor had. Nevertheless, Michael was no easy nut to crack. He continued to keep his jury sequestered; he was nowhere near ready for a verdict of any kind.

Early in December arrived his second Van Dyke: *The Mansion,* a lovely lime-green illustrated edition. This book spawned some exceedingly disturbing questions about his inner motivations. Of what value, really, was his life? When was the last time he had ever done anything for someone without expecting something in return? For such a small book, it certainly stirred up some difficult-to-answer questions.

March brought a book he had often talked about reading but never had the temerity to tackle: Victor Hugo's forbidding *Les Miserables:* almost 1,500 pages unabridged! He wondered why. Why such a literary classic following what he had been sent before? He didn't wonder long; the story of Jean Valjean was a story of redemption, the story of a man who climbed out of hell—the first Christ-figure he could ever remember seeing in French literature. By now, he was beginning to look for fictional characters who exhibited, in some manner, Christian values.

At the end of the book was a brief note:

No other book for six months. Review.

He did . . . but he felt terribly abused, sorely missing the expected package in June.

By the time September's leaves began to fall, he was in a state of intense longing. Certainly, after *Les Miserables*, and after a half-year wait, it would have to be a blockbuster. To his amazement and disgust, it was a slim mass-market paperback with the thoroughly unappetizing title of *Mere Christianity*. The author he knew of but had never read: C. S. Lewis.

Swallowing his negative feelings with great difficulty, he gingerly tested Lewis's Jordan River with his toes. As he stepped further in, he was quite literally overwhelmed. Every argument he had ever thrown up as a barrier to God was systematically and thoroughly demolished. He had had no idea that God and Christianity were any more than an amalgamation of feelings. For the first time, he was able to conceptualize God with his *mind*.

Whoever was sending him the books was either feeling sorry for making him wait so long or punishing him by literally burying him in print. He was kindly given two weeks to digest *Mere Christianity*, and then began the nonstop barrage of his soul. First came three shells in a row: Lewis's space trilogy: *Out of the Silent Planet, Perelandra,* and *That Hideous Strength.* At first, Michael, like so many other readers of the books, enjoyed the plot solely on the science fiction level. Then he wryly observed to himself that Lewis had set him up. Woven into the story was God and His plan of salvation.

The trilogy was followed by Lewis's *Screwtape Letters.* How Michael laughed as he read this one! How incredibly wily was the Great Antagonist. And how slyly Lewis had reversed the roles in order to shake up all his simplistic assumptions about the battles between Good and Evil.

A week later: another shell—*The Four Loves.* In it, Michael found himself reevaluating almost all of his friendships in life. That was but the beginning: Then Lewis challenged him to explore the possibilities of a friendship with the Eternal.

Two shells then came in succession: *Surprised by Joy* and *A Grief Observed.* At long last, he was able to learn more about Lewis the man. Not only that, but how Lewis, introduced to the joys of nuptial love late in life, then faced the untimely death of his bride. How Lewis, in his wracking grief, almost lost his way—almost turned away God Himself . . . . Paralleling Lewis's searing loss of his beloved was Michael's loss of Ginevra. He relived it once again, bone-wrenching in its intensity, more so than Lewis's, for he had not Lewis's God to turn to in the darkest hour.

The final seven shells came in the form of what appeared to be, at first glance, a series of books for children: Lewis's Chronicles of Narnia. It took Michael some time to figure out why he had been sent this series last, after such heavyweights. About halfway through, he fully realized just how powerful a manifestation of the attributes of Christ was Aslan the lion. By the moving conclusion of *The Last Battle,* the 15 shells from Lewis's howitzer had made mere rubble out of what was left of Michael's defense system.

Then came a beautiful edition of the Phillips translation of the New Testament. On the flyleaf, in neat black calligraphy, was this line:

May this book help to make your new year truly new.

He read the New Testament with a receptive attitude, taking a month to complete it. One morning, following a concert in Florence, he rose very early and walked to the Arno River to watch the sunrise. As he leaned against a lamppost, his thoughts did an audit of the past three years.

He was belatedly discovering that a life without God just wasn't worth living: in fact, nothing, he now concluded, had any lasting meaning divorced from a higher power. He looked around, mentally scrutinizing the lives of family members, friends, and colleagues in the music world. He noted the devastating divorce statistics, the splintered homes, and the resulting flotsam of loneliness and despair. Without God, he now concluded, no human relationship was likely to last very long.

Nevertheless, even now that he was thoroughly convinced in his mind that God represented the only way out of his dead-end existence, he bullheadedly balked at crossing the line out of the Dark into the Light.

The day before Easter of that tenth year, there came another old book, an expensive English first edition of Francis Thompson's poems. Inside, on the endsheet, was this coda to the faceless three-year friendship:

> Dear Michael,
>
> For almost three years now,
> you have never been out of my
> thoughts and prayers.
>
> I hope that these books have come
> to mean to you what they do to me.
> This is your last book.
>
> Please read "The Hound of Heaven."
> The rest is up to you.
>
> Your Friend

Immediately, he turned to the long poem and immersed himself in Thompson's lines. Although some of the words were a bit antiquated and jarred a little, nevertheless he felt that the lines were written laser-straight to him, especially those near the poem's gripping conclusion—for Michael identified totally with Thompson's own epic flight from the pursuing celestial Hound:

> Whom will you find to love ignoble thee

Save Me, save only Me?
All which I took from thee I did but take,
Not for thy harms,
But just that thou might'st seek it in My arms.
All which thy child's mistake
Fancies as lost, I have stored for thee at home.
Rise, clasp My hand, and come!

These lines broke him . . . and he fell to his knees.

It was the morning after, and Michael awakened to the first Easter of the rest of his life. Needing very much to be alone, he decided to head for the family chalet near Mt. Blanc. How fortunate, he mused, that the rest of the family was skiing at St. Moritz that week.

Two hours before he got there, it began to snow, but his Porsche, itself born during a bitterly cold German winter, growled its delight as it devoured the road to Chamonix. It was snowing even harder when he arrived at the chalet, where Michael was greeted with delight by Jacques and Marie, the caretakers.

A meal was served adjacent to a roaring fire in the great alpine fireplace. Afterwards, thoroughly satisfied, he leaned back in his favorite chair and looked out at the vista of falling snow.

He felt, he finally concluded, as if sometime in the night he had been reborn. It was as if all his life he had been carrying a staggeringly heavy backpack, a backpack into which some cruel overseer had dropped yet another five-pound brick each January 1 of his life, for as far back as he could remember. And now suddenly, he was *free!* What a paradoxical revelation that was: that the long-feared surrender to God resulted not in straitjacketed servitude but the most euphoric freedom he had ever imagined.

Looking back at the years of his life, he now recognized he had been fighting God every step of the way . . . but God, refusing to give up on him, had merely kept His distance. Michael went to his suitcase, reached for that already precious book of poems, returned to his seat by the fire, and turned again to that riveting first stanza:

> I fled Him, down the nights and down the days;
> I fled Him, down the arches of the years;
> I fled Him, down the labyrinthine ways
> Of my own mind, and in the midst of tears
> I hid from Him, and under running laughter.
>
> Up vistaed hopes I sped;
> And shot, precipitated
> Adown Titanic glooms of chastened fears,
> From those strong Feet that followed, followed after.
> But with unhurrying chase,
> And unperturbed pace,
> Deliberate speed, majestic instancy,
> They beat—and a Voice beat
> More instant than the Feet—
> "All things betray thee, who betrayest Me!"

He turned away, unable, because of a blurring of his vision, to read on. "How many years I have lost!" he sighed.

Years during which the frenetic pace of his life caused the Pursuing Hound to drop back sadly. Years during which he proudly strutted, wearing the tinsel crown of popularity. . . . And then that flimsy bit of ephemera was taken away, and the long descent into the maelstrom had taken place. It had been in his darkest hour, when he actually felt Ultimate Night reaching for him, that he plainly and distinctly heard his Pursuer again.

For almost three years now that Pursuer had drawn ever closer. There had been a strange meshing: the Voice in the crucifixion earthquake who spoke to Artaban, the Power that defied the Ally in the Dan Matthews story, the Force revealed through the pulsating strings of "Mine Cremona," the Presence that through the Bishop's incredible act of forgiveness and compassion saved the shackled life of Jean Valjean, the Angel who showed John Weightman's pitiful mansion to him, Malacandra of the Perelandra story and Aslan in the Narnia series . . . as he read "The Hound of Heaven," all the foregoing lost their distinctiveness and merged into the pursuing Hound. They were one and the same.

Michael resonated with a strange new power, a power he had never experienced before. It was as if, during the night, in his badly crippled power station (a generating facility to which, over the years, one incoming line after another had been cut, until he was reduced to but one frail piece of frayed wire that alone kept him from blackout), a new cable, with the capacity to illuminate an entire world, had been snaked down the dusty stairs, and then plugged in.

Then from far back (even before his descent into hell), two images emerged out of the mists of time, one visual and one aural: the tear-stained face of the Only Woman . . . and the throbbing notes of "Meditation."

Tingling all over, he stood up and walked over to the grand piano always kept in the lodge for his practicing needs, lifted up the lid, seated himself on the bench, and looked up. Humbly, he asked the question: "Am I ready at last, Lord?"

Then he reached for the keys and began to play. As his fingers swept back and forth, something else occurred. For the first time in over nine years, he was able—without printed music—to replay in his mind every note, every intonation he and Ginevra had heard in that far-off bell tower of Votivkirche. Not only that, but the sterility was gone! The current that had been turned on inside him leaped to his hands and fingers.

At last . . . he was ready.

Michael immediately discarded the fall concert repertoire, chosen as it had been merely for showmanship reasons, and substituted a new musical menu. Ever so carefully, as a master chef prepares a banquet for royalty, he selected his individual items. In fact, he agonized over them, for each number must not only mesh with all the others but enhance as well, gradually building into a crescendo that would trumpet a musical vision of his new life.

Much more complicated was the matter of his new recording. How could he stop the process at such a late date? Not surprisingly, when he met with Polygram management and dropped his bombshell, they were furious. Only with much effort was he able to calm them down and that on a premise they strongly doubted: that his replacement would be so much better that they would be more than compensated for double the expected production expense.

He walked out of their offices in a very subdued mood. If he had retained any illusions about how low his musical stock had sunk, that meeting would have graphically settled the question. If his new recording failed to sell well, he would almost certainly be dropped from the label.

He memorized all the numbers before making his trial recording; this way, he was able to give his undivided attention to interpretation before wrapping up the process. Only after he was thoroughly satisfied with the results did he have it recorded and then hand-carried by his agent to Deutsche Gramophone/Polygram management.

He didn't have to wait very long; only minutes after they played his pilot recording, Michael received a long-distance phone call from the president himself. Michael had known him for years and knew him to be a very tough man indeed. Recognizing full well that he and the company lived and died by the bottom line, he was used to making decisions for the most pragmatic of reasons. Recording artists feared him because he had a way of telling the unvarnished truth sans embellishments or grace-notes. . . . And now he was on the line.

Initially almost speechless, he finally recovered and blurted out, "What has happened, Michael? For years now, your recordings have seemed—pardon my candidness, but you know blunt me—a bit tinny, fluffy, sometimes listless, and even a bit . . . uh . . . for want of a better word, "peevish," more or less as if you were irritably going through the motions again, but with little idea why.

"Now, here, on the other hand, comes a recording that sounded to us like you woke up one morning and decided to belatedly take control of your life and career; that there were new and exciting ways of interpreting music—interpreting with power and beauty . . . and, I might add, Michael . . . a promise of depth and seasoning we quite frankly no longer believed was in you! . . . *What has happened?*"

That incredible summer passed in a blur of activity. The long ebb over at last, the incoming tidal forces of Michael's life now thundered up the beaches of the musical world. Deutsche Gramophone management and employees worked around the clock to process, release, and then market what they firmly believed would be the greatest recording of his career. Word leaked out even before it was released; consequently, there was a run on it when it hit the market. All of this translated into enthusiastic interest in his fall concert schedule.

Early in August, before the recording had been released, Michael phoned his New York agent, who could hardly contain himself about the new bookings that were flooding in for the North American tour the following spring. Michael, after first swearing him to secrecy, told him that he was entrusting to his care the most delicate assignment of their long association—one which, if botched, would result in irreparable damage. The agent promised.

He wanted of him three things: to trace the whereabouts of a certain lady (taking great pains to ensure that the lady in question would not be aware of the search process); to find out if the lady had married; to process a mailing (the contents to be adjusted according to whether the lady had married or not).

Meanwhile, Ginevra played the waiting game, a very hard game to play. The frustration level had been steadily building for almost three years. . . . When would she know?

Within a year after mailing her first book, she felt reasonably confident that he was reading what she had sent. But she had little data upon which to base her assumptions. During the second year, little snips of information about possible change in Devereaux appeared here and there. Nothing significant, really, but enough to give her hope.

She had knelt down by her bed that memorable morning before she mailed Thompson's poems. In her heartfelt supplication, she voiced her conviction that, with this book, she had now done all that was in her power to do. The rest was up to Him. Then she drove down the mountain to the Boulder Post Office and sent it to her New York relayer—and returned home to wait.

It was several months before the Devereaux-related excitement in the music world began to build. Her heart beat a lilting allegro the day she first heard about the growing interest in Michael's new recording. She could hardly wait to get a copy.

Then came the day when, in her mailbox, there appeared a little yellow piece of paper indicating that a registered piece of mail was waiting for her in the post office. It turned out to be a very large package from an unknown source in New York.

Not until she had returned to her chalet did she open it. Initially, she was almost certain that one of her former students was playing a joke on her, for the box was disproportionately light. She quickly discovered the reason: it was jammed full with wadded-up paper. Her room was half full of paper before she discovered the strange-shaped box at the very bottom of the mailing carton. What could it be? Who could it be from?

In this box, obviously packed with great care, were four items, each separated by a hard cardboard divider: a perfect flame-red rose in a sealed moisture-tight container, Michael's new Deutsche Gramophone recording, a publicity poster of a concert program that read as follows:

MICHAEL DEVEREAUX
FIRST CHRISTMAS EVE CONCERT
VIENNA OPERA HOUSE

(followed by other data giving exact time and date), and—at the very bottom, in an exquisite gold box—a front-section ticket to the concert.

Fearing lest someone in the standing section should take her place before she reached her seat, Ginevra asked an usher to escort her to the third row during the enthusiastic applause following Bach's "Italian Concerto." Michael, who had turned to acknowledge the applause, caught the motion: the beautiful woman coming down the aisle. And she was wearing a flame-red rose. Even in Vienna, a city known for its beautiful women, she was a sight to pin dreams on.

How terribly grateful he was to the audience for continuing to clap, for that gave him time to restore his badly damaged equilibrium. It was passing strange, mused Michael. For years now, both his greatest dream and his greatest nightmare were one and the same: that Ginevra would actually show up for one of his concerts. The nightmare had to do with his deep-seated fear that her presence in the audience would inevitably destroy his concentration, and with it the concert itself.

And now, here she was! If he ever needed a higher power, he needed it now. Briefly, he bowed his head. When he raised it, he felt again this new sense of serenity, peace, and command.

Leaving the baroque world of Bach, he now turned to César Franck, a composer of romantic music but with baroque connections. Michael had felt him to be a perfect bridge from Bach to Martin and Prokofiev. As he began to play Franck's "Prelude: Chorale et Fugue," he settled down to making this the greatest concert of his career. He had sometimes envied the great ones their announced conviction that, for each, the greatest concert was always the very next one on the schedule—they never took a free ride on their laurels. Only this season he had joined the masters, belatedly recognizing that the greatest thanks he could ever give his Maker would be to extend his powers to the limits, every time he performed, regardless of how large or how small the crowd.

The Opera House audience had quickly recognized the almost mind-boggling change in attitude. The last time he had played here, reviewers had unkindly but accurately declared him washed up. So desperate for success of any kind had he become that he openly pandered to what few people still came. It was really pathetic; he would edge out onto the platform like an abused puppy, cringing lest he be kicked again. Not surprisingly, what he apparently expected, he got.

Now, there was never any question as to who was in control. Soon, he would stride purposefully onto the stage, with a pleasant look on his face, and gracefully bow. He would often change his attire between sections; that added a visual extra to the auditory. His attire was always impeccable, newly cleaned and pressed, and he was neither over- nor underdressed for the occasion.

But neither was he proud, recognizing just how fragile is the line between success and failure, and how terribly difficult it is to stay at the top once you get there. Nor did he anymore grovel or play to the galleries. The attitude he now projected was quite simply: "I'm so pleased you honored me by coming out tonight. I have prepared long and hard for this occasion. Consequently it is both my intent and my expectation that we shall share the greatest musical hour and a half of our lifetimes."

Ginevra felt herself becoming part of a living, breathing island in time. Every concert performed well is a magic moment during which outside life temporarily ceases to be. Great music is, after all, outside of time and not subject to its rules. Thus it was that Ginevra, like the Viennese audience, lost all sense of identity as Devereaux's playing became all the reality they were to know for some time.

These weren't just notes pried from a reluctant piano; this was life itself, life with all its frustrations and complexities.

With such power and conviction did César Franck speak from the grave that they stood applauding for three minutes at the end of the first half. In fact, disregarding Opera House protocol, a number of the younger members of the audience swarmed onto the stage and surrounded Michael before he could get backstage. The new Michael stopped, and with a pleasant look on his face all the while, autographed every last program that was shoved at him. As one of these autograph seekers, jubilant of face, came back to Ginevra's row, she saw him proudly showing the program to his parents. Michael had taken the trouble to learn each person's name so he could inscribe each one personally!

Michael's tux was wringing wet. As for the gleaming black Boersendorfer, Michael had attacked it with such superhuman energy that it begged for the soothing balm of a piano tuner's ministrations; hence it was wheeled out for a badly needed rest. In its place was the monarch of the city's Steinway grands. Michael had specifically requested this living nine feet of history. No one knew for sure just how old it was, but it had for years been the pride and joy of Horowitz. Rubinstein would play here on no other, and it was even rumored that the great Paderewski performed on it. Michael, like all real artists, deeply loved his favorite instruments. Like the fabled Velveteen Rabbit, when an instrument such as this Steinway has brought so much happiness, fulfillment, meaning, and love into life over the years, it ceases to be just a piano and approaches personhood. Thus it was that Michael, before it was wheeled in, had a heart-to-heart chat with it.

A stagehand, watching the scene, didn't even lift an eyebrow. Concert musicians were all a loony bunch.

Only after a great deal of soul-searching had Michael decided to open the second half of his concert with Swiss-born Frank Martin's "Eight Preludes." He had long appreciated and loved Martin's fresh approach to music, his lyrical euphonies. Martin reminded Michael of the American composer Howard Hanson—he often had a difficult time choosing which one to include in a given repertoire; but this season, it was Martin's turn.

More and more sure of himself, Michael only gained in power as he retold Martin's story. By the time he finished the Preludes, he owned Vienna. The deafening applause rolled on and on and nobody appeared willing to sit down.

Finally, the house quiet once again, a microphone was brought out. Michael stepped up to speak.

"Ladies and gentlemen," he began, "I have a substitution to make. As you know, I am scheduled to perform Prokofiev's Sonata #6 in A Major, Opus 82 as my concluding number . . . but I hope you will not be *too* disappointed"—and here he smiled his boyish grin—"if I substitute a piece I composed, a piece that has never before been performed in public."

He paused, then continued: "Ten years ago tonight, in this fair city, this piece of music was born . . . but it was not completed until late this spring. I have been saving it for tonight." And here, he dared to glance in the direction of Ginevra.

"The title is . . . 'Variations on a Theme by Massenet.'"

Nothing in Michael's composing experience had been more difficult than deciding what to do with "Meditation." And the difficulties did not fall away with his conversion. He still had some tough decisions to face: Should his variations consist merely of creative side trips from that one melodic base? By doing so, he knew he could dazzle. Should the variations be limited to musical proof that he and his Maker were now friends? With neither was he satisfied.

Of all the epiphanies he had ever experienced, none could compare with the one born to him one "God's in His heaven / All's right with the world" spring morning: a realization that he could create a counterpart to what Massenet had done with the "Meditation" intermezzo, a fusion of earthly love with the divine. Belatedly, he recognized a great truth: God does not come to us in the abstract; He comes to us through flesh and blood. We do not initially fall in love with God as a principle; rather, we first fall in love with human beings whose lives radiate friendship with the divine. It is only then that we seek out God on our own.

Ginevra was such a prototype—that is why he had fallen in love with her. And he had little doubt in his mind but that it was she who had choreographed his conversion. No one else he had ever known would have cared enough to institute and carry out such a flawless plan of action. Besides, some of the book choices made him mighty suspicious.

Michael had also recognized what all true artists do sooner or later: that their greatest work must come from within, from known experience. If he was to endow his variations with power akin to the original, they must emanate from the joys and sorrows that made him what he was . . . and since she and God were inextricably woven together in Michael's multi-hued bolt of life, then woven together they must remain throughout the composition.

It would not be acceptable for her to distance herself and pretend she could judge what he had become dispassionately. No, Ginevra must enter into the world he had composed . . . and decide at the other end whether or not she would stay.

In Ginevra's mind, everything seemed to harken back to that cold night in the tower of Votivkirche, for it was there that two lives, only hours from oneness, had seen the cable of their intertwining selves unravel in only seconds.

Furthermore, there was more than God holding them apart. More than her romanticism as compared to his realism. That far-off exchange of words had highlighted for her some significant problems that, left unresolved, would preclude marriage even if Michael had been converted.

Essentially, it all came down to these. Michael had laughed at and ridiculed her deepest-felt feelings. Had made light of her tears. Had shown a complete absence of empathy. Worse yet, he exhibited a clear-cut absence of the one most crucial character trait in the universe: kindness.

Also, at no time since she had known him had she ever seen him admit in any way that he was wrong about anything. Compounding the problem, he had refused to disclose to her his true identity.

There had been a locked door halfway down to his heart.

There had been another locked door halfway up to his soul.

As far as she knew, both doors were still closed.

But if they ever were to be unlocked . . . "Meditation" would be the key.

With a soft-as-a-mother's-touch pianissimo, Michael begins to play. So softly that there appears to be no breaks at all between the notes, but rather a continuous skein of melodic sound. For the first time in Michael's career, there is a flowing oneness with the piano: impossible to tell where flesh, blood, and breath end and where wood, ivory, and metal join.

Ginevra cannot help but feel tense in spite of blurred fingers weaving dreams around her. Deep down, she knows that what occurs during this piece of music will have a profound effect upon the rest of her life. And the rest of Michael's life.

But she didn't travel so many thousands of miles just to be a referee or a critic. If their two worlds are ever to be one, she must leave her safe seat in the audience and step into the world of Michael's composition. Strangely enough—and living proof that it is the "small" things in life that are often the most significant—Michael's exhibition of kindness to the young people who blocked his exit during intermission strongly predisposes her in his favor.

How beautifully his arpeggios flow, cascading as serenely as alpine brooks singing their way down to the sea. All nature appears to be at peace. As Michael plays, she can envision the birds' wake-up calls, the falling rain and drifting snow, the sighing of her dear pines, and the endless journey of the stars. The world is a beautiful place, and love is in the air.

Suddenly, she stiffens: Certainly those are bells she is hearing. Yes, Christmas bells, flooding the universe with joy. She listens intently as their pealing grows ever louder—then *that theme!* It begins to mesh with the bells, but only for an instant. Right in the middle of it, there is an ominous shift from major to minor key, and from harmony to dissonance. And the bells! In that self-same instant the pealing joy ceases and is replaced by tolling sorrow. How uncannily perfect is Michael's capture of that moment when all the joy in their world went sour.

The dissonance and tolling eventually give way to a classical potpourri. Here and there she recognizes snatches of well-known themes, some of them from piano concertos. But the notes are clipped off short and played perfunctorily: more or less as if the pianist doesn't much care how they sound as long as they all get played in record time. Several times, the Theme tries to edge in . . . but each time it is rudely repulsed.

Now it is that Dvorak's "New World Symphony" thunders in. Aha! At last, some resolution! Some affirmation! Not so; it quickly becomes apparent that this paean to a brave new world is, ironically, in steady retreat instead of advancing to triumph. Almost it seems to her as if it were a retrograde "Bolero," its theme progressively diminishing in power instead of increasing. Once again, "Meditation" seeks entry; once again, it is unceremoniously disposed of.

By now, Ginevra is deciphering Michael's musical code quite well; vividly revealed has been the progressive deterioration of Michael both as a person and as a pianist. From the moment in the cathedral tower when the bells began to toll, every variation that followed has dealt with the stages of his fall.

Then, clouds close in, thunder rumbles in the east, lightning strikes short-circuit the sky—and the rain falls. Torrents of it. Darkness sweeps in, and with it all the hells loose on this turbulent planet. Ginevra shivers as Michael stays in minor keys, mourning all the sadness and pain in the universe.

The winds gradually increase to hurricane strength. Far ahead of her—for she is exposed to the elements too—she sees Michael, almost out of sight in the gloom, retreating from the storm. She follows and attempts to call to him, but to no avail; the tempest swallows the words before they can be formed. Then the black clouds close in, and she loses sight of him altogether.

As the hurricane reaches ultimate strength, major keys are in full flight from the minors. It does not seem possible that any force on earth can save Michael from destruction.

It is now, in the darkest midnight, when the few majors left are making their last stand, when she has all but conceded victory to the Dark Power—that she again hears the strains of Thaïs' Theme! How can such a frail thing possibly survive against the legions of Darkness? But almost unbelievably . . . it does.

At this instant, Ginevra chances to look with wide-open eyes at—not Michael the pianist but Michael the man. He has clearly forgotten all about the world, the concert audience, even her. In his total identification with the struggle for his soul, he is playing for only two people: himself, the penitent sinner—and God. . . .

With Michael's surrender, the tide turns at last. The storm rages on, but the enemy is now unmistakably in retreat. Dissonance and minors contest every step of the battlefield, trying vainly to hold off the invading Light. . . . Then victorious majors begin sweeping the field.

Ginevra discovers in all this a great truth. It is minors that reveal the full beauty of majors. Had she not heard "Meditation" sobbing on the ropes of a minor key, she would never have realized the limitless power of God. It is the minor key that gives texture and beauty to the major . . . and it is dissonance that, by contrast, reveals the glory of harmony. It is sorrow that brings our wandering feet back to God.

Finally, with the mists beginning to dissipate and the sun to break through, the Theme reappears, but alone for the first time. Now it is that Ginevra feels the full upward pull of the music . . . for "Meditation" soars heavenward with such passion, pathos, and power that gravity is powerless to restrain it.

And Ginevra, her choice made, reaches up, and with Michael, climbs the stairs of heaven to God.

———————— • ————————

This story is dedicated to my dearly beloved brother Romayne, who himself is a living embodiment of all that is finest in the concert piano profession—and who lived in, and loved, Vienna for almost a third of a century. He often performed in Votivkirche.

Massenet's "Meditation" (composed as a bridge between the secular and spiritual realms of our lives) has moved me as has no other piece of music in my lifetime. It was while listening to Zamfir's pan flute rendition of it that this story was born.

About the Contributors

Frances Ancker and **Cynthia Hope**, both of Canada, wrote "Last Day on Earth" in the 1890s. Today almost nothing is known about them.

Faith Baldwin, early in the twentieth century, was one of America's most cherished authors—and one of the most prolific. Among her best-sellers are *Three Women, Honor Bound,* and *First National.*

Annie E. S. Beard, an early folk historian, chronicled the true story of Grandmother's quilt to preserve it for posterity. She probably wrote the story during or shortly after the close of the Civil War (1865–1875). Little else is known about her or her other writings.

Katherine D. Cather wrote prolifically from 1915 to 1925. Her niche is unique in Americana: stories about famous people when they were young. Her books include *Boyhood Stories of Famous Men, Girlhood Stories of Famous Women,* and *Younger Days of Famous Writers.* She also wrote books dealing with the educating power of stories, especially in terms of ethical and spiritual values.

Felicia Buttz Clark (born in 1862) painted vivid word pictures with her pen in such works as *The Cripple of Nuremberg, The Sword of Garibaldi,* and *Laughing Water.*

W. L. Colby. After an exhaustive search, I was unable to find any information on this author.

Eunice Creager wrote for inspirational magazines around the 1890s and early 1900s.

Hartley F. Dailey, a freelance writer from Ohio, has been writing family stories for almost 50 years.

Paul Deutschman, a New Yorker himself, continues to chronicle the undying interest in his memorable story "It Happened on the Brooklyn Subway." Mr. Deutschman, one of the most famous correspondents to come out of World War II, wrote for *Life, Coronet, Reader's Digest, American Magazine, Colliers,* and *Harper.* He also was a mainstay with *Holiday.*

367

Annie Hamilton Donnell, early in the twentieth century, was one of the most loved family writers in America. Most of her stories deal with bringing together orphans and potential parents.

Anna Brownell Dunaway wrote greeting card messages, short stories, and a book. Little is known about her today.

Ella Enslow, like "Christy" of television fame, gave her all as a teacher in isolated Appalachia. In the mid-1930s, she collected her memories, and they were published as *Schoolhouse in the Foothills*.

John Thompson Faris (1871–1949) was a well-known Presbyterian clergyman, editor, and author who specialized in western history. Among his books are *Winning the Oregon Country, The Alaskan Pathfinder,* and *On the Trail of the Pioneers.*

Zona Gale (1874–1938), Portage, Wis., novelist, short-story writer, dramatist, and poet, was awarded the Pulitzer prize for her landmark play *Miss Lulu Bell* in 1920. Like Theodore Dreiser and Sinclair Lewis, she was of the Realist School of Literature; but unlike them, her characters operate in a world where the scriptural moral and ethical code of behavior remains central. In Gale's world, family, friendship, and fidelity are as essential to happiness and fulfillment as is love.

Hamlin Garland (1860–1940) was born in a Wisconsin log cabin one year before the Civil War. Although a teacher, his real love was writing. His subject was the people he knew best, those intrepid souls who somehow survived the changing seasons in the Great Plains. No greater or more honest stories have come out of America's heartland, and *Main-Traveled Roads* (1891), from which "A Day's Pleasure" comes, is a masterpiece. Garland's autobiography is the powerful *A Son of the Middle Border* (1917). He was awarded a Pulitzer prize for *A Daughter of the Middle Border* (1921).

Frontier writer **Zane Grey** (1872–1939) was a voracious collector of stories. For 30 years, he spent several months each year on the trail in western states, mostly on horseback. Each night after the evening meal, Grey would listen to true stories about the people who had lived on that particular part of the frontier—and he would write them down. Later, many of them would appear in his books and short stories. The complete story of Monty Price appears in one of Grey's greatest books, *Light of Western Stars.*

Jefferson Lee Harbour (1854–1931) was a prolific short-story writer, penning more than 700. From 1884 to 1901, he was associate editor of one of America's most beloved family magazines, *The Youth's Companion.*

Mary Sherman Hilbert, a prolific freelance writer from Washington State, continues to write memorable stories.

Florence C. Kantz. After an exhaustive search, I was unable to find any information on this author.

Fannie H. Kilbourne (born in 1890) was one of the best-known writers of her time and contributed regularly to the family magazines of her day.

Thomas Morris Longstreth was born only 31 years after the close of the Civil War. He grew up around people who had lived through the war; they shared their memories with anyone who would listen. Out of those conversations emerged such Longstreth books as *Trial by Wilderness, Two Rivers Meet in Concord,* and *Tad Lincoln: The President's Son.*

Guy de Maupassant (1850–1893) was a tormented writer who died at age 43, a victim of poor lifestyle choices. But what he wrote was honest: life as he saw it in his day-to-day interactions with people. In that respect, no greater story has ever been penned than "The Necklace."

Mabel McKee, early in the twentieth century, was responsible for some of the most memorable inspirational literature in print. Little is known about her today.

Louise Redfield Peattie (1900–1965) married the well-known writer Donald Culross Peattie (1898–1964), of Chicago. Both wrote and published prolifically, in many cases as coauthors.

Helen Peck. After an exhaustive search, I was unable to find any information on this author.

Grace Richmond (1866–1959) was loved for her short stories as well as her books (*Strawberry Acres, The Twenty-fourth of June,* the *Red Pepper* books, *Foursquare,* etc.).

Linda Harrington Steinke is an Alberta homemaker, rancher, and freelance writer.

G. E. Wallace's niche was unique: stories dealing with that intangible line between success and failure, both in terms of career and lifestyle. Little is known about him (or her) as a person or writer.

Leonard Wibberley—actually **Patrick O'Connor**—was born in Dublin in 1915. Much of his later life was spent in the United States or on the road as a correspondent or editor with the *Daily Mirror,* the *London Evening News,* the *Los Angeles Times,* and the Associated Press.

Besides his many short stories, his works include children's books such as *Little League Family;* biographies such as *The Life of Winston Churchill* and a four-volume life of Thomas Jefferson entitled *Man of Liberty;* and longer works such as the best-selling satire *The Mouse That Roared.*

C. M. Williams. After an exhaustive search, I was unable to find any information on this author.

Acknowledgments

"His 'Innymunt.'" Author and original source unknown. Published in *The Youth's Instructor*, Dec. 1, 1914. Text used by permission.

"A Sandpiper to Bring You Joy," by Mary Sherman Hilbert. Published in *Our Family*, Oct. 1979, and in *Reader's Digest*, June 1980. Reprinted by permission of the author and by the Reader's Digest Association, Inc.

"Their Word of Honor," by Grace Richmond. Published in *The Youth's Instructor*, June 12, 1934, and in *Their Word of Honor and Other Stories*, © 1940, Review & Herald Publishing Association, Takoma Park, Maryland. Text used by permission.

"It Happened on the Brooklyn Subway," by Paul Deutschman. Published in *Reader's Digest*, May 1949. Copyright © 1949 by Paul Deutschman. Reprinted by permission of Regina Ryan Publishing Enterprises, Inc., 251 Central Park West, New York, NY 10024, and by the Reader's Digest Association, Inc.

"A Lesson in Forgiveness," by T. Morris Longstreth. Published in *The Youth's Instructor*, Feb. 10, 1925, and in *Their Word of Honor and Other Stories*, © 1940, Review & Herald Publishing Association, Takoma Park, Maryland. Text used by permission.

"Inkspot," by Louise Redfield Peattie. Published in *The Youth's Instructor*, Sept. 16, 1930. Text used by permission.

"The Necklace," by Guy de Maupassant. Original English source and date of publication unknown.

"The Night of the Storm," by Zona Gale. Published in *Scholastic,* Apr. 21, 1934. Text used by permission. If anyone can provide knowledge of the first publication source of this old story, please relay this information to Joe L. Wheeler, care of Focus on the Family.

"Letter to Edith," by Faith Baldwin (Faith Cuthrell). Published in *Good Housekeeping,* July 1940. Reprinted by permission of Harold Ober Associates, Inc. Copyright © 1940 by Faith Baldwin. Copyright renewed in 1976.

"The Rejected Stone," by Felicia Buttz Clark. Published in *The Youth's Instructor*, Sept. 14, 1926. Text used by permission.

"Last Day on Earth," by Frances Ancker and Cynthia Hope. Reprinted by permission of the Toronto Star Syndicate.

"When Mozart Raced with Marie Antoinette," by Katherine D. Cather. Published in *The Youth's Instructor,* Sept. 29, 1914. Text used by permission.

"Beautiful Living," by Mabel McKee. Published in *The Youth's Instructor,* May 29, 1929. Reprinted by permission of Fleming H. Revell, a division of Baker Book House, Grand Rapids, Mich.

"The Captive Outfielder," by Leonard Wibberley. Published in *The Saturday Evening Post,* Mar. 25, 1961. Reprinted by permission of McIntosh and Otis, Inc.

"Two Courageous Missionary Brides," by John T. Faris. Published in *The Youth's Instructor,* Apr. 18, 1916. Text used by permission.

"At the Eleventh Hour," by Eunice Creager. Published in *The Youth's Instructor,* Apr. 18, 1916. Text used by permission.

"God Never Forgets," by Florence C. Kantz. Published in *The Youth's Instructor,* July 2, 1940. Text used by permission.

"Purple and Fine Linen," by Anna Brownell Dunaway. Published in *The Youth's Instructor,* July 14, 1925. Text used by permission.

"The Boy on the Running Board," by Annie Hamilton Donnell. Published in *The Youth's Instructor,* Oct. 18, 1921. Text used by permission.

"Overnight Guest," by Hartley F. Dailey. Published in *Sunshine,* Feb. 1963. Reprinted by permission of the author and Garth Henrichs, publisher of Sunshine Publications.

"Little Johnny Slept Here," by C. M. Williams. Reprinted with permission from *Reader's Digest,* Feb. 1971. Copyright © 1971 by the Reader's Digest Association, Inc.

"Birthdays Are Lovely." Author unknown. Published in *The Youth's Instructor,* July 24, 1928. Text used by permission.

"Monty Price's Nightingale," by Zane Grey. Published in *Success,* Apr. 1924. Copyright © 1978 by Zane Grey, Inc. Reprinted by permission.

"The Breakwater on Elk Creek," by G. E. Wallace. Published in *The Youth's Instructor,* July 26, 1938, and in *Red Letter Day and Other Stories,* © 1942 by Review & Herald Publishing Association, Takoma Park, Maryland. Text used by permission.

The Story of
Joe L. Wheeler, Ph.D.

Joe Wheeler's earliest childhood memories are of stories—more specifically, of listening to his mother tell stories. And as soon as he was able to read, Wheeler recalls following her around the house, relentlessly reading his storybooks to her.

Shortly after turning eight, Wheeler's parents moved from their home in Napa Valley, California, to Latin America as missionaries. There his mother taught him at home, encouraging him to "devour entire libraries" wherever and whenever he could.

At 16, Wheeler left his family and returned to California to attend Monterey Bay Academy near Santa Cruz. It had, at one time, been used as an army base. When the army moved out, it left its library. Over the next two years, Joe Wheeler read the entire collection.

It comes as no surprise, then, that Wheeler majored in English and history in college, later securing master's degrees in both, as well as a Ph.D. in English, from Vanderbilt University. He became a teacher and continued the tradition his mother began when he was small—he read stories to his students.

Today, Joe Wheeler is an English professor at Columbia Union College in Takoma Park, Maryland. He is also Senior Fellow for Cultural Studies, Center for the New West in Denver, Colorado. He is founder and executive director of the Zane Grey's West Society, as well as compiler and editor of the popular *Christmas in My Heart* series for Review & Herald, Doubleday, Dell, and Bantam.

He and his wife, Connie, are the parents of two grown children and make their home in Arnold, Maryland.

Photo by Joel Springer
(chief photographer for Review & Herald)

Coda

We appreciate hearing from our readers. If you have any comments, positive or negative, about this collection, or have any stories you would like us to include in future collections, please send them to

Joe L. Wheeler, Ph.D.
c/o Focus on the Family
Colorado Springs, CO 80920